SECRETS, LIES, AND PROMISES

A Novel

Signe A. Dayhoff, PhD

Secrets, Lies, and Promises
by Signe A. Dayhoff, PhD
Copyright © 2021 by Signe A. Dayhoff, PhD
Published by Effectiveness-Plus Publications LLC
80 Paseo de San Antonio
Placitas, New Mexico 87043-8735

Cover Illustration by fiverr.com/nevzapravdu
Cover by http://www.bookclaw.com

ISBN: 978-0-9985324-5-5

ACKNOWLEDGMENTS

The author wishes to acknowledge the assistance of Dr. Jennifer Smith, DMV, for repeatedly sharing her veterinary medical expertise. JesseV@detectives.com who answered all my questions about what private detectives do, can do, and how they do it. And HelenJ@justanswer.com who provided me with information about intellectual property.

Also, I want to express my appreciation to Anne Lane, Karlene Spivak, Linda McAllister, Carlie Klepach, Katrin Kornblom, Marilyn Cokefair Westbye, James Shannon, Leslie Day-Ebert, "Jack Daye" (pseudonym for an upcoming writer), and Reid Bandeen (who is indeed a very fine landscape painter and shows in various galleries around New Mexico) who allowed me to use their names for my fictional characters.

1

As she was nearing her destination on foot, an urgent-sounding voice ambushed her.

"Please, Miss! Could you help me?"

Suddenly, a sixteen-ounce Starbucks paper coffee cup was shoved into her face. She had been walking along the left side of Charles Street toward Beacon in downtown Boston. Rearing back startled, she saw the speaker. He was a tall, thin, unshaven man in his late twenties, dressed in soiled military fatigues, with "Patrick" stitched above his right-side shirt pocket, wearing beige ear muffs and sunglasses. He was swaying to and fro, seemingly having difficulty maintaining his balance. As he leaned backwards, his left hand momentarily braced against the back of a wood and wrought iron bench. It was in front of the redbrick building containing the Wine & Cheese Shop. Then he collapsed onto the seat. Given his lack of coordination, she thought he probably hadn't intended to assault her. While a whiff of his breath was bad, there was no scent of alcohol.

Dressed in her charcoal gray business pant suit, she was on her way to her office, which was above the Starbucks at the corner of Charles and Beacon, across from the Boston Common. Immediately, she dug into her wallet, which was inside her shoulder-bag briefcase, for change. As she dropped a handful of larger coins into his upheld cup, they made a big splash. Hot brown droplets emerged and showered her hand.

"Oh, damn! I'm so sorry," replied Charley, grimacing. "I misunderstood."

Tilting his head as if ready to say something, he tried to stand. But his movement skewed his equilibrium, making it more likely he would topple over forward instead. He reached out and clutched her upper arm causing more of his coffee to spill, barely missing her jacket. It nearly threw her off-balance. She dropped her weight into her knees to stabilize herself and tried to look unconcerned. Even as fear was racing her heart, she knew she had to keep the situation low key. If she couldn't handle it, all she had to do was alert the other pedestrians and business owners around her. Acknowledging them as she passed them daily, she knew they would lend her a hand.

Pulling him upright, she slowly walked him over to the curb of the one-way street. There stood one of the many mature trees which had been planted intermittently in rectangular plots, surrounded by ornate black wire fencing. As she helped him lean against it, he released her arm.

"Please. It's my head!" He raised his head slightly to look her in the face. "The noise, the light, the pain. I need help. Can you help me? Please?"

Through his dark lenses, she could see his eyes welling up, imploring her. With his shoulder against the tree, he lowered his head again to press the hot container to his right temple. However, in doing so, his lower body began to slip from the tree trunk. Using her foot as she held his arm again, Charley nudged his combat boots toward the tree. When she had temporarily steadied him, she released his arm. He raised his head to look at her.

"You wouldn't be a doctor, would you?"

She shook her head and said, "No, sorry."

"How about a lawyer? I need a good lawyer too."

With his body braced against the smooth-barked tree, he tried to shift the coffee cup to his other hand but lost his balance. As he started to slide down the trunk, he reached instead for her upper arm again. His fingers burned her clothing into her flesh as he struggled to stand up straight. She responded by leaning back to allow him to regain a standing position. It was obvious he wanted to look Charley in the eye as he rendered a restrained, but sob-tinged, account of his situation.

"A month ago, I got back from Afghanistan. I'm not getting my benefits. I've been robbed in shelters. Repeatedly. Now I have no place to sleep. My head hurts so bad I can't sleep anyway. A concussion bomb nearly killed me. I can't think straight. I'm dizzy and sick all the time. I can't go on much longer like this. Sometimes I want to die. Please, Miss, can you help me?"

Something clicked and Charley nodded. What he was saying about his head was familiar. She had heard about that when she visited an old physician friend at the VA Hospital where many of the veterans there suffered from traumatic brain injuries, TBIs.

"I think I understand."

She gently tried to remove his hand from her arm. His fingers were strong and unwilling to release as he tried to lock his knees to pull himself up, erect. It was as if he were frantically hanging onto a log in raging whitewater approaching boulder-strewn rapids. Because he was still on the verge of falling over, Charley quickly slipped her arm under his to help stabilize him. When she smiled kindly at him, he relaxed a little, got his feet directly under him, and finally let go.

"I'm not a lawyer either but maybe I can still help you a little. Let me look."

With his free hand he took off his dark glasses, squinted, and looked at her hopefully as she reached into her briefcase again to pull out a card to give to him. It was for the Massachusetts Department of Veterans' Services at 600 Washington Street. One of the partners at her firm, Anne Lane, volunteered with veterans who were re-integrating after combat and had given out the service's cards.

After he scanned it, holding it closer than farther away, she began to inch him along the redbrick sidewalk to Beacon Street. Keeping his head aslant, he quickly slipped on his sunglasses. Their bodies wove together through the pedestrian stream like amiable drunks. Several of her acquaintances who passed looked at her as if to ask if she needed help. She slightly shook her head and smiled her appreciation.

A few minutes later they were at the corner where she braced him against the tall black light pole which displayed the green Charles and Beacon street signs near the top. He wrapped his free arm around it. That enabled her to let go so she could flag down a cab. When the taxi arrived, she helped the veteran into the back. Leaning in, she gave the driver two twenties and directions.

"I'd appreciate it if you'd take Private Patrick here, just back from Afghanistan, to Mass. General's ER, the one on Fruit Street, and make sure he gets inside okay *and is seen as soon as possible*. This is a little extra for your kindness and time. Thanks."

The older cabbie, who had a Purple Heart and a Vietnam Service Medal pinned to his windshield visor, nodded knowingly, smiled at his big tip, then became serious.

"No problem. By the way, if he has his DD214, the Armed Forces Report of Transfer or Discharge, they'll probably want to connect him with the VA Hospital in Jamaica Plain after he's treated. But I'm not sure of the exact procedure these days."

"Thank you, Miss," Patrick replied, reaching out his free hand to shake hers.

"Do you have your discharge papers?" she asked.

"Yeah," he responded as he pulled out a folded document from his breast pocket. "Wait! I don't know your name."

"It's Charley."

"Oh?" His face reddened and he lowered his head as a tear began to roll down his scruffy face. "My best buddy was Charlie. He saved my life. A sniper's bullet almost got me. He pulled me away. Just in time. We were ducks … in a shooting gallery. Then he was killed … in the bomb blast … that nearly got me too."

He looked up at her with a tiny smile hardly creasing his bristled cheeks.

"You must be an angel sent to help me. I can't thank you enough."

Charley smiled too. He reminded her of an abused puppy still hoping for a hint of kindness. As she backed up to close the door, he shakily placed the coffee cup between his thighs, pressed both hands against his temples, and mumbled, not looking in her direction.

"I'm sorry I frightened you before."

"Not a problem. You're going to see some doctors now. Do whatever they say so you can feel better soon. And, be sure to contact that veterans' agency—the card I gave you—about your benefits," she whispered with another warm smile.

She thanked the cabbie again for his help then shut the vehicle's back door. As the
cab drove off, her eyes followed it sadly. She hoped the hospital would really help him. She had read that according to the Defense Department and the Veteran's Brain Injury Center about twenty-two percent of all combat casualties were from brain injuries.

As far as she was concerned, TBIs were the worst type of injury for military people—or anyone else for that matter—because they were so hard to treat. Too often with them were physical, psychological, and social consequences which could be devastating. These contributed to a significantly increased risk of suicide for veterans. Wondering how many casualties with TBIs were discovered by medical professionals in time and properly treated so the vets could have a chance at an acceptable recovery, she sighed and continued on her way to her second-floor office at 66 Beacon.

Charlotte "Charley" Eyre was a political image marketing consultant, with a degree in Political Science with Communication, and a concentration in "Campaigns and Elections," from Northeastern University. For ten years she had been part of a three-person agency in Boston. Her partners, Karlene Washington and Anne Lane, and she had met when they all had attended the "Campaign Strategy and Politics" and "Mass Media" courses at NU. Each of them idealistically wanted to stop political campaigns from being waged in the proverbial pigsty.

Karlene had been one of the first black female news directors and videographers in Boston while Anne had been a former educational psychology doctoral student and adult educator. Since their special experience and talents dovetailed with Charley's interpersonal communication and social influence expertise, they felt that together they could be the vanguard in making political campaigns cleaner and more honest again.

Their three-room agency, Ultimate Strategy, was geared to create campaign structure and strategies. Primarily, they provided image management through polling and focus groups and persuasive ads in all media. They were moderately successful given their strong competition in the Northeast corridor. What they felt made them stand apart, however, was that they made a difference with innovation, honesty, and integrity. Their agency dealt with carefully-vetted political campaigns. Specifically, they worked with local and state-wide candidates, causes, and groups.

Charley's part of the business required a lot of one- and two-day travel to meet with and acquire clients. After a decade of doing this, she preferred to have a savvy junior executive with great interview skills take over the task. But, at present, their agency didn't have the budget for that. It bothered her that her recent, increasingly harried schedule kept her away from what else she loved: her large, ring-tailed, short-haired, silver Siamese-Tabby-cross cat, "Little Bit," as well as her abstract painting, article writing, and personal political activism.

While Karlene, Anne, and Charley were all politically active, they worked more privately, behind the scenes, with marketing consultation and ad concepts. They were particularly involved in women's issues, such as getting the Equal Rights Amendment passed and helping more women, and women of color, achieve elective office. But they tried to avoid situations which could label the firm as politically biased. With clients, they related more to specific issues than party affiliation, although they tended to eschew any extreme positions or causes which conflicted with their own individual senses of what was fair and democratic.

What was most notable about Charley's firm was their strong desire to be untouched by the taint of political chicanery. While she and her partners represented somewhat different religious beliefs, what they had in common was possessing high principles. These were inculcated into them at an early age by parents who emphasized the values of character and honesty and espoused support for causes of justice and equality for all.

That, however, did not stop others from foisting their religious judgment upon them as Charley and her partners had quickly found out after they had taken on a candidate for state senator who privately happened to be non-theist. When some more extreme religious people discovered his background, they came after Ultimate Strategy for what they labelled as their "un-Christian, irreligious" credo in promoting him.

Having created a campaign for a so-called "non-Christian," Ultimate Strategy had been confronted, questioned, and berated by zealots as the personification of evil. They spread the word publicly, in the newspapers, blogs, and on social media, that the agency should be avoided because they were "sinful for promoting the ungodly." That small group picketed on the sidewalk beneath their office numerous times, handing out leaflets to passersby, stating "Beware! Ultimate Strategy is anti-Jesus and aiding and abetting the Prince of Darkness."

Karlene, Anne, and Charley were thunderstruck but did nothing about it. However, upon hearing about this, the Boston branch of the American Civil Liberties Union threw their backing to the firm and the candidate, stating in the media that "all citizens had a right to run for office, irrespective of their religious affiliation and beliefs or lack thereof." Unfortunately, the attempted boycott gave some prospective clients pause. The experience also created a temporary divide among the partners as to what degree outsiders should be allowed to dictate whom they'd take on as clients.

Charley's agency had a reputation for integrity. Up to that point, it had dealt primarily with run of the mill candidates, more by chance than on purpose. Consequently, it had been financially in the black for its first eight years. But starting two years ago, new factors were insinuating themselves into their future accounting calculus. The economy had begun to fluctuate. The non-theist client controversy had cut into the number of new clients they were attracting. Karlene had heard from associates that some people felt uncomfortable being seen dealing with anyone deemed publicly to be "non-Christian." Anne said that most people she knew didn't really care one way or another but didn't want to be associated with people who might prompt negative associations, especially when they were contemplating a campaign.

Over this time period as well, national political campaigns whose strategies and tactics were becoming less honest and transparent distressed, angered, and discouraged the partners. While Charley wanted to remain optimistic that things would eventually right themselves or even off, she worried because she was hearing gossip that that the aggressively-combative approach was likewise insinuating itself into state and local campaigns. As a result, her agency's version of political marketing, research, and strategy consultation was beginning to look, to an increasing number of politicians-to-be, as not hostile and bellicose enough. They indicated to the partners that pugnacity was necessary and the only effective avenue to enable them to win, and win big.

What was clearly happening was that there was a resurgence of the 1970s and 1980s no-holds barred type of campaigning that South Carolinian Lee Atwater had advocated and wielded for Republicans many years past. His was the epitome of belligerent, saber-rattling, slimy political campaigning that Charley, Karlene, and Anne abhorred and fought against.

Atwater had worked for Strom Thurman, Ronald Reagan, and George H. W. Bush, among others. His bag of sadistic, attack-dog-style dirty tricks were not aimed just at winning. They were aimed at totally annihilating his clients' opponents by using some of the worst political smears in U.S. history.

His George H. W. Bush campaign against Massachusetts Governor Michael Dukakis was one example. Atwater made wild, unsubstantiated accusations about Dukakis's personal life, from his allegedly having had a mental illness to his wife, Kitty, having "burned the American flag" in protest to the Vietnam War. But the worst of it was the racist, rape-oriented, fear-mongering Willie Horton ads which essentially transplanted Horton's scary image for Dukakis's in the minds of many voters, facilitating his loss.

However, the ultimate sin that stood out for Charley as repugnantly beyond the pale was his making sadistic fun of a candidate who as a sixteen-year-old suicidal student had experienced electroshock treatments for his depression. That was something which the candidate had already shared openly with his constituents. Still, Atwater savagely joked about his having been "hooked up to jumper cables" in order to dismiss him and obscure the real campaign issues he represented. This sad era of political marketing at its worst was later documented in 2008 in *Boogie Man: The Lee Atwater Story* after Atwater had died at the age forty in 1991 of brain cancer.

On the anniversary of Atwater's demise just after Ultimate Strategy had been created, Charley, Karlene, and Anne opened a mini-bottle of Champagne in their new office to raise their glasses. It was not to celebrate Atwater's death but the hope that with his death his cutthroat legacy would no longer sustain traction to harm people, arbitrarily destroy campaigns, and bury important issues. And, that Ultimate Strategy would become the vanguard of the future for cleaner political marketing.

"May his unconscionable political campaign approach never show signs of being on the rise again," said Karlene.

Anne nodded, "Yes, may we never again have such an open acceptance of maliciousness and unethicality that winning is not just the goal of a campaign but one to be achieved in *any* way possible."

"And while we have a battle ahead of us as we establish Ultimate Strategy as the shining example of innovative and successful political marketing," Charley added, "let us never forget that we have the grit, determination, persistence, and talent to make us a firm to be reckoned with."

With that they had clinked their glasses to campaign ingenuity, their righteous sword of honesty and integrity rising to smite any residual effects of that wickedness. However, eight years later, they found themselves pitted against a strong revitalization of the Atwater legacy which was significantly negatively impacting their business.

In the last two years Ultimate Strategy's business had begun to slip market share. As the firm saw what was rushing toward them on the horizon, they knew they needed additional help. What they wanted was to bring in another person to act as an executive assistant who could do some of the more routine tasks so the partners could concentrate fulltime on the advancement of their respective campaign projects and seeking new clients. This person would specifically allow Charley not to spend over twelve hours a day at the office trying to find new ways to reach and motivate their public to hire them. A Type-A personality, Charley particularly felt compelled not to take time to sleep. The partners were all being dogged by anxiety and fatigue. But, once again, they didn't have the budget to recruit someone.

It was a conflict that plagued Charley because she also wanted to have time to write more articles about political marketing consultation to inform and persuade the public about the creeping, unethical trends. She already had had several controversial articles on that topic in the *Boston Business Journal* which had drawn positive responses, at least from some corners. More to the point, after each one, there had been a small flurry of new clients. She had even started a book on the current market's hunger for effective sleaze. It would have been good advertising for the firm. But it was languishing, having been untouched for months, as Charley and her partners struggled for the agency's survival.

Over this time as Charley and her partners had thought they could still accomplish amazing, successful campaigns through their form of political consulting, more and more of their prospective clients were aligning themselves with Atwater's modus operandi. As such, those clients were expecting lies and deceptions, rather than clever, influential, truthful strategies, to out-smart and out-match their opponents. Ultimate Strategy's developing predicament was that they didn't know what they could do about this looming political inclination, much less address it as they wanted in order to stay in business. Even though political marketing was a lucrative area, their firm was burdened by having to constantly counteract other small firms' use of name calling, negativity, deception, disinformation, altered reality, and lack of facts. Too often, they found that the public was beginning to *demand* those elements in political ads and speeches.

As a result of these shifting beliefs about what was acceptable, Charley saw larger Boston agencies as well beginning to incorporate them. But that meant that competing for clients would become even harder than it already was and, perhaps, eventually, nearly impossible. In an age of perceived entitlement, more clients wanted what they thought was the quickest and easiest way to achieve their goal. They had only to see the successful results of those who used the Atwater "whatever works to seize and hold the voters' attention" approach. And if that meant their taking the low road, then so be it because their mantra was, "if everyone else is doing it, they have to do it too in order to compete and survive."

Anyone who gave credence to a different approach was labeled as out of touch, impractical, ineffectual, and a loser. Consequently, Ultimate Strategy after ten years was no longer being considered, as it had been, a "really good horse to bet on if you want to win with your character intact."

Given the situation, the partners had begun contemplating the possibility of moving out of the Boston area, maybe to another state. But that would have been a last-ditch effort to keep the agency alive *if* the trend hadn't already blanketed every large city.

"This situation is so crazy," said Karlene. "What we have is good. It works. And better still, it lets me sleep at night. I know we're losing clients and not picking up new ones rapidly enough to keep us going but I'm just not ready to hang up my strategic marketing spurs yet."

Anne nodded her head in agreement.

"Unless we knew for sure there were enough clients elsewhere, moving sounds like a too-costly and risky maneuver. We're at the hub of political marketing activity now so if we can't make it here, … While I grant you that things *are* looking darker by the week, I'm also not willing to give it up yet either. I say we hang here until the end of the year."

"Okay," Charley replied. "We'll see if we can get the agency back on a firmer financial footing. But … if what seems to be the inevitable occurs, … we'll know we gave it a damned good try."

They'd decided to stick it out at their present location until the end of the year or for as long as the agency remained in the black. They high-fived each other and returned to work. While outwardly bullish, none of them was inwardly optimistic about their prospects or making it through that many more months.

As Charley mulled over the strong possibility of having to close the firm, whether at the end of the year or perhaps sooner, she found a pink telephone message on her desk. Her primary care physician, Dr. Katrin Kornblom, had called her earlier when Charley was on the other phone scheduling candidate flyers and bumper stickers with a printing firm. The message stated Kornblom wanted Charley to call her. Charley knew it had to be about the results of her most recent mammogram. She felt her intestines clench.

Off and on for over a decade her mammograms had shown anomalies but her physicians couldn't decide if they were malignant or not. Since neither Charley nor her primary care physician had ever felt a lump and no x-ray technician had ever detected one, her doctor felt it was reasonable not to refer Charley just yet to a surgeon for a needle biopsy.

Periodically, she had gone through a series of 3D mammograms and ultrasounds, performed every six months, for potential breast cancer. After each series, the professional decision that was made was to do nothing. When Charley called her doctor back, she expected the worst.

Dr. Kornblom answered, "Charley, sorry but we still don't know what these two spots are. They *may* only be a density of fibrous breast material. But whatever they are, they still don't appear to be growing in any way. We'll just have to continue to monitor them."

Charley sighed deeply. While that was positive, she didn't find it comforting because once again nothing had been resolved. In addition, recently she had read that there wasn't enough clinical evidence as yet to conclude that the 3D mammogram truly reduced the risk of dying of breast cancer more than a standard mammogram alone. Moreover, it stated it was possible for the 3Ds to miss very small areas of cancer or ones that were difficult to see. Damned if you do and damned if you don't, she thought. At least, she could go back to having her mammograms every twelve months.

In the meantime, however, she would worry about what all the extra radiation from the 3D machine might precipitate. It could trigger some random cancer in her breast or somewhere else in her body. The last time she had her 3D mammogram she shared her concern with the technician, half-jokingly.

"I'm surprised after all this radiation that I don't glow in the dark."

The technician who had heard that disguised fear many times before smiled and nodded knowingly.

Concerned that this possible disaster might burst forth at any time, she had bought a health DNA test kit from one of the highly-promoted genealogical sites. She didn't really want her DNA recorded anywhere because, depending upon what it might reveal, the data could be used against her with respect to retaining her health insurance or getting life or disability insurance at some time. She wouldn't be the first person to suffer discrimination as a result of the documentation of having a so-called "pre-existing condition," also known as a "pre-disposition to some disease" which might never show up clinically. Despite her conflicting concerns, she followed instructions in the small box, spit saliva into the enclosed tube, and mailed it back.

Two weeks later when she received the results, she was surprised. While she had expected the report to show her something about her recurring mammogram problem, it didn't. Maybe that was good. She knew that none of her now-deceased female relatives had had breast or ovarian cancer or had documented the BRCA1 or BRCA2 gene mutations. That made her hopeful that this fact eliminated her from the five- to ten percent of breast cancers that were heritable.

Since the results didn't answer her question about how her breast aberrations had come about, she still wondered if they could have been a fluke of Nature. Caused during mitosis when a cell's chromosomes split to form two cells. Or, scar tissue from some injury she had sustained as an active child. The test gave her no clue so she put her cancer worry on the back burner. But what the DNA test *did* reveal was shocking.

It stated unequivocally that she was going to develop early-onset Alzheimer's Disease, possibly as early as in her thirties but by her sixties. Early-onset Alzheimer's was rare. According to the most recent research that she found, it was an inherited change in one of three genes: Amyloid precursor protein on Chromosome 21; Presenilin 1 on Chromosome 14; or Presenilin 2 on Chromosome 1. Charley had no idea what specifically that genetic babble meant except that it would have a devastating impact on her life.

But that made no sense. She couldn't believe it. No breast cancer but an early senile dementia? It was as if she had just exchanged one deadly problem for another. What, she wondered, would she do? Maybe she should have the test re-done in case it was a false positive. While she knew it was foolish not to, she felt it was such an overwhelming prediction that she didn't want to risk it being confirmed, especially at that time. With her business sagging, it felt as if fate were playing a cruel joke on her. Suddenly, she had learned that she had a very short future ahead of her, irrespective of breast cancer.

Unable to push the new health concern out of her mind, she soon began losing what little sleep she got. She began forgetting names. She had always had a well-honed memory, an ability she had further developed, which she depended upon for doing research and keeping straight all details of clients' campaigns. Was that, she worried, the beginning of her tragic Alzheimer's end. Or was that reflective of the stereotypical syndrome that seemed to affect many new medical residents: seeing in themselves the symptoms of every new disease they encountered? Or was it just plain lack of sleep? When she described her symptoms to Dr. Kornblom, without mentioning the DNA test results, she received a prescription for a benzodiazepine, Ativan.

However, shortly thereafter, as fewer and fewer clients were signing up with Ultimate Strategy, she began feeling negative, confused, and depressed. Suicidal ideation was threatening to creep in. It was only when she forced herself to google the drug that she discovered that what she was experiencing was possibly its frequent side effects. She tapered off the dosage and felt a little better.

Yet, she continued to fight intermittent bouts of mild depression about her life. There were too few rays of sunshine penetrating the deepening emotional gloom. Despite the difficulty, she knew she had to fight it. She wanted to be like Lozen, the female Chiricahua Apache warrior and prophet, the so-called "Apache Joan of Arc," she had read about. She had fought beside her brother, the prominent chief Victorio, and Geronimo to recapture Native Americans' land stolen by the U.S. government. She was an inspiring Native American "Wonder Woman."

In the following weeks, as much as she wanted to re-test her DNA for Alzheimer's, she couldn't push herself to do it. Every time she thought about it, she rejected the idea. She knew she wasn't being rational or logical—characteristics she prided herself on representing—but it didn't matter. Already at a low ebb, she couldn't risk having her potentially very negative future etched in marble. As a result, she waited … but never stopped worrying about it subconsciously.

Charley no longer had any immediate family to provide any kind of emotional support about this. Her mother and father had been killed in a fiery crash on the Mystic Valley Parkway. They had been on their way to their home in Medford after visiting Charley in Boston. A gasoline tanker truck side-swiped them on the icy pavement, rupturing its tank, and pinning their car against the guardrail as the truck exploded.

The only one currently who was very close to her was her painting mentor, Amie Benison. However, because she was in the process of making plans to move to New Mexico, taking trips there to look over real estate in different towns where she might eventually settle, she was less available physically to Charley. Not wanting to play victim or interfere with Amie's plans, Charley kept her dire health prediction to herself.

Likewise occupying her mind was the business proposal Amie had recently made to her as Ultimate Strategy was sinking into a morass. If she accepted, she would follow Amie to the Southwest. It was inviting but Charley was on the fence. She felt doomed and didn't know if she wanted to move considering her pending disastrous health situation. Even though she was exhausted from trying to help keep their business above water, she couldn't see herself doing anything but political image consulting fulltime, which was not what Amie had in mind.

Because of her work addiction Charley's dance card no longer held any names. Social engagements had dwindled to nothing, even with her partners and friends because every time they asked her, she begged off to do work. Her compulsive personality made her look as if she were on amphetamines as her world was seemingly crumbling around her. Meeting men and dating were out of the question. Her only real company was her beloved cat. In her few hours not at work, she was a near-recluse.

Depressed, tired, and contemplating her diminishing future, she was ripe for gravitating toward any overly-attentive, forty-five-year-old man who exuded gallons of sticky charm when he imposed himself upon her.

3

It was early afternoon when Charley left the office to meet a client-to-be. Mares tail clouds, like spidery fingers, scudded across the cornflower blue sky on a modestly cooling breeze. It was the perfect day to leisurely stroll around the Frog Pond on the Boston Common and converse with David Phillips' two whimsical, bug-eyed, life-sized bronze frog sculptures. They were seated just outside the Tadpole Playground on the edge of the pond. One was "Donny," a fisherman with a pole, seated on a tackle box beside a can of worms, and the other was "Angela," a froggy version of Rodin's *The Thinker.* But neither had sticky tongues to dart at prey and reel them back into their mouths which Charley liked to imagine them frequently doing between comments.

Above the playground gate was a fun gatekeeper frog, "David," with one arm raised in welcome. He was frequently decorated for the holidays and special events, and was the one who greeted the children, inviting them to come in. Inside the playground were Phillips' snorkel frog, "Joann," the lifeguard frog, "Charlie," with whistle and life ring buoy for the little tadpole statues, and a sunbathing frog, "Skippy," with its hands casually clasped behind its head. Along the playground's black metal fence were mounted two-dimensional frogs on illustrated panels, the result of collaboration of artist Mark Cooper and the children of Dorchester's Citizens Elementary School. There was also a large mosaic medallion in the walkway with a lurking bullfrog which was created by Lilli Ann and Marvin Rosenberg. It all took Charley to an enjoyable alternate universe.

When business was healthier, Charley used to escape to the Frog Pond at lunch time whenever she could tear herself away from work. That was where she truly wanted to be today. But lately, her work time was so essential that she had to forgo her moments of ribbit conversation, which she sorely missed. Having one of Phillips' full-size, short-bodied, tailless amphibians would have been a delight for both Charley and Little Bit.

Dressed in her stylish, gray linen twill business pant suit and eggshell-colored silk blouse, with her shoulder-length red hair pulled back from her face in a French twist, she arrived fifteen minutes early for her one o'clock meeting. It was at the Hilton Boston Hotel near Logan Airport. As she waited, seated in the glass-framed, spacious lobby, which was filled with lush, tall tropical plants and wrapped around a ship's figurehead at its center, she reviewed the information about the man she was to meet. He was a real estate executive from Conway, New Hampshire, who wanted to run for a state senate seat there. Suddenly a man she didn't recognize approached her.

Speaking rapidly, he said, "I saw you alone, was drawn to you like a moth to a flame, because you are so extremely attractive. You have the most amazing smile. It lights up the lobby. Smile again for me?"

Frowning, Charley looked up at him slowly, considering whether to laugh or not. He was six feet tall, athletic-looking with angular features, light brown hair, hazel eyes, a neatly-trimmed beard and moustache, and wearing a dark brown sport jacket and tan slacks. His attire blended in with the abstract carpet of brown circles on a beige background. She glanced back at the photo attached to the real estate exec's résumé. The stranger was not a match for the short, slightly heavy man for whom she waited.

While this man was very attractive, he sounded slightly unhinged in his assault on her. She quickly looked around to see if it were some kind of on-camera prank to record how she would respond. She thought those jokes were embarrassingly cruel. But she saw nothing to suggest it. Before she could say anything, he continued.

"You know that somewhere in the world there's a right girl for every boy. I guess I found the one for me before I even met her. I knew instantly it was my destiny to meet you."

Charley looked surprised then began to laugh, shaking her head.

"You know that's from the musical *On the Town*."

He looked a little sheepish for an instant then regained his composure.

"Admit it. It did get your attention and broke the ice though, didn't it," he grinned.

Looking up through her eyebrows with a questioning smile, she shook her head.

"Seriously? Does that cheesy, over-the-top pick-up approach *actually* work?"

He spread his arms apart, palms forward and looked down over his person as he smiled broadly.

"What do you think?"

She laughed, "You do not want to know what I think," and went back to her reading.

He sat down on one of the tall-backed, brown leather armchairs beside her in the conversation grouping where she had situated herself near the lobby entrance.

"I just registered for a room for a two-day international CGI conference that's being held here," he said taking a deep breath. "Now you know why I'm here. How about you? You're not here just to royally grace the lobby's décor, like another figurehead, I gather."

As handsome as he was, he reminded Charley of the oil slick in the Gulf of Mexico resulting from the British Petroleum disaster. His self-possession seemed to ooze arrogance which she found off-putting. Still, she chuckled to herself, she couldn't believe she was talking with the mirror-possessed epitome of "I'm too sexy for my shirt." But the truth was that she didn't have anything else to do for the moment as she waited. She could take the plunge and try to converse, for a few minutes. At a minimum it might be good for a couple of laughs later on.

"I'm waiting for a prospective client."

"Ah," he smiled and rattled on. "Brains and beauty. An amazing combination. Now you have to tell me more than that. So, what exactly do you do? Perhaps an entrepreneur? Financial analyst? Fashion magnate? Neurosurgeon? Nuclear physicist?"

My God! How affected was this guy? Charley wondered if he was ever off-stage.

"I'm a political image marketer."

"Oh, really?" His voice dropped. "And, ... what precisely does a ... 'political image marketer' ... do?"

His smirking was purposely obvious so she chose to ignore him and not play his game.

"My firm helps build clever, squeaky-clean campaigns for those who want to win their elections for office with professionalism and integrity."

"Really? 'Squeaky clean'? Are you serious?" He laughed out loud. "My dear," he continued looking at her like a teacher ready to correct an uneducated pupil, "that's so old hat. You must be kidding. It went out with pot-bellied stoves and cracker barrels. You can't really believe there is still a market for that idealistic claptrap," he stated more than asked, his right eyebrow raised as he shook his head.

She pursed her lips and debated whether to respond, asking herself if she should waste her breath on such a patronizing, pompous jerk. Before she could open her mouth, however, he dismissed her possible response.

"Well, never mind. I'm Jefferson R. Smith, at your service." If he hadn't been seated, she could have pictured him standing, simultaneously clicking his heels together and bending from the waist as if he were a member of European royalty presenting himself.

Charley frowned and asked herself if his name wasn't the moniker of a notorious con artist in the Old West for whom a festival wake was held annually in Skagway, Alaska?

"What does the 'R' stand for?"

"'Randall.' Why do you ask?"

If she wasn't mistaken, the Old West grifter's middle name was named "Randolph." She suspected, with a laugh, that in this case that was close enough.

His speech accelerated to sixty miles per hour.

"I'm a recognized CGI—computer generated images, in case you didn't know—consultant for architectural design firms, though I'm expanding. I cover the Northeast. You've likely heard of me and the amazing work I do."

"No," she smiled, swallowing a laugh, "I can't say that I have."

"That's very humorous. Anyway, I'm here specifically to conduct the leadership session at this conference. Leadership is so lacking these days. Someone has to help lift up the profession and that's why I'm here. I'm the best person to do that."

Charley stifled a guffaw.

"How very lucky they are then to have *you* to 'enlighten and lift them up.'"

"Yes, that's true. And you? I'm sure you have some absolutely fascinating things you could share with me, that is, besides, what you do with," he cleared his throat, "well, 'politics.' You need to tell me about yourself."

Charley ignored another putdown. She sighed and muttered to herself.

"How do I manage to attract these narcissistic winners!"

Checking her watch, she saw that her prospective client was running late. She was already prepared for him and wasn't sure now if she really wanted to spend the rest of her free time continuing that poor excuse for a conversation. It was too campy and pseudo-urbane. Moreover, it was quickly becoming apparent there wasn't much hope for it to be worthwhile, even for an eye-rolling story to share with her partners.

As she went back to her reading, he suddenly surprised he by speaking without all his previous pretense. It was like a swoosh from an ocean wave, wiping away all the calligraphy in the sand he had previously written with its characteristic flourishes. Assuming she'd be interested, he began sharing some of his history. He said he was born in Concord, not far from the Old Manse where Transcendental poet Ralph Waldo Emerson drafted his essay *Nature*. He crowed that his interests, which were extensive, spanned the arts, marketing, sciences, and technology: a regular Renaissance man.

While his quick turnabout unnerved her a little, she was glad he was finally letting his motorcycle-mouth idle a little. His high energy plus his affectation were too much to put up with for long. It reminded her of how she felt as a child from eating too much Hallowe'en Candy Corn.

Since some of these topics he touched on were actually near to her heart, she began to relax a little as she looked for openings in which to respond. But, as she soon discovered, they were too infrequent; he still hadn't given up the stage.

As he tangentially touched upon one interest and then another, he came across as superficial. She couldn't figure out how much of what he said represented reality. It occurred to her that perhaps he was very insecure and had cultivated this worldly-wise, devil-may-care attitude to protect his vulnerable self-esteem. But, aside from that passing thought, she really didn't care.

Everything he said was spiced with what he must have considered to be wit. But his idea of humor tended toward flippancy and disrespect. She thought this was questionable. But, at the same time, his personality seemed to sparkle as if he were enjoying himself immensely and, perhaps, wanted to share that enjoyment. Charley felt a peculiar push-pull which made her uncomfortable.

Moreover, what had at first appeared as "vivaciousness," now felt like serious nervous energy. As she forced herself to listen to him rave about his personal and professional life, she felt the desire to escape. Go to the ladies' lounge. Get a cup of coffee. Or quaff a bitter cup of hemlock to the dregs.

Even though he had tapered off on his fake compliments to her, his bragging lingered. As he talked at length about his experience and professional CGI designs, he brazenly offered to help make her political marketing agency firm "so much better" through his information technology expertise, which he "knew" she desperately needed in order to succeed. That came out of left field and irritated her thoroughly. While she wanted to set him straight on his insulting, know-nothing assessment of what she did, she decided to say nothing. His level of conceit was incredible. Since her appointment would be arriving soon, Charley felt that contradicting this ignoramus was simply not worth her time or effort.

But just as she was getting ready to tell him she needed to continue her preparatory reading, the conversation jarringly shifted as he segued to a different topic: her. He began to prompt Charley to talk more intimately about herself. It didn't feel like a natural progression of a conversation's give and take. Moreover, he sounded more anxious than eager. Perplexed, she was caught short. Most of the strange men she had had the displeasure of having these initial encounters with had wanted only to monopolize the conversation to talk exclusively about themselves, almost as if she weren't present. While it was almost gratifying that he had shifted gears, he had done so without any finesse.

As he did, Charley noticed that he was now visually focusing entirely on her, disconcertingly staring at her. His pupils were dilated as he held her fast. It was disturbing at first. She asked herself what it could mean. Was it suggesting he had had too many double-espressos this morning or was he actually attracted to her? She had read at one time that humans' pupils dilated when a person was absorbed in something or someone. She felt as if he were trying to hypnotize her or look directly into her soul. While it was disquieting, it was, at the same time, also strangely appealing. She didn't like him but almost felt drawn to him.

As her prospective client entered the lobby, he looked around, and seeing her, rushed toward her, gushing with apologies.

"I'm so sorry to be late. My flight was hit by strong head winds which made getting here on time impossible."

They shook hands. At that point Jefferson stood and paused. Charley wondered if he would now revert to his previous stagecraft by stiffly bending at the waist, reaching for her hand, and kissing it gallantly. To her relief he instead whipped out his business card from his wallet. She took it and hesitated for a minute, deciding if she wanted to politely return the gesture. Almost groaning, she gave him hers. As he turned to walk away, he looked back and gave Charley a lowered-eyelid seductive look. How, she puzzled, was she supposed to read all that theatricality? If he had intended to keep her off balance with all that manipulation, he had done exactly that.

In the meanwhile, her prospective client had seated himself in another leather chair beside her. Sparks of enthusiasm were emanating from him as he grinned. Welcoming him, Charley began to further discuss what her firm could do for his campaign, reminding him of what she had previously discussed at length with him over the phone. She reviewed the campaign examples that were on Ultimate Strategy's website: press releases, print and broadcast ads, flyers, bumper stickers, brochures, diagrams of what a campaign structure generally needed to contain, candidate websites, and typical speech elements. Some of these possibilities could be designed for his individual campaign. She also surprised him with the results of a brief survey she had conducted of what a random sampling of his constituents had revealed of their thoughts about him and his concerns. Exuberant, he said he was ready to sign up then and there. That was one in the plus-column for Ultimate Strategy.

As Charley was on her way back to her office, she thought about what had transpired with Jefferson. Despite his eventual, seeming interest in what she said, it still felt as though the interaction had been not only unnatural but also calculated. Furthermore, his presumptuousness about her business offended her. He knew absolutely nothing about her firm, what it did, and had done successfully. Yet, he had high-handedly thought it appropriate to suggest that her firm was deficient in some way. While she knew there was always room for improvement, he seemed to have made the unwarranted assumption that she and her partners were ignorant or dumb, "more hobby-oriented than real business people." He didn't ask but implied that she and her partners didn't know what CGI methods were, hadn't tried any, or didn't know how to use them effectively. His whole approach was smug, aggressive, and disagreeable. Charley wanted to tell him that it was not a smart or persuasive marketing tack to take but decided there was no reason to bother. He wouldn't have heard her.

Later that evening in her apartment as fatigue from a long day settled in on her, she wondered, over a glass of white wine, if his encounter represented some hidden agenda, like a half-baked sales tactic. Or if he was just practicing his come-on lines to flex his warped idea of sophisticated machismo? Had anything he had said been sincere? After their conversation had gotten well underway, had he actually enjoyed talking to her? In spite of Charley's ego acutely wanting to believe that he had, she was reluctant to accept it. Too much of the interchange had had the flavor of a low-budget 1950s attempt at a "witty" romance flick that she wouldn't have wasted theater-style buttered popcorn on. But still …

It was a puzzle. And while she liked solving puzzles of all kinds, she wasn't sure she wanted to keep toying with this one. She hadn't met anyone quite like him before and now couldn't quite decide what he was about or trying to accomplish. Her first predilection was to forget him. Something whispered to her that he was bad news. But at the same time his seeming contradictions intrigued her. They tickled her need to decode what he'd presented. Down deep she knew that dismissing him was not going to be as easy as she had originally thought.

Over the next several weeks, Jefferson pursued Charley with numerous phone calls, email, and texts, each overflowing with earnestness and studded with smatterings of public performance. On the one hand, it felt distressing. But on the other, it was almost flattering. Because she couldn't quite decide what to make of it all, she kept putting him off. In spite of it, he was unrelenting.

After a while, she began to wonder if, perhaps, she might have been too critical of him. Maybe he wasn't a total buffoon; maybe he just initially came on that way. Maybe he was just anxious or shy and overcompensating for it. Maybe she should ignore some of what had bothered her about him at their first meeting, even though she knew that her first impressions might truly tell the tale. And yet, even if she could forgive and ignore all the stagey techniques, what she couldn't quite relinquish was his negative comments and his overbearing business-related suggestions which had kept cropping up. She didn't know why but his pushiness still rankled.

In his daily communications he pressed her to accompany him to art museums and galleries he especially liked and wanted to share with her. That had a speck of appeal. Because of her having been so consumed with keeping the business afloat, she hadn't taken off any time, for longer than she could remember, for even a little divertissement. When she allowed herself to think about it, she longed to act like a truant for a little while, to play hooky, relax, and have some fun. She knew that obsessing about the business and working all the time was neither healthy nor emotionally smart. Down deep, she acknowledged she deserved a break. Unsure if that were the right move, however, she finally agreed to a Saturday afternoon of "leisurely art exploration" and was looking forward it. But much to her unexpected exasperation, it did not play out as she had envisioned.

The day had started early and became a mad whirl of constant movement, rushing by foot and cab from one art museum to another, from one art gallery to another. Except for Jefferson seeming to need to relieve himself every ninety minutes at the nearest restroom, they barely stopped along the way to take a breath. Charley's requests—then demands—to slow down, even pause in between locations, or get something to eat or drink, went unheeded. This annoyed and gnawed at her.

By late afternoon Charley's energy was sapped from all the bustle of activity … and she was on the verge of dehydration and starvation. The expression that came to mind to describe it—something her father used to say—was "her stomach thought her throat had been cut." Even though she had been wearing comfortable shoes, her feet hurt. After the last photographic display, of the works of Gordon Parks, she was more than ready to go home. She couldn't wait to soak her feet, have a cool glass of Chardonnay, snuggle with Little Bit, order in a pizza, and watch a DVD of *Monty Python and the Holy Grail*. That would have been perfect. She luxuriated in the thought.

However, Jefferson had already made reservations for 5:30 p.m. at the posh Menton restaurant on Congress Street, near the Institute of Contemporary Art, so they could have some artistically-executed French-Italian hybrid cuisine. Even though she had never been there before, she had heard about their amazing wine program and delicacies. While it sounded interesting, something that she'd like to explore some time, she would have given almost anything for it to have been any *other* time.

By their arrival at the restaurant, Jefferson, who had been jet-propelled since the morning, was now at a low ebb, as if he had run out of gas. He seemed unimpressed that they were seated immediately even though it was getting busy. To Charley simply having the opportunity to sit down felt incredibly good. But Jefferson didn't sit. Instead, he excused himself, ostensibly to go make a phone call. While he was gone, she put her feet on the seat of the opposite chair, which was concealed by the table cloth, drank nearly all the water in her glass, eyed the glass carafe with more, and sighed in relief.

As she waited, she casually looked around at the constant stream of customers presenting themselves in twos, both overly- and under-dressed. When that became old, she decided that she might as well use the time productively to check out what the menu had to offer, besides their expertly-crafted cocktails, as had been written about in the *Boston Globe*. There was a panoply from which to choose, but, in spite of it, she still wanted to go home. Since she knew they weren't going anywhere else soon, she eventually settled on the ocean trout with its two delicate vegetable accoutrements. While all the entrées did sound delicious, in her state of enervation they didn't sound as good as a thin-crust, brick-oven, North End Regina Pizzeria pizza.

As she waited, having to ask the waiter who had arrived again to take their orders to come back, she noted Jefferson had been gone nearly fifteen minutes. She was beginning to feel as if she'd been abandoned and, happily, might need to call a cab for herself. When he returned, hurrying toward their table, he seemed like a new person. Gone was his listlessness. Super-upbeat again, he now moved like a frantic rock drummer. She guessed it had been a very successful phone call.

As Charley was ticking off what she was ready to order, he speed-read the menu. When the waiter reappeared, Jefferson claimed, a bit too loudly, that nothing really appealed to him at the moment. He was not particularly hungry after all. Charley was stunned. Feeling self-conscious, she didn't quite know what to do. Maybe that meant she could go home soon after all.

"Wait a minute. You said you were starving since we'd skipped lunch. Eating here makes no sense if you're not hungry. Why don't you just take me home? It has been a very long day and I'm really tired. Actually, I'd prefer that."

He jubilantly dismissed her suggestions, picked out a full bottle of a rare vintage from a lesser-known vineyard from the wine list, then, as soon as it arrived with her meal, had several full glasses of wine in succession. While Charley was feeling non-plussed, she ate her beautiful but spare meal. As she dined, he spent his time at the table in a world all his own, discussing each activity they had participated in that afternoon. He examined each museum's architecture, what he would do to change it, and the galleries' outstanding exhibits—each from all angles—and assessed their value. This was all done in a machine-gun, tutorial-like presentation as if he were running late in class and expected Charley to listen raptly and take notes for a pop quiz later.

After her meal and his having imbibed more than three-quarters of the bottle of wine to her one half-glass, Charley eschewed having one of the luscious desserts she had previously contemplated as compensation for having given up her pizza and her peaceful evening's solitude. While she was eager to depart, it turned out she was not as eager as he was. After leaving an enormous tip with a pronounced noblesse oblige, he hastened her out of the restaurant to finish their date with a fast taxi ride back to his large apartment near Storrow Drive. She begged off, repeatedly saying, "I really prefer to go directly home now, thanks. Maybe some other time," but he chose again not to hear anything she said. It galled her but she chose not to make a scene in the cab.

Once in his large apartment, she found herself being further entertained by his stories of his CGI adventures. Charley couldn't figure out what was going on. In the back of her mind something kept irritating her. Subconsciously, it teased her to address it. Whatever it was, it was enticing, like a missing filling in a tooth that constantly and perversely drew her tongue to explore it.

So, when he ultimately drove her to her door and asked her out for the following Saturday, she was confused and undecided. She wanted to say "no," but at the same time something unseen forced her to say "yes." Maybe this day had been a fluke, she hoped, that he'd been overly anxious about it. Just maybe next time wouldn't be so bad.

From there on, their relationship hydroplaned along on choppy waters as he started again to prod her to have her office employ his CGI suggestions. Explaining that she wanted to keep her work separate from his, she struggled with his increasing pressure to mingle the two. It wasn't long before Jefferson began to complain that he had presented so many of his "innovative ideas" to Charley's firm gratis but she and her partners were unwilling to even give any one of them a try.

"It strikes me as ungrateful and impolite for you to reject out of hand all my generous offers."

It was troublesome having to remind him that just because his ideas were offered didn't mean that Charley, Karlene, and Anne had to act on them.

"While we appreciate your offers, we're long-time professionals in our own field. We know what has worked for us, gotten us clients, and given us deserved recognition, and what hasn't."

When that didn't stop his carping, to be polite they took away time from their own projects to carefully analyze, evaluate, and give feedback on two of his smaller suggestions, which they could quickly do.

"After analyzing them," Karlene told him when they all met at Ultimate Strategy, "we have had to reject your proposed projects because either they don't fit our agency's approach or we have already tried them and they didn't work for us."

Anne added, "We hope you'll also understand that just because you're Charley's friend doesn't mean that we will employ whatever you propose. It has to fit us."

This announcement irritated him enormously and he made sure Charley knew it.

As conflicted as her relationship with Jefferson seemed to be to Charley, she felt that in some small way it buoyed her during the week when she was inundated with nearly "scrounging" for new clients. She felt it was his intermittent high-flying exhilaration—his energy and eagerness—that rendered her more optimistic. She needed that.

As he inadvertently assisted her to exude more enthusiasm, she began to take back some leisure time. It felt good to give herself a small break to do something other than work all the time. She convinced herself it was no longer necessary to spend up to fourteen hours a day, every day, in the office even as business was slipping further. After all, with more relaxation and sleep she could feel less depressed and do a better job at work. She used to do other things when the business was solidly in the black, like painting and running, but hadn't done either in ages. She needed something fun.

In the interim, while they couldn't hire another executive for client interviews, they could employ a college business major as an administrative intern to allow Charley to cut back on her hours, actually eat dinner, play with Little Bit, and go to bed earlier than 2 a.m. Feeling more upbeat, she'd put that on her to-do list.

But, at the same time, her relationship with Jefferson was beginning to alternate between brilliant sunshine and Stygian darkness. The sunshine had drawn her in and trapped her into something moonless and claustrophobic she didn't understand or like. While she compartmentalized and enjoyed this sunshine component, she struggled to understand and deal effectively with these worrisome indistinct areas.

4

Charley had been painting since childhood, taking lessons from her highly-regarded, successful painting mentor, Amie Benison. Amie was the perfect example of "she believed she could so she did." As a youngster, Charley had been considered accomplished, having received awards from art competitions she had entered.

Most of Charley's art subjects were innovative, intricate, layered abstracts, often including Cubist presentations of Nature and liquids in motion, which she did with brush and palette knife. Amie Benison had also taught Charley to work on and copy Amie's own works. She had said her reproducing these abstracts was an important skill Charley could use to broaden her perspective and approach. Amie tried to expose Charley to a wide array of skills and techniques. Learning from Amie had expanded Charley's knowledge and flexibility enormously. Like a sponge, Charley absorbed every inventive molecule offered by Amie and applied them in novel ways. Unbeknownst to Charley at that time, it would have a substantial impact on her, her art, and her life later on.

As a result of her early artistic development when she was a teenager, she had been offered a scholarship to the prestigious Rhode Island School of Design in Providence which, much to Amie's disappointment, Charley turned down. Amie couldn't believe it and pleaded with Charley to change her mind.

"This is a huge honor. They don't give out their prestigious scholarships like jelly beans. Most people have to pay for the privilege to attend. You're my first protégé to have been offered a placement. What they offer is incredible. You can learn so much there, so much more than I alone can teach you. Please reconsider. For both of us."

Charley loved to paint, wanted to paint, and really needed to paint. She felt it opened up an important and dazzling avenue of self-expression for her. She also loved Amie like the doting aunt she never had and would try almost anything she asked of her painting talent, except that.

What Charley didn't tell Amie was that her father had repeatedly discouraged her from painting for a living, that it was a "bad business" for her, irrespective of her artistic reputation which was already blossoming.

"You would have to present and sell yourself. First to become a 'recognized artist.' Then to hawk and sell your works to the public. It would be very hard. It wouldn't be spending all your time painting. You don't have the kind of New York City chutzpah you'd need to do that. Whatever talent you have wouldn't be enough by itself. As a result, you would probably end up starving in a garret in Soho on welfare."

His lack of confidence in her assertiveness and artistic ability undermined her so that she finally acceded to him, relegating her painting to a hobby. With her father against painting as an occupation, she couldn't have gone to this elite school for the arts and not gone into art as a career afterward. That had seemed fraudulent to her.

As she contemplated his objection, she wondered if he had thought that she would find it too personal, egotistical, and crass to actually sell her own paintings. Later she also wondered how he had reacted to her ultimately choosing a "real" career where she was always having to present and sell herself and her political marketing company. He never said. She doubted he'd have seen the incongruity in it. In spite of her love for her political marketing career, for succeeding years painting had continued to tug at her sleeve and her heart.

When Charley picked a non-art occupation, it struck her as odd that it was political science, which seemed diametrically opposed to painting. However, that interest had evolved from her observing how some political campaigns and elections seemed to have become sullied, unethical, and questionable. When a candidate whose views she supported was vilified, being politically drawn and quartered with deception and outrageous lies while the pros and cons of the election's issues were being trampled in the mud, she felt called to get involved. Over time her pursuit of doing what she saw as the right thing nearly took on the vestments of a holy cause.

Providing quality, integrity, ingenuity, and inspiration in political and other campaigns was something she felt was disappearing, having gone the way of the vacuum tube. Though she knew her political consultancy wasn't likely to eliminate most of the scummy practices which many others considered necessary to *win at all costs,* she wanted to show that candidates with well-expressed issues, presented truthfully and innovatively, emphasizing real benefits to their audiences, could engage and change peoples' beliefs and behaviors on issues and candidates to make things better.

5

Jefferson had begun to constantly press Charley to move in with him. In view of their off-again, on-again weekend relationship, she saw no benefit to doing so. She liked where she was. However, in her despondency she was growing tired of his nagging and her having to resist him. His sizable and bright apartment was on the second floor at Mt. Vernon and Otis Streets, with large windows overlooking the Charles River and Hatch Memorial Shell. In his more upbeat moments, he reminded her about the enjoyable music drifting in from the open-air concerts and how much more space she would have. Her having to drive to work and the daily hassle of finding a parking spot wasn't part of his promotional effort. Despite his enthusiasm, she felt down deep that her moving would be making a poor bargain. She had always valued her freedom to do what she wanted when she wanted. Part of her felt her independence and privacy would be infringed upon by giving up her *own* smaller, but comfortable, apartment.

Hers was a five hundred square-foot, one-bedroom apartment with hardwood floors, washer-drier combination, large closets, patio, and a garage. The ambiance was cozy, tranquil, and private. Located off narrow Branch Street, her classic redbrick building was covered in ivy, with vines cascading over the redbrick walls surrounding it, and falling nearly to the redbrick sidewalks below. Heavily-treed, the property was like a green island off Charles Street and a short walking distance to her office. She always felt she belonged there. It was where she could say "hi" to her neighbors and if she needed anything, there was always someone to give her a hand. She could easily access city transportation to anywhere within minutes if she didn't want to drive.

But, still, the other part of her felt that, for all of Jefferson's vices, she had found someone who seemed to care, most of the time and in his own way. Feeling particularly emotionally deprived with all that was going on with her business and her health status up in the air, she needed that more than ever. It was then that she tried to convince herself that if it didn't work out, she could always go back to where she had been and not have to drive to work. Swirling in this desperate magical thinking, she submerged her concerns, threw caution to the imprudent winds, and said "yes."

Over the ten years in her own place, Charley had accumulated so much more than she had figured she'd have to address. She would have to stash her furniture, CDS, DVDs, DVD/tape player, television, small kitchen appliances, pots and pans, dishes, linens, and hundreds of books in a storage unit. Worried about the humidity level and temperature-control of such a unit, she would store her multitude of finished paintings in the ideal conditions of Amie's studio on her property in Chestnut Hill, in Newton, near the Hammond Pond Reservation. As she immersed herself in the packing and transfer of her belongings to storage, she realized what an enormous task she had undertaken. Her interest in moving was rapidly dwindling. Besides, it was taking more time than she wanted or expected to devote to it in the light of the campaigns on which she was still working. Sleep and her acuity at work were again suffering.

After she had finished hauling all her personal property to the storage unit and scrubbed the apartment, she stood in its bare confines, taking it all in. Sadness engulfed her. She looked out the living room window and remembered how the snowflakes had covered the ivy in delicate and intricate crystalline patterns which she had tried to commit to canvas. Her attempted copy of an Alexander Calder mobile, done as a teenager, had hung from the ceiling in the foyer and which moved languidly with the slightest breeze. The wine parties Karlene, Anne, and she had there on the patio in the early days of Ultimate Strategy when they were still full of unquenchable idealism and so ready to meet the world head on. The corner in her living room where Little Bit climbed and jumped about on her six-foot tall, gray carpet-covered cat tree with all its hidey-holes and platforms, acting like a jungle cat, was empty.

Little Bit had been Charley's constant companion and alter-ego for all of her nineteen years. Charley had found this almost-stunted runt of the litter at a cat rescue shelter where she had been passed over repeatedly for adoption because of her perceived abnormalities. Those factors immediately drew Charley's attention to her. For some reason, maybe because she was a fighter, Charley identified with this bright-eyed but often-ignored little ball of fuzz. However, with almost twenty-four-hour continuing care, good nutrition, necessary and appropriate exercise, and lots of love, Little Bit blossomed. Moreover, she exceeded all of Charley's expectations for her.

Suddenly Charley felt untethered, free floating, at a loss. It was as if she had divorced herself from everything that had held any meaning for her.

"If that's true," she repeatedly asked herself, "why in the world am I doing this?"

Realizing her quandary, she was not sure what she could do. How could she back out of the move after telling Jefferson she would join him? She had spent days not working enough on business in order to move out of her apartment. Everything but her clothing, unfinished canvases, painting supplies, and Little Bit had been stored away. Gone was that level of comfort she relied upon in her own little sanctum sanctorum. And the worst part of it was her treasured apartment was gone. She couldn't back out now because she had nowhere else to go. She couldn't believe she had carelessly done that to herself. Was it, she asked herself, some form of masochistic punishment?

As she finished saying good-bye to her apartment, Charley had reconciled herself to her decision to move and was determined to make the most of it. However, within weeks of Charley and Little

Bit taking up residence with Jefferson, things dramatically began to change.

Later, looking back, she thought she should have recognized that it was to be expected. After all, before the move they had been seeing each other only on the weekends and for only a few hours each week. They hardly knew each other and had experienced very little of each other together over longer periods of time. Now they were thrown together almost all the time in the evenings as well as on those weekends which no longer boasted involvement in interesting activities. For Charley it was like the physiological shock of being tossed into a nearly-frozen pond.

What was more evident to her now was how aspects of his personality seemed to change, such as his socially agreeable, respectful persona, and even the vestiges of sharing that she had come to expect from their weekly dates. These behaviors seemed to dissipate and resurge unexpectedly. She couldn't tell if it were her presence, once she had been installed in his apartment, that precipitated his moods waxing and waning, or if it were his general demeanor which she had not encountered, much less assessed, before.

Suddenly, she was experiencing whatever-it-was up-close and personal. One minute he could be depressed, angry, and ravenously hungry and a few minutes later depending upon what he did in the interim, he could be almost manically happy, considerate, understanding, and disinterested in eating anything at all. One minute he could be praising her and the next he could be spewing sarcasm at her. She thought back to their first meeting when she had initially tried hard to convince herself that his flippancy was really clever. Now it was revealing itself as the true hostility and cruelty it was.

The more she witnessed his emotionally erratic changes, the more confusing they became. During the day, he was apparently upbeat and constantly on the go. But in the evening, he was often the opposite. Whatever hadn't gone well at work slithered home with him where it encircled and constricted Charley python-like as he continued to grouse about it and lay blame everywhere.

One evening after they'd nearly had a fight because of his constant evening irritation with everything, he retired to his office. Ten minutes later when he returned, he was energized. Buoyant, he couldn't have been happier with his life and business. The next thing she knew, he wanted to again discuss CGI projects for Ultimate Strategy and kept at it for an hour and a half until Charley could successfully pull herself away when he seemed to have depleted his reserves.

At first Charley tried to be sympathetic with these odd flip-flops, which she didn't understand. But after a while, she tired of dealing with them. It wasn't her responsibility to keep the atmosphere calm and peaceful. What she quickly discovered was that the only way to keep him on a relatively even keel in the evenings, even when he was slowing down, was to agree with whatever he said and did. In other words, she was never to contradict him or disagree with anything he uttered. She was to be, in essence, a yes-person. It was exasperating. That was definitely not Charley. And never would be.

It wasn't until that realization that she fully confronted the degree to which his mood could spike and sink, almost on schedule. Really up after breakfast and really down by dinner, unless …

More often she was also seeing intermittent anxiety and aggression looming with his approaching down moments. In his more subdued moods, he began again to complain about all he had offered to her firm by way of video ideas to help her acquire the new clients which she had indicated she wanted and needed. Whenever he'd start that rant, it seemed to trigger something for him. Sometimes instead of continuing, he'd retire to his office and return minutes later a fully-changed individual, up to the challenge.

It was then that he'd launch into his zealous, much-repeated presentation for her on how best her agency could address their issues and needs. He stated he had the strategies to counter any competitor. He had the video styles that would be the most acceptable to their clients' audiences. "Even an idiot," he stressed a bit too pointedly, "could succeed with them.

"With animations and music," he further insisted, "your clients could better and more intimately reach their audiences, pinpoint their concerns, and effectively respond to them. It would enable you to more imaginatively market yourself to these potential clients. It's the *only* thing that could save your agency."

Early on, each time this transformation occurred and he'd again begun his full-bore harangue, Charley had listened as civilly as she could to his tiresome exhortations. Initially, she still had tried to explain that while she thought his ideas were interesting, her firm was already quite imaginative in their campaign executions and that his proposals were currently too expansive or expensive for their small agency to handle.

He always chose to ignore that fact, elbowed himself forward, and enthusiastically dashed along. As time wore on, he began adding "reasons" for Charley's firm losing ground in their marketing niche.

"Your approach is stale like an old attic. It's horse-and-buggy old-fashioned, for today's market which requires aggressive, in-your-face freshness. You seemingly go out of your way to do the same stupid, prissy things over and over, each time expecting them to work and succeed. If you can't get smart and do what today's savvy program requires, your business deserves to die an ignominious death."

"That's an invalid assumption!" was all she could utter as she shouted inside her head, "You are such a flamingly arrogant, stupid twit!"

Bored by his ceaseless lectures, she ignored most of what he repeated. Regardless of how he presented it, it was not going to work. But, when she once again didn't relent, accept, and endorse any of his proposals, he seemed to lose patience.

No matter how often he tried to bully and intimidate her, he knew those tactics likewise were not going to work. But, in spite of it, he wouldn't—or couldn't—acknowledge defeat. However, one particular evening before he disappeared into his office, he added a warning note.

"I'm sharing with you my vast, superior experience, expertise, strategies, and tactics that have worked over and over for larger firms than yours. And what do you do? In your ignorance and stupidity, you simply toss them aside like garbage. You're on notice as of this moment that I will not tolerate that any longer."

This time Charley snapped. "Ignorant and stupid?" She clenched her jaw, trying to keep control, "You—" The phrase "arrogant asshole" was being prepared to be expressed but she held it fast because of his anger. Instead, she addressed the issue. "You do NOT have a clue about my business. And, furthermore, *I'm* the one who won't tolerate your insults any longer."

Charley was fed up with his rancorous accusations. But at the same time, she didn't want to say too much which could provide fodder for further arguments, or worse. She could see his face contorted with rage and could feel the increasing heat. Things were escalating. Suddenly he was no longer just berating her; he was threatening her. There was no question that he meant what he said and she was at risk. He was unpredictable. As he left the room, he was clenching his fists, knuckles white.

Seated alone at his long, mahogany dining table, she felt trapped, overpowered, and shellshocked. This realization smacked her with a tsunami's wall of water which was striving to batter and drown her if she didn't go with the flow. It was apparent that she could no longer put up with his outbursts and tantrums. While he had never physically abused her, it was a short distance from verbal to physical abuse. Whenever he had lectured her, they both invariably went to bed angry, with him spending most of those nights either awake in bed or pacing around his apartment. And this evening was no different. Charley was afraid to go to bed to sleep for fear of what he might do.

Chilled by his ultimatum, she had to finally acknowledge, as she lay in bed alert to every sound, that she had made a very big mistake. What she wanted more than anything else at this moment was to be able to magically click her ruby slippers together three times and go back home. But "There's no place like home" rang hollow for her. If only she had remained rationally-focused enough to have held on to her much-loved apartment as she had previously decided. How, she asked, could she have been so incredibly dumb to have let it go?

6

Karlene and Anne had been leery of Jefferson from when he first arrived at their office ostensibly for a CGI-related overview of their business. Their first impressions told them something was wrong. Despite his always being upbeat with them, he didn't come across to them as genuine. Most of the things he said to them felt false, as if he were slathering them with soft-soap. His turbo-charged patter indicated to them that he had an ulterior motive that wasn't in their best interest. He was trying to steamroller them into something. Without a doubt, they knew he was too self-centered to be trustworthy.

While they had wanted to communicate that to Charley, they didn't want to create a rift if they didn't have to. As far as they could tell, she seemed outwardly satisfied with her relationship with him. Instead, they decided together to wait until they all were having a problem with what he was doing or wanted to do. Then they would carefully introduce their concerns to her. In the meantime, they vowed to stay vigilant.

While Charley was searching for another apartment, the firm did accept one of his minor CGI marketing project suggestions just to see if he really had anything on the ball. He was thrilled and repeatedly lauded them for their "perspicacity." His condescension, though expected, chafed but they chose to ignore it. Immediately, he was like a child who couldn't begin to work on it fast enough. Given a free hand to execute it within their pre-determined budget, he moved like a person on fire, his feet barely touching the floor as he bounded around, throwing out his scintillating ideas to impress them. Their hope was that he'd just disappear into wherever he did his work and leave them to theirs … and return *only* when he was finished. And if they were very lucky, with something productive.

Over six weeks' time, however, despite his constant popping in and out of their office with repetitive questions and excuses, nothing he did seemed to be working quite right for him, irrespective of how he configured and had to reconfigure the project. That struck them as distressing and unprofessional.

Unbeknownst to Karlene and Anne, at night in his apartment he was frequently despondent, anxious, and rarely sleeping a full night if at all. His thinking seemed murky. By the project's deadline, one that he had imposed on himself, he was looking haggard and exhausted as well as unable to demonstrate his promised results. No matter how Ultimate Strategy would examine what he presented, there was no way to measure an increase in clients, a noticeable and acceptable return on investment, or more efficiency than already existed.

When he saw the final figures on his finished project in their office with Karlene and Anne present as well, he became irate and blamed Charley personally. Grasping for excuses, he began to sound paranoid.

"This approach has been shown repeatedly to work. If only I had had my way totally, without you amateurs' interference and a ridiculous budget, it would have been wildly successful. You purposely made sure it wouldn't work. I want to see the real figures!"

"Wait a minute!" Karlene countered. Everyone was tired of accepting his tirades. "You had your own way. You were in complete charge. You knew what the budget was at the very beginning before you accepted the project. You knew the details and boundaries. You said you had plenty of time in which to do it."

"That's not so! You're twisting it."

"If you had needed more, you had only to put that in your plan. So, if there was a problem, it was up to *you* to adjust your proposal to adapt to it. You never told us at any stage of the project that there was a problem. And, to set the record straight, these *are* the real figures."

He wasn't pleased that she was contradicting his flimsy excuses.

"I'm the CGI expert and you're not. Your expectations were way out of line with the likely results of the program. You should know better than to expect marketing miracles from a short-term project."

Anne broke in, "That's crap. You're the one who said it would show positive results in that time frame."

Jefferson's face was glowing crimson as he hyperventilated and made fists.

"That's the problem working with amateurs. They constantly monitor your work, ignorantly interfere, have totally unrealistic expectations, and doom it all to failure!"

Karlene and Anne shook their heads. Charley ignored his pathetic rationalizations. She was busy evaluating the execution of an escape plan. While she didn't want to go to a hotel and spend any extra money that could go into the business if necessary, she felt she was taking a large risk staying where she was. Visions of her former domicile haunted her. She wanted to cry at her loss.

Back in his apartment she increasingly noticed that he was continuing to lose weight and not sleeping. She, likewise, was losing sleep as a result and it showed. Annoyed with whatever Charley said and did, Jefferson began questioning her motives for what he perceived as her ill treatment of him.

"You've been stealing my CGI ideas. That's why you've said you rejected them."

When she made the mistake of responding to him, that they hadn't stolen any of his ideas, his temper flared. His face flushed. Veins stood out in his forehead. It was then she noticed that his eyes looked very bloodshot. Breathing hard, he fortunately chose to go into his office instead of retaliating. Her heart raced as she contemplated not only the level of risk to her but also what she should do at the moment.

Even though he was smiling when he returned, Charley knew from then on that she had to bide her time, keeping out of his way and mostly to herself, as she checked the "For Rent" pages. She still hadn't found any apartment in the city she could afford. The ones she could afford were way out in the suburbs—north, west, and south—and would take up too much time each day commuting, time she felt she couldn't waste.

The next Saturday morning he wasn't his ebullient self. Instead, he seemed very anxious, striding back and forth in the living room, wearing a track in the colorful Oriental runner near the front door. As Charley was quietly fixing Little Bit's breakfast in the galley kitchen, Jefferson was muttering to himself as he strode.

"He said he'd be here. Where is he? You can't depend upon anybody."

"Can I help?" automatically called Charley. The moment she did, she knew she should have just kept quiet.

"No, *you* can't help!" he shouted. "I'm waiting for a colleague with some important plans I need for a project I'm proposing for people who fully understand the true depth of the professional experience and expertise I have to offer."

Charley corralled Little Bit, fed her on the kitchen floor, then tiptoed to the living room corner near the picture windows which overlooked the water where she had had her easel set up. Just as she was cleaning her brushes so she could put them away as part of her readying herself to move out, Jefferson exploded. He began to throw any small objects within his grasp against the living room wall.

"That goddamn son of a bitch bastard! He knows I need it!"

Little Bit ran from the kitchen and hid under Charley's easel, ears erect, eyes nearly bulging out of her head. Fortunately, he hadn't hit her with any of the pieces of pottery that he had smashed that now littered the hardwood floor. He had scared the cat so badly that she tried to wedge herself under his mahogany hutch beside Charley's easel and became stuck, increasing her panic. When Charley couldn't coax her to reverse course to try to squeeze herself out, Charley began to carefully pull her out. Her spine grated against the lower rail of the front frame. As the cat cried piteously, Charley's eyes swam in teary guilt.

Twenty minutes later, when his colleague finally knocked, Jefferson threw the remaining decorative dish in his hand to the floor and raced to answer the door. Standing there was a young man in a black hoodie, jeans, and running shoes who handed over a bulky manila envelope to Jefferson. In the meanwhile, Charley had painfully disengaged Little Bit. But no sooner free, the cat ran under the chocolate-brown leather sofa and hid there, frozen against the wall. Jefferson, grunted, and headed to his office with his envelope in tow. But before he closed his door, he looked back at Charley and angrily shouted to her.

"That goddamn cat doesn't belong here in *my* apartment. I want her the fuck out! Now!"

Charley absorbed it with increasing agitation. The warning sirens were blaring louder and more frequently now as things were rapidly regressing. Before she did anything else, she carefully moved the heavy sofa away from the wall, peeled Little Bit off the charcoal gray, acanthus leaf William Morris wallpaper. Then she held her close, gently trying to soothe her panic and abraded spine. She needed to act.

In the beginning, she had been worried that even though Jefferson tended to simply ignore the cat, he might purposely, or unintentionally, harm her when he was distraught. Now that he had portentously targeted Little Bit, Charley knew she needed to remove her *immediately,* irrespective of when she could remove herself from the premises. She'd figure out something.

Dipping into her pocket for her cellphone, she called Karlene and asked her for temporary cat help. A feline lover, she agreed in an instant. Guessing there was a problem, Karlene stated that her mother was staying for a while so she didn't have any room for another human guest. After thanking her for her intuition, Charley asked Anne about the possibility of staying a few days. She discovered that Anne had just taken on a roommate to split expenses because of their business decline.

It had become readily apparent to Charley that Jefferson's initial attraction to her had more likely been based on finding an opportunity in which he could take control of promoting a professional political marketing firm than on his attraction to her personally. It was probably a way for him to expand his reputation and résumé as well as elevate himself financially and status-wise as an information technology, CGI, and data marketing expert. That would be a plus in Boston's esteemed, competitive scene. That realization hurt. With everything that was going on she had wanted so badly to believe otherwise and had talked herself into it, despite that little voice in her head continuing to whisper, "Beware."

As Ultimate Strategy continued to lose ground, Charley slowly slipped onto the outskirts of a deeper depression. Each fleeting thought she had negatively chased away the next one. Everything seemed maddingly oblique. Even Amie's weekly, normally-uplifting painting sessions, now that she was back from New Mexico house hunting, didn't seem to be able to penetrate this shadowy veil hanging over her. When she finally accepted that she couldn't do this alone, she revealed the situation to Amie.

"Leave him," Amie begged. "Think about Little Bit and her safety. Think about *your* safety. He's mercurial and has serious problems. And you already have enough on your plate to deal with without him adding to it."

"Believe me," Charley said, "I've been working on it but finding an apartment is taking longer than I expected. Right now, everything feels so unworkable and lost."

Charley blushed magenta as she felt humiliated disclosing her failures in so many areas. She knew she should have left him the moment he started to treat her badly. But, no, she had not only put up with his perilously unpredictable behavior for far too long but also wasn't making the necessary progress fast enough to move out. It was obvious that she had to stop looking for an apartment and get whatever she could manage to live with, including the YWCA if necessary.

"I'm glad you told me because I knew something was wrong. I know it's hard to deal with but it can only get worse. He's like two people, Jekyll and Hyde. He's treating you like a punching bag. Let *me* help you get out of this. You can stay with me. We'll discuss my Southwest moving plans tomorrow. Okay?"

Before Amie's offer, Charley was feeling desperate to do something—anything—as soon as possible. She had had to restrain herself from acting impulsively, like immediately moving into an inexpensive motel as far west as Framingham. But even with Amie's home to go to now, she knew she couldn't just blithely walk out of Jefferson's apartment with her possessions in hand. It would not be safe. The reality was that when she left, she had to do it surreptitiously so there would not be a dangerous confrontation. Amie was right. Jefferson seemed unbalanced and couldn't be trusted not to harm her. If she could manage it, it would be safer to wait until the right moment.

Until she could make her move, she thought that her increasing travel to secure more needed clients could help keep her away from Jefferson for days at a time. To protect Little Bit longer term, she would move the cat from Karlene's to camp out with Amie and her large, long-haired, black cat, "Saatchi." Furthermore, when she wasn't traveling, she could leave for work even earlier and come home even later. She hoped his current sleep habits wouldn't interfere.

As a result, maybe she and Jefferson would barely see each other. Maybe she could sleep in a chair in his extra room. Since he would be pre-occupied with other things, those maneuvers could help reduce their interactions and tension … if she had to stay there much longer. She only wished she could start to move her possessions out that instant.

As a contingency, in case something came up and Amie couldn't have her move in with her right away, Charley looked into possible motel vacancies. But that idea turned out to be a bust, at least for a while, because there were several conventions in town or coming to town which resulted in no room availability even into the nearby suburbs.

As Charley waited to hear Amie's upcoming schedule for moving, she allowed herself to fully recognize the emotional pit she had slipped into and took a few minutes in her office to wallow in a quagmire of "poor me."

"My business is dying. I'm going to have Alzheimer's and, maybe, breast cancer. Little Bit has become a sad, frightened cat. I gave up my ideal apartment which had been a steal financially and an island of peace and contentment." Shaking her head, she recalled, "I stumbled upon it when an economic downturn had rendered rents incredibly low and had held on to it. I will never find such a huge bargain again. Since then, the in-town rents have become exorbitant.

"My so-called relationship with Jefferson has been like bathing in toxic waste. It's made me ill physically and emotionally. Beyond rationality, I wanted him to be something he wasn't—a 'diamond among men.' Despite his polish, he had so many irredeemable flaws. Unlike a diamond, he didn't sparkle gray and white brilliance on the inside and reflect a fire of a rainbow of colors onto other surfaces. His colors were hidden on the inside, like a hunk of glass. He was simulated and just plain fake.

"And I acted like a dunce by giving up myself and my right to be respected for some imaginary affection. I put myself in a position to be treated like an object. I was merely a means to an end for him. He never really cared about me as me. That's so humiliating.

"Okay, I admit it," she said to herself as she finished. "It was something I felt I needed to, wanted to do at the time. It was a big risk I was willing to take then. It turned out to be an even bigger mistake than I thought it might be. I'm correcting that now. The only rehab for such stupidity is not repeating it."

Having given herself permission to have made a big error, she felt somewhat relieved. In spite of it, her depression was still attempting to dance around the edges of her mind, tantalizing her to give in to it. But Amie had provided her hope so she vowed she'd be damned if she would give in. Even though she temporarily felt as though she just didn't care about anything, she knew down deep she did. She cared for and about Little Bit. Her feline alter-ego had strength, not from physical capacity but from an indomitable will. If she could survive this grievous situation, so could Charley.

When Charley saw her mentor the next day for lunch, Amie shared her plan. It was one Charley knew could work. That was a huge relief. Now it was just a matter of when she could implement it.

While she tried to do her work on ongoing campaigns, she still had to deal with her peripheral sense of foreboding. She had to find the right time to move out of Jefferson's apartment. She knew that if he had the chance, he would try to stop her even though she wasn't giving him the jobs he wanted to showcase his talents. Maybe it was a matter of control. It certainly wasn't that they had any kind of salvageable relationship. Whatever his reason, she knew he'd try to hang onto her, or maybe worse. She had to be very cautious.

Because she wanted her partners to know the details of her efforts to leave Jefferson, after inquiring about bunking with them, Charley explained her circumstances. That finally gave them the opportunity to admit that from the outset they had been confused by her actions as they pertained to him and the firm. His arrogant attempted intrusion into their business affairs showed he was more concerned about himself than what they were all working to accomplish.

"We were worried about you," exclaimed Karlene.

"You know we are completely on your side and will help in any way we can," added Anne.

Charley hugged them both, glad she had fully shared her situation with them. She was beginning to feel even better about her plans. As expected, Amie's solution was solid and would be relatively easy to execute. Charley was eager to get it underway but had to wait for the most opportune time.

That moment materialized shortly when Jefferson left for a two-day CGI convention in Hartford, Connecticut. As soon as he had departed and she had checked to make sure his car was really gone, she began to pack. It would take several trips to Chestnut Hill even though her possessions there seemed pitifully few. She had all her business attire and other clothing, her in-process paintings, some of which were still wet, her art supplies, and the rest of Little Bit's paraphernalia she hadn't already transferred.

When she arrived for the last time at his apartment, she left him a farewell message, locked the front door, and shoved the keys under it. Now she didn't have to worry about being there to have to argue with the volatile Mr. Hyde about her decision to leave. However, there was still one small snag. She couldn't totally disengage herself from him just yet. But, luckily, that interaction would be at her office, not on his home turf.

The firm had contracted with him to perform another simple, albeit non-CGI, project for them. It was his writing an article for the *Boston Business Journal* about their firm's imaginative involvement with a Boston charity. While under other, less urgent circumstances, Charley would have been the one to write it for *BBJ*. However, she once again had been spending upwards of twelve hours a day on a campaign, that was likely to be her last, for the Mayor of Lynn, Massachusetts, who was being smeared in the media by his primary opponent. And her two partners were occupied with what might be their last campaigns or political marketing tasks as well. Unlike so many of Jefferson's proposed marketing ideas, this one seemed reasonable because Charley had seen some of his published writing in local papers. She regarded his news reportage as very good and well-suited to their article.

The contract deadline for the article was approaching. Once it was in the agency's hands, they would blue pencil it for inaccuracies before submitting it to one of Charley's contacts at the paper. While that positive piece was unlikely to save the agency, it wouldn't hurt either. Besides it would highlight what wonders Karlene, Anne, and Charley had wrought to make the charity event a super-success.

His doing the article, however, meant that Charley would have to continue to deal with him until he handed in the finished product, or failed to do so. She wasn't sure how his concentration was doing these days due to his ongoing insomnia but he had been given plenty of time in which to complete the task. At a minimum their interaction would be only for a few minutes. With witnesses present he was probably not going to do anything untoward or violent.

As the article deadline neared, he came to the office upbeat, wearing shades, his skin looking gray, making extravagant apologies and bringing Charley flowers and candy, reverting to his greasy compliments to ask her to return. It was awkward and only for show considering how really angry he was with her for having moved out in such a calculated way. He knew if he had been there, she wouldn't and couldn't have left. He was the only one to make those decisions. His left eyebrow twitched each time he re-considered her actions.

But in spite of all his unexpected excuses for possibly not completing the project on time, Charley and partners were not about to let him out of his legal contract: He'd be paid only for an acceptable, finished article when it was due. If he didn't finish it, then it was just too bad for him. They decided not to bother to hold him legally to the contract if he defaulted. It wasn't worth the hassle at that juncture. Instead, if necessary, Charley would work on it late at night and first thing in the mornings to have it published as soon as possible.

Not surprisingly, it did arrive on the last day at the last moment before they closed the office that evening, by an email attachment. Charley thought it was more credible that he had delayed it on purpose to make a point. But she felt it was probably important for him to finish it to have the credit for work on a project for her political marketing firm. He could add that to his résumé. All she cared was that it was finished … and it was actually well done. To her surprise there was nary a single sneer. Charley signed his check and snail-mailed it to him, bidding him a not-so-fond adieu as she dropped it into the postbox.

"The mark of gross stupidity, Jefferson, is thinking you are always brilliantly correct and everyone else is still crawling out of the primordial ooze."

Following Amie's suggestion, Charley moved into Amie's house, which Amie was planning to put up for sale in six months or fewer. When Amie finally did put it up for sale, Charley would have to give final consideration to Amie's other proposal about leaving Boston to follow her to the Southwest. It would all depend upon if Ultimate Strategy were still treading water or back on dry land at that time. Six months was a long time and the company was already sinking fast.

Amie's proposal for a new business venture felt like an escapist's pipedream. It was so inviting. They'd work and paint together to showcase and sell their respective artwork. Charley would become a "real" painter, a professional artist. What she had always desired. That meant no more hobby painting. The idea thrilled her. Suddenly she thought about her father. It was too bad he couldn't see her succeed in what he had so roundly denigrated. She let herself wonder what would have transpired if he hadn't bad-mouthed it ages ago. It didn't matter. For her now it would be upward and onward.

7

The *BBJ* article was about The Animal Rescue League of Boston (ARL), which described Ultimate Strategy's pro bono marketing work with this top-rated charity. ARL provided quality veterinary care, adoption, and rescue programs that confronted the root cause of animal cruelty and neglect through community programs, as well as police investigations and public advocacy. What Charley and her partners had done was consult with ARL on their next big push for donations by conceiving new and different ways to reach the animal-loving public, past adopters, potential foster parents and adopters, and financially-endowed benefactors.

They acquired sponsors for all their programs. One program offered two fee-for-entry contests for the best one hundred animal stories. For adults the stories were at least two hundred and fifty words, but no more than five hundred, about animals they had adopted from ARL. The one for children, depending upon age, was from twenty-five to one hundred words. These stories would be published for ARL as two books and made available for purchase with the authors' names emblazoned on them. Children could also provide their drawing of their adopted animal to accompany their story in the children's book.

They had had a contest for the best photos of adopted cats and dogs in adorable poses which would also be made into a coloring book for children, which likewise would be for sale. In addition, there was a recorded "Stupid Dog Trick" contest for children, with the resulting fun videos available for purchase.

There was a seminar on how to quickly teach dogs and cats ten tricks; a survey which would detail a person's personality makeup and lifestyle to match that to either the dog or cat species, a specific breed, and a particular animal. Posters with adoptable animal pictures. Adoptable animal t-shirts for children. And an adoptable animal parade where the public could see then meet those animals seeking loving homes in an animal café setting. They offered booklets for a small price to fosters and adopters on how to care for dogs and cats at their different stages of life, from newborns to seniors, so they could feel more comfortable caring for any new animals.

One of the highlights was a silent auction of animal artwork—which ranged from paintings, etchings, sculpture of all kinds and materials, pottery, quilts, embroidery, weavings, greeting cards, posters, to photos, etc.—which artists and animal owners had contributed. Furthermore, with the assistance of a lawyer friend of Charley and the Cummings School of Veterinary Medicine at Tufts University, they helped create an updated manual for the public which formally established protocols to identify and report suspected animal cruelty throughout Massachusetts and provided guidelines and methods for making rescues and keeping animals loved and healthy.

As a result of their hard work, the media coverage, which they had planned and arranged, was extensive. They had initially raised over seventy-five-thousand dollars from the public and a quarter of a million from philanthropists for The Animal Rescue League of Boston, with more expected as the contributed-to animal books were published. Charley, Karlene, Anne, and even Little Bit had worked their magic with donors. Everyone was very pleased with what they had accomplished.

8

Then, just as Charley moved into Amie's home, she was viciously attacked in the tabloid press. A national political strategy firm which was trying to further expand its influence and client base began waging war with Ultimate Strategy generally, but with Charley specifically. Without any real evidence, it accused her personally of being a con artist who unethically was putting her own corrupt financial interests ahead of her clients' campaigns to the detriment of her clients and their success.

In particular, this agency claimed, "Charlotte Eyre has charged scandalous fees and produced shoddy, underhanded, often bordering on illegal, results instead of the quality service she promised and that her clients deserved. They stated that was not new. She had quietly fleeced clients for the last ten years with her questionable campaigns."

They allegedly backed up their claims with "testimonies" of individuals who asserted they had been Charley's clients, and who further hinted she was anti-religion, racist, and, perhaps, even a Communist. The big problem with all that was that their client references, to a person, had never been Charley's or her firm's clients, and had never even spoken with them.

After the impressive response to the ARL article, Charley was appalled that these unsupported and unsupportable lies had been published. Furthermore, these claims and that attack made no sense to her whatsoever. Ultimate Strategy was merely a speck in the political image consulting landscape and probably wouldn't be around much longer anyway. It had only one office, and that was in Boston. Most of what they did was for single candidates and groups scattered about in New England. They were hardly competition for this national firm.

The attack was a conundrum until a colleague mentioned Charley's recently acquired state-politician-to-be and his considerable value to any political marketing agency which handled him. After that, she looked even harder for old articles and sought gossip from many more corners about him. She had already realized he was *that* special. She knew he was an up-and-comer: good-looking with a "dazzling smile," charismatic, smart, well-educated, monied, with a well-known family. But she hadn't as yet seen him as having the potential of a new JFK, worthy of a large cult following. If she hadn't been so distracted by everything else, she probably would have because she was known for her background investigation thoroughness. He had important contacts in high places and possessed the innate ability to connect with the so-called "common people." Some early articles and old pols saw him as having apparent unlimited political and financial prospects. They even touted his political future in Congressional terms, and "beyond."

Before the lie-based article came out, when they had met for the second time, he had told Charley her firm was special to him.

"I'm choosing your firm for my first campaign because I want it to be super-clean and sincerely clever. Also, I want to prove myself without all the backroom politics. My campaign will not be about secret planning, exercising control, and using dirty tricks and payoffs to rig an election."

That was a breath of fresh air to Charley.

So maybe the reason for this monstrous assault was that the national firm, Winning Campaigns, had badly wanted to sign him up. But what she learned a short time later was that the onslaught probably also had to do with an opinion piece she had published in *BBJ*. It had been about some public relations and political marketing firms using perception management as the primary propaganda tool of their campaigns. She had bemoaned the adverse effect it had on political marketing as a profession and how it had negatively, unfairly influenced election results with its fake polls and lies.

From her research, it had also become more apparent that perception management was slowly, silently insinuating itself into local, state, and national political actions and policies. She imagined that it would, in the not-too-distant future, be the new norm in what was fast becoming a war of "information," not of facts.

Perception management, which originated in the U.S. military as part of their Psyops program, was a technique which provided "selective information"—deception, distortion, dishonesty, disinformation, fabrication, and falsehood—to influence the emotions, motives, and objective reasoning of a target audience in order to advance a desired behavioral change. Those who managed perceptions in these campaigns were not *spinning* facts, like so-called "spin doctors" who presented information in biased ways. Instead, they were *creating* the "facts," using conspiracy theories, identity biases, alternative realities for truth. In other words, trending politics toward dystopian extremism. This was definitely not something that the political marketing firms which used it wanted discussed in the press. Not if they wanted their campaigns to be believed as gospel, accepted, and embraced that their candidates honestly cared for their constituents' issues.

The article's publication had created a stir and controversy for a week. But since specific firms could not be named, without risking an expensive, retaliatory law suit, the impact of her microscopically-examined examples of their use of lies and deception was short-lived. But it had created a distinct impression and made Charley and Ultimate Strategy stand apart, for good but also for ill.

Her recent state senate client, when confronted with these blatant lies about Charley, was conflicted. While he had liked her and her agency's approach because he too was idealistic enough to want to try to avoid the negative, psychological character assassination campaigns of the larger companies, Winning Campaigns' crusade against Charley had contaminated the local and regional media, social media, and blogs with constant detrimental rumors and stories. Those close to the client were very concerned as were a growing number of his enthusiastic supporters. His first campaign with the "ethically questionable" Charley was seen as too risky, irrespective of the virginal image he wanted to portray in his first public introduction.

Winning Campaigns, which had contacted him, repeatedly informed him, by showing him the results of the spurious polls and focus groups they had ostensibly conducted, that his reputation would be irredeemably blemished by staying with Charley's firm. He surely didn't need that kind of stain on his emerging record. They emphasized he would figuratively die on the vine before he even had a chance to bloom politically, much less bear fruit. That, they informed him, was something a young politician like him simply couldn't afford to let happen. As a result, Winning Campaigns said they would save him by helping him with his current campaign, initially gratis. Furthermore, they were willing to guide and assist him in every aspect of the planning of his splendid future of success which they guaranteed he would have with them.

With regret and concern, he left Charley as she was suing Winning Campaigns for libel. A month later, Charley won her suit against Winning Campaign. Having already done their calculated damage, they saw no reason to fight it. Her reputation had been trashed. While the truth when laid bare was recognized and understandable, it didn't necessarily change anything.

Fortunately, Ultimate Strategy had hardly been touched by the article. And yet, prospective clients stayed away. Old clients who valued what the firm had done for them previously still had Karlene and Anne provide services for them as long as those services wouldn't be associated publicly with Charley or the firm by name in any way. Their arthritic business was barely limping along. If it had been having trouble swimming in storm-tossed waters before, it was now being fitted with cement booties to guarantee its sinking to its watery grave.

When Winning Campaigns recanted in the tabloid, as part of the settlement agreement that they had reached with Charley, they stated that all they had claimed about Charley had since been "determined to be untrue, that sources had lied to them." Naturally, the notice of settlement and national firm's recanting did not make the front page where all the accusations had been boldly printed. Instead, they had been buried seventeen pages back with the crossword puzzle. Likewise, that had become a mere side note on the Internet, if it were mentioned at all. Even the *Boston Globe*'s own investigation, reported on page two, which acquitted Charley of all charges made no meaningful difference given all the harm that had already been inflicted. None of it mattered any longer. There was no coming back at that point for Charley.

"Maybe," Charley chuckled cynically, "I should be glad they didn't also label me as a 'blood-drinking, child-sex-trafficking, fascist animal abuser' just for good measure."

What was ironic was that Charley had, before she and her partners opened their own agency, briefly toyed with becoming a part of an existing national firm. But the idea of being merely a cog in a large firm, having to do whatever trickled down to her, "ethical, slimy, or in between," spending all her days slogging routinely, not contributing creative input, didn't appeal to her. She wanted to have the freedom to decide what campaigns *she* would choose to work on and how to handle them.

When she, Karlene, and Anne had first started the agency, Charley had already been courted by several such firms because of two spectacular campaigns she had run on her own. One was to help pass a bill in the Massachusetts legislature to prevent genetic discrimination in health insurance and the other was a bill to require that pre-existing conditions be covered by all health insurance plans issued in the state. Ironically it was Winning Campaigns at that time that had pressed Charley the hardest to join them.

But now she discovered that she was persona non grata for all of those same large firms. Several maverick political strategists did ask her to join them. However, their soiled reputations preceded them. They were willing to do *anything at all* to win a campaign, and had already done so more than once. That would have required her to be willing to chuck her principles and integrity in order to join them for nothing more than a paycheck. Slugging it out with other firms' campaigns meant she'd have to get down and dirty, wrestling in the malicious, unscrupulous Atwood mud. To try to survive in one of these hothouses of mendacity was not a viable option for her. The reality was that she could no longer operate as a political strategist in Boston.

After checking out the possibilities elsewhere in Massachusetts, she determined that because of her notoriety if she wanted to continue with her current profession, she would have to move to another state and re-establish herself where she was hopefully as yet unknown. But given the echoes of the charges against her by Winning Campaigns, which, she discovered, were persisting after all this, she knew she was likely to never be an "unknown" in her field. There seemed little sense in her struggling to keep her anonymous participation in Ultimate Strategy's already-lurching business alive even as an outside consultant because of her newly-acquired "demonic stigma."

It reminded her of how she felt on her first day of second grade. It started with everything being right with the world. Wearing new shoes and her first pair of jeans, she felt very confident, eager for school, and ready for anything. When the students hit the playground for recess, a wandering dog greeted her. This was a good sign too because she loved animals. But no sooner had she started to pet its head than it leisurely lifted its leg and pissed onto her shoes. Startled, she jumped back, tripped over a clump of grass, and fell, landing on her bottom directly in a fresh pile of dog feces. No doubt another gift from this friendly animal. There was no way for her to go home to change. She scrubbed as best she could in the restroom, leaving her jeans aromatic and wet as if she'd had her own accident. There was nothing she could do at the moment for her soggy shoes. For the rest of the day no one wanted to be near her. And for days after, her school mates tended to regard her suspiciously, sniffing to check her out first before joining her in any activity.

Finally, having decided to sign the agency over to her partners, Charley talked with them, suggesting possibly changing the firm's name to try to plunge ahead to recoup some of their losses. That appeared unlikely since their so-called "passé" principled business was going down for the third time in spite of all their Herculean efforts.

It all seemed so unfair to them. Charley, like Karlene and Anne, had toiled to create the agency out of empty space, sweat, tenacity, imagination, and integrity. They were entrepreneurs doing whatever it took to develop an agency that was a credit to themselves and their community. It was now that they all truly began to feel the loss and grieved. Guilt soon overhung Charley's thoughts of leaving. Yet, after having been portrayed as a Typhoid Mary, her association even as a silent partner could mean death to any remote chance of the business regenerating any semblance of its former self.

While Karlene and Anne seemed relieved with Charley's decision to sever their connection, they also knew that without divine intervention, and even changing the firm's name, old and new clients wouldn't start breaking down the door again any time soon, and maybe never would. They reluctantly acknowledged that their "take the high road" ethical approach essentially had become "unfashionable" to too many people who lusted for a win any way it could be achieved. The impetus of political marketing had emphatically become "the end justifies the means." In spite of it all, Karlene and Anne desperately clung to the idea of hanging on until the end of the year, to give it one more old Northeastern University try. Go, Huskies!

9

After a short time, Amie notified Charley that it was time for her to put her house on the market. After all that had occurred in Boston, Charley was not only ready but also hungry to make that big move to New Mexico. The artistic proposition she had received from Amie had since become even more attractive. With Amie's house in a seller's market in Massachusetts and houses in a buyer's market in New Mexico, it took her only a week to locate a house in Glorieta.

It was nineteen miles southeast of Santa Fe, located in the Sangre de Cristo Mountain foothills. Flying out to inspect it, she bought it just barely before she would have a sales contract on her own home. Through her Santa Fe realtor, she also collected photos and descriptions of similar houses for Charley to consider. Because of Little Bit's age and health Charley didn't want to fly to New Mexico to inspect the properties in person before moving. She felt she could do that once she was there.

Before Charley had left Ultimate Strategy for good, as she finished everything that was still pending, Amie had urged her to start readying herself for her own move. In other words, be prepared to depart Massachusetts as soon as possible because several buyers had shown interest in Amie's Chestnut Hill property. By the time a sales contract would be coming up, a closing would not be far behind. Charley could possibly have a month at the most in which to be ready, but two weeks was a more realistic probability given how fast things were moving.

After having left Jefferson's apartment, Little Bit had recovered from her chaotic life with his violent paroxysms but it was suddenly becoming clear that she was beginning to show her years. What

Charley had not noticed before, because of Jefferson's frenzied milieu and Little Bit's anxious panting in response to it, was that her cat's breathing was beginning to sound particularly labored when she moved around. In addition to her panting, she had begun coughing. At first, Charley ascribed that to Little Bit being allergic to Saatchi or whatever was in Amie's house or barn. Charley had moved her property from the storage unit to the barn as she decided what to move West with her and what to sell or store. She had made an appointment for her cat at VCA Brookline Animal Hospital to address her problem.

Nevertheless, as the days dragged by, Little Bit was not only getting sluggish but also was having difficulty exercising and walking. She was obviously grappling with something serious and it was worsening fast. Her once-hefty appetite had dropped off. When she meowed, her gums look pale. That was it. Charley wasn't going to wait for the appointment next week. She immediately took her to VCA's emergency clinic.

After carefully examining the cat, doing x-rays, and making a diagnostic assessment, the veterinarian, Dr. Marilyn Cokefair, looked grim.

"I'm sorry to have to tell you that Little Bit has severe congestive heart disease and it appears to be worsening fast." The vet furrowed her brow. "I can detect fluid building up in her lungs. She'll need to be on multiple medications to help her."

Charley swallowed hard and her mind went blank.

"She'll need Furosamine to promote diuresis—urine secretion— and regulate fluid retention. To help her stressed heart pump better she'll need Pimobendan."

Tears rolled down Charley's cheeks and stained her denim shirt.

"And further to assist her heart to beat more easily and more efficiently, she'll need Enalapril. It will relax her blood vessels so her high blood pressure will decrease to allow the blood and oxygen to flow to the heart more effectively. Hopefully, it will also reduce further fluid build-up in the lungs."

Charley looked at Little Bit, focused objectively on her for the first time, and finally recognized how her beautiful silver coat had seemingly overnight begun to look unkempt and matted despite its short length. She had to acknowledge that the cat no longer delighted in being brushed and combed and, sadly, would crawl away from Charley when she attempted to do it. She had to admit that there were many things Little Bit could no longer do, like roll onto herself to groom her tummy or inner back legs because it interfered with her breathing. As a result, snuggling with Charley was rarely of interest even though Charley coaxed her and tried putting her on her lap or in bed with her. Any extra movement, either on her own or from Charley moving her, made it harder for her to breath.

All the individual behaviors Charley had been noticing, but, perhaps, trying to dismiss because of what they could mean, coalesced into a realization that her cat was on her last legs. Little Bit could no longer enjoy much of what she had loved since the very beginning when she likewise could barely get around on her own, but for a totally different reason.

As the following days revealed, the continuing dosages of medications had less than salutary results. Despite what they were prescribed to do, they didn't seem to make her any more comfortable. Even though Charley knew better, she wanted instantaneous positive results which weren't forthcoming. After a week, this didn't bode well. Dr. Cokefair carefully increased the dosages. Charley didn't want her fur baby to keep struggling to breathe, unable to act as a cat should. She wanted her relaxed and contented, in any way she could achieve that for her. At Charley's request, the vet shaved a place on Little Bit's rear right leg for a pain-med patch to ease her distress because giving her another pain med, buprenorphine, by mouth tended to make her choke and panic her.

Once settled on a well-padded kitty bed on the floor, Little Bit would accept Charley's petting in moderation as long as it didn't require her to move. Still, she never seemed to be her old congenial self even with her loving human companion stroking her gently and not putting any pressure on her back in case it might interfere with her breathing. It was clear that if she had had to do much moving to ask for or receive her due, she would have chosen to continue to lie there quietly, unpetted.

Charley brought her food and water to her and placed a low-sided litter pan close by so she could relieve herself without too much exertion. As it became necessary, Charley would carefully place Little Bit, holding on to her front and back legs only, in the pan. Because of the use of diuretics, Little Bit needed to urinate often.

Now it seemed that Little Bit was responding primarily internally, to her lungs and heart being overwhelmed, rather than to her surroundings and Charley. Soon it was all too clear that the coronary-disease medications were not sufficient to allow her compromised heart to deal with the pulmonary fluid accumulation. Charley was undecided about what to do and when to do it. If only she could find a way to increase Little Bit's physical ease for as long as possible so the two of them together could enjoy the short time she had left.

In the meantime, Amie had discovered several especially good real estate listings which she had emailed to Charley. When Charley wasn't talking quietly with Little Bit or offering her a special tidbit, like canned tuna broth, she checked out each house. She took the virtual tours, sent emails asking questions about costs of utilities and taxes of the several real estate agents associated with the listings, and checked on mortgage possibilities. Tentatively she had decided on one smaller home, with room enough for an office and studio, which also would be in close proximity to the one Amie was buying. That convenience was important. She made her decision, spurred on by not wanting to take too much time away from Little Bit. Contacting the real estate agent for the house, she made an offer on it. The sellers, who were nearly finished building a house in Pahrump, Nevada, were eager to sell and accepted Charley's offer in one day.

Charley then asked the agent to hire a house inspector. While the buyers offered to have her use their previous inspector, that wouldn't work for Charley. She needed her own, independent inspector. Her parents had made that mistake with their first house and ended up with "missed" cracks in the house foundation, water damage in a basement wall, and a mold problem that weren't discovered until after they had closed on the house.

Charley shared with Amie her housing activities and that Little Bit's illness would most probably postpone her own move to New Mexico, but not by much.

"Don't worry. I'll be sure to be out of your house before the end of the month so there won't be any problem with the new owners moving in."

"That's fine. I'll stipulate in the contract an extra week for you to leave. The new owners are moving from New Jersey and don't have a tight schedule."

Even though Charley had been enthusiastic about moving, when Little Bit demonstrated her serious condition, everything seemed to be turned upside down. There was no way Little Bit could agreeably survive a long drive to Santa Fe. If necessary, as time drew close, Charley would move out of Amie's house to a motel to see Little Bit as comfortable as possible through her last days.

Whenever Charley sat beside her best-friend feline, Little Bit looked at her human companion with half-closed eyes before dropping off to sleep again. She slept most of the day, unlike before when Charley was around. Charley watched as her chest rose and fell, still working hard even on the maxed-out level of heart meds and the replaced opioid patch to keep her as pain-free as possible. As she catered to Little Bit's diminishing needs, she continually asked herself.

"How cruel and thoughtless am I by keeping Little Bit around me because I don't want to let go?"

She knew the answer and she felt selfish and guilty. She just didn't want to say "good-bye" to her most loyal friend ... but, at the same time, she didn't want her dearest friend to suffer either.

When it was obvious that Little Bit's time was quickly drawing near, Charley picked up the cat in her kitty bed and placed it on a puppy pad she had spread on the bed beside her each night. And every night just before the cat closed her eyes, Little Bit would exert herself to raise a limp paw to touch Charley's nearby face. Charley would touch the cat's face in return and smile as cheerfully as she could, despite choking up, knowing this might be the last thing her companion would see.

She always said, "I love you, Little Bit. You're the *best* kitty ever."

But in spite of all of Charley's loving care, Little Bit's heart could no longer deal with the strain of the fluids in which her lungs were drowning. One night shortly after her last visit with Dr. Cokefair where Little Bit had been sedated, she silently slipped away. Her kitty mom, awakened from her twilight sleep by a deep sighing sound, lovingly caressed her as she passed.

Charley felt robbed of the one true loving companion of her life, the one who always brought out the best in her. She always made her feel good about herself: lovable and capable. Her closest, sweetest, most nonjudgmental friend—even more so than Amie—was gone ... forever. Little Bit would never again snuggle warmly on Charley's lap, purring, and then crawl up her chest to put her front paws on Charley's shoulders to lick her chin as if to say, "It's okay, Mom. We'll get through this together ... somehow."

Charley felt immobilized. Suddenly everything that she had tried to suppress that had happened this last year burst forth like a dam, submerging her in a bottomless pool of sadness and blameworthiness. Doing anything now seemed pointless to her. Why bother to move? What was left for her? Even though she had known Little Bit would die ... sometime, she hadn't truly come to grips with it in her heart. Her heart had a hole in it so gaping that a U.S. Navy fleet of two or more squadrons of small warships could charge the waves through it.

Now it seemed to Charley to have taken too much time for her to have come to the stark realization that she had to escape her former living situation or else. As a consequence of her reticence in dealing with Jefferson, Little Bit had suffered so much anxiety and fear before her kitty mom mobilized the fortitude to move out. How could she have done that to her cat? She had failed and lost her furry pal. And with her now gone, there seemed to be nothing left for Charley.

The proposal her painting mentor had made to her had sounded wild and fun but that was before her cat-involved world had crashed in on itself. Everything suddenly sounded like a fantasy or a mirage, unlikely if not impossible, purely wishful thinking. Was she really willing to make the move for something that sounded so improbable? Becoming a "best-selling artist," that career her father said could never be?

Through her hot tears, she felt her heart drop. Her chest felt tight, compressed by reality. Nothing made sense. Nothing mattered. She had Alzheimer's. Maybe breast cancer. She had been crucified in the press. Lost her business, and, maybe, her former life career. And now she had lost the best of her, Little Bit. Spiraling downward into a deep hole, she uttered what she had finally revealed to herself.

"Everything meaningful is gone ... forever."

After kissing Little Bit's head, she left her warm, inert body on the bed, grabbed her car keys and driver's license, and drove north, seeking the right spot. For some odd reason Charles Stuart came to mind. Indicted as the double-murderer of his wife and unborn child for an insurance policy on her, in 1990 he leapt from the three-span, two-tiered Tobin Bridge which crossed the Mystic River, connecting Boston to Chelsea.

Traveling northbound onto the Tobin, she parked on the lower level of the cantilevered-truss bridge in the right-most of the three lanes. There she left her identification and keys on the passenger seat of the car, praying no police would see that she was parked illegally before she could fulfill her mission. The toll plaza had been closed in the 1980s so no one was staffing the roadway. Strangely, there was only intermittent traffic on this busy two-mile stretch at 11 p.m. Climbing the railing between the green trusses, she was about to throw her right leg farther over it when she heard a piercing cry of extreme pain.

Leaning back momentarily on her left foot to keep her balance, she spied limping toward her from the north a small, pale smoke-colored, short-haired cat, as it moved awkwardly forward. It looked like a wraith except that its left back leg was bloodied and dragging. It was making odd vocalizations interspersed with high-pitched cat yelps, begging her for help, as it slowly approached.

Charley automatically switched gears. Something in her soul required her to address this situation. She had a duty to help this poor, injured creature. Not only rescue but also transport it to the nearest veterinary clinic for immediate care. Unlocking her right leg from the rail, she pulled it back, to ready herself to capture the cat. But no sooner did she have both feet on the pavement, than the animal had vanished from view. She looked around. Where could it be? Intently, she listened for its crying but heard nothing. That made no sense to her.

Confused and verging on panic, she started to search for the animal. Walking yards in one direction then yards in the other, on both sides of the bridge, she couldn't locate it. Even though its back leg had been bloody, she couldn't find a single blood droplet, much less a trail of them, which she had expected. But the blood on its leg had looked wet to her. That was incongruous. Where, she pondered, could this badly injured feline have gone? There was no place for a cat to hide along the bridge that Charley could observe. But she was not about to give up looking.

After twenty minutes of searching on foot, she got back in her car to continue her hunt. But she could find no sign as she glided along backward to the on-ramp and then forward at barely five miles per hour toward the off-ramp, scanning every visible inch of the roadway and railings. Stopping, she found her frustration, bewilderment, and anxiety for the cat had replaced her despair. She shook her head, amazed at what she had been prepared to do before the cat appeared.

"That was damned stupid. For a smart person, that was not a good solution, Charley," she whispered to herself, almost laughing, incredulous she had even contemplated it. "Never again, no matter what. Little Bit would never have approved. She had been a real fighter who didn't give up but did what she had to do. She hung on 'til the absolute end for me. Her love for me gave me strength. And now my love for her can give me courage to go on. That's the least I can do for her."

Having been discouraged from jumping that night, she exited the bridge and then drove back south on its upper level to Amie's house. There she wrapped Little Bit in the puppy pad that was on the bed and fell asleep cradling her.

The next morning over strong coffee she calmly re-examined her previous plan to move. In reality, there was nothing left for her in Boston. And New Mexico had the advantage of being someplace new and different. She had read that the people there valued the arts and that countless well-known modern and contemporary artists lived and made names for themselves there in the various pueblos as well as in Taos, Santa Fe, Corrales, and Placitas, where they had formed important artist communities.

Unsuccessfully holding tears at bay, Charley talked to herself.

"In someplace new I can re-evaluate my present and future and begin to make a plan for it. It could be a fresh start with fresh thinking. Painting with Amie and whatever else I can do, hopefully with marketing. It could work. And Little Bit would approve."

Even on the unimaginable off-chance that her mentor's proposal didn't work out, since it did sound a little crazy, Charley felt she could use the disengagement to set up some version of her own political consulting practice. That was, if news of her illegitimate "shame" had not stretched to New Mexico. What exactly would happen at that point would be uncertain, but she suspected she could figure it out without breaking a sweat. She had done it before so she could do it again. She had to. In her mind she raised a fist of power.

"There are lots of ways to go with my extensive experience and expertise," she added optimistically.

After all, she was strong, smart, inventive, and had overcome large obstacles before. She gave herself a thumbs up and smiled at that sneaking hint of confidence.

As soon as Little Bit had been cremated by the Animal Rescue League and Charley had collected the ashes, she contacted Amie to inform her she would soon be on the way. Then she began to finish packing. This time, *everything* she owned that she cared about was going with her. This included all her previously finished paintings which she had had stored with Amie.

However, before she left Boston forever, she galvanized her resolve and finally made an appointment at Beth Israel Deaconess HealthCare, a short distance away on Boylston Street, "because it's the smart thing to do," she told herself. She thought she really ought to have the DNA tests done to either confirm or disprove her upcoming Alzheimer's threat. Time was running short. While she waited for the results, she experienced intermittent palpitations. She'd given it fourteen days and hoped that had been enough. The response had to arrive before she left. She couldn't hang around.

It was on the day before she was to leave that her results arrived. Opening the envelope required more courage than she thought she could muster. With her hand shaking, she used a thumb nail to unfasten it quickly, pretending she was pulling a bandage off a wound fast to reduce the pain. But it never really worked that way.

After double-checking their results with two separate tests to make sure, their geneticist revealed what they'd found.

"Dear Ms. Eyre:

"There is no indication that genetically you are likely develop Alzheimer's early-onset or Alzheimer's at any time. The original Alzheimer's DNA finding was a false positive. That is not to say you could never develop some form of Alzheimer's or senile dementia. However, were you to develop the disease at some time in the future, it would be more likely the result of some random occurrence, a confluence of factors.

"While at-home DNA tests which are approved by the FDA and meet U.S. standards for Clinical Laboratory Improvement Amendments (CLIA) may tell you that you are more likely to have a certain disease, they cannot predict—tell you with any degree of certainty—that you will have that disease. There are too many other factors that influence whether you might have it, and if so to what degree, such as your life style, habits, and how your body responds to the environment.

"It is important to be aware that some private, at-home DNA tests may be sold without proof that they work as advertised. I hope this has been helpful and answered your questions."
"Best regards,
"Leslie Day-Ebert, MD, PhD"

Charley threw the letter into the air and whooped.

"I can't believe I waited so long to check it. I could have avoided all this anxiety."

That was a pathetic lie. She hadn't wanted to have it etched in granite that she was going to be losing her personhood any time soon, not with everything else life had recently thrown at her. Suddenly she laughed, then shook her head. That was the first hopeful sound she had uttered since she had taken Little Bit on a leash to the Boston Common Frog Pond, a couple of months before Winning Campaigns had destroyed her name in business. Maybe things were actually looking up at long last.

That was one pressing thing off her mind. But what about her breast abnormalities?

"Well," she mused, "I have had these images for ages. Maybe it's serious and maybe it isn't. None of my physicians has seemed unduly concerned after each series of these diagnostic tests. Each time they have said they've found no discernible measurable changes. So, it looks as if I'll merely need to continue my annual mammogram schedule and regular breast self-examinations. Okay, Charley, since you've done all you can, there's no need to continue to worry about it needlessly."

She had to conclude that it was time to put her previously distressed and unhappy life behind her and start brand new.

"On to the land of cacti, sun-parched skin, painting, … and a reinvigorated life."

Because she didn't want to haul a trailer behind her car for two thousand one hundred and eighty miles, she contracted with Allied Van Lines to pack what she hadn't as yet packed and move her belongings. Before she let them in, she had had to get rid of anything she hadn't used in a year but kept essential pieces of furniture, like her three Stickley pieces of Mission furniture: a tile-topped cocktail table and two Carlisle-style end tables. She also disposed of any hazardous materials and anything perishable. Sadly, she gave away to Karlene and Anne some of her indoor plants which she loved. She couldn't take them all in her car, only her variegated philodendron, a "Rise and Shine" bright yellow miniature rose, a weeping fig, and a Christmas cactus. They would ride in the back of the car, shaded, making sure they were safe from extreme heat or leaf-burn. Little Bit, in a small brass urn, and an album of photographs of her from over the years would keep Charley company up front.

As she had learned from her parents who had at one time early in their marriage not done this and rued the result, she made a careful, numbered inventory of everything to be moved. This would give her a detailed way to assess that all items shipped had been delivered. Having a list of missing or damaged items would then enable her to file a damage claim with the mover or an insurance claim with her own insurer. After she had taken a day to complete that, she let the movers in.

When they were all finished, Charley was surprised by how little space her possessions took up in wooden moving crates in the massive trailer, even though she was taking all her important belongings. Next, she steeled herself for her butt-numbing thirty-three-hour drive to Glorieta.

10

Amie and Charley's houses were situated only four hundred feet apart in the middle of Glorieta, a small village covering seven point six miles with sixty-eight people per square mile, twenty minutes out of Santa Fe. The town sat at an elevation of seven thousand four hundred and thirty-one feet and was punctuated by mature spruce, Douglas and white firs. The ambiance was wild and private, with few adjacent houses. Charley would bunk with Amie and Saatchi for a day or two while she awaited the moving van and then would quickly tuck herself into her new home.

At night Saatchi curled up with Charley in the second bedroom. She started with lying on Charley's pillow which she kneaded, lulling Charley into sleep. Then she gravitated to her right shoulder and ended up crawling up on Charley's chest, where she stuck her nose into Charley's as she purred. While Charley was present, Saatchi enjoyed taking over her bed territory. Because Little Bit had loved to knead soft bedding and furniture areas as well as parts of Charley's anatomy, Charley wondered if cats were doing it to recall the contentment of initiating suckling with their mother. In reality, it didn't matter if that were it or if it represented something else entirely. Charley just enjoyed the cat's pleasing touch, movements, and sound.

Simultaneously, Charley planned to discover what she might be able to do to work with her political marketing background as she and Amie started Amie's plan. Maybe she could offer telephone coaching. She wanted to make that decision as soon as possible in order to rapidly inaugurate her new business. That was the Big If: if her notoriety hadn't spread all the way to New Mexico as well. Since

Santa Fe was the capitol of New Mexico, there were lots of politicians of all stripes, in the legislature and locally, as well as the less politically-habituated surrounding areas, who could use her brand of help. And New Mexico's largest city, Albuquerque, with over five hundred sixty thousand population, was only sixty-four miles south on Interstate 25.

In three-days' time she had fully moved into her seven hundred square-foot pueblo-style house. At the entrance there was a Spanish arched, cedar-stained, plain, heavy-wood front door with large black wrought-iron decorative straps. Mimicking an actual adobe structure in stucco, it had thick, round-edged walls in a natural earth color inside and outside with small square windows, with frames and muntins painted in cedar stain, set deeply into the outside. Inside the ceiling was natural cedar tongue-and-groove wood with bark-shaved ceiling beams, which extended through the interior walls to project into the outside (vigas). The roof appeared flat but sloped slightly to direct rain to two wooden, metal-reinforced drain projections (canales), on each side of the house with a French drain below. In the back was a wide porch (portale) laid in unfinished brick in a herringbone pattern, its tongue-and-groove roof supported by three rough-hewn wooden posts.

Throughout the house the floors were set in a goldish-red brick which were laid out in a dramatic sunburst design. In the living room were a beehive fireplace (kiva) in the corner, benches built into the walls (bancos), and arched niches (nichos) in the walls for displaying art objects. Multi-colored decorative Mexican accent tile adorned counters and back splashes in the kitchen and bathroom, around the opening of the fireplace, and along all the lower walls where baseboard molding would have been in traditional New England houses. Overall, it had a comfy, slightly exotic, feeling that Charley liked.

The room she would use for her studio had a northern exposure which was ideal. It would provide indirect or reflected light which would produce controlled and cool value shifts, subtle color changes in the paint because it would not be affected by the sun moving through the studio at different angles during the day. Detached from the house at the rear and at a right angle to it was a two-hundred-fifty square-foot electrified pueblo-style, stucco-ed outbuilding, the same color as the house, that would be just right for her office. There was a separate entrance on its long side at the end of the building. It was set off from the house by delicate New Mexican willows, a curving, sunset-colored pebbled walkway, and a native-flower garden in silvery blue and yellow on either side, paralleling it. Charley was very pleased. It was close enough to be convenient but separate enough to be professional if she chose to have clients come.

As soon as she moved in, she began surveying what area politicians and future politicians were doing and not doing to set up and achieve their election campaigns. Using her mother's maiden name, she made up flyers stating she was doing research on political campaign strategies. These she paid the newspapers and the various state and local periodicals to place within their pages. Responses were to be sent to a post box she rented at the Santa Fe UPS Store. Her goal was to learn what political strategizing needs people in the area had that weren't being filled.

What she discovered through her online research was that the legislators didn't serve all the time. The legislature met in regular session on the third Tuesday in January of each odd-numbered year. Regular sessions were limited to sixty calendar days, but every other year it was thirty days. Massachusetts legislative sessions likewise occurred every two years beginning on odd-numbered years.

The survey results fascinated her. She found that, in general, there was no way for young politicians to do their basic campaign marketing at a cost-effective price. Most admitted, with detectable embarrassment, that they couldn't afford a full-scale political image- or campaign strategy consultant so they were bootstrapping, and not always successfully. What Charley also learned was that some of the neophytes had already met with the bigger names around the area, but to no avail. To their disappointment they found that their return on investment simply didn't make it advisable for them to purchase any of these more well-established, comprehensive services from the notables.

Some indicated that their being not as computer research- and poll savvy as they thought they needed to be in order to work with a less expensive consultant was a problem. And others who didn't have the time to do all that was required to work with a minimum-service professional likewise felt at a loss. While they all knew they needed to be involved in their campaigns, they had not as yet figured out how to balance the different aspects of their lives satisfactorily with a campaign.

Consequently, Charley had a website quickly designed, almost the identical twin of her former-agency site, substituting Santa Fe and Glorieta photos for the Boston ones, to address these survey results indicating the politicians' most basic research and consulting needs. She notified all who had participated in the survey of what she had to offer to them. Emphasizing how these beginners could spend their time and money better laying the groundwork and building their campaigns, she promoted the use of sound, imaginative, influential marketing copy with someone with ten years of experience in a Northeast political nerve center.

But what clinched it for many, who began to send her emails seeking further information, was that Charley offered to consult over the phone, do teleseminars, employ web conference calls, and provide power point slides directly to them to minimize the time they had to take away from their jobs, businesses, or homes.

Most of what Charley would provide to them was their political marketing education and a way for them to then educate their public about what they did, how they differed from their local political opponents, the trust, integrity, and honesty they offered, as well as the benefits they would provide if chosen the public's new state legislator, mayor, or local council member. The benefits, determined by survey, would be what was most important and appealing to their constituency, whether social, civic, justice, financial, and/or environmental. All this would be done by keeping their campaign before the public continually and creatively in order to supersede their competition.

After Charley had set up her coaching practice, she felt confident that she could continue more or less as she had in Boston. At the same time, she would continue to work with Amie on Amie's and her own paintings, as per the proposal. Things were looking up.

In a week's time she had her first client. Surprisingly, they had met standing in line at a bank on Cerrillos Road in Santa Fe. Through their conversation about her being a newcomer, she found out many bits of information about how she could learn more about what was going on politically in Santa Fe specifically and New Mexico generally. She also shared her related background.

"Funny you should be involved in political campaigns," responded the man in front of her in line. "I want to run for the board of education but haven't a clue how to do it. I'm Al Cordova by the way," he announced with hearty handshake.

She gave him her new business card and heard back from him in two days. Stating he found her website illuminating and encouraging, he enthusiastically signed up for coaching, her writing copy for him, and strategy implementation.

It took Charley three weeks to research, create, broadcast the image of Al's fit for the office, and roll out his campaign. She had a basic website developed for him which asked for his constituency's comments. The feedback for him coming in was mostly positive. They both were gratified. Charley felt good about her new start which suggested lots of potential for business growth.

When Al won his election, she was thrilled but exhausted and quickly realized that after Boston, she no longer wanted to be involved in the campaign implementation as well. It was too much work even for a small election. But more importantly, it wasn't wise, just in case word of her Boston downfall became known. Being further behind the scenes was financially and personally safer. What she now really preferred was offering only private consultation and instruction. Feeling good about this, she re-tailored her website.

However, what she didn't know at the time was that her first political marketing client in Santa Fe would be her last.

After Al won, she took out a business ad in the *Santa Fe New Mexican,* or simply *New Mexican,* a daily paper often referred to as "the West's oldest newspaper," having printed its first issue in 1849. In her ad, chancing to use "C. H. Eyre" instead of her full name, she touted the benefits her political campaign experience and expertise in education, research, and image consultation, which she had rolled into her coaching practice. She stressed that campaign structure and image skills were essential to new politicians. Making reference to past accomplishments, she did not refer to her recent client because he had not given her permission to do so.

By chance her ad which ran for five weeks happened to catch the eye of a New Mexico State House reporter who recognized her name from an online article on "politicswise.com" a month before. Curious if this were the same person, he promptly began to investigate. There had been lots of coverage, especially in Boston and around New England, on what had transpired as well as the controversy that had ensued. As a result, he wrote a straight-forward, page-two piece about Charley's appearance in Santa Fe. At length it described her successful history, the wide-ranging accusations against her, winning her libel suit, her company slipping competitively, and her leaving what remained of her business and Boston to resurface in Santa Fe.

Charley was not happy to have it all dredged up again, although what was written was accurate, and not slanted. However, what happened two days later was precisely what she had feared. The paper published a "Letter to the Editor" responding to the article about her. It was from someone she assumed was a powerful political force in New Mexico, who also was probably involved in most of the important campaigns in the state. In his letter he stated that while he "sympathized" with Charley's plight after her having had a well-regarded small Massachusetts agency, which had created some noteworthy campaigns, he questioned her successfully running campaigns in New Mexico.

"I'm surprised Eyre has come here to set up her political marketing practice. Does she think that New Mexicans would not have heard about the astounding and serious accusations made against her back East? Despite her having won her lawsuit against Winning Campaigns, I can't help wondering if there wasn't a scintilla of truth to the many claims of unethicality made against her and her agency. Because of what political consultants do to manage public opinion to get their candidates elected, too often one finds that where there is smoke there is fire. I'm not suggesting we rush to judgment about Eyre. I'm open to seeing what Eyre can do to rehabilitate herself and make New Mexico proud of her. With that in mind, I welcome her and wish her good luck. But given her alleged shady past, I fear she may need more than a super-abundance of it."

Charley was stunned. He had implied she was a crook and urged everyone to beware of her as if she were a convicted felon. Before Charley had even established her business, the article and letter together had rung the death knell on her efforts.

As she later learned what she had suspected, nearly everyone in politics who wanted to get ahead in the New Mexico power structure knew it was imperative to stay on the good side of this political power player. Even though she was exceedingly small potatoes by comparison and no competition for him and his firm, he had just drawn a line in the sand around her and essentially provided a stark warning to her potential clients:

"All political newbies and you old timers as well, you can look but don't touch. If you need political help of any kind, you come to me. It would be unwise to be brushed with the lingering black mark of her widely-reported unethicality and illegality."

She was flummoxed. She had barely started a brand-new life and suddenly her integrity had been questioned and she was rendered persona non grata here too.

"But why?" she asked. "I'm just not important enough to be concerned with. Besides," as she had since discovered from her research, "he practically owns political marketing consultation and all it entails from local to state campaigns, not only in New Mexico but also in the entire Southwest."

She could picture this head honcho on a throne-like chair with all his calculating acolytes seated at his feet, looking up at him with rapt attention, absorbing every precious gesture and syllable from on high, lusting for whatever he had to offer them.

"Crap! All I'm offering is coaching on campaign education."

Again, it wasn't until a while later that she discovered that he was also a part of the upper echelon of Winning Campaigns which had so successfully libeled her. This second take down, likewise, was not by chance but further vindictiveness for her article on "perception management."

In her newly open-for-business office, Charley contemplated what to do next. Re-assessing her business position from every angle, she knew she could no longer be effective or make money doing what she had done successfully for a decade. Now anything associated with her name was bound for failure because of the stain. Even a paid blog or newsletter was out of the question. She'd been tarred and feathered to a fare thee well. Her new website as designed was useless. Moreover, it appeared there was nothing else she could she do to modify or restructure it for anything else if she used her own name on it.

At the same time, she didn't want to take it down. She'd paid a website designer handsomely to set it up, had purchased a domain name, and created a merchant account to handle payments. Maybe, she shook her head in dismay, she should wait in case something else occurred to her. As unlikely as that might be, she felt it was not beyond the realm of possibility. Well, she hoped so anyway. She needed a good stream of income. It was obvious that one wouldn't come immediately from her painting. But, were there any other reasonable options available to her? Standing on a street corner in sheer tulle teddy and a smile wasn't one of them.

While Charley was taking a shower the next morning, she remembered something a U.S. ski team physical therapist named Jess had said to Olympian ski jumper, Nick Fairall, who had had a jump accident which rendered him a paraplegic and mired in deep depression.

"The injury doesn't change who you are. You can still do whatever you want to do. You might have to do it slightly differently."

In other words, there were no limitations to what he could do. He just had to apply some sort of adaptation to it. Motivated by that, the former ski jumper adapted a water ski to let him ski which gave him a similar speed-infused thrill to ski jumping. Then he began to compete which he loved. Soon he was doing many other such things as well.

"Adaptation" was the answer. Charley knew she was good at that. At that very moment something flashed before her. Maybe she could adapt it after all. The idea was not only self-evident but also potentially very productive. It could be a real winner and she knew exactly what to do. The benefits were clear. She had only to sell Amie on it.

Feeling optimistic that it was workable, she wouldn't broach Amie about it until she had done her research first. She needed answers for herself as well as for Amie's possible queries and concerns. Things, she thought, might be looking up after all.

After she was dressed, she began searching "Amie Benison." To her considerable surprise she learned that Amie did not have a personal or business website. However, there was page after page of individual links to her on the different search engines. They were for galleries that sold her works, well-known locations of various named paintings, articles about her, her education, reviews of her style of painting, things that she'd done, places she had lived, who her students were and what they were doing now, and so much more. There needed to be in a central site for access to all relevant information about Amie and her paintings. Amie needed to promote herself so her public could more easily purchase her paintings and have her do commissions for them.

"Amie," Charley thought out loud, "damn, girl, you *really* need this website and someone who knows exactly how to successfully market you with bells and whistles."

While Charley would first have to get Amie on board, she could then re-create the website to promote Amie's painting events, showings, and make available ancillary products (like posters, prints, a book of Amie's work, and whatever else came to mind) whenever they created them, and more.

As expected, Amie wholeheartedly agreed. She was overjoyed that Charley would take on the distasteful task. She admitted that she had had neither the time nor the inclination to work with a designer, be a webmaster, or market herself. In fact, her understanding of marketing wasn't just deficient, it was non-existent, especially when compared with Charley's. Charley chuckled, suspiciously wondering if that had been Amie's plan all along.

Within a week's time Charley's website designer, Geoff Slattery, had converted Charley's site to Amie's, with a new domain name, re-named payment gateway, links to articles and galleries, and placement on all the Internet's important search engines as well as on useful social media sites, like Facebook, Instagram, and Pinterest. For all practical purposes, the infamous "Charlotte Eyre, Political Marketing Consultant" had disappeared from public view. She had dropped out of Santa Fe and, as far as anyone knew, off the face of the earth. Geoff made sure there was no recoverable connection between her name, her old Glorieta site, and Amie's website. A new dawn and a new day.

For the next year Charley divided her time between painting for herself and Amie and becoming increasingly involved in the business of marketing and selling art. Anonymously applying her skills to expose Amie's art to the world was child's play. In the future she hoped Amie would offer painting instruction videos through the website which she thought would be fun. It was something she would have liked to do herself but hadn't as yet figured out how she could do it without using her own name or image. Either way, that project would require much planning and careful execution. But if she could create the videos, they could be another effective and profitable sales technique for them. Charley found she was overflowing with ideas to successfully market Amie. Soon they'd be on the road and on the map. That was the epitome of adaptation.

Until her marketing would help draw larger numbers of people to the site to imaginatively tweak their interests, the "amiebenison.com" website did enough to help them stay in the black, but barely. While website visits were always increasing, painting sales had dropped off during the summer, when people were vacationing. Fortunately, they were ramping up again as fall approached.

As Charley worked with Amie to determine what new products would be of the most interest to her aficionados, she did a website survey. Then she added the most popular items as quickly as possible. As a result, business was improving. Charley managed this part of the business out of the office in her own house. Online sales and shipping kept Charley busy when she wasn't painting with Amie in Amie's style as she had done over the years. Most of her painting with Amie was done in Amie's studio which was more convenient for them both. However, it would soon become a necessity.

Slowly Charley had begun to notice physical changes in Amie. They were primarily in the little things she did ... or ... seemed to have difficulty doing. At first, she didn't think too much of them. What she noticed initially looked like occasional physical quirks. Amie would go to pick up a tube of paint and her hand would miss it. But Charley thought that everyone had such lapses from inattention. Individually, these movements were nothing of any consequence. But more and more, as Charley began considering them altogether, she became puzzled and concerned.

As the months rolled on, Charley saw that Amie was beginning to need her assistance for minor everyday tasks. This was even extending more frequently into Amie's painting. Because something was out of kilter, Charley's spending equal time at both their houses could no longer work for her. She had to hang around Amie's for longer times each day in order to help her with various tasks.

When Charley observed that Amie's hands were beginning to wave back and forth, interfering with her applying paint to her canvas, she asked if Amie wanted her to complete that part of the painting and let Amie continue to instruct her. Amie agreed. Charley worried what these movements meant for Amie's health, as well as for their partnership. Whatever was going on was getting progressively worse. When she shared her concern and suggested that Amie see a doctor to determine what might be wrong, Amie dismissed the idea with a wave of her shaky hand.

She said, "It's nothing to worry about. I'm just tired."

But Charley knew that wasn't the real problem.

Bit by bit, whatever was going on with Amie was becoming more obvious. If it continued its trajectory, at some point Amie would be unable to do what was required of her to live her life. This unnamed condition was becoming a disability, one which would undoubtedly require Charley not only to paint for Amie but also to take care of her and Saatchi. Assuming that was likely to happen, Charley knew that at some point it would probably mean having a home care assistant live with or visit Amie daily in order to attend to her and her cat's physical and emotional needs. She wished she knew what was going on to cause this situation. It would have been useful to be aware of the possible consequences and implications for them both to prepare to deal with it.

That nearly constant presence of Charley in Amie's home would not be a problem as far as Amie's cat was concerned. Saatchi had already adopted Charley. When she wasn't magnetized to Charley's legs when walking, she was at her side whether she was still or moving about painting. Like a puppy, she double-stepped to mimic

Charley's stride when her newly adopted human companion walked around the studio and house.

For the moment Charley would have to create a schedule that would allow her to be at her office processing Amie's website orders as well as in her studio finishing her own painting projects and then spend the rest of the time with Amie, painting and caring for her and her cat. But the help Amie needed was increasingly becoming for more than just her painting and assisting make their dinners or dressing her. But when Charley suggested hiring someone to assist Amie with little things, Amie looked panic-stricken. She vehemently refused. No one could know. Charley didn't understand her fear.

It was clear that Amie also needed healthcare assistance. When taking a shower, she seemed less steady on her feet. Charley had bars and a centrally-placed, weighted plastic chair with arms installed in the shower. She also raised the seat on the toilet and placed a heavy-duty safety frame on either side of it for balance support. When Amie wanted to brush her teeth, she was having difficulty putting a layer of toothpaste on her brush without dripping it into the sink and smearing the rest on her chin as the toothbrush missed her mouth. Attempting to make coffee for them one morning, Amie dropped most of the ground coffee onto the counter instead of into the paper filter then nearly smashed the glass carafe against the coffee machine when trying to put it on the heating element. Charley didn't know what to do.

It was at that point that Charley and Amie together decided that Charley should totally move in with her. That way they could paint fulltime when Amie was feeling up to it. But Charley would still have to continue to go back to her own house daily to check out everything as well as handle inventory, sales, and shipping.

But as the months chugged haltingly along, Charley realized sadly that selling her house made more sense. She could no longer be there to enjoy it. Besides, she was worried about someone breaking in if it looked deserted. It was also a financial drain, costing her in mortgage, insurance, taxes, and utilities. The upside of selling it was that the sale price would bolster her bank account which,

Charley suspected, could be strained as Amie got worse and wasn't doing her painting. Charley decided to do it, but not just yet. She wanted to wait for the right moment to present itself, and hoped she'd recognize it when it did.

By the beginning of the next year Amie was becoming the primary focus of Charley's time and attention. Amie needed help getting out of bed and chairs. She could no longer successfully drive her car, shop, vacuum, do her laundry, or tend to most of Saatchi's needs, although she desperately tried to take care of them herself. Her inability to do the simplest things frustrated and angered her. Charley could see how disheartened and depressed Amie was becoming as something was strangely overtaking her, thwarting her by interfering with her most basic functioning.

Painting more and more for Amie while taking care of sales, and Amie, had become time-consuming and often difficult. Even though Charley's time to do other things had been diminished, she cobbled together time to work on her own paintings. Her abstracts were elaborating on her long-time subjects, fluids in motion, Cubist visions of Nature, and unusual natural earth patterns as viewed from a satellite. These she would keep under wraps until the time was right to introduce them. At the moment, she didn't want to distract attention from selling Amie's paintings.

Early on when Charley was still in Boston, she had made a point of no longer using her real name on her paintings. Instead, she used "Mana," her nickname for her mother, meaning "spiritual life force" in Polynesian. She didn't want her artistic endeavors to publicly and negatively affect, or interfere with, her political marketing professional status. She had noticed that people tended to think of consultants as high-commitment, logical, high-knowledge "professionals" whereas artists tended to be stereotyped as emotional, unreliable, flighty "dilettantes" with no business or marketing sense. And now, after her having been raked over the political marketing coals in Santa Fe, she wasn't about to sign her own notorious name to them either.

Soon Charley had to admit to herself that she could not do everything for Amie by herself. Her painting for Amie, which she was doing totally now, and caring for her as she was developing some kind of physical condition, superseded any other scheduled activities. Up to this instant, she still hadn't a clue what was wrong with Amie. Searching online, she saw several conditions that matched some of her symptoms. Once again, she urged Amie to see a doctor. But Amie said she had no intention to do so.

"I already know what it is."

"But you need more assistance than I can provide. Please help me help you."

Recognizing that her body was becoming less under her personal control, Amie said she'd think about it and let Charley know. Charley hoped it would be shortly, before things got much worse.

11

When Amie finally revealed the cause of her involuntary physical movements, Charley was simultaneously astonished, angry, and disappointed. Part of her felt she had been hoodwinked. Why couldn't Amie have told her before she had begun to show symptoms. Charley was there for her friend. She wouldn't have left her; Amie should have known that. But, more importantly, it was Charley's decision alone to make about what she was going to do in this situation. Having been informed of this only when Amie was already in great need somehow seemed unfair, even though Charley could grudgingly somewhat understand why Amie hadn't revealed it sooner.

As Amie reluctantly disclosed, she was suffering from a terminal, degenerative, neurological condition called Huntington's Disease, inherited from her father. Charley was aghast. She had heard of it but knew little about it other than it was very bad.

"It is from a DNA defect in a single gene on Chromosome 4 where there are thirty-six or more repetitions of a single amino acid sequence (CAG, representing cytosine, adenine, and guanine). Larger numbers of repeats tend to produce a more rapid decline. It's an autosomal dominant disorder. That means a person needs to receive only one copy of the defective gene, from one parent, in order to develop the disorder. Each child in the family where one parent has the disease gene has a fifty percent chance of inheriting it. It tends to show itself in adults starting around the age of forty, but can be lots younger."

"Oh, Amie, I'm so sorry. Are you absolutely sure that's what your problem is?"

"I saw the same symptoms in my father. But do I know for sure? There is no way of knowing for sure aside from having a genetic test, which is primarily suggestive, *or* until the specific clinical symptoms begin to show themselves, as they are doing now."

Sighing, Amie went out to the patio to sit on her wrought iron bench to watch the hummingbirds sip nectar from her many brightly-colored tubular flowers. She had planted them just after she had moved in specifically to attract these iridescent aerial acrobats. In the meanwhile, Charley spent a half-hour doing research on Huntington's Disease.

She learned that Huntington's interfered with the sufferer's muscular coordination, cognition, and mood. As she had observed, Amie increasingly was unable to hold any object as steady as she needed to in order to use it. That was because she couldn't stop her hands from making slow, writhing, snake-like movements. These movements were called "athetosis." Huntington's also produced jerky involuntary movements of the body which were called "chorea," perhaps because someone at one time thought they looked like purposeless, gawky dance-like movements. Charley had not witnessed that yet. Neither had she discerned any signs of cognitive or mood aberrations. All Amie's symptoms, especially diminution of balance and ability to walk, would be expected to significantly worsen over time.

Charley was thunderstruck to find that the disease tended to progress to death in ten to thirty years with the individual in the late stage likely to be confined to a bed and unable to speak, drink, or eat on his or her own. That seemed inconceivable. Amie had always been so active, so full of fun and life. It seemed so unfair that such a highly talented artist was being cut down so cruelly in her prime.

The end tended to be prolonged. That meant that Amie might be aware only of being unable to fully respond to her environment as well as to Charley and Saatchi's presence. Or, she might not be aware of anything at all, as far as anyone could tell. Charley felt devastated by this pronouncement. It sounded like a hellacious future into which to be trapped.

Why, she wondered, would anyone choose to have a pre-dispositional genetic test for this horrible disease? But after she read in detail about the testing, she could understand that for some it might make sense. Still, it didn't sound all that sanguine to her. There were essentially three emotional ways that sufferers, like Amie, tended to respond to the idea of being tested and shown they were likely to have Huntington's.

One was taking the test in order to know their likely Huntington's future. This would allow them to rationally and emotionally prepare for the worst and get their business and life in order. Even living with this sword hanging by a fine wire over their heads, they could still choose to enjoy life as much as possible, knowing there probably wasn't as much time left as they had initially hoped to have.

Another was not taking the test and, therefore, not knowing. They could then choose to live as if no problem existed. But if it did, it left them unprepared for its occurrence and its consequences.

And the last was not taking the test and merely assuming that they had the terminal disease. For them that meant living their entire life expecting the worst, making it the negative centerpiece of their thoughts, behaviors, and existence. And all-too-often that+ attitude sabotaged everything positive they did or had the opportunity to do because down deep they felt "why bother?"

Even though the first choice sounded like the "best" of three as far as Charley was concerned for herself, none was all that great. Amie had obviously chosen the second option and it seemed to have worked for her psychologically, thus far.

Further research told Charley that while there was currently no treatment for Huntington's, in 2016 an international genetics team out of the Health Center at the University College, London, had begun trials to see if they could reduce the production of the harmful mutant protein, *huntingtin*, which had been discovered to cause Huntington's. By 2019, the randomized, double-blind Phase I-IIA clinical trials of their new gene therapy drug had indicated that the drug was safe and was successfully lowering the levels of the abnormal protein in diseased patients. The next clinical phase would be administering the drug monthly to a very large group of enrolled Huntington's patients by injecting it directly into their cerebrospinal fluid to make sure it was safe and effective for most people with Huntington's. With the goal of silencing the mutant gene, geneticists believed that they might be able to alleviate Huntington's patients' suffering, even if they couldn't eliminate the gene itself.

That was of particular interest to Charley for Amie. She thought it might be remotely possible to enroll Amie into their trials, *if* she would be willing to do it. Given that Amie had indicated that she didn't want anyone to know about her disease, that was, perhaps, unlikely. But, then again, as Charley observed, these trials were well underway. Even if Amie couldn't, or wouldn't, be in the clinical program at the current point in the evaluation research, Charley would try to keep track of the progress of the experimental trials in case she could get Amie treated.

She had no idea if Amie would find that acceptable given her privacy concerns. It was a long shot given the progression of her symptoms and what time Amie might have left. But, at the same time, who knew when they might make the treatment available to others. Even though it might be an iffy proposition, Charley would be sure to monitor what was published about it in the medical journals and press just in case Amie would agree.

12

For years Amie had been not only giving her protégé lessons on her particular technique of computer modeling her painting subjects before painting them but also hinting at Charley using them for Amie at some time in the future. And after she saw unequivocal evidence of Huntington's in herself, she hoped that Charley would be inclined to take over the painting for her totally when she no longer could. Then she would make suggestions as to subject, colors, etc., for as long as possible. Her hope was that Charley would see that as a real opportunity for her, and not a burden.

Amie felt that she had been upfront from the beginning about wanting Charley to take over her painting as her physical condition worsened. However, earlier when Amie referred to it and Charley had agreed, she had unknowingly made the assumption that Amie was referring to her physical debilitation due to unanticipated old-age health problems, which would be far in the future. She had had no understanding of or indication that Amie's mental, emotional, and physical health would degenerate well before that time.

Embarrassed about having kept her condition secret for so long, Amie explained.

"I didn't want the possible prediction to be true. I didn't want to live my life as if it were a tragic death sentence. It was possible I might have missed the bullet. Had a very mild clinical case. Or developed it but very late in life."

Charley fully understood not wanting a medical prediction to be true though she still felt a slight twinge about Amie's not having shared anything before, even about her future concern. After much discussion, they made a business agreement. Amie would have Charley do all of Amie's paintings now which Amie would oversee.

They felt that legally and ethically it would be very similar to what painters had done for centuries and were comfortable with it.

During the Italian Renaissance, in the studio of Verrocchio for example, the apprentices/assistants may have done works for their master under his name. At that time guild rules for artists allowed the master to sign as his own any work which emerged from his shop. "Authenticity" in the modern sense was not at issue. A master's signature was a sign that a work met his standards of quality, no matter who had actually painted it under his tutelage. That, however, later led to concerns about some of Verrocchio paintings, such as the *Madonna and Child with a Pomegranate,* dated 1475/1480, which was in his style. But, the experts debated, was it really his own work? As a result, there existed the puzzle of whether it was painted by Verrocchio himself or Lorenzo di Credi, an artist he had trained.

Charley was not going to be copying Old Masters' works and selling them as originals, like Han van Meegeren, the Dutch painter and portraitist, who in the 1930s and 1940s sold $60 million worth of fake Vermeers to everyone from Hermann Göring to the government of Netherlands. Johannes Vermeer was the 17th Century Dutch Baroque Period painter and premier artist who specialized in domestic interior scenes of middle-class life. Because of Van Meegeren's "artistic genius," he had been considered to be one of the most ingenious art forgers of the 20th Century.

What Amie was having Charley do didn't fit their definition of art forgery because Charley had been painting on, and often completing, Amie's canvases for her with her permission for years. In essence, she had been "ghosting" Amie's work for her, with Amie giving it her own authenticity. As far as Amie was concerned, Charley had been producing, and would continue to produce, the artist's intellectual property for her.

However, after the time when Amie would die, Charley knew she couldn't start any new "Amie Benison" paintings with Amie's signature. Even with a contract between them for Charley to act as Amie, producing brand new works then would very likely be considered fraud, whether anyone knew of Amie's death or not. Charley thought that it might merely be questionable but still didn't want to put herself in a tenuous position. She had already suffered enough negative public scrutiny even though, in this case, she would legally be acting as "Amie Benison."

Before the disease had significantly progressed, Amie was concerned about Charley's signature matching her own as Amie was losing further control of her hands. She didn't want anyone to think someone was faking her paintings. At one point, as Charley was perfecting Amie's signature, Charley had suggested making a rubber stamp for Amie's painting signature, just in case. They tried it. But when the stamped signature not only didn't look enough like a real signature on paintings but also effected a smeary mess, they both dropped that idea. Instead, they decided, the flat stamp could be used for other things, such as side products "by Amie" that they would develop. Over time Charley's duplication of Amie's former signature became natural and flawless. In the interim, no signature could be said to look unrealistic or illegitimate. Amie made sure of that.

Saatchi's famous paw-print signature which accompanied Amie's was another story. Saatchi's contribution had happened by accident the day following her adoption by Amie from the Boston animal shelter. Since then, Amie's in-demand abstract art had always had a distinctive small black cat paw print from her cat, Saatchi, as part of her signature.

As a kitten, the bedraggled-looking ball of long hair had tried climbing onto the stool that Amie used when painting. Amie hadn't paid much attention to those attempts since Saatchi was so small and ungainly. However, as Amie soon discovered, "Where there's a will ….," even for kittens. As soon as Saatchi could attain the stool seat, she leaned forward toward the easel. With that her balance disappeared. To save herself she threw out her right front paw which landed on the wet canvas at the lower right-hand corner.

When Amie returned, she spotted the desecration. Just as she was about to use a brush to smooth it over, she stopped. There was something intriguing about the blurry shape. Using black paint, she filled in the paw print so it was more well-defined and then added her signature in front of it, all on the horizontal. It had a cachet she liked. From then on, she decided, that would be the official Amie Benison signature. But how, she wondered, would she duplicate it?

When she immediately scrutinized the kitten, she found that the furry vandal seemed very proud of what she had done in making an impression on the interesting object. Furthermore, she appeared eager to do it again. To the cat's exasperation, Amie did not want the kitten trying to or doing it again. She might knock the canvas and easel over, smear the paint or get dirt, dust, and long strands of cat hair on it. That was a habit in the making she did not want to support, in spite of how cute Saatchi had been about her first accomplishment.

Besides, it was risky for Saatchi's health. No matter how carefully Amie could clean the paint off Saatchi's pads, claws, fur, and between her toes, there was always the possibility of a residue left which Amie did not want the cat to lick. Fortunately, when it first happened, Amie had been using acrylic paint which was easier to clean than oil paint.

"But supposing I had been using oil paint?" Amie had asked herself aloud. "I would have had to use turpentine on the paw to remove the paint and risk serious consequences."

She knew that turpentine was toxic to cats, even after washing the area with soap and water, because it was quickly and easily absorbed through the skin. Amie considered that too hazardous for a possible repetition.

From then on Amie kept her easel away from anything that Saatchi could use as a springboard to leaping at and touching a work in progress or one drying.

The problem to solve was how to re-create the pawprint without using Saatchi and giving it the right depth and look. When Amie mentioned it to Charley, it was Charley who suggested creating a plaster mold of Saatchi's right front paw and then making a rubber duplicate of her four digital pads and metacarpal pad combined from it. The resulting small rubber appendage which was flexible worked satisfactorily for years. All it required was for Amie or Charley to paint the resulting impression in black. Charley saved the plaster mold for whenever the rubber paw-print needed to be replaced in the future.

Amie's art was vaguely reminiscent of fractal abstract wall art on canvas but not a computer-created photograph. She used the computer's software algorithms to generate the models of what she generally wanted because she found this faster than using charcoal to sketch and alter the shapes. Then she painted them with brush and pallet knife in oil or acrylic on canvas and made her own changes as she went along.

Most of her art represented roiling agitation where upheaval poured forth to effect transformation. They had the appearance of colorful raging smoke and fire, tumultuous storm clouds, and dark, strangely twisted, roughly undulating non-storm asperitas clouds with varying textures, created by different thicknesses of paint layers and paint additives.

Early on Amie had also played with creating cosmic nebulae. While, at that time, she thought a multi-colored nebula would be interesting subject matter, she found it very flat, static, lacking in strong emotional content, despite her giving the dust and ionized gas three-dimensionality within their stellar background. She had even tried duplicating huge Portuguese and Hawaiian surfing waves. But while her two experimental abstract wave paintings done in blues, greens, and white had action and power, they seemed too controlled, predictable, and commonplace for what she wanted to portray.

Her primary principle was that her paintings should reflect Nature at its most elemental and emotion-grabbing. Full of turmoil. She identified more with the disquieting effect of an angry, explosive environment and its resulting metamorphosis. In that vein nothing in her paintings of it should be too colorful or unnatural. Consequently, the colors she favored were white, gray, brown, ocher, yellow, black, orange, and orange-red depending upon whether she was representing fire, smoke, or clouds. Her aficionados agreed. Because her sixty-inch-wide paintings were best for depicting this turbulence, that size had become her most popular, though her thirty-six-inch-wide paintings were a close second.

She felt her paintings were a testament to her philosophy that turbulence was a life force and an opportunity to create and implement change.

Because Amie and Charley were both increasingly becoming concerned about Charley's rendering of Amie's paintings ever being found out, the two had decided to go beyond their original verbal contractual agreement. They would form a non-profit company in Amie Benison's name to protect Charley. Charley did all the research, with the help of several online legal sites, and created the complex, comprehensive written contract. It would address all the business associated with Amie and all her signature works.

Initially, both their names were on the company's checking account but the checks required only one signature. Once Charley sold her house, the checks would be changed to Amie's name only as Charley "ceased to be" in Santa Fe. Charley would handle their business as Amie which would continue even beyond Amie's death.

If she understood correctly what she'd read, it appeared to Charley that legally, where a person was appointed to act as another person's agent for *all* legal purposes, that person could sign all legally significant documents on behalf of the other person. Written like a notarized power of attorney, it expressively allowed Charley to use Amie's name and signature on legal documents. This would include the use of the artist's painting signature, the 3D rubber paw-print model, and the flat rubber stamp of Amie's full signature with paw print which was being used on letterhead, website design, business checks, as a logo for promotional materials, and for whatever else they later decided to add. In essence, via the document, Amie was "authenticating" Charley's work as Amie's as well as her acting in all respects as the artist herself.

It would allow Charley and Amie to eventually literally switch identities, from legal documentation to overall appearance. That meant Charley would physically represent and/or "impersonate" Amie Benison in a non-exploitive, non-fraudulent way, in any circumstance required for business and non-business as Amie's condition worsened. While Amie wanted her artistry and legacy to continue, at the same time she wanted to prevent her condition from being associated with "the artist Amie Benison." Hopefully if Charley were wrong about any of what she understood to be permissible, her interpretation would not end up legally biting her in the butt.

Amie was becoming even more apprehensive about anyone, from friends to gallery owners to purchasers to doctors, to the public in general, knowing about her condition or that she personally was no longer doing all, or even any, of the actual painting of her Amie Benison masterpieces. As far as she was concerned, everything Charley had ever done or would ever do on Amie's paintings, irrespective of the degree, was Amie's work and was to be promoted and sold as such, even as Charley would become the sole, authentic producer of her works.

While there was a certain absurdity to their switching identities, and all that entailed, Charley also felt it possessed a modicum of high-mindedness. It was the goal and the noble efforts toward achieving it that mattered. While it didn't seem to trouble Amie because she would live on in Charley with her legacy intact, Charley had two minor qualms. One was about lying and having to keep every nitpicking detail about Amie's pre-Huntington's life straight so she wouldn't make egregious mistakes and potentially be found out. The other was about discarding her own identity.

By assuming Amie's life, she at first felt she was giving up an aspect of her personhood: her name and her history. However, as she contemplated it over time, she recognized that there really wasn't that much to hang on to in her own life where Charley had essentially had to "vanish." She was still who she was in mind, body, and spirit. Everything that made her who the person she was remained intact even though she was wearing a costume to act a role. That could work out okay after all.

Now she only hoped, with a slight chuckle, that as a result of making this identity switch, they wouldn't risk being squashed by the karmic backlash.

13

Things were moving along for Charley as well as one could expect given the increasing demands on her time, until one late, heavily-shadowed afternoon. It was then that Amie decided to break free from participating in the studio—participation which was diminishing by the day—to act on her own. She hadn't been off her property in what to her seemed like years and she was tired of Charley's secretly monitoring her activities, occasionally imposing on her what she could and couldn't do. While she still knew that Charley was doing that only for Amie's safety and well-being, she felt she had to take back her own indispensable independence in some way. Today was going to be the day.

Because driving was one thing she was no longer allowed to do because of her involuntary movements and decreasing lack of coordination, that was what she wanted most dearly to do. Just one more time she needed to feel herself behind the wheel, directing all that horsepower; feeling the road rush beneath her, and the wind whipping through her hair. That, she anticipated, would very probably be her last hurrah. Her last spate of real hands-on freedom.

She decided she wouldn't go far, just ride through the seven thousand five-hundred-foot pine and conifer mountain forest. It was always so much cooler there, with dappled light playing optical tricks among the dark green branches and the air sharp and pungent with resinous fragrance. Maybe she'd stop along the side the road to step onto the pine needle carpet to hear it crunch under foot. It would be like giving life-saving oxygen to a person suffering from hypoxia. Excitement buoyed her mood. Surging adrenaline pushed her to reclaim her life.

Charley, who was armed with Amie's identification, had taken Amie's standard-shift, metallic-orange Honda Fit to get groceries. Fortunately for Amie, Charley's red Toyota Corolla, which was parked near the house, was an automatic. That meant she didn't have to constantly shift, coordinating hands and feet, and screamingly grind the gears of her own car which she was no longer able to drive. Amie slid behind the Corolla's steering wheel. Haphazardly she adjusted the seat and mirror and turned on the engine. For a minute she resonated to its surge then purr. Before she stepped on the accelerator, she sighed with a smile of satisfaction. Attempting to place her hands firmly on the steering wheel, she shakily moved the gear lever to drive, swung her right foot toward the gas pedal, catching it by an inch, then took off.

Even though she had somewhat stayed on the dirt driveway until she met Log House Road below, her slowing the car was hit or miss because she couldn't keep her foot on the brake pedal or press it with the force required. By chance, there was no traffic to deal with on the short connecting road or anyone to see her. The Corolla responding to her involuntary arm movements tended to sway from side to side on the asphalt, making the driver look inebriated. Finally, she haltingly turned right, north-bound onto Fire Station Road to drive the one mile to the forest.

Only scattered housing greeted her as she awkwardly made her way to her destination. No sooner had she passed a large, terracotta-colored building with four warehouse-like white doors on her left than she had reached the actual fire road. Leaving the pavement, she entered, rolling uncomfortably over the cattle guard. Her right arm began to wave about, pushing the steering wheel to the left. The car was still moving, now along the dirt road. Trying to correct her path, her left elbow jostled the wheel. Together her elbow and right hand erratically tried to re-orient the vehicle. But as she did, her right foot hit the accelerator hard. It slipped, becoming wedged between the gas and brake pedals. The vehicle shuddered … and sped up. The car took over. As she tried to grab the steering wheel, the Toyota lurched left.

Racing, it hurtled into a mature pine. The ear-piercing screech was quickly followed by a heavy thud. Hammered, the moist wood gave way. Its lower limbs rammed through the laminated windshield, shattering the glass. Shards flew inward, bombarding Amie. Just missing her right eye, they imbedded themselves in her face. Branches stabbed and raked her left cheek. Tons of metal vanquished the tree, plummeting its top. The now-displaced car roof hung precariously mere inches above her head. The engine still seething, the crumpled vehicle came to rest.

Simultaneously, the airbag inflated, pinning Amie as the front end of the car crumpled into an accordion's bellows. The dashboard thrust toward her. The steering wheel pressed against the airbag. She gasped for breath. Her left arm flopped numbly as her right leg was locked, grotesquely twisted. She felt her face bloody, dripping, and disfigured as darkness closed in on her.

Hearing the loud grinding and crunch of metal on wood, the occupants of the last building on the left ran outside to check. The building housed the fire and rescue station. Seeing the near obliteration of the vehicle, two hurried to Amie to see if they could begin helping as the others raced to retrieve their rescue vehicle.

Emergency vehicles converged on the scene within minutes along with a notified New Mexico State Police car which was patrolling in the area. The fire department's rescue personnel had with them all equipment necessary to extricate a person from the twisted, sharp metal. After their assessment of the tortuous front-end wreckage, they used the "jaws of life," piston-rod hydraulic cutters, spreaders, and rams, to slowly cut, disentangle, and gently pry open Amie's metal coffin. The EMTs then checked her pupils and spoke to her. But she couldn't hear them.

After only fifteen minutes on this older model car, the rescuers carefully extracted her bleeding and fractured body. Unconscious and on oxygen, she was then rushed by the ambulance, which was now standing by, to Christus St. Vincent Regional Medical Center Hospital for immediate surgery. She was identified as "Amie Benison" from her Social Security card in her wallet. She had forgotten to include it with her other personal documents she had given to Charley. Since she was supposed to remain homebound, she didn't as yet have any of Charley's identification on her.

Because she was driving Charley's car, the police contacted Charley who had just returned to her home first from shopping. In Amie's Honda she hastened to the hospital. There she had to wait for untold hours in Amie's assigned room—which was not in the Intensive Care Unit—until Amie was back from surgery. She heard there had been a serious bus accident which had already taken up their ten ICU beds.

Amie was a specter of her former self. Her left arm and right leg had been broken in several places. Broken ribs had barely missed puncturing her lungs. Her torn, now-lopsided face was temporarily stitched together, except for her large, deep cheek wound. It would require daily negative pressure therapy to draw out fluid and infection through a sealed dressing over it which was attached to a gentle vacuum. Her entire face would require extensive plastic surgery later to reconstruct, smooth out, and re-balance her slightly askew features.

Surrounded by cables attached to monitors for respiration, pulse, and heart rate, a catheter to collect urine, and an IV pole for slowly administering bags of intravenous antibiotics and pain medications, Amie looked critical and fragile. That evening a gowned, masked Charley was allowed to sleep in a lounge chair in Amie's small, spartan room where she kept a bedside vigil. It would be a couple of days before Amie would be fully conscious and able to try to talk, despite her bandaged, patchwork-quilt face, to tell Charley what had happened.

When she did come around, she recognized Charley. Almost immediately, she began to mumble something. When a nurse wasn't present, Charley leaned close to hear what Amie was attempting to say. Even though her voice was muffled by the sutures, bandages, pain, and the tube for the negative pressure unit, Charley could hear the panic in her voice. Amie sounded desperate.

"Charley, … no one … can know … what really … happened."

"Amie, *I* don't know what happened."

"You … have … to tell … the police … a cougar … dashed out … in front … of me. … I swerved … to avoid it. … That's how … I smashed … into … a tree."

"Okay, but what really happened?"

"You're …going … to be … mad."

"No, I'm not. It's too late for that. So?"

"Wanted … to drive … one more … time. … Thought … I could … control … the car. … Couldn't. … Sorry … demolished … your car."

"Let's not worry about that. The insurance will cover it. I'm just glad you're going to be okay. Let's just get you on the road to recovery and out of here. But you have to promise me, no more attempted joyrides."

"No … more."

Because there had been no sign of alcohol or drugs in Amie's system when she was tested at the hospital, there was never a question about her having had control of her faculties and the vehicle at the time. After Charley wrote out Amie's tale of the accident for the police, they reported it as one of those unforeseeable, random occurrences that couldn't have been avoided.

Fortunately for Amie, her tremors were less observable when she was anesthetized and as she lay unconscious in her room. And when she was awake, she remembered about her Huntington's and tried to keep her right arm under the covers, despite her intravenous tubing, so any excessive movement wouldn't be detectable.

The casts on her upper left arm and her left wrist were both made of molded plastic and fabric, for necessary re-adjustment since the arm didn't need to be immobilized. Her upright positioning in bed was awkward and kept that arm from waving very much. Her right leg, which was swollen, was in a splint until the swelling went down. Then it would have a plaster cast. It likewise didn't move very much. As far as Charley and Amie could tell, no one commented on any involuntary movement. Thus, as far as they knew, her underlying condition had not been detected, much less recorded.

Before Charley left her side for a while to get back to work, Amie also wanted her to make it known publicly, after the accident had hit the papers, that she had decided to not take part in any public or gallery events as she recovered in solitude. This was even though she hadn't been in public for some time because of her increasingly observable neurological symptoms. However, she felt the need to remind her public that she was still around and wanted to be back with them as soon as possible.

"Tell them," she said, asking Charley to quote her as saying, "I expect … to continue … painting … as I … recover."

Via an email press release, Charley, using Amie's name, "informed" the media of the artist's decision. It stated that because of her extended recovery, Amie would not personally be showing up at Vida Hermosa Gallery on Canyon Road for events of her work for a number of months so don't forget her. Furthermore, the artist would not do interviews during her hiatus.

It was more than her severe facial injuries and continuing reconstructive surgeries that would interfere with interviews. It was also that her underlying disorder had already begun affecting her speech. At times it left her sounding slightly muted. She was also concerned that as her condition worsened, there might be long pauses in between words or inappropriate word choices, as had happened with her father.

For when there would be any necessary in-person interactions, Charley had to learn to speak like Amie. Consequently, Charley had been practicing Amie's style of communication, her tone of voice, her range, inflection, use of idiomatic phrases, and her nonverbal behavior, especially her gestures when speaking. But even with all this, she did not as yet feel she could sound enough like Amie to tackle those interviews. But that was only half of it. As she was taking on Amie's persona, she would have to make herself look physically more like her as well as duplicate her walk and movements. She didn't want to be seen as Charley Eyre ever again. Amie would be Charley.

The PR release mentioned that as soon as she regained her strength, she would also continue show more of her works at Vida Hermosa. In the interim, her website would remain active for all but commissions. For that secluded amount of time most of her communication would be via mail, email, text, and later by phone, when, unbeknownst to them, Charley could confidently emulate Amie's voice to speak for her, especially with those who had known Amie's voice before. Therefore, the release didn't give out the unlisted home landline or cell phone numbers in order to keep the press and public at arm's length. However, the website's separate phone number was public. Charley, as a webmaster named "Bronte," her favorite author's name, would have to deal with any journalists calling as well as continue dealing with those people placing orders. The gallery had already promised not to call her. After sufficient time for Amie's recovery, Charley would take paintings to the gallery, presenting herself to the owner as Amie.

Over Amie's many months of recovery, Amie and Charley began to exchange their appearances. While Charley was 5'5" and Amie was 5'7", Charley's height could be altered easily by wearing platform shoes. Their ages, however, were eleven years apart. Charley was thirty-five and Amie was forty-six. After all Amie's required reconstructive surgeries, any facial age difference would be erased. Both were on the slim side although Charley looked more athletic, having been a competitive runner in her earlier life in Boston who had continued to stay active when she could fit it in, which was less and less all the time. While Charley was right-handed, Amie was left-handed. But the breaks in Amie's left arm and wrist, and any "resulting nerve damage," could explain her having to switch hands and ostensibly re-learn to paint with her right hand.

Charley had shoulder-length red hair and Amie had short brunette hair. To make the transformation Charley had to cut and dye her hair to match Amie's. Because Amie's hair was tousled in a more Bohemian style with a lot of natural body, Charley also had to have a light permanent to emulate it. With luck, the changes suited Charley's face shape and coloring.

Relinquishing her professional-style of suits, tailored slacks, business blouses, and jackets, Charley assumed Amie's dull-colored, unconstructed, natural fabric attire, which generally ranged from cotton tunics to loose-legged linen slacks. Since she wore contacts while Amie wore glasses, she had her own eye prescription made into Amie's rimless eyeglasses' style as well.

At first, Charley had thought very reluctantly that she might have to have collagen and dermal fillers added to her face to change her appearance to look more like Amie. But after Amie's accident and face alterations, she quickly and cheerfully disposed of that idea as no longer being necessary. In addition, many years had passed since those early photos of Amie were taken. Over the decades, Amie had naturally changed as she aged. What Charley discovered was that just using makeup, she could make herself resemble the old pictures of Amie enough to get away with any upcoming physical impersonations in public.

As Charley was rapidly becoming Amie in every way possible, she knew that for the most part the former Charlotte Eyre was disappearing. Amie who was now "Charley" no longer appeared in public. Nonetheless, there would come a time when she would have to appear, in a manner of speaking.

14

Following Amie's release from the hospital, she had a lot of healing to do, especially from her deep cheek wound and her series of facial surgeries. Her fractured bones took only a few months. Overall, her recovery was unspectacular. With Amie back in Glorieta, Charley hoped everything would be all right for a while. But that wasn't to be.

Now more clinically clued in to Amie's behavior, Charley noticed Amie was beginning to demonstrate apathy, loss of energy and initiative. Nothing seemed to interest her. At first, Charley thought it was the emotional result of the accident and disfigurement. But when she urged Amie to re-immerse herself in her home activities and she lackadaisically tried, the results were awkward and frustrating. Amie too observed the changes and wanted to believe it was because her upper left arm and wrist having been in casts for so long. Being stiff made sense. But, later, she sadly confided to Charley that she recognized the behavioral alteration and recalled that she had also seen that most common change in her father as his Huntington's progressed.

Amie was also beginning to show signs of impaired judgment, poor self-care, and a blunting of her emotions. Change seemed to be moving too fast to be related to the consequences of her accident. However, Charley did wonder if all the anesthesia Amie had endured for her multiple surgeries had had a negative effect on her brain. Or, if she had endured some brain injury that wasn't detected in the hospital. But, then again, the MRI could have detected Huntington's changes in the brain. It was lucky they hadn't done it. In her research to answer her questions she didn't find anything online to support that effect of anesthesia. Unfortunately, like half of those with Huntington's, Amie was also beginning to express some depression, anxiety, and irritability. Although, she had shown no signs of hallucinations or delusions … yet.

It was at this time that Amie received a phone call that panicked her. It was Saturday afternoon when a police officer called to say that she, Amie Benison, had missed her State jury duty and a warrant was being issued for her arrest. Charley was in the Honda grocery shopping and doing other errands for Amie so Amie answered the phone. The call set off agitation and a sense of dread. Amie told herself she couldn't be arrested. She hadn't fully recovered from her accident. They would see her underlying physical secret. She couldn't go to jail. How could she take care of herself there? Everyone would know she could no longer paint, that she had become like a limp stalk of celery, collapsing into a heap of flailing body parts. Charley's and her plan would disappear like the dust in New Mexico's hot, oppressive desert winds. Everyone would remember her for her incapacity instead of her artistic talent. They wouldn't buy Charley's paintings which were done for her. The world was caving in and disintegrating around her. She couldn't let that happen.

After sending her through a series of department officials, the caller told her.

"You can pay a $926 fine and then go to court on Monday to finish clearing it up."

Amie's mind went blank. Anxiety was bathing her in sweat. She could smell her armpits become acrid. She knew there was no way she could go to court to clear it up. Charley would have to do it as Amie. But would Charley do it? She felt on the verge of hysteria. How, she wondered, could she get the money as soon as possible to avoid this contretemps. This was the weekend. The banks wouldn't be open until Monday. Any moment a cop could knock on her door and haul her off to the pokey.

As she hyperventilated gripping the receiver, she tried not to cry into it, her voice quivering. Hearing her, the caller spoke soothingly to reassure her all was not lost.

"If you could provide another $100 in addition to the $926, I will personally take care of your paperwork for you to save you from having to spend a long, exhausting day at the courthouse, tangled in confusing red tape. If you'll allow me to help you, I can do it now and make sure that the officers who already have the warrant won't come for you."

It took Amie a moment to digest this reprieve. Thrilled by his concern and kind offer, she agreed, "Oh, yes, yes," and scrawled, nearly illegibly whenever the pen and paper happened to meet, the dictated directions on where to send a Moneygram wire. Feeling more relieved, she suddenly realized that she couldn't get the money without Charley's help. But she had no idea when Charley would be home. Furthermore, she had no idea where she could get a wire to send the money. Was such a place in Santa Fe? And was it open on a Saturday?

When Charley returned twenty minutes later with bags of groceries, pots of colorful butterfly-alluring perennials, and artistic supplies, Amie was crying, distraught. Slowly, with gentle prodding from Charley, she tentatively shared the problem, becoming frightened all over again. Charley looked askance at Amie. What she said sounded peculiar to her. Did her friend have this right? She was called by the police who were going to arrest her for not showing up for jury duty? Charley was sure that something was incorrect, that Amie had misheard or there had been a mistake. After spending a half-hour calming Amie, telling her she would take care of it all, Charley began an Internet investigation.

Checking legal sites, she discovered first that a summons for jury duty always came by U.S. mail. Since it was Charley who always picked up the mail, she would have known of such a summons. But she hadn't seen any such judicial mail, whether Federal or State. Second, if Amie, who had been randomly selected from the jury pool based on her driver's license or voter registration, didn't appear for duty, she would receive a second notice, one of "Failure to Appear" or "Delinquency," from the court. That also would be by regular mail. Third, if Amie then offered the court no valid excuse for not having appeared for jury duty, it was then that the court could issue an arrest warrant *or* impose a fine.

What was certain was that there wouldn't be any fine imposed until *after* Amie had appeared in open court to respond to the notice. There certainly would never be a phone call from either the court or police demanding payment without going through the normally-required judicial channels. Neither law enforcement nor the courts would ask for a Moneygram to satisfy a fine. Moreover, they most assuredly would not ask her to also pay them to fix a problem that only she, or perhaps her attorney, could fix. The situation shrieked "scam."

When Charley reported this to the Santa Fe Police Department, she learned that it was indeed a scam, one being perpetrated by prisoners in southern state prisons. What they would do was call, often in the late afternoon, hoping no one was home, to leave a message using a spoofed local police phone caller ID. When the person called back, an app directed the caller to an automated answering center which had recorded, "You have reached Santa Fe Police Department" (or whatever was the receiver's local PD) and would provide a menu of buttons to press for different police matters, one being "Court Services Division." When the caller pressed that number, the call would be directed to a prisoner who, using an app of local police calls as background noise, talked with the caller, explaining the process of how to resolve the problem and secure the money to pay the "bond" or "fine."

While the FBI had gotten convictions of prisoners in 2017 in this scam, the scam had been appearing in other places since then. Charley was stunned yet relieved she had been able to keep Amie from becoming a victim of this million-dollar-plus fraud.

As her disease progressed, Amie became unable to tightly control more of her body movement. Her head began to wobble more, making her look like a slow-motion bobblehead. While she could still walk, her gait exhibited a lack of balance and coordination. Her hands and arms often refused to do precisely what she wanted them to do, instead waving around. Her flexibility with thought, emotion, behavior, and action had a tendency to get stuck, repeating itself. At times when Charley arrived home from doing errands, Amie would welcome her back over and over, as if it were the first time each time.

From her ongoing research on it, Charley knew that behavioral changes were a major aspect of Huntington's though their symptoms could exhibit significant variability of type and severity among individuals and over time. These behaviors could disrupt family life as well as social relationships.

At first Amie's behavioral symptoms were mild and had little impact on her social functioning with Charley. However, as her symptoms worsened over the following months, her impulse control decreased. She would have outbursts, strangled screaming for her lunch when she didn't spot it immediately at twelve noon on the kitchen table. Charley thought these could be related to Amie's anger and frustration over her losing control of her body and mind. But slowly, Amie's awareness of her own abilities and her behavior seemed to change as well. She had difficulties processing thoughts, finding words, and learning new information. Her hostility was palpable.

Because Amie needed Charley around all the time, her going back and forth to her own house to handle online business no longer made any sense. The time was now, Charley decided, to sell her house. Sadly, she listed her comfy little home with its finished outbuilding and beautiful, well-tended, landscaped grounds with the local real estate agent who had sold her the house. Before the agent had a videographer create a new three-sixty tour of the house, Charley moved everything associated with their online business, which was doing well in spite of the circumstances, to Amie's house and organized it in a backroom Amie didn't use. This especially would provide privacy and quiet for when Charley finally began to teach.

Since Charley had set up their website, she, as Amie, had expanded the business to include Charley's instruction in painting with masterclass videos which she created at night once Amie had gone to sleep. Thus far, Charley had nineteen students who shared their progress via Skype or email attachments. Charley also coached them by webinars at prescribed intervals. She was enjoying watching their advancements. At some time in the future, she might even be able to conduct her classes in person. Because she was a people person and was deriving so much pleasure from teaching, in-person was something to which she really looked forward.

One afternoon while Amie was taking a nap, Charley took the chance of running to the grocery store to get salad and taco makings for a dinner she had promised Amie but had forgotten earlier. Disappointing her would most probably create more tantrums. But as she was returning home, a patrol car crawled up behind her and started its siren wailing. Charley's heart jumped. Pulling over, she rolled down the driver's side window, took the insurance card for the car out of the glove compartment, and removed Amie's license from her wallet. As Charley began to sweat, the officer in blue approached.

"I'd like to see your driver's license and insurance."

Charley handed them to him with trepidation. This was the first time she was showing Amie's license to anyone.

"Your name is Amie Benison?"

"Yes, sir." She took a gulp of air.

"This doesn't look a lot like you." He scanned her face, referring to the license mug shot.

"That's because I was in a car accident and had to have several plastic surgeries. You must have read about it. I tried to avoid a mountain lion in Glorieta and wrapped myself around a tree just off Fire Station Road."

"Oh, you're *that* Amie Benison. You were very lucky to get out of that alive."

"Yes, I know. It wasn't until much later that I learned how close I'd come to kissing it all good-bye."

Charley was taking short breaths and smiling while trying to appear pleasant and relaxed.

"Did you know your license is no longer valid?"

Charley swallowed hard and felt sweat form between her breasts and begin to drip. Her brain went blank. Oh, Lord, she thought, he knows I'm not Amie. What do I do now?

"I beg your pardon. What?"

"You need to have your license renewed as soon as possible."

"Oh! My God! You're right. With all the necessary reconstructive surgery I've had I totally forgot. But it's probably just as well since my face has just recently fully healed. At least my renewed license picture will actually look like me as I am now."

Charley exhaled.

He acknowledged her comment by nodding.

Wanting to leave now that she had promised to take care of it, Charley started the engine. But the cop hadn't moved.

"Wait a minute, Ms. Benison. That's not why I stopped you."

Embarrassed, Charley looked at him, her heart galloping.

"Oh, of course not. What's the problem, officer?"

"Your left rear taillight is flickering. You need to have it fixed."

"Darn. Thank you for spotting it. I'll get on it right away. it." She took another slug of air. "Anything else, officer?"

"No, that's all. Just get your license renewed. And I'm glad to see you have recovered from your accident."

She smiled and said, "Thanks."

He nodded again at Charley then walked back to his car where he sat for a moment as Charley started to breathe again and let her cannonading heart begin to calm down. As she pulled away, she saw in her rear-view mirror that he was still sitting there. She felt a twinge.

15

Fortunately, there had been several good offers on Charley's house. She took the highest one, sold it immediately, and moved all the rest of her possessions, other than most of the furniture which she donated to Goodwill Industries on Cerrillos Road, into Amie's house. As she did, things seemed to be happening even faster with Amie's health. Soon Amie could no longer successfully care for herself. Getting something to eat or drink, dressing herself, showering, washing her hair, or successfully sitting herself down squarely on the toilet even with the side safety rails to grasp was hard for her to achieve. Moreover, as this occurred, she was displaying more irritability and was less willing to be physically assisted—or as she seemed to see it, "controlled." Shortly, she began to complain about everything she couldn't do by herself. Charley felt forlorn for her. Amie's ability to function productively and her former personality were fading fast.

It was obvious that Charley could no longer provide what was necessary for Amie. Besides, caring fulltime for Amie by herself had cut seriously into the time Charley needed not only to paint for Amie but also to handle the website, work on the instruction videos, coach, and process and ship orders for the recently-added calendars and posters of Amie's best-known paintings. Her work, which she had come to love more by the day, was necessary to continue to bring in income enough to cover any additional costs for Amie. Any interference with it had to be avoided.

Their current income demonstrated a dramatic difference from what Charley had earned as a political image consultant and Amie had earned from her painting sales and her part-time college and other instruction. Before her professional life in Boston had changed for the worse, Charley had been earning low six figures with the expectation of easily increasing that as the firm continued to grow and expand. Amie's had been in the middle six figures much of which she had invested. Their current bank account was healthy, especially after the sale of Charley's house, but it wouldn't be for long if Charley had to spend all her time being Amie's fulltime nurse and maid. She knew that research had shown that over sixty-six percent of bankruptcies resulted from medical issues: the high cost of care and time out from work. She didn't want them to be a statistic.

Quickly it became incumbent upon Charley to have Amie admitted to an assisted-living facility. With Amie's agreement, Charley would do this using Amie's name and Amie would be admitted under Charley's. So far, their identity switch was working.

Occasionally Charley wondered if anyone would consider that "perpetuating a fraud?" But, why, she always answered the question, would anyone care if Amie were really Charley and vice versa? Amie had agreed to everything and Charley would religiously pay the bills for her. There was no harm, no foul. Once again, she dismissed it as a problem. Besides, in this situation, practicality superseded everything else. There was no question that Amie would not allow being admitted under her own name.

Afterall, it wasn't as if Amie were simply going into a hospital for a short stay to cure her of some bacterial infection or fix another broken limb. This well-known artist had a degenerative disease and was going to be living in assisted care because of it. There was no way that word wouldn't get out. Since Charley had solemnly promised Amie to protect her, she couldn't risk having Amie's name besmirched, even slightly. Everything they had worked so hard for would be lost if that happened.

Charley had excellent, albeit expensive, health insurance so that wasn't a problem either. Staying healthy could be exorbitant. Amie did too which left Charley in good stead in case she needed any medical care, even something that went beyond the run of the mill health problems. They were luckier than ninety percent of people in the U.S.

Strangely, it wasn't until Charley thought about her using Amie's health insurance that a potential problem occurred to her. What if she had to go to the Santa Fe hospital for a situation requiring a blood test? Did she and Amie have the same blood type? Hopefully, they'd test Charley first. If not, she could receive the wrong blood. What if someone spotted that there was a difference between what her blood type revealed with what was recorded for Amie's hospitalization and surgery? But that wouldn't be an issue if Charley didn't go to that medical facility or went to an individual doctor who had no privileges at Amie's hospital, and, therefore, no access to her medical records there.

After a fitful night, contemplating possible complications, she decided that was a problem but she was simply creating worries for herself now about circumstances that might not exist. Even though she hadn't covered all the bases, this wasn't a real stumbling block … at least for the moment … she prayed.

Having located one of the very few assisted-living facilities nearby that accepted Huntington's sufferers, Charley reviewed it online and contacted state agencies to get their critiques. Their rating was excellent with no complaints registered with the state or local Better Business Bureau. Everything they did and what they offered to make residence there as comfortable and therapeutic as possible seemed first-class.

Charley had to work hard to keep Amie upbeat about it and have her admitted. Providing accurate medical information was essential. But that was difficult since Amie had never shared her condition or her family's condition with anyone. And her stay at the hospital didn't indicate anything useful with respect to the disease. Fortunately, the home accepted Charley's description of Amie's problem with movements, cognition, mood, and behavior, as well as her father's history of having had Huntington's. That was a relief and a step in the right direction for both of them. Things were looking up.

16

At Sunflower Homes, the assisted-living facility just off Airport Road, Amie would be carefully observed and monitored, especially for frequent violent behavior which was not currently in evidence, to further cement her diagnosis. As a result of what looked like a clean slate, Amie was allowed to do whatever she wanted, within reason, at the home. Specifically, she was encouraged to enjoy social activities and provided with jigsaw puzzles, games, and supplies for any artistic or other hobbies she might wish to pursue.

Each resident had a ten-by-twelve, single room which pleased Amie. She still had the flexibility to choose what she wanted for her meals, how to spend and live most of her time, and how to decorate her bedroom's light-aqua-tinted-walls room. Amie had one of her own smaller paintings hung on the wall across from the foot of her bed so she could enjoy it when she woke up in the morning. What it represented was her former, but rapidly disappearing, self and previous life.

Then to further make her space as personal as possible, she could add plants she would take care of, knickknacks, books, stuffed animals, and anything else, within reason. Even though Amie loved plants but had never been an indoor plant person, Charley purchased a small barrel cactus, with downward-curved golden spines which sprouted cheery yellow blooms and didn't require much maintenance, that she could keep on her sunny window sill. Regretfully, Amie couldn't keep real animals of any kind, even an ant farm or "sea monkeys." Consequently, Charley gave her an enlarged color photo she had taken of Saatchi and had it placed in a plain silver frame which Amie could keep on her night table.

Charley hoped she would be willing to accept this cat substitute, knowing full well that Amie couldn't hug, kiss, and play with it as if it were the real and present Saatchi. That was likely to be too abstract for Amie to understand and accept. But, then again, a photograph of Little Bit, Charley knew, would have been a poor substitute for her cat if her cat were still alive. Despite somewhat ambiguous regulations to the contrary, Charley would try to sneak Saatchi in for a visit whenever possible.

The primary restriction at the home for Amie was regarding leaving the facility without permission. The staff and manager indicated repeatedly they were particularly concerned about residents wandering off. This irritated and challenged Amie. She had always been a free spirit, doing whatever, whenever it occurred to her. If there were anything that she could not abide, it was constraint, particularly if it were through regulation and regimentation.

This A-one facility was up-to-date with all that someone in Amie's situation would require. They provided psychological therapy to help Amie control her behavioral problems, develop coping strategies, and adapt her expectations during the progression of the disease. She received physical therapy to help her enhance her strength, flexibility, balance, and coordination. The exercises were geared to help her maintain mobility for as long as possible and reduce the risk of her falling. And her speech therapy was to help improve her ability to speak clearly and to teach her to use communication devices—such as a board covered with pictures of everyday items and activities—for when she could no longer speak. It addressed difficulties Amie would encounter when the muscles she used in eating and swallowing began to fail her. The staff also provided her with any psychotropic medication they believed she required for her condition.

To start with, their staff psychiatrist, Dr. Roland Valdez, who came by every couple of weeks, prescribed Ritalin, a psychostimulant, for what he determined was, as he described it, a "shroud of apathy which had encircled her." But the medication made Amie feel agitated and anxious. Furthermore, she began having insomnia which she had never had before. Unable to sleep, she launched into wandering the halls of the facility in the early morning hours. That concerned the staff. She might fall unobserved. She might inspect the rooms of other residents and get caught inside, unable to free herself, creating resident panic. She might check out the supply closets, mess up the order of things, and take gloves, syringes, or incontinence products. Even though she had never shown any interest in the piano, she might choose to start banging on it, awakening everyone who was not sedated. And maybe she'd go into the kitchen to make something to eat, use the stove, and set herself and/or the room on fire. It all caterwauled liability.

When staff informed Valdez that Amie was showing signs of anxiety, the psychiatrist dropped the Ritalin and prescribed a SSRI, a selective serotonin reuptake inhibitor, to increase the neurotransmitter serotonin in her brain to help regulate her mood, emotion, sleep, and appetite. They started her on Paxil but no sooner had she begun taking it, she felt as if she were crawling the walls. It was like anxiety on steroids. Weeks went by before she received relief. Next, they tried Celexa which left her feeling on edge but not as bad as on Paxil. Amie had to repeatedly ask staff for relief. To get Amie to "shut up," as one aide confided to Charley much later on, Valdez followed it with Lexapro. This finally calmed her anxiety sufficiently that she quit complaining about it, to everyone's relief.

For her physical problems, like her involuntary jerking and writhing, there was a range of medications that could be prescribed. The psychiatrist first tried Xenazine but it triggered depression, restlessness, and nausea. Next, he tried Haldol but this worsened her muscle contractions, leaving her with cramps in her arms and legs. Then came Thorazine, an anti-psychotic being used off-label, which made her muscles rigid, leaving her like a marble statue.

At the beginning, Amie had complained to Charley about each new drug as it was tried on her. Charley tried to calm her and explain that they were searching for the best way to individually help her. But Amie expressed her skepticism about their having a clue about what they were doing. Charley wished she had more background on these particular drugs and their effects. She vowed to do some reading on them.

On several occasions Amie looked discouraged.

"I'm being treated like a white rat in a high school research project. Can't you do something about it?"

As the trials of drug switching went on, Amie began to speak less about her depressing medication tribulations. But from the expressions on her face when Charley visited her, Charley could tell Amie was frustrated and angry about being on a drug assembly line, which Charley cynically interpreted as meaning "this unnecessary, haphazard pharmaceutical experimentation" on her. While Charley empathized, she didn't know what else she or they could do.

Charley's evolving impression was that the standard procedure in the home was giving whatever was on Valdez's priority list of oldies but goodies. She had seen this before with an elderly friend in a nursing home. But in her elderly friend's case, they first gave her an anti-anxiety drug for her sense of unease as well as a sedative, whether she had sleep problems of not. Then when there were negative side effects to the medications, rather than take her off the first drugs, they gave her more drugs to curb the side effects. As a result, it didn't take long before that created more problems with side effects and the drugs having synergistic reactions. Her nursing home friend was left lethargic and apathetic all the time. More dead than alive and on a downward slide.

When Charley had looked up her friend's drugs online, she knew there was a serious problem. Calling herself her friend's daughter, she demanded they take her off several of the drugs. Furthermore, if a drug had negative side-effects for "her mother," they were to take her off that drug and find something else instead. There was to be no further stacking of drugs. Somehow, to Charley and her friend's relief, it worked. Her friend, soon on only one appropriate drug, became her old lively self again.

It was well-known that giving elderly people non-essential drugs could mask or make worse their health problems. Just piling on drugs on anyone struck Charley as being incredibly stupid, dangerous, and lazy. But too often it was a convenient habit in some such homes. At least, they weren't doing that with Amie. However, Charley would continue to carefully monitor what they were doing at Sunflower just in case.

As her faculties began to desert her, Amie communicated to Charley that she felt that she had been reasonably fine before they began experimenting on her. Her own assessment of her condition was that basically she was unable to control her movements and knew it. And the rest of what she perceived the problem to be was merely her emotional expression of that lack of control and what it meant to her in her life. While that held some truth, it wasn't the whole story which Amie could no longer see. She further expressed herself in a scattered, idea-shifting way.

"I won't be a guinea pig any longer. They can't continue to experiment on me. I know my rights. I won't let them make me run a maze for a scrap of cheese. The next thing you know they'll bore holes into my skull. Implant electrodes in my brain to control me. They want to make me a robot. That's what Jeffrey Dahmer and the Nazis did in the concentration camps."

Consequently, she began balking and physically refusing each new drug and vociferously complaining about its side effects and lack of efficacy. This was a situation that didn't please the home staff, although they tried hard not to show their unhappiness with Amie to Charley. As far as Charley knew, everything about Amie's living at Sunflower was going better than expected. But what they really wanted, that Amie wasn't giving them or intending to give them, was a good, quiet, compliant resident who created no trouble for them even when a difficulty required it.

On top of this, Valdez appeared to label everything Amie complained about as a "psychological symptom" of her neurological condition. Despite Amie's refusal to continue to be a paragon of acquiescence, the introduction of new drugs did not cease. Amie became more hostile, lashing out verbally whenever she could.

Next the benzodiazepine, Klonopin, which had been shown to reduce chorea, was given her. While it had a small positive effect on her movement, it also made her a zombie cognitively, where she had even more difficulty putting thoughts and words together. Her vociferous complaints of her head feeling as it were stuffed with cotton interfering with her ability to make a sentence led the psychiatrist to abandon it. Not to be deterred, he tried a few more medications to address her uncontrolled movements.

Finally, she received a carefully-controlled regimen of Risperdal which had been used to treat mood disorders, including violent outbursts and delusions. To Amie's surprise and the staff's delight, it also quieted her involuntary movements enough to enable her to get around more normally. Strangely, but thankfully, Risperdal's common side effects of sudden, jerky, involuntary motions of the head, neck, arms, eyes, and body didn't further amplify Amie's chorea. Valdez felt vindicated after all he had endured with Amie. And she experienced a new sense of freedom at the home. With that her complaints and her fragmentary speech dwindled.

For the first time in a long time, she was able to move around on her own enough to allow her to do some things she wanted to do with her body. Now she could eat at the dining table without knocking over her glass and dropping food from her therapeutically-large, heavy fork or spoon. She could walk around the home without stumbling, colliding with walls, and falling. Moreover, most of her brain fogginess had been eliminated as had been her anxiety.

However, she was still somewhat confused about what had or had not happened and unable to clearly remember the past or, occasionally, what she wanted from moment to moment. In addition, some depression remained. This was especially with regard to her wishful feeling that she should be in her own home. Sadly, she also believed that Charley and Saatchi never came by.

Instead, she became convinced they had abandoned her in this "prison."

Still, in a less frequent lucid moment Amie indicated to Charley the next time she visited that over all she felt almost triumphant. She was, in essence, like Rocky Balboa as he ran up the seventy-two stone steps to the entrance to the Philadelphia Museum of Art. Free. Unbeaten. Charley hoped it would last.

From the very beginning of Amie's stay at the home, Charley felt guilty about no longer being able to care for her friend. Even worse was having had to put her in a facility, despite Amie's having acceded to going. Furthermore, now, every time she saw her, Amie begged, crying, to be released early, paroled.

"I'll be good. I'll do whatever you want. I won't be a burden. Oh, please. Please, please, please take me out of here."

17

Because of Amie's continuing pleas, Charley felt torn and conflicted. It also reminded her what her own mother had made her promise years ago, well before her mother was ever likely to need such assistance.

What her mother made Charley promise was that if she ever could no longer care for herself that Charley would not put her in a nursing home. Early on, when she first asked, Charley had no idea why she was so adamant about it. Although, over time, it became obvious to her that it must have been related to her grandfather finally having to place her grandmother in a nursing home when she had developed inoperable brain cancer and resulting uncontrollable dementia in her seventy-ninth year. As hard as he tried, he couldn't care for her at home and couldn't afford to bring in fulltime nursing assistance which she required for all her needs. Charley's mother had complained bitterly about her mother's nursing home care, or lack of it, but she couldn't care physically or financially for her mother herself either.

Charley's mother was still young and healthy with no expectation, that Charley knew of, that she would ever require that kind of care. If Charley's dad died and, therefore, wouldn't be there to help his wife, Charley would certainly have found a way to assist her. She saw that as her sacred duty. In spite of the less than confidence-building comments her father tended to make to her, that would have gone for assisting him as well in that position.

"Promise me—please—that no matter what you'll never put me in a nursing home," she beseeched Charley. "I saw how your grandmother was treated when she went into one. Just the thought of it scares me to death. Even in those that are well-run, not warehouses, you have no personal control. No independence. No say. You're like an object, not a person, to be tolerated and manipulated—*dealt* with."

"But, Mom, there's nothing to worry about. You eat healthy, exercise, don't smoke, and don't drink to excess. You'll be around for a long time … with Dad."

"Charley, darling, things happen that you can't foresee. I could develop incapacitating arthritis, Parkinson's, severe heart disease, or terminal cancer. I could have a serious fall and destroy my hips or back. It could be anything. I don't want to spend my last days being tended to by strict-scheduled strangers in an impersonal environment where I might lie in urine-soaked sheets for hours, getting bed sores, until someone finally came by to change the linen. I'd rather shoot myself."

"Mom, I would never let that happen to you. I understand how you feel about being independent and in control of your life."

"I know it's asking a lot but do this one last thing for me. I haven't asked much of you before but I need to ask this of you now. Promise me you'll never let me be treated like that. Promise you'll keep me in my home somehow, no matter what."

That was a tough promise to make. Charley promised her, feeling she would likely have the resources to keep her mother in her own home, where she would be the most comfortable and independent-feeling, with round-the-clock nursing assistance or whatever else she required. If her political image marketing firm continued its upward trend, that would not be a problem financially. The less-desirable alternative, should a situation arise necessitating it, would be taking her into Charley's own small apartment with part-time assistance.

In her apartment Charley knew she personally would have to provide similar care for her mother. Her participation in it would help keep their relationship warm and close. She knew it would be too easy for her mother to feel like an unwanted guest and a burden if she didn't. But, at the same time, given the requirements of Charley's work, that would be very difficult because she still traveled. Either way, she would find a solution to deal with the details in the best way possible should that situation actually occur. But, as it ironically turned out, the car accident involving her parents rendered that promise null and void well in advance of her needing to fulfill it.

Charley continued to visit Amie every other day for a half-hour and often brought Saatchi with her. Visiting and checking on Amie had begun to cut into the time Charley needed to paint for Amie and run their business because with each visit Amie begged for more time together. But Charley had to balance her time with Amie and her time making money to cover Amie's expenses. As Amie pressured Charley to stay longer and longer, each visit became more emotional and awkward. While Charley had no plans to change her visitation, she was concerned about Amie's behavior and what it might mean about her condition, as well as for her continuing to stay at Sunflower. As much as she wanted Amie to be as free as possible at the home, she also didn't want her to create any management problems. So far as Charley knew, things still looked okay with respect to that worry.

Professional care for Amie was going to continue to be very expensive, and likely to increase over time. And there was no way to know how long Amie would stay at the home. Charley hoped it would be for as long as possible, for as long as it was helpful to both Amie and her. What her research had disconcertingly shown her was that there was only a tiny handful of facilities anywhere, and especially around the New Mexico area, that took individuals with Huntington's.

As a general rule, long-term care facilities, assisted-living homes, and nursing homes dealt with old age infirmities, but not Huntington's. Many, she discovered, were not even familiar with the neurological disease. That shocked Charley. If Amie's anger and frustration, and potential behavioral outbursts, became too much for Sunflower to handle, Charley didn't know what she could do to place Amie somewhere else to get her the specific, essential care she needed. According to the Huntington's Disease Society of America website, if you knew you'd need a long-term-care facility, you had better start looking and interviewing early … very early because it was likely to be a long, exasperating undertaking to find one.

As a result of the progression of her disease, Amie could no longer cognitively take into her understanding what had happened to her relatives, particularly those where their brains had degenerated and their personalities and lives disintegrated. Memories, good and bad, were no longer hers to dissect and consider, much less apply to her own situation. There was no longer any personal identification or comfort for her in them as there had been in the past. Bit by bit, everything that made Amie the old Amie was evaporating.

Despite her becoming atomized into disconnected, disorganized parts, she could still feel the pull of the freedom which had always been an overarching desire for her. As a young person, she had been rebellious, marching and protesting for whatever social concern she embraced, from minorities, women, animals, nuclear power, to the climate and environment. As an artist, she had taken on a more laissez-faire, individualistic approach to life and her work. She expected to be able to take whatever life presented to her on her own terms. Always having been a free soul, she chafed at being observed, monitored, and managed for no reason she could see. She didn't have a problem so others had no reason to treat her as if they had a problem with her.

Amie hadn't been at the assisted-living facility seven months when increasing obstreperous behavior became a predicament for management. Her living constraints were out of sync with her sense of control which she had always assumed would continue until she died. The more she felt her former sense of herself slipping away, the more she struggled to find ways to recapture it. Momentous or inconsequential, it was anything that would make her feel she was still Amie, the unfettered individual she once was. As she stared out the windows of the home, observing the native plants that challenged the aridity, the outdoors spoke to her. She identified with it and urgently needed to re-immerse herself in Nature.

That business about asking for and receiving "permission to leave the premises" she knew was just so much bull. It was supposed to make the home sound more friendly, flexible, and adapted to the residents' needs and desires. But no resident had ever received a hall pass to sashay through the front door while Amie was there. Watching, Amie had never seen anyone—not a single resident who was not comatose, sedated, or circling the drain of senility—just leave. But she knew that others, like her, wanted to in their heart of hearts. Any mentally-alert resident who actually passed through that door to the outside did so only with a relative or friend acting as the responsible guardian in supervision. They were taken out like a dog that needed to be walked. But never casually with a nurse or tech from Sunflower. And, most assuredly, never ever on their own.

She had begun to see herself as a POW, maybe a kidnap hostage, bound up in the chains of others' commands and demands. It was then that she undertook to formulate a plan for how she'd slip out through the front door when no one was looking. Her emotional focus was suddenly becoming one-track. It was on the six-paneled, honey-colored oak door which was usually double-locked by the staff and opened only when a visitor came to see a resident. It was like TV's 1966-1973 *Mission: Impossible.* Her mission, should she decide to accept it, was to await that tiny instance when the door was unlocked and everyone else was occupied, not looking. It was then that she would leave … flee … escape.

There was no debate about it. She was asserting her independence and taking her freedom into her own hands. Before it was too late.

18

While these images of her prison break-out took on a more calculated behavioral dimension, she also took to teasing the staff, daring them to "catch me if you can." Even though she couldn't think clearly about how and when to maneuver past visitors and staff, a more primitive urge to make a run for it took over. It was like a reversion to something ancient or ancestral in her brain. Part of her felt she had become a trapped animal, exploring her cage for any sign of weakness she could exploit. That required that she was always on the alert for any opportunity to break loose and bolt.

But what Amie didn't, and couldn't, realize as she assessed her chances for making her flight to freedom was that her actions would become a large management and schedule complication for the facility. Allowing residents to walk freely in the neighborhood or beyond would disrupt everything because everything had to be organized and programmed, with interruptions to a minimum. Staff had duties which didn't include search and rescue. There was no time set aside to scour the neighborhood for wandering residents.

Once she would get herself outside, she could envision herself ambling down the street away from the facility. Her balance and ambulatory problems would no longer be a difficulty. The only thing that would matter would be that she was her old self again. And by the time the staff would have noticed she was missing, she would have traveled nearly a mile toward town or into a bordering development, looking at house styles and landscapes ... whatever took her fancy at the moment.

Maybe she'd pick some native wildflowers, like the yellow daisy-like Perky Sue, the long-stalked orange Porter's globe mallow covered with flowers along the stem, or the white trumpet-shaped flowers of the Datura, also called "Jimson weed," in the sandy lots along the sidewalk. Maybe she would cross the street to check out the arroyos, the steep-sided gullies which were formed by the action of fast-flowing water from fall monsoon season rains in that dry land. Maybe she'd enjoy the blazing sun on her face and feel the sand-clotted winds rumple her hair, all to be at one with the universe. And maybe she'd just walk and walk and walk until she encountered something new and unexpected. It would be an adventure. She wanted it. She needed it to feel real, a person again. And then it happened.

It was one o'clock. The residents had finished their lunch at the long, oak table which required two leaf extensions, at the other end of the dining room/living room combination. Visitors were beginning to arrive. As a group of five visitors entered and took up the over-stuffed chairs in the conversation groupings to await their resident friends and relatives, she edged near the door. When the staff went to residents' rooms to escort them to meet their respective visitors, Amie slipped out.

What she first experienced was the breeze that kissed her skin. It was soft and sweet despite the warm dryness sprinkled with grit. She smiled. Her nervous system seemed filled with sensuous delight. As she walked from under the porte cochère, where visitors arrived and waited to be admitted after they had parked their cars, she felt the sun on her face and reveled in it. It was like a shot of golden adrenaline. It tasted like honey comb. Invigorated, she turned to her right, past the planted four-foot blue-green agave. Its spear-like tips at the ends of its three-foot-long, fleshy leaves seemed to point out directions she could follow as she ambled to the concrete sidewalk. There she turned left and started her long-sought-after journey.

She was feeling unbound at last. Nothing felt diminished … because she couldn't remember anything to which to compare it. Being in Nature seemed to make her see things more clearly today. It was like a narcotic. She made a note to herself to be sure to do this any time she could. It would be worth *anything* she had to pay for this fix.

After crossing the street and traveling about a quarter of a mile west, she approached a housing development. It was one with cloned, single-story beige stucco buildings, each with a red-tile roof, on less than a quarter of an acre, all xeriscaped with gray, rounded, two-inch Mexican beach pebbles, dotted with cacti and succulents, but no trees. Not even a single desert willow with its pink orchid-like flowers, a vitex with its purple spikes, or even a fragrant shrub-like globe of blue lavender. It was austere, as grim as her life felt at the home.

It was not that she had expected to see one of the dramatically-unusual constructions by New Mexico's outstanding architect Bart Prince, like his steel-pole-elevated "Snake House" in Rio Rancho. That was an elongated string of box-like rooms each separated by a narrow-windowed hallway she had once seen on the Web. But these development buildings were like a pueblo-style version of Levittown's twenty-seven-step-assembly-line houses, each one the same as the next. At least her own place, which she missed and longed to return to, had some individuality. In addition, her house was isolated from other houses to a degree and surrounded by shady New Mexico olives, Siberian elms, piñon pines, and huge fragrant purple and white lilacs.

She even had a black locust that was on its way to becoming eighty feet tall one day. Its fragrant white cascading flowers reminded her of the scent of orange blossoms. But what she really liked about it was its two-to-four-inch-long hanging black seed pods that attracted quail, grouse, song birds, and deer from autumn to early spring. Also, small wildlife often took advantage of the tree's thorn-covered branches to nest in safety. Her trees provided not only shade but also distinctive landscaping. She had made a point of having her yard's other plantings all perennials, like agastache, lupines, bee balm, cardinal flower, and butterfly bush, which would attract the bees, butterflies, moths, hummingbirds, and all manner of beneficial insects.

As she approached a paved road on her right, she turned into the housing development's first entrance and sauntered on in. How sad, she thought as she walked along, that everything looked so bland. These interchangeable domiciles were like little boxes. Very ticky-tacky.

Suddenly she had a rare flash of remembrance. In 1962 Malvina Reynolds wrote the song *Little Boxes*, which Pete Seeger made famous in 1963. It was all about the development of suburbia which exemplified the conformist attitudes of the middle-class. How strange, she thought, that she should have remembered having heard that. Sometime in the past. But it disappeared from her as quickly as it had appeared.

As she rambled along, she suddenly spotted a collarless, dirty and matted Tabby cat making its way around the outer perimeter of a yard. It looked emaciated, neglected, perhaps ill, and unquestionably homeless to Amie. If it had a home, those people obviously didn't take care of it. Maybe it had been abandoned. Or, maybe, it was feral. She scrambled over the unwieldy yard's surface, knocking rocks out of place where the yard met the sidewalk wall. Scooping up the cat, she slipped and nearly slid onto the sidewalk-less road.

Regaining her footing while still holding her prize, she retraced her steps to the main drag where she stood, contemplating what to do next. She could take the cat back to Sunflower but she was sure they'd reject it. She had sensed that when Saatchi visited for only thirty minutes, never leaving her or Charley's lap, management was not all that pleased. Its staff members always wore expressions of irritation but no one said anything directly to Charley about it which made it hard to respond to. Instead of taking the cat back there, she decided to wait to see if a police car would come by. She could have them take possession of the cat and drop it off at a no-kill animal rescue shelter. That, she felt, was the better plan.

Leaning against the concrete block retaining wall surrounding the development, she waited forty minutes in hopes of seeing a black-and-white. If one didn't appear soon, she knew she had no other choice than to take the animal to Sunflower and plead with the obdurate staff to place a phone call to a shelter. She wasn't confident that alternative would turn out well, but …

Just then, a patrol car fortuitously approached, one that was not on its regular beat. She flagged it down. As she walked to the passenger's window, the police officer seated there electronically rolled it down. Raising up the cat, she stated quietly that she had just found the poor animal which was in dire need of assistance.

"It's homeless and needs help," she said. "Could you take it to the nearest no-kill animal rescue shelter? I'd do it if I had a car. I can't keep it because I can't have any animals where I live."

The ragged-looking cat which had curled up comfortably in her arms, was rubbing its head against her shoulder, and was purring loudly as if it had claimed Amie as its haloed protector.

It was during Amie's interaction with the police that two of the home's female staff members who seemed joined at the hip, that Charley had thought of as "Frick and Frack," arrived in their car. Upon noticing Amie, they pulled in and parked behind the cruiser. As they alighted and approached her, they were smiling but appeared unsure of how to address the situation. There was clearly a sense of determination on their faces, that they had to explain their reason for being there. Their aim was to convey to the police as calmly as possible, being careful not to accuse Amie or upset her in any way, that they were there to escort Amie back home.

"Has Amie done anything wrong, Officer?"

"No. Why do you ask? She just wanted to talk to us. Who are you?"

"I'm sorry if she has been bothering you. She lives with us at Sunflower and seems to have momentarily wandered away without letting us know."

The two police officers in the squad car looked questioning. First at the normal-looking Amie and then at the two residence staffers. The cop who was speaking frowned.

"Bothering us? She wasn't bothering us. Why would you think that?"

Amie was standing quietly by the front quarter panel on the passenger side still cradling the cat which was in kitty seventh heaven. A shadow of annoyance began to reveal itself in her set expression and stiffening body. The staffers were trying to look as open-faced and casual as possible. They knew it wouldn't do for the police to think that people with mental health issues were roaming around aimlessly, taking pets from people's yards, and waving down police cars, on a whim.

Finally, the cop spoke to Amie who was slowly shaking her head.

"Is there some other kind of problem you also want to talk about?"

Amie screwed up her face, shook her head definitively, responding, "No, thanks, it was just the cat—," but she was cut off by the taller of the two staffers.

"Now, Amie, you know you can't just take the cat from someone's yard. And you know you can't take it home with you. Sunflower has rules about that sort of thing."

Cocking her head to the side, Amie stared at her, wanting to tell her to mind her own business. She answered with emphasis as if talking to a recalcitrant child.

"I'm saving a homeless cat, not stealing it. I'm arranging to send it to a shelter. This has nothing to do with Sunflower … or with you."

The cop beside Amie, who happened to help with cat and dog adoptions in Santa Fe at PetSmart on weekends, looked quizzical. He spoke to the staffers.

"It looks to me as if you have thoroughly misunderstood the situation."

The taller staff member looked confused, as if she were suddenly aware that they had addressed the situation the wrong way, that maybe she should have just indicated that the three of them were out for a walk and Amie had drifted off from them, following the cat. But, then again, they were in a car and Amie was on foot.

"All I meant was," she began, "that she shouldn't have gone off on her own to someplace new, shouldn't have taken the cat, and she shouldn't have bothered you."

The police officer raised his eyebrows as he looked up at "Frick." Then he spoke to her with a hint of irritation.

"I don't see what your problem is, aside from your condescending attitude. You're acting like you're her keeper. Are you?"

"Well, uh, no. We were just concerned—"

"Okay, then." He began to open his door to take the cat from Amie.

The staffers fidgeted. They trembled at the accusation but they were caught without an empathetic response.

Looking at Amie, he asked, "Are you going to be okay?"

Amie half-heartedly nodded with a sigh. She was feeling annoyed that her first outing had been turned into a big fiasco. She had already decided that the next time she slipped out, she'd go east, in the other direction, and maybe avoid all of this brouhaha. Then, as if an afterthought, Amie almost smirked at her prison guards' discomfort.

"Thank you, Officers," she said to the cop and his partner, smiling, as she reached around the opened door to hand the cat to the officer, giving it one more gentle scratch under the chin as she did. "I appreciate your concern and assistance."

She could tell her guards were agonizing, intensely wanting to explain that Amie had illegally eased herself out of the home. But, at the same time, someplace in Amie's patchy brain, she knew they did not want to make her look like an escaped basket case and themselves as supremely incompetent for not watching over and controlling her. It wasn't just the public relations that worried them. It was the home's liability as well as their jobs being on the line. After the police car pulled away, Amie unhappily joined the staffers in their car.

Once they were back at Sunflower, the obviously aggrieved manager of the home spoke with Amie about the necessity of not leaving the building.

"Amie, you know there are rules about leaving on your own. Those rules are for your own protection, to keep you safe. When you leave without permission, no one knows where you are. Then we have to search to find you. We don't want you to get lost or hurt. So please don't leave again without permission from one of the nurses."

Amie almost chuckled. She knew that "permission" was a crock. Sometime, she thought, she'd actually have to ask for it just to document what a blatant lie it was. But now wasn't the time. Her meds were wearing off and her thoughts were dashing here and there. For her short trip she had been able to actually converse and sound normal. But, she wondered, would she be able to do that again?

Every day she seemed to be slipping a little bit more despite the Risperdal. And, somehow, she knew, regardless of her cognitive diminution, she wouldn't have that many more escapes in her. She was like a clock running down, slowly ticking away what was left of the rest of her life's recognition. She'd have to act fast to make her future ventures a reality before it was too late.

19

After the cat-rescue incident, the staff at the home took turns explicitly watching Amie when she was in the front room between one and four o'clock visiting hours with the only viable access to the outside. The only other door was in the kitchen which was rarely opened except for removing garbage or accepting grocery and supply deliveries. Escaping by that door was beyond the realm of possibility. The kitchen was always occupied by staff taking coffee breaks or cooks making meals.

Amie would continue to taunt the staff when she knew they were looking. She would ease toward door and hang there to see what they would do as a result. From the expressions on their faces, that was more trouble than they wanted to have to deal with. It pleased her. She still had a crumb of control. One afternoon she sidled up to the home manager and asked if she could have permission to leave. The woman was taken aback. Amie had the idea that no one had ever actually asked her before.

"Oh, not now! Talk to me later. I have an order to see to in the kitchen."

After that, if Amie began to approach her again, she scurried off to handle something "important" elsewhere in the building. Amie felt it would have been laughable if it hadn't been so hypocritically pathetic.

It took another three weeks before Amie could slip out again, unseen. This time while she could feel the sun on her face, she couldn't assign a value to it. The wild flowers which now looked dull to her didn't beg to be observed and picked. No skittering animals or insects caught and held her attention. The world around her presented itself in gray tones, something like the brooding somberness of a 1950s' black-and-white Swedish film, and had less of a meaningful impact. Somehow, she didn't feel in touch with it. Her senses felt tamped down. She couldn't conjure up her previous enthusiasm. That left a lingering note of melancholy that she couldn't place.

But today she was on an important errand. It was a little fuzzy around the edges but she knew there was something she had to do. It was more than a fix. It was a humanitarian operation. As part of it, she had taken her untouched lunch with her, still on its plate, which she held out in front of her, covered by a cloth napkin, as if she were serving a meal.

After walking a mile in the opposite direction of the development, she came to a solitary, small stick-built house with brown-seared privet shrubs around it that no longer needed watering and one straggly Siberian elm which at one time had provided shade to the parched-looking house. There she stopped at the front door. Calling out a name from her past, she knocked until the wary resident, not recognizing the name, came to the door. Opening it only a crack to see what the noise was about, a middle-aged woman dressed in gray sweats peered out. Amie offered the startled home owner her turkey sandwich with an apple and slice of dill pickle.

"I heard," Amie said sympathetically to the confused woman, as she pulled back the napkin to show her, "that they took you off Medicaid. That was so unfair, so cruel. I'm sorry about your state of destitution. I brought you something to eat. I'm sorry it couldn't be more right now. I will bring you dinner later and anything else you need. You can let me know whatever that is then."

Before Amie could say anything else, the woman reached back from the partially-open door to grab her iPhone resting on a small table nearby to call the authorities. Just then, the two previous residence staffers arrived again.

Taking Amie by the elbow to turn her away, the taller one, Amie's "Frick," spoke to the homeowner.

"We're sorry Amie bothered you. She mistook you for an old friend she thought had moved here. We'll see if we can help her find her friend."

The woman's face reflected skepticism and a barely-concealed anxiety. What did that mean? Was that person a mental case? Would it happen again? Should she be afraid? It was all too strange. After she closed the door, the staffers escorted Amie to their waiting car and drove her back to the home.

Hints of delusions were now peeking out more frequently from behind her previously semi-cooperative mask. Idiosyncratic beliefs increasingly prompted her to behave in unusual and unacceptable ways. For some reason the Risperdal was no longer as effective as it had been for her delusions, though it still helped decrease her involuntary movements. When Dr. Valdez was called in, he still had a list of some thirteen drugs he could try for her delusions, such as Clozaril, Seroquel, Geodon, and Zyprexa. He approached Amie patronizingly.

"Now, Amie, you don't want people to think you're crazy by doing all these odd things, do you?"

Amie just looked at him, stunned, then irritated.

"Crazy things? What are you talking about?"

"You know, taking cats and visiting strangers with food."

"It's not crazy to rescue a starving cat or wanting to help an old friend in need. What's crazy about compassion and being humane?" She paused for a moment. An aha expression covered her face. "Oh, I know what you're doing." She began to hyperventilate. "You're trying to talk me into being in your military experiments. I know about the psychedelics you want to use to try to drive me mad. I know I'm not crazy and you can't make me crazy. I'm an American citizen. I have rights. You can't force me."

But the more he tried to placate and coax her into taking the new trial of medications, the more afraid and wildly resistant she became. Amie still saw herself as his prisoner guinea pig where he was the equivalent of a "Dr. Josef Mengele." Only now he was heading the 1950s and 1960s U.S. Army Intelligence's secret, uncontrolled experiments with lethal nerve agents, mescaline, psilocybin, and LSD to see what could be used as an enhanced interrogation technique. Ostensibly, they were interested in whether use of these drugs by the enemy could make soldiers reveal military secrets. Amie knew she had a big secret but they couldn't make her reveal it. Even though she could barely remember what it was, she knew that no matter how they tried, it was hers—alone—forever.

Quickly this was making her an even more unwelcome resident at Sunflower unless she could be forced to take each new medication or potentially be sedated for the better part of the day. When Charley finally found out about it, she strenuously opposed it. But after several more episodes, one particularly where at midnight when everyone was asleep, Amie stripped-teased to her birthday suit in the living room raucously singing "I'm Just a Girl Who Can't Say No" from *Oklahoma*, auditioning for her role in a new stage production of the musical, Charley was informed that Amie had to comply or leave.

"She's a bad role model for other residents and is upsetting everything here," explained the house manager, trying to cover her exasperation. "We have tolerated her for as long as we can but her behavior simply can no longer be tolerated. She has to be out of here in two days' time … period. The only alternative is to require her, by force if necessary, to be on a new anti-delusion med or sedation for control."

"By force?" Charley shook her head. "No bloody way!" she sputtered.

She knew that kind of maneuver would only make Amie even angrier and more motivated to regain her independence in any way possible, even if the drug might ultimately reduce, or potentially eliminate, her delusions. It could also make her a zombie. The alternative? Sedation most of the time? That had to be illegal or, at least, unethical. As much as Charley really wanted Amie to stay at Sunflower, she simply could not allow such an outrage to come to pass. That wasn't living. That was intolerable.

Amie sat unmoving, intractable, on her bed, clutching the bedspread beneath her, as she watched Charley pack all her clothing and personal items. Focusing on her few paltry possessions, she saw what was left of her life being relegated to a few empty cardboard boxes. For an instant, she felt overwhelmed with a sadness which competed with her anxiety. Then again … she was finally leaving.

But, immediately, she knew that these boxes weren't going to be saved for her. They were going to be tossed, the first step toward making her vanish from the home's books. That way they could send her to the gas chamber to get rid of her once and for all. Thoughts appeared, registered, and disappeared. She felt confused and afraid.

As Charley finished packing, she could see the turmoil on Amie's face. She tried again to explain, to make her understand, that she was going back to her own house. That that was where she had said she really wanted to be. But nothing seemed to be reaching her. Leaving her attached to her bed, Charley took Amie's boxed possessions out to the car, opened the hatch, and placed them in the back. Once again in Amie's room, now she had to entice her to go outside as well.

"Saatchi has been looking forward to seeing you. She's at your house waiting for you to return there. Would you like to see your cat?"

Amie looked bewildered for a moment and then smiled.

"We have to go outside to get into the car to drive to your home to see her. Are you ready?"

Amie rose and allowed Charley to escort her through Sunflower to that magical front door. As they approached it, Amie began to look questioning, as if she wanted to smile but was afraid that she was wrong about why she should do it. Were they really leaving? As they stepped over the threshold of the opened door into the outside, she began to grin a little. Once inside the awaiting car, she began to relax, smiling from ear to ear. It was obvious that she had finally been released. Someplace in her brain she knew that meant she was being freed. Someplace within her body she felt that what was left of her soul was rejoicing. She knew her Dr. Mengele could no longer play his evil games with her mind. No more.

20

When the car began to roll along the paved driveway, which meant Amie was leaving Sunflower, the rolling sensation tapped into the glorious feeling she had had when she had first escaped, when she had convinced the police officer to rescue the cat. But the sensation passed in an instant. The buoyant mood it had engendered slipped away too. That memory of triumph had dissolved well before she reached her formerly-desired destination.

Once at her own home, she tried to re-acclimate to it, but it was more difficult than she had imagined. It had the ambiance of "home" but it seemed less familiar and less comfortable somehow. While she knew she wanted to be "home," whatever that meant, it felt as though someone had made a mistake. She had been taken to the wrong house, even though everything was the same as before she'd left.

Charley was totally at sea about what to do next. Now that Amie was back, what would she do to care for and handle her? If she hadn't been able to do what was necessary for her before Sunflower, how could she possibly do so now that things had gotten so much worse over Amie's time in assisted-living? Charley needed to find someplace else to take her … and do it yesterday.

Sunflower hadn't given her a clue that things were so unsatisfactory with Amie there that she was at risk of being evicted. No one had spoken directly to her about these recurring management issues when she visited, which was certainly frequent enough for them to have had the opportunity, over and over again. Moreover, she was only an email or phone call away. They gave her no time to locate someplace else appropriate for Amie. It was at this moment of disorientation that she remembered that the

Huntington's Disease Society of America had warned about the difficulty of finding placements.

Charley was incensed. It had been Sunflower's responsibility to inform her when they perceived things weren't going well, that Amie's continued residence there was at risk because of her behavior. Maybe, if they had, Charley thought, she could have had time to make an informed decision about what to do next. But, irrespective, they should have told her of Amie's repeated absences and/or misbehaviors. But, no. Instead, they slapped her in the face with an order to vacate, almost immediately. It was like *not* having been alerted by the local weather bureau that radar indicated a tornado they had been following was barreling directly toward your house alone and that you should take shelter in the cellar in the next few minutes if you wanted to live.

In essence, they had merely dumped Amie in Charley's lap and wiped their hands of her. Not very professional, and very crude, she thought. Besides, their contract said they would keep Charley apprised of Amie's progress, regression, and any minor or major troublesome behavior. It occurred to Charley that maybe they were counting on the guardians or relatives of the resident who was being given the heave-ho being so discombobulated, suddenly being burdened with trying to find a new placement as soon as possible, that they wouldn't sue.

Charley knew she didn't have the time at present to bring suit. Slow-dragging legal action was the last thing on her mind. She knew that *if* she could finally find someplace suitable, it was unlikely that she would have the energy, much less the inclination, to pursue litigation. She did wonder, however, how many times Sunflower had pulled that stunt on residents and caught a lucky break on that score.

While she frantically tried to locate another long-term care facility, she was aware that nothing could conceivably happen immediately. Assuming she could actually find another place, the bureaucratic red tape after that always took minimally anywhere from ten days to two weeks, especially where health or disability insurance was involved and medical documentation had to copied, sent, examined, assessed, and approved.

As long as Amie stayed at her home—until Charley could find an acceptable resolution—she would have to be almost a captive. There had to be restrictions on her activities. She couldn't be allowed to wander from the house or attempt to use the car. That would be awkward, rife with complications, and prospectively dangerous. But there was no reason to expect that Amie would choose to accede to Charley's dictates. Especially, if she were able to recall that it was happening in her *own* house.

Daily Charley tried to duplicate Amie's schedule at Sunflower. Regularity seemed important, especially where her medications, meals, activities, and sleep were concerned. She didn't want to do anything that would upset Amie's circadian rhythms which might create further problems. With Amie's Risperdal no longer adequately handling her delusions, Charley found she had to spend a lot of time trying to keep track of what Amie was doing. Likewise, trying to disabuse her of what she believed was the situation at any given moment. She knew she truly had her work cut out for her.

One time, all of a sudden, Amie started packing her large, polycarbonate wheeled suitcase, throwing anything she could get her hands on into the hinge-strained bag. As Charley approached Amie's bedroom to check on Amie, she found her mumbling, frenetically emptying dresser drawers onto the bed. Then she saw Charley.

"I have to catch an early flight to Los Angeles to appear at the Hammer Museum, near UCLA. They're having a showing of my works this week. And I have to give a presentation and receive an award. I need to get to the airport right away."

Late one afternoon Charley couldn't find Amie until she heard the sound of something pounding on metal. Tracking it to the garage, Charley found Amie crying and wailing, banging on the Honda's hatch, trying to open and get inside it.

"Davy, it's me, Amie," she breathlessly called. "You locked yourself inside. I can't get you out because Mommy has the key.

And I can't find her. Don't die. We're having S'mores this afternoon."

Charley tried to calm her as she lifted the unlocked hatch for Amie to see its contents.

"There's no one in here, Amie. Davy is safe. He got out all by himself and went home. You can stop worrying now."

She pulled Amie away, as Amie tried to go back to check the back of the car one more time. Charley guided her to the living room sofa to sit down where Saatchi immediately jumped onto her lap and began her diesel-engine purr. Saatchi always helped enormously. Amie was like another person when petting and cuddling her cat. It was as if some strong connection of sound and touch triggered the comforting effect of oxytocin production in her hypothalamus which created a sense of empathy and a loving relationship. Sometimes that euphoria could last as long as ten minutes. Then Amie began pleading to go outside.

"All I want to do is watch the birds. The butterflies. The ground squirrels. There can't be anything wrong with that, can there? I want to smell the flowers. I love flowers. Please."

As much as she hated the prospect of allowing it, Charley began to wonder if there were some reasonable, safe way in which she could do it. But she knew that irrespective of whatever Amie might promise about sitting or walking in the back garden, that wouldn't be all that she'd do. Something else would occur to her. She might take the notion to hike up the road to the forest to see is she could spy any owls. Or something beyond that location would attract her attention. She might hear a neighbor's horse whinny and want to check to see that it had feed and water. She might spot a coyote or raccoon in the distance that appeared to beckon her to follow to its den to see its babies. And if any of that happened, then everything before that would slip from her mind. She could disappear and become lost.

That meant that if Amie were to go outside, Charley would have to be with her and, if necessary, wrestle her back into the yard. Charley didn't want to have to get physical with her, to force her back inside. That would be unacceptable, even if it could work. Furthermore, it would enrage Amie.

But it wouldn't be as bad as the alternative of chaining her up outside. The idea of putting a safety harness on her on a long lead attached to a wire running from one Siberian elm across the property to another to restrain her like a dog was distasteful. And she didn't want to lock her inside either, angering her, though that was likely the best solution overall. Even though Amie had already been through the circumstance of strangers locking the doors in a strange place, this felt different. Charley doing it in Amie's own home smacked of arguable behavior. Yet, she had to do whatever was necessary to protect them both. When Amie began clamoring all the time to go outside, Charley's attempts to distract her were only minimally helpful.

Occasionally, Amie's behavior became physically wild, like throwing all their non-painting inventory in the studio out of the cabinets onto the floor because she said it was time for spring cleaning. That put Charley even more behind in her intermittent handling and shipping of orders. When Amie made a move toward the paintings which were stored in a corner, Charley made a grab for her but Amie just stood and looked

"Who paints?" she asked. "At one time I knew someone who painted."

On one occasion when Charley was taking a shower, Amie had awkwardly tried to make Charley and herself scrambled eggs, bacon, and toast for breakfast. But she dropped the heavy iron skillet, splashing bacon grease onto the burner and stove top, causing a fire. Confused and frightened, she tried to run outside. Because the French doors were locked. She ran against them again and again until the wood around the single lock splintered, giving way.

It wasn't until Charley emerged from the bathroom that she saw the billowing black smoke. Using a large stew pot lid to cover the burner, she turned it off and ran to grab the fire extinguisher that she kept hanging on the wall near the door to the garage. As a result of her quick thinking, she put out the flames before the walls and cabinets were scorched. About to clean up the grease, she spotted the French doors wide open. She knew Amie had plunged through them to run into the back garden.

After a few minutes searching, she saw her hiding among the lavender shrubs, crouched down behind the concrete birdbath.

"Fire's out, Amie," called Charley calmly as she approached her. "It was just an accident. You can come in the house now and we'll have your nice breakfast."

Amie continued to hide, unwilling to move. Getting her attention, Charley worked to distract her by pointing out the mourning dove which was perched on the side of the nest of twigs it had made on the branch of the evergreen, near the doors. Since the eggs had hatched earlier, little charcoal beaks, now wide open perpetually awaiting food, were poking above the nest rim in readiness.

As Amie was rising from her crouch, she spoke to Charley, tears threatening to overflow her lower eyelids.

"Loved ones can't always live in your heart forever."

It was an unexpected moment of fleeting awareness. It struck Charley with great sorrow because soon Amie would no longer know about or even feel again that deep connection that she had had with all those who had cared for her and for whom she had cared. Suppressing a sigh, Charley nodded with a smile, put her arm around Amie's shoulders, and escorted her back into the kitchen. After she had scrubbed up the grease from the stove top and floor, they had the reheated, overcooked breakfast.

Before doing the dishes, Charley called a carpenter to replace the French doors. He also installed a deadbolt lock in one door leaf and secure flush bolts in both doors to make them more resistant.

There were times when Amie seemed in a world all her own and other times when she was almost her old self, just in a diminished capacity. While she never spoke of loss again, she repeated her frantic concern that absolutely no one could ever know about her degenerating condition.

"You promised that not a single soul would learn about this. It's a secret. I hope you're keeping your word."

While Charley reassured her, it seemed that she hadn't convinced Amie because she remained anxious and continued to bring it up. At least that showed some lingering link between the present and recent past.

Things were obviously changing again. Now when Amie didn't get her way, she physically showed her frustration and anger. Knocking furniture over and pulling dishes out of the kitchen cabinets became her way to make her point. Control issues were resurfacing as manipulation. Charley, worried about Saatchi being hurt, wasn't sure how to deal with it. She didn't want to allow such behavior but she also didn't want to try to physically subdue Amie either. She wondered how many ways there were that she could distract Amie to stop her and if they'd continue to work. Following that first incident, Charley experienced an undercurrent of worry about how she could keep all three of them free from harm in the house. Visions of fist-smashed windows and more accidental or intentional fires swirled around her mind as possibilities occurring before she found another living place for Amie.

Another month slogged by as Charley continued her search for *any* solution that would help Amie. In the meanwhile, she had become afraid of leaving Amie alone at the house. She could picture finding the house in total disarray, on fire, or Amie having left for parts unknown. She was also afraid of taking Amie with her when she had to run errands. On the one hand, she couldn't take her into stores for fear of what she might do. Besides, Amie didn't want anyone to see her. On the other, she couldn't keep her strapped into the passenger seat without risking loud, public- and police-involving screaming tantrums which would be more than a little difficult to explain. And there also the possibility of her managing to unstrap herself and simply walking away.

In Charley's ongoing exploration for help, she had additionally been searching for a part-time professional as a stopgap measure to help her deal with Amie until she could locate a permanent solution. Finding someone with experience with Huntington's, however, had been no easy task. Consequently, it felt like a true miracle when a psychiatric nurse who had the necessary experience all of a sudden appeared. To Charley it was as if Mary Poppins, in the form of Julia Anaya, had sailed out of the sky using her parrot-headed umbrella and landed on her doorstep as a "spoonful of sugar."

Now with appropriate help, Charley could feel more comfortable that Amie was safe and being cared for. Anaya could also get refills of medications, using Valdez's prescriptions from Sunflower. However, Charley didn't know what Anaya could do about Amie's involuntary movements which appeared to be trying to make a comeback as Risperdal was losing its overall effectiveness. That was a knotty problem.

At last, Charley could get back fulltime to painting and handling their business, both of which were rapidly slipping out of her control. To her great embarrassment orders to be shipped had piled up with repeated inquiries coming from customers. That required Charley to apologize and have to lie about the reason for delay. Multiple canvases were still unfinished and demanding her attention if she wanted to have them ready to replace others which had been sold at the galleries.

On several occasions Amie repeated her previous concerns about privacy, now in front of the nurse.

"You promised that not a single soul would learn about this. I hope you're keeping your word."

Anaya looked puzzled and asked Amie what she meant but Amie just firmly pressed her lips together and shook her head. That was a secret about something she couldn't remember that she would never reveal, even if tortured. When Anaya had the opportunity, she took Charley aside and asked her about it.

"Oh, that." Charley paused a moment, seeking a believable response. As Amie's car accident flashed into mind, she recalled her old friend, Dorian, back in the Boston area, a horticulturist whose hobby was automobile racing. That could work.

"She was an avid race car driver. She's referring to race accident she had at the Seekonk Speedway in Massachusetts. She had always prided herself on her expert driving abilities—thinking of herself as a combination of Danica Patrick and Janet Guthrie," as Dorian had asserted. "They were the only two women who had driven in both the Daytona 500 and the Indianapolis 500. So, when she spun out on the oil- and rain-slick figure-eight track and crashed into the grandstand, she felt humiliated. It's her deep, dark secret. She doesn't want anyone to know about her mortifying loss of control that day." Even though Charley had witnessed it, Dorian never spoke of it again.

Anaya nodded knowingly. Charley hoped that the nurse was satisfied with her borrowed explanation and wouldn't inquire further.

As Amie appeared to worsen, Charley re-thought her "promise" not to do any more paintings "signed by Amie" after her death. It wasn't so much a promise to Amie as it was to herself. It occurred to her that since she was still acting as Amie and promoting Amie's work on Amie's website, she couldn't have "Amie" suddenly stop doing her paintings after the real Amie died. After all, her style was continuing to attract a large following. The question was could she continue, somehow? And if so, how could she do it ethically?

The first idea that sprang to mind was starting a slew of canvases—as many as she could manage—in Amie's painting style with her signature already painted on them. If they were started, and partially done, well before Amie died, they weren't really started *after* her death. But was that a distinction without a difference? She thought that solution was probably reasonable, considering, but would have to give it some more thought.

21

After more weeks of frustrating google searches, phone calls to various health- and mental health departments in the state, and intake interviews, Charley was finally able to have Amie admitted to the state facility, New Mexico Psychiatric Institute (NMPI), in La Cienega, which now had an opening. As she had been listed for Sunflower, Amie was registered under Charley's name. Charley had another little twinge of abstract concern, since this was a governmental service as opposed to Sunflower's private service, that maybe admitting Amie under a false name was doing a nifty two-step around the outer edges of legality. But, then again, she thought, so what? She simply could not do otherwise. As much as she had fought against the "ends justifying the means" political marketing approach in her business, she felt this was different and absolutely necessary. Besides, after everything that had already occurred, she really didn't give a damn.

Patting herself on the back and feeling somewhat sanctimonious, she muttered to herself.

"Saving Amie and her reputation while at the same time not harming anyone is more than worthy of special dispensation."

While Charley was in Glorieta working, Amie would be established at the second state-owned and -operated, and publicly-funded, psychiatric hospital in New Mexico which offered inpatient care for adult psychiatric patients at one of its five clinical divisions. It was one of the state's major regional licensed long-term nursing care providers for the elderly and disabled residents. Patients were aged eighteen and older, suffering from a "major mental illness that severely impaired their functioning, ability to be maintained in the community, and who represented as an imminent danger to self and/or others."

Once Amie was admitted on paper, she would be evaluated by a disciplinary treatment team. Because Amie had no family, significant others, or guardians Charley would participate. Within seventy-two hours other team members would complete a discipline-specific assessment to be used in the development of a master treatment plan with the participation of the patient within seven days. Then the psychiatrist, a Dr. Idris Harris, who would lead the treatment team, would identify the necessary interventions, and, with the medical practitioner, would prescribe medications and any necessary tests or treatment to be performed. Progress would then be frequently reviewed for its meeting the treatment goals. It would be the nursing staff which would monitor Amie and coordinate treatment interventions as well as help her process her moods and feelings.

The facility, which consisted of multiple redbrick, red-roofed, two-story buildings on mature-treed, rolling lawns, was about twenty-nine miles west of Glorieta. This took Charley about a half-hour to reach as she wended her way through southern Santa Fe, taking Los Piños Road to Route 548. This was the beginning of Charley's three days a week visiting schedule to check on Amie and keep their connection alive and well for as long as possible.

After Amie arrived and was permanently settled in her new room with all her clothing, books, and favorite objects, a nurse guided her to the activity room where Charley met her with a big hug. Amie didn't respond to it. Instead, she falteringly sat down on an orange molded plastic chair by a large plate glass window, one of many that ran along the perimeter of the spacious, bright, linoleum-floored room.

"Where is Saatchi?" Amie asked. "You have to promise to bring her to see me. Please." Then she looked confused. "When did I see her last? It seems like years. I want to see and hold my cat."

However, Amie had seen her cat that morning, only an hour before she moved into the facility fulltime. When Charley produced the eight-and-a-half-by-eleven photo of Saatchi in the silver frame for her, Amie began to cry.

"I miss Saatchi so much."

She reflexively tried to wipe her face with her slowly waving hand but missed it twice. Charley offered a tissue for her running nose. Amie didn't reach for and seemed to ignore it. Charley tried to place it in her moving hand but it fell to the floor when Amie chose not to or couldn't grip it. Risperdal seemed to have become increasingly ineffective in controlling her movements. Charley hoped they could safely increase the dosage or easily find something else that would work.

"You must bring her to see me now. Not to visit but to live here with me. I want her. I need her. She's all I have left."

As she rapidly but cumbrously stood, she knocked over her chair, and grabbed at Charley, partially to keep her balance.

"You'll take care of it, won't you?" she begged, hanging on. "You need to bring her to me. She needs her mom. My sad little kitten."

Her hands slipped down from Charley's arms as she folded into a momentary squatting position before dropping onto the floor. Everything, her head, arms, and legs, seemed to be in slow motion. Charley lowered both hands and bent over to assist Amie to get her feet under her but her body wouldn't or couldn't cooperate. Kneeling and struggling to pull Amie forward to get her right knee under her, Charley started Amie's body moving upward. She could see that Amie was trying her best to facilitate the movement to get herself erect. As she shakily stood, she grabbed hold of Charley's body again until her standing was finally achieved

Then Amie seemed to leave the present, having mentally meandered somewhere else into her own thoughts. It was as if she had forgotten Charley was still there. Charley guided her to another chair to keep her from falling over again. Then when she was seated squarely on the chair and less at risk of toppling, she looked out the window.

Speaking Amie's name but getting no response, Charley touched Amie's shoulder. Amie showed no awareness. Charley stepped back and, feeling insensitive doing it, waved her hand in front of Amie's face to get her attention. In spite of receiving no response, Charley spoke to her again.

"Amie, I understand you wanting Saatchi with you all the time but I don't think she can live here with you. I'll check to make sure. However, I promise to bring her as often as possible, whenever NMPI allows it. Is that okay with you?"

No response.

"I have to go now but I'll see you again day after tomorrow. All right?"

If Amie heard, she didn't respond. Distressed, Charley walked away slowly, looking back over her shoulder. Stopping for a moment, she wondered if there were something that she might do to animate Amie, to try to tickle any other embedded positive memories into awareness. But nothing came to mind. The situation was frustrating. She wanted to make things better for Amie but wasn't sure she even could.

As she approached Amie's Honda, it suddenly occurred to her that music could conceivably help. She recalled having seen a half-hour documentary on Alzheimer's that demonstrated that music could reach those suffering from that disease. While she had no idea if it would resonate with someone with Huntington's, it seemed worthwhile to give it a try. Maybe she could use it to find a way to re-connect with Amie, maybe even communicate with her. Or, perhaps, more importantly, just spark whatever was left of access to Amie's previous life. While Amie could no longer pursue happiness, maybe she could discover a flicker of joy.

"For my next visit," Charley spoke aloud with a grin, "I will definitely bring a radio to see if it has any detectable beneficial effect on her."

Amie had always loved music. It seemed reasonable to Charley that she just might be able to tap into some buried recollections. Charley left feeling slightly cheered. There might be something she could do to reach Amie after all, before her personhood dissolved completely.

When Charley occasionally felt a wisp of disquietude about Amie being recognized or Charley appearing enough like Amie, she thought about what Huntington's had wrought on Amie physically and emotionally. Her appearance had changed radically. Her face had become gaunt, angular, and slightly distorted due to muscle contracture of her lower jaw. Her eye movement had become somewhat erratic. Due to weight loss, her long bony arms and legs seemed to hang out her sleeves and pantlegs, making her look scarecrow-like. Her short dark hair had grown longer and was now threaded with strands of white, adding to her decreasing recognizability as the original Amie, especially when compared to any of her early photos.

Amie had been eccentric about having her photograph taken, even snapshots. On those rare occasions when she was photographed for business, she always held up Saatchi next to her face so that only a third of her face or her profile was revealed. Many felt she did that to lend an air of mystery to her. While Amie liked that hypothesis, in reality, as she had expressed to Charley, the true reason was that she felt being photographed in general was an intrusion into her privacy and a form of objectification, but she would do it for business because it was necessary. She couldn't understand people constantly taking and publicly sharing selfies.

Expanding on that thought, she had then explained that she had heard claims that some indigenous peoples felt that having a photograph taken of themselves "stole their soul." She said she was skeptical and that was probably the interpretation of the non-native person. Instead, she felt it was more likely the result of their simply not wanting to allow non-native strangers to take advantage of them, to continue to use them as had been done historically all over the globe. That their personal images weren't something native peoples necessarily wished or chose to share with non-native others. And if they did, she added, that they'd probably want to control it and, perhaps, even desire to be appropriately compensated for it. Which she thought was more than reasonable.

For her next visit, Charley brought a small, portable AM/FM radio with a handle and tuned it to the classical station, KHFM, ninety-five point five on the dial. As Mozart's 1787 *Eine Kleine Nachtmusik* was played by a chamber ensemble, Amie who was seated in a chair by the window in the activity room became somewhat enlivened. She moved as best she could, while keeping her balance, as she responded to the tempo of the music. Charley was delightfully surprised. It was stimulating Amie and amazingly held sway until the piece finished.

After a while, Charley changed the station to jazz. They were playing Dave Brubeck's 1959 composition, *Blue Rondo à la Turk*. It was the original recording by the Dave Brubeck Quartet with Brubeck on piano, Paul Desmond on alto sax, Eugene Wright on bass, and Joe Morella on drums. This made Amie start to try to move her whole body. She had had CDs of all of Brubeck's albums. While she couldn't reproduce the 9/8 and 4/4 beats taken from Turkish aksak time signatures, which were characterized by unequal beats, her arms and feet perceptibly swayed and jumped with the music.

It seemed to influence some part of her deep within her brain where she still lived. Whether she would do this to all music or only music she knew and/or liked didn't matter. Amie reacted positively and Charley was thrilled. When Charley tried to talk to Amie with the music on, Amie ignored her. Maybe, she thought, the music didn't also open up a channel for communication which Charley hoped she could use. Although, maybe it eventually would? But, more to the point, maybe Amie simply didn't want to interrupt her immersion in the music to interact in any way with anyone.

Irrespective of whatever it might have been, it didn't really matter. She gave Amie the radio which, holding on to the handle, she tried to hug to her bosom as the station followed with two Stan Getz best-sellers. It was Getz teaming with Charlie Byrd in 1962 on *Jazz Samba,* and then *Desafinado* for which Getz won a Grammy for Best Jazz Performance in 1963.

As Amie's condition continued downhill, Charley now visited her only once a week. A lucid and responsive Amie, which was only intermittently lurking before, had quickly begun to grow faint. The music stations still affected her internally to a degree as demonstrated by slight, almost-rhythmic movements of her hands. But, slowly the brain's nerve-cell-destroying disease was rendering Amie less able to move voluntarily at all. Even if Charley couldn't see the impact of the music on Amie, she fervently hoped that it was still reaching her … somewhere. Charley could only wish that was the situation for Amie's sake.

No longer were the larger, heavy-handled fork and spoon Charley had purchased for Amie allowing her to feed herself effectively. Finding her mouth with a spoonful of applesauce had quickly become nearly impossible. Trying to use the fork more often than not had ended with her stabbing herself in the cheek. To Charley and Amie's despair Amie soon had to be fed.

It wasn't much longer before she seemed to not recognize Charley at all. While Charley knew she was probably being perceived as a stranger, she wondered if Saatchi could still break through the nearly impenetrable, biochemically-induced mental barrier. Even though she had been asked not to bring the cat, for her next visit she had sneaked Saatchi in by way of a black backpack she was wearing. When Amie saw the cat Charley presented to her, she tried to throw her arms around her to pet her like a long-lost friend. But she wasn't successful. Charley placed Saatchi on her lap and helped direct Amie's constantly moving hands toward the cat until she could touch her.

"You gorgeous thing," she cooed. "I love cats. I wish I had a cat of my own."

"It's Saatchi."

"Saatchi? What's Saatchi?"

"The cat."

"The cat?" she mumbled, not seeming to show any recognition of either label.

That was the last time she spoke to Charley or recognized the cat as being present.

As Saatchi was growing more elderly, she had decided that she didn't want to go to the psychiatric facility with any frequency to see Amie, especially in Charley's knapsack. But she had never liked riding in a vehicle because something in her inner ear triggered car sickness. As she had aged, her negative response to this kind of motion became more frequent and stressful. Increasingly when the cat had finally arrived to see Amie, Charley could see she felt miserable. She stayed that way during her visit and arrived home nauseous. Her black velvet face took on a pond-scum cast. When Charley discovered both that Saatchi could no longer tolerate visits to see Amie and Amie no longer recognized her cat, she no longer tried to sneak her in, sparing Saatchi the torment. After that, she rarely took her out in the car again except to go to the vet.

Without her ever showing any further awareness of her environment, in less than a year Amie was in a near-vegetative state. From that point it took only a few months for her to then expire, leaving Charley both distraught and glad for Amie to finally be spared the ongoing torture. Her death was attributed to aspiration pneumonia.

As Charley further discovered, her pneumonia all too frequently happened with late-stage Huntington's patients. When Amie could no longer eat or drink, she had been equipped with a percutaneous endoscopic gastrostomy (PEG), a gastric feeding tube which was placed through the abdominal wall into the stomach. Into this tube her caregivers poured prescribed amounts of a liquid nutrition, fluids, and medications. Even though she was no longer taking in liquids by mouth because her swallow muscles had ceased to work, saliva was still easily sliding down her throat and sometimes entering her lungs.

Her epiglottis, the leaf-shaped cartilage flap which was located at the top of her larynx, would have, under normal circumstances, prevented the saliva from reaching her lungs. But it too had ceased to function properly. It was designed to seal off the windpipe when a person ate or drank in order to prevent that material from being accidentally inhaled, instead of entering the esophagus. But when Amie's voice box, or vocal folds, moved involuntarily, as happened in Huntington's, aspiration could occur.

Coughing up this material could have helped if only Amie had been able to do so. Unfortunately, since she couldn't, bacteria had begun to grow in her lungs and caused an infection. Coughing, however, wasn't a guarantee of removing it. So even if she could have coughed, she might not have been able to bring up the mucus with the bacteria, or enough of it.

Despite having been on intravenous antibiotics and extra oxygen via a cannula, as she had once before for this particular medical problem, this time Amie's pneumonia overwhelmed her. But, even if it hadn't happened the second time, it might well have happened the next time or the time after that. Once saliva was no longer prevented from entering her lungs, aspiration was expected to happen again and again.

Since Amie had had no family, she had no will. Instead of having testamentary instructions that all her worldly possessions should be given to Charley after her death, Amie, when she was still of sound mind enough to do it, had conveyed everything to her protégé and best friend directly. Pretending to be Amie, Charley saw to Amie's cremation under the name of "Charlotte Eyre." As per Amie's early-expressed wishes, Charley received then sprinkled Amie's ashes at the property line of her yard, the mountain foothills that Amie had loved. Whenever Amie's beloved Saatchi died, Charley would see to it that the cat would join her previous painting companion in adding to the enrichment of the soil for the native vegetation.

Amie had provided Charley with two bequests for her to act on following her death. They included anonymous annual donations of the artist's half of the painting and ancillary profits to the Huntington's Disease Foundation and to a designated local no-kill animal rescue organization, for as long as the profits continued. Then after Charley's death, any profits from the business before it folded would be split between the Huntington's Disease Foundation and the non-profit no-kill animal shelter with a local lawyer, Allen Caperton, as executor, overseeing disbursement.

Shortly after Amie had been admitted to the psychiatric facility, Charley had thought long and hard about the previously considered possibility of starting as many canvases as she could in Amie's style with Amie's signature. Weighing the pros and cons, she finally decided she would. The more canvases she started, each about a quarter to a third painted and signed, the more time she would have to sell Amie's paintings and the more she would have to donate to Amie's charities as well as keep herself going.

Consequently, the studio was swamped with unfinished paintings. As the number of Amie's canvases later began to dwindle, Charley could very slowly taper off their sales, leaving just enough paintings to cover several sales a year for a number of years. In the interim, her paintings by Mana would become available and eventually take their place as the primary "Amie Benison" painting website and gallery output.

Months went by swimmingly with Charley painting, instructing, processing orders for Amie's artistic output, and caring for the ageing black cat which had long ago become her own fur child. She also cared for the hummingbird garden and planted milkweed to attract the rapidly-disappearing monarch butterflies. As soon as she could, she would add production of her own paintings to the business. She had become Amie Benison totally.

Charley had marveled at how over time she had so easily discarded "Charlotte Eyre" like a pair of worn, holey sneakers and adapted to being Amie Benison. While she occasionally missed having long red hair and well-tailored clothing, that exact persona had been dead and properly buried for years.

But then, something frighteningly absurd occurred to drop those discarded, threadbare sneakers right back on her doorstep.

22

Because Charley had totally forgotten about cancelling her email on her own computer, which she had continued to use primarily for research, she was shocked when one suddenly arrived. Someone calling him- or herself "avengerforamie" was threatening her. This message claimed he or she knew for a fact that "Amie's fabulous paintings" were being "forged," and that she, Charlotte Eyre, was the one responsible for it. Moreover, he or she was going to expose her unless …

The way the email was emotionally expressed about Amie suggested to Charley that the sender was probably someone who was strongly enamored of Amie, and, perhaps, a male. Despite the villainous accusations about Charley's alleged crimes, there was something almost chivalric about his asserted need to protect Amie. It was as if this "avenger for Amie" thought of himself as having a responsibility to the knights' honor code to save Amie from being devoured by the fire-breathing-dragon-forger.

"I'm going to correct this situation because someone so talented and beloved as Amie Benison deserves to be rescued from a scavenging fake like you."

This person stated that he could prove that some of Amie's paintings over the years hadn't been done by Amie at all because he could spot inconsistencies in her signature. Charley shook her head and wanted to laugh out loud at this nonsense. There was no way she could take him seriously, but still it was a threat, and one directed at her.

"The recent signatures don't match the signatures on her older works. I know that means they've been forged. And you're the person who has been forging them."

He said he had collected and loved Amie's paintings for a decade and wouldn't stand for her being harmed in any way, especially not financially and artistically.

"You have to pay for your crimes. I want you to buy back all your forgeries, confess to the authorities about what you've done, and pay the legal price for your sins. If you don't do so within ten days, I will publish an exposé of your felonious behavior. All your forgeries will be revealed. You will be an even greater outcast. And I can guarantee you will go to prison for a long time for your larceny."

The first thing Charley noticed, besides its sounding bonkers to her, was that there was a big logic problem with what he was threatening to do. If she didn't buy back her copies and confess, he would see to it that *all* of Amie's existing paintings, wherein these "forgeries" allegedly were hidden, would be questioned. What he didn't seem to understand was that if *all* of Amie's paintings were to be questioned, that would be highly likely to cast a pall upon her works in general and significantly devalue them. That sounded like a terrible risk to take if he really cared about Amie, her paintings, and her artistic legacy.

There was no way he could possibly determine that forgeries existed. Yet, if he made these ill-considered claims in public, he could indelibly hurt the Amie Benison business. Not only that, he would also re-surface Eyre's name to be re-tarred. Charley didn't want her original self to be revived because it would require her to have to figure out how to address the issue with her two separate personalities, or even Amie's death as "Charlotte Eyre."

This was a conundrum. She had to determine how she should respond to the email, *if* she should respond to it at all. Ideas brightly arrived and darkly withdrew. At first, Charley examined having Amie respond to indicate that "Charlotte Eyre" had already died. But why would Amie respond to an email on Charley's computer? Besides, that wouldn't demonstrate to the blackmailer that Eyre couldn't have been forging them before she died. The threat was so harebrained that she just wanted to ignore it. However, he seemed so positive that he could "prove" someone had been forging Amie's paintings and was intent upon speaking out to reveal it.

If Charley communicated with him, claiming innocence, that would let him know that she was alive and, therefore, able to do what he was accusing her of. Moreover, there was no reason to think he would believe her claim of innocence. He was certain she was a master criminal. As such, she would most certainly lie about doing it.

With a pang of dismay, she felt there must be a brilliant—or even half-assed—way to handle it and hoped it would magically appear. All she knew was that she'd have to do the "something" before his deadline. If not, it could become an unholy mess. That it required her immediate attention annoyed her.

But why, it suddenly occurred to her, had he given her ten days? To contact the alleged buyers of her alleged forgeries? Or might it say something about him? That his location wasn't Santa Fe? Or his level of so-called proof was lacking and he was still trying to find ways to support his unsupported contention? No matter what his deadline meant, she felt ten days could give her plenty of time to counter it if she started doing so right away. That meant she needed a particularly clever plan to execute to address it.

As she struggled to formulate something, she kept consoling herself that there was no way he could publicly charge forgery based on some painting signatures varying slightly over Amie's career. Would any legitimate newspaper risk a suit for libel by accepting his claim without having solid scientific evidence? Since absolutely none existed, it seemed improbable. Still, it was intimidating to have the authenticity of Amie's paintings questioned, as well as having Eyre resuscitated. She wished she could merely laugh at it.

A day later, Charley received an email from the blackmailer warning her that he had further support for the forgery contention … and her time was running out.

"In case you didn't believe me, I'm having expert analyses done of Amie Benison's paintings with the different signatures that are showing not only significant stylistic differences but also chemical differences between her early and later works."

"What the …?" Charley gaped.

That was not only ridiculous but also a total fabrication. Amie's early and later paintings were done precisely the same way with the same materials, paint compositions and canvases, whether done by Amie, by both of them, or by Charley alone before and after Amie's death.

Once Charley could get beyond the subject of the emails, she noticed that there were a couple of figures of speech in them having nothing to do with Amie, that reminded her vaguely of someone. She furrowed her brow and thought hard about it. Making herself a cup of wild cherry herbal tea, she sat at the kitchen table to mull it over. She wondered if the blackmailer possibly could be Jefferson. She rolled that around in her mind for a few seconds then discarded it.

"That makes zero sense." She talked to herself. "What the blackmailer presented sounds as if he had never met 'Charlotte Eyre.' It is more like he had used a pin to randomly pick her out of a list of people with some relationship to Amie, plus the fact she is also living in Santa Fe."

Even though the legalese used made her remember how Jefferson always tried to sound smarter than he was, she had never heard him try to sound like a lawyer. Moreover, she couldn't conjure up any rationale for his doing that. On the off-chance she was wrong, she checked him out online to see if he were unemployed and desperate.

What she found was that since she had left Boston, he had associated himself with another political marketing firm, Ames & Burlington, in the city. While he might have enjoyed her being slammed in the Boston and New Mexico papers, he would have been less happy about the demise of her reputation and business. With her defamed, the two projects he had done for Ultimate Strategy would no longer be a positive for his résumé. Consequently, he was likely to leave her best forgotten. Besides, after all this time, his trying to make Charley's life miserable was too outlandish to be believable.

Jefferson was a purpose person. First, last, and always he was about himself and attaining his concrete goals. He did what moved him as quickly as possible toward whatever he wanted to achieve. If he had had a guiding problem-solving principle, it would have been simplicity. He was all for being parsimonious, practical, and doing things in the simplest, most direct way possible. This blackmail attempt didn't fit him. The scheme was too emotional, contrived, and impractical. There was nothing of substance to be gained by it. Furthermore, he had had no relationship with Amie whatsoever. And he certainly was no aficionado of her abstracts.

By the next day, Charley had worked out a plan that might stop the blackmailer without her having to respond in any way as "Charley" to his threat. But, if she were to implement it in time, she would have to get cracking to get it all in place as fast as possible. Now that she was being proactive, she felt more in control ... and even a touch optimistic.

And yet there was a lingering concern about him giving the newspaper *anything* negative about her that they might publish. However, the published Santa Fe newspaper article about her, as she was loath to recall, had portrayed a factual picture of her Boston debacle. She could have survived that even if it took a while. What had destroyed any chance that she might have had to re-establish her former political image marketing business in New Mexico was only the nastily-speculative "Letter to the Editor." So, there was no reason to think the paper would publish anything as fact without reliable sources for credibility, even regarding her previously notorious self.

23

.

That afternoon as the blackmailer was driving around Santa Fe, he caught sight of the personalized license plate, "Amie B" on an orangey-gold, five-door Honda Fit which was parked in front of an art supplies shop. He was only several yards from his "artist supreme," almost close enough to touch her vehicle. As he slowed way down to attempt to take a snap shot of the plate with his cell phone, someone came out of the store. He decided to snap her instead. A car horn blared behind him. Startled, he dropped his cell into his crotch and missed taking a shot of the person who was undoubtedly Amie. He was beside himself with exasperation.

He wanted it so badly to be she that he drove around the corner, parked momentarily, and pulled the yellowed, early newspaper photo of Amie from his glove compartment to make a comparison. There was no question in his mind. It was his adored Amie. But he didn't have time now to circle the block again to try to get that photo of her today. He had a business appointment calling to him and he hadn't given himself extra time to get there. He felt he should have calculated this possibility. He vowed he'd be more flexible next time he was driving around the city, especially when near any store he had discovered she frequented.

While he had done lots of research on Amie's paintings, his investigation hadn't started with his now in-process, newspaper exposé on the assumed forgery of her works. Instead, it had commenced as a bountiful series of love notes he had written as a paean to Amie which he had entitled *The Passion of Amie Benison*. After he had arrived in Santa Fe, he was exceedingly eager to contact her. Although, because of her accident recovery, she always seemed just beyond his reach. His overarching goal was to tell her of his abiding deep feelings … and that he was writing a book as an homage to her.

However, when he suddenly perceived what he assessed to be signature variations, he knew he had been blessed with a divinely-inspired task. He was to be the one who ferreted out her fraudulent competitor and the one to eliminate that scourge. As soon as he could, he would also tell her of his clever discovery and his plan to bring her forger to justice.

What had initiated the blackmailer's obsession with Amie and her paintings was when he had acquired through eBay an early Benison painting of rolling fire. The seller guaranteed it was an original, that she had bought it from the artist, but could provide only a snapshot of a faded handwritten sales slip as provenance, or authentication. Even though he had never cared for abstract art before, he was bewitched by the work. It stirred something inside him. He wanted to collect more and larger works. He didn't know if it was the style, subject matter, or colors that intrigued him. But it didn't really matter. He just needed to have more of it.

The next thing he knew, he had begun going to galleries, checking out flea markets, and online and offline auctions for more of her work. He began to feel jealous of anyone who had more of her pieces. He felt they didn't deserve them because they didn't truly appreciate what they passionately shouted and what went into them. They were a living part of the artist not an inanimate decoration, not something to hang on a wall to cover nail holes or brag about to others.

Because his secret interest in Amie's work had become too precious to reveal to anyone, he never told a soul about it, though he longed to. From staring at her works, he felt he had come to know the artist intimately. Through her paintings, she spoke fervidly to him. No one else could possibly understand the depth and breadth of his feelings. It was an ardent connection that he and the artist alone psychically shared.

Then all of a sudden something strange happened. Whenever he spotted one of her works, rather than buying it straight away and racing home to project himself into it to be loved and absorbed by it, he began to scrutinize it. He had no notion of what had prompted that single-minded change. Maybe, he thought, it was because he was becoming a connoisseur of her work and of the artist herself. But now that his focus had been inextricably drawn to her signatures, he began to perceive slight variations in Amie's painted name from canvas to canvas. That alarmed him. It screamed forgery.

As his concern propelled him, it wasn't long before he found what he feared. The signatures from canvas to canvas were not identical. That felt like a momentous aha. It was significantly more than just the fact that people in general never wrote their names precisely the same way each time. He told himself that what he had "unearthed" meant that something was very wrong, that some scurrilous cur was actually counterfeiting her masterpieces. He was beyond outraged, wanting to rectify it in any way he could, immediately.

As a result, the more he concentrated on the signatures of her various works, the more consumed he became about what he thought he saw and what he was certain it meant. There was no doubt. Amie Benison's works were being reproduced. And he alone was the one who had to investigate and resolve it as soon as possible. He had to make things right for her ... for the both of them. It would be precisely what she'd want and for which she would be most grateful.

All that had begun well before Amie's Huntington's had interfered with her painting and Charley having permanently taken over painting for Amie. While his concern was growing, he hadn't as yet decided what to do about it. All he knew was that he had to do something. He asked himself if he should track down an art expert to assess the paintings. While he wanted to have an analyst empirically demonstrate that someone was financially raping his beloved artist via forgery, he didn't want to allow anyone to trespass through his secret world with their technological boots.

His questions and assumptions about variations in her signature didn't take into account Amie's auto accident because, he told himself, it wasn't relevant. He had convinced himself that it had occurred *after* he had spotted the signature inconsistencies. As a result, he saw himself as a divinely-inspired sleuth, exploring, probing, assessing, and revealing the truth of these unthinkable thefts, all for Amie.

In his new role of an amateur art forgery detective, the blackmailer had read at length about many of the art forgeries that had been discovered. One that intrigued him had started with the controversy about the German Renaissance master Lucas Cranach's 1531 *Venus*. There had been questions about its attribution to Cranach so a scientific analysis had been done and revealed it to be a forgery. Because of the increasing number of expensive art forgeries, Sotheby's Auction House had brought in James Martin who was considered the "arbiter of authenticity." As a result of his firm, Orion Analytical Conservation Science, he had become the art world's most famous art detective.

Using scientific equipment, like giant x-ray fluorescence, a spectrometer pump for infrared, a Fourier-transform infrared microscope, and a scanning stereo electron microscope, Martin could determine the true age of the masterpiece by the true age of its components. What he did was look at what chemicals constituted the pigments and the binder as well as the canvas. Sotheby's bought Martin's company and Martin as the only in-house fraud-busting organization which would demonstrate they could prove if any masterpiece were genuine or otherwise. As a result, Sotheby's offered a five-year guarantee of the refund price if any object they sold as authentic was later proved to be counterfeit.

In his off-work hours the blackmailer had begun his worshipful book on Amie which covered Vermont, Boston, and Santa Fe, anywhere that Amie was known to have lived and painted. Because of her move to Santa Fe, he chose a publisher, Nova Libre, located there. He felt they would be very interested in a loving, intimate portrait of that well-known artist who now lived not only in the state but also just outside their city. He had found that while they published all genres, they focused on works about New Mexico and New Mexicans. They had just released one on the engineering of buildings of the Ancestral Puebloan people. An upcoming one was on the effect of the psychological collusion in the relationship between Georgia O'Keeffe and Alfred Stieglitz on O'Keeffe's painting. Because of the blackmailer's intimate relationship with Benison, he felt his book was sure to be scooped up for their top seasonal listings.

He believed a book about Amie and dedicated to her would further endear him to her. Nova Libre had shown an initial interest in his project as he described it. But when he happened to off-handedly mention that he was also investigating what looked like forgeries of her work for an article he wanted to write, their ears perked up.

"While your bio of Amie Benison sounds interesting," responded James Shannon, his prospective publishing rep, "a book investigating possible forgeries of her work could really create a stir. Exposés and controversies tend to be big sellers. We would be more inclined to want to handle *that* book. However, our decision to publish would be predicated upon what your investigation analytically reveals. Your investigation must fully answer the question that a book title like, *Who Really Painted Amie Benison's Works?* would ask."

Conflict swirled around him. He wanted to do a book for Amie that embraced their connection and how much he admired and appreciated her. The article, however, was merely to reveal Eyre as the forger and force her to stop defrauding Amie. While that attention-grabbing title could be used for his article as well, he didn't want to expand that article into a book. That was not his goal. Not for his beloved Amie.

When he had first begun his investigation into the forgeries, he had no idea who the perpetrator could be. He felt it must be someone who had been close to Amie, perhaps someone who had studied with her. It never occurred to him that someone who had no relationship with or proximity to Amie might be doing it, like Van Meegeren copying Vermeers three centuries later.

Plowing through his thick collection of her press clippings, he looked for and discovered a mention of protégés she had had in the Boston area. One of her protégés, he thought, would be more likely to be the forger than anyone else. He wondered if that person were a real artist in his or her own right or an artistically-inadequate-but-brilliant-technician, as many known art forgers had been.

In an old article in the *Boston Globe* "Arts Section," there was a list of names of recognizable, and unrecognizable, painters who had worked with Amie. One who had studied with her the longest, had won awards all her own, but either was not painting now or not painting under her own name, was Charlotte Eyre. Googling her, he found, to his surprise, that she had been one who had been considered likely to succeed in the art world. If so, he thought, where were her works? He found nothing about her paintings after her teen years. However, what he did find was the scandal and "Letter to the Editor" in the Santa Fe paper which claimed that she was an "unethical business person" who was now living in the city. That cinched it for him. He knew she was the culprit, the one who had been living off his Amie's talent and hard work.

That meant his duty and path were clear. He had to create an easily implementable plan that would ultimately haul her into court. He would accuse her of the forgeries and then reveal that he had a tell-all article about it in the works. If she didn't buy back her knock-offs and then confess to the authorities, he'd have the tell-all published for all to see. That would show her she couldn't continue to get away with her misdeeds.

But … much to his disgruntlement, he found himself caught on the horns of a gut-wrenching dilemma. He wanted to dazzle Amie with not only how much he cherished her with his biographical book but also how he had brilliantly foiled the counterfeiter of her works with his article. Unfortunately, while the newspaper he had contacted was interested in his exposé, so was his prospective book publisher. His literary love letter had fallen through the cracks and evanesced, distressing him but, at the same time, motivating him.

As if that weren't enough, irrespective of what progress he had asserted to the newspaper and Nova Libre, his investigation was currently stalled. Nothing he had found had provided him with the necessary empirical evidence to *prove* Amie's works had been forged. When Shannon described what an acceptable exposé had to contain, the blackmailer became enraged. His "proof," according to the publishing company, was fundamentally non-existent. What he'd gathered to date was merely his perceptions—pure conjecture—without any merit if he couldn't provide scientific evidence to back up his extraordinary claims. So, despite his having photographs of what he considered signature differences, he couldn't as yet show that these differences actually represented anything fraudulent. The psychic pain was all-encompassing.

As he looked at how James Martin had analyzed the fakes of old paintings, he thought that he too could look at the pigment Amie and her forger used. Surely, there would be signs of age or differences in the chemical compounds used which would somehow represent inaccuracies.

However, there was a hitch. While the numerous books he had read all said that one could discern differences in modern copies of Old Masters, no one said anything about determining differences in copies of works that had been done in the Twentieth and Twenty-First Centuries where, they claimed, paints and pigments were nearly identical. The one exception, perhaps, was where lead or zinc was added to the oil paints for softness or sculptural effect. This was particularly evident with white oil paint which was an important component of Amie's paintings.

Exploring this avenue, he found that titanium white was considered the most popular white because it reflected light, appeared bright, had a softer consistency, neutral bias, was non-yellowing, and had no lead. Whereas, lead white, the world's oldest manufactured pigment, introduced in ancient Greece, had the benefits of being flexible, durable, and non-cracking. But that wasn't all. There was also the use of linseed oil, safflower oil, or poppy seed oil which could be added to create transparency as well to shorten (linseed oil) or lengthen (safflower or poppy seed oil) the paint's drying time. As a result, in order to discern any differences in the pigments used in Amie's paintings, he knew he'd still have to submit a few of her earlier and later paintings for a real analysis.

Ready to contact Martin's company, by chance he turned up the fact that artists were known to try different paints for different textures, temperatures of hue, tinting strength, and drying times in different paintings. Furthermore, while canvas age in copies of older paintings could be a clue to forgery, there was likely no difference between canvases used in the Twentieth and Twenty-First Centuries. Painting supplies had been standard for innumerable decades.

As a consequence, determining a modern painting to be a forgery had fewer ways to prove it, other than, perhaps, direction of palette knife usage, stylistic brush strokes, or unintentional finger prints in the paint. But he hadn't observed any difference in brush or even palette knife strokes he could document. Since he saw nothing written on these other ways, not even on James Martin's website, he had no idea what they might be. That left him stumped as to how he could demonstrate empirically that Amie Benison's works were the subject of forgery. He could simply go ahead and state that it was so even without credible, reliable support, but no reputable newspaper or book publisher was going to risk publishing it in that circumstance.

Unbeknownst to Charley, the blackmailer had had disappointing discussions with his two publishers-to-be. The newspaper expressed chagrin that his article wasn't farther along than an outline. And while he hinted that he knew who the "forger" was, he likewise could not present one scintilla of proof either that any of Amie Benison's paintings had been forged or that the specified person was the forger.

"You know," said Shannon, when he spoke again with him at Nova Libre, "unless you have excellent evidence of what you claim, we at Nova Libre could be sued by Charlotte Eyre, *and especially* by Amie Benison, for libel. And they'd win. It could be financially devastating to us. We're not willing to publish anything that smacks of sheer speculation. So, unless you can give us substantial, indisputable scientific proof that these forgeries exist and have been done by Charlotte Eyre, we regret we cannot publish your forgery book."

Hiding his disappointment at their incredible short-sightedness and unwillingness to acknowledge what he could so clearly see, he departed, still trying to resolve the difficulty. But once he was back at his office, he sent his next email to Charley to set up a meeting at La Posada de Santa Fe Resort and Spa, on E. Palace Avenue, on the patio by the pool. Since she wouldn't know about his current publishing dilemma, he could continue to threaten her, pressing her hard such that she would be convinced that his exposé publication was imminent, as was her being arrested for her flagrant crimes. She would have to act as he desired.

24

After having carefully calculated what her blackmailer was looking for, Charley had loosely devised a plan which she hoped would undercut his claims by countering anything that could even remotely support his allegations. It was political campaign strategizing all over again. Her plan was to make a presentation which would be public and attention-grabbing and hit all the essential points. It would not only immunize her followers but also erase any concerns others in general might have as to the validity of the blackmailer's assertions, should he actually try to publicly disprove the authenticity of some of Amie's works. Accordingly, she would remind her audience of what she had been through and that her painting, as an expression of her imagination, talent, skill, and life circumstance, often showed miniscule differences from canvas to canvas, which most fans understood, and, perhaps, even expected and enjoyed.

It took her two days to create this presentation and set it up as to date, time, and space with her primary gallery. Within the blackmailer's deadline, this gave her less than eight days in which to implement and present it. In spite of her feeling reasonably confident that she had theoretically covered all the bases, she was anxious about having all the necessary physical arrangements come together smoothly.

At this juncture, with the blackmailer breathing down her neck, she also had to remain calm and remember that she had already become Amie naturally in her videos, coaching calls, and in-person interactions. With all her fine-tuning, imitation "perfection" wasn't required. Besides, her followers would be at the event to support her. Thus, *if* she could get everything done by the proposed date of her event, it could work for all: the attending audience, the media, gallery owners, and the blackmailer.

Suddenly, she had to laugh when she thought back to when she and Amie switched identities. It was then she had thought that there was no way she could plausibly pretend to be Amie, much less have her impersonation be believed. It was incredible how much had changed since then. Now there was no doubt.

When Charley received the blackmailer's email invitation to meet at La Posada, she shook her head. Could he really be so deluded as to think she'd meet him? She had no intention of confronting him. As far as she was concerned, she no longer was Charlotte Eyre. A metamorphosis had taken place. She was now Amie. Poor, maligned Eyre had disappeared in a whiff of sulfur, and with any luck, would never to be seen or heard from again. Or if anyone carefully checked, which she hoped they wouldn't, she had died in La Cienega. She wondered why he had chosen that place in which to meet. It was so public. Was he trying to impress her or show he was unafraid and meant business?

When the blackmailer arrived at the patio, he couldn't find anyone who looked anything like any of Amie's former protégés, according to the early photo of her entourage, or to Charley's small photo which was revealed on links to the former-Ultimate Strategy. Getting an iced tea, he waited, and waited, and waited. An hour went by with no one appearing. He was beside himself with anger. That sent him straight to the local computer café he's used before where he sent Charley another threatening email.

"You have fewer than ten days. If you don't do as I say, I'm publishing my exposé. I'm having the police arrest you for perpetrating a fraud. Your days of counterfeiting Amie Benison's paintings are numbered."

If he decided to act before his ten-day time frame was up, before she could do her presentation to counter it, there appeared to be no good way she could prevent him from unleashing all the expected negative fall-out. If he could somehow make his newsworthy but conjectural case to the authorities, they could possibly skip over his not having any real evidence and merely plow ahead. Not reasonable but possible. She had already experienced with her political image marketing that even a whisper of "smoke" could be devastating.

It was now, before the event, that she needed to have "Amie" contact the blackmailer on Amie's own computer to see if *she* could set him straight. The event then could be the frosting on the cake.

"Dear avengerforamie, I have heard from my former student, Charlotte Eyre, that you think she is forging my works. I can't for the life of me understand how you could have come to that outlandish and erroneous conclusion. But I can guarantee you that it absolutely is *not* so, and that no one has ever replicated my work under my name.

"You are making outrageous claims and threats based on invalid assumptions. I'm sure you think you are helping me but, in reality, you're very definitely are not. Your wild accusations could hurt her and me, my reputation, and the value of my lifetime of art. Every painting with my name on it, from the very beginning, has been done by me, and only by me.

"Because I wouldn't tolerate forgery of my work for one moment, my attorney is always on the lookout for such crimes. He and I have unequivocally found nothing representing itself as my work that isn't my work. All my work has secretly placed codes by which to identify it.

"My attorney and I are hereby directing you to immediately cease and desist all your actions regarding your claim as well as your threatening emails to my dear friend and former student. She is quite ill, having been so since before she left Boston, and you are unduly distressing and assaulting her. I won't tolerate that. We would appreciate your co-operation in this matter so we don't have to address this further legally which we will if necessary. Sincerely, Amie Benison."

When Charley had contacted Vida Hermosa, she arranged for a gala of her paintings. It would celebrate Amie coming out of seclusion by giving a special unveiling of some of her newer works. Also, she had asked that the gallery make sure that the press was informed so they would attend in order to this particular "noted local artist" would receive the local and state coverage she deserved regarding her amazing recovery and previously unseen paintings.

After that, Charley worked tirelessly on the event set up, from printing and distributing announcements; sending press releases to the newspapers and broadcast stations nationally and personally inviting art critics and independent film makers to cover it. She collected most of her new and a few of Amie's older, infrequently-seen examples of her paintings and hung them in the gallery and created all the space she needed for the different activities she had in mind. To chart her recent history, she had four essential photos enlarged. To entice as many notables as possible from Santa Fe, Albuquerque, and beyond, she ordered canapés and Champagne for refreshments. In her announcements she had also promised a renewal of her painting demonstrations which had been very popular in the past. By the seventh day Charley was dragging from exhaustion but, at least, she hadn't heard further from the blackmailer. Furthermore, she hadn't seen anything about her or Amie with respect to painting forgeries in the paper. She hoped that portended that things were looking up.

For the gallery function on Saturday evening at 5:30 p.m. Charley wore pancake makeup in Amie's skin tone, which was only slightly more olive than Charley's. It also made her look a little more as the artist had earlier on before her car accident, but a little older. It was ostensibly to cover some of Amie's accident scars which plastic surgery, skin grafts, and, dermabrasion hadn't as yet totally erased. Over time they would heal completely and be, for all intents and purposes, nearly invisible. After that, she felt her skin tone would have been slightly altered any way. Then she would no longer bother with that makeup. That was something she would discuss.

The gathering garnered a huge crowd, more than the twenty-five hundred square-foot gallery could safely hold, with the overflow having to stand on the sidewalk outside the gallery's front windows waiting to find space inside and slip in. Reporters and newscasters were also present, perhaps more for the Champagne than for covering an artist's re-emergence. Seated on a stool toward the right rear of the large room, with photos behind her on easels, and Saatchi on her lap, Charley talked about the recent challenges to Amie's work. She told of her disfiguring auto accident—which they might have read about several years back, the reconstructive arm, leg, and facial surgery, and particularly having had to retrain herself to write and paint with her right hand due to nerve damage in her left.

"If any of you have noticed slight changes in my paintings to my signature over time," she looked her audience over and smiled, "that's why. But seriously," she chuckled, shrugging her shoulders with her palms out, "who writes their name the same way twice? Besides, some people are ambidextrous. That sounds dangerous."

The audience laughed.

Behind her were enlargements of the photos to which she referred. One was the first newspaper photo ever of her with her paw-print-signature cat, Saatchi. Because it had been enlarged from a reprographic halftone, using dots varying in either size or space to generate a gradient-like effect, it was like a colorless, pale Roy Lichtenstein painting without the defining, character-producing black lines. Up close, it looked like a mass of shades of gray. Only at a distance of at least eight-to-ten feet was it truly discernible as a photo of early Amie.

One was of her first gallery painting, life-size in full color. One was of her destroyed car which was split screen with her severely and disturbingly disfigured, bloody face and broken body as she lay on the ambulance gurney before having all her surgeries. And the final one was of her newest painting, likewise life-size in full color.

As she discussed each photo, she stroked her black cat. Saatchi was definitely getting on in years and cheerless after having had to leave the comfort of her home. Charley had gotten some dimenhydrinate to prevent her nausea from riding in the car. However, it hadn't changed her attitude about crowds. As the cat scanned those congregated, she pulled back her upper lip and gave an unimpressive hiss. That properly indicated her displeasure with the disquiet of a large group of people crowded around her, as well as with her having had to travel by car to that location, with or without a resulting upset stomach and vomiting.

Wearing a newer and pressed version of Amie's expected colorless, loose outfit, Charley joked with her audience that she had toyed with the idea of acquiring a more flamboyant fashion style after the accident, going more colorful, because she had been given a new lease on life after surviving the near-fatal crash.

"But that had not been previous identity. In other words, I chose not to change my overall style in order to perk up my spirits during my difficult recovery. Just being in Santa Fe with people who love my work was enough. This was because I wanted, instead, to feel as though nothing had really changed. I was still Amie Benison in heart, spirit, and, thanks to you, portrayer of whatever talent I still possessed. But maybe someday, now that I've recovered, I might just entertain a little change and get a *little* flamboyant. What do you think?"

Her audience applauded.

"I also want to thank all of you who kindly sent me your best wishes for a speedy recovery to my website email. They meant a lot and truly helped."

Then she referred to the early picture the press had taken of her.

"While I looked a little different then—if you're too close, you may have to squint a little to actually see me—I'm still the old Amie Benison now. But more importantly, my painting and my subject matter, which you've communicated in the past you like, has not changed. Though at some point I might venture into other subjects as well. Who knows?" She smiled. "Change is opportunity and growth. But the old Amie will still hang around no matter what else I may do."

More applause.

She was intimately sharing with her "people" so they would understand, sympathize, and accept any minor differences the blackmailer "claimed" existed. While she didn't mention it, she was hoping that the media coverage of this get-together would contradict most of the blackmailer's allegation points, satisfy him, and get him to back off in case Amie's email hadn't already accomplished that.

"Even though I'm mostly recovered, I still have some leg pain which requires me to sit on a stool this evening rather than stand for long periods of time. I sometimes wonder if they put me back together using baling wire and chewing gum."

Her audience laughed, knowingly.

"As a result, I have decided to remain a little less public and just concentrate on my painting … and other activities you may like. So, I may be doing such evenings as this only infrequently."

The audience responded, "Aww."

"However, I am so delighted we all could get together here tonight because these events are individually such fun. I hope you will understand.

The crowd answered, "Yes." "You bet."

"Okay. Do any of you still want to take painting lessons with me?"

More applause and a roar of "yeses."

"For those of you who want to take lessons with me and may not know, I am currently doing online instruction and coaching."

More applause and hooting.

"I may even start doing them in person." She gave them a glowing smile. "Things change. In some ways for the better."

More applause.

Then she added that given her great body of work she was thinking about creating a coffee table book.

"This will be of my most popular paintings as well as some of the newer ones you may not have seen yet. Some of them are here tonight." She pointed to others that were hung on the wall to her left. "And, yes, the book will have a section on Saatchi, my painting partner, who has become a celebrity in her own right."

The audience smiled broadly. But at the mention of her name Saatchi wriggled, causing Charley to stand and let the cat have the stool where she curled up, her face in the opposite direction of those assembled.

"For those of you who have not accessed my website lately, it has been expanded to provide other products for you all to enjoy, such as posters and wrapping paper. I've had requests for t-shirts and scarves as well. I'm thinking about that. Moreover, I thought you'd like to know, I have been approached by Finest Art Reproductions about having my works also available in fine art reproduction prints."

The throng, while drinking and noshing, oohed loudly.

"I'm considering it but am disinclined to do it just yet because I've been so busy keeping up with my painting and your orders. By the way," she announced cheerfully, "there is going to be a survey on my website, 'amiebenison.com,' where you can weigh in on having access to fine prints. Vida Hermosa," she looked to the gallery owner to her right, "informs me they will mat and frame them for you."

Tom Fetzer, who was wearing a name tag and standing ten feet from her, smiled and nodded to the large group which again elicited applause.

"Next we'll do a painting demonstration of fire and smoke. So, grab some more refreshment. There's plenty of bubbly. Get your questions ready. But first, Tom has an announcement. Then we'll head to the rear corner where my easel is set up."

As Charley waited, holding Saatchi, Tom addressed the crowd.

"Don't forget that next Saturday plein air oil painter Reid Bandeen, of Placitas, will be here presenting his positively luminous landscapes of New Mexico. You will not want to miss that either. If you're on our newsletter list, you will receive further info by email. If you're not the list, please sign up at the desk at the front before you leave tonight."

After her gallery gala, a week went by with no emails to Charley from the blackmailer and no response to Amie's cease-and-desist demand. She hoped that meant that he had either attended the gala or read about what she had revealed during her presentation and that it had put some of his preposterous speculations to rest.

Frequently scanning the papers for scandalous articles about Charley in reference to Amie, she also checked out book news. To date she hadn't read anything of note. That was encouraging but, then again, getting a book published the old-fashioned way took a lot of time. The alternative was having it done digitally upon demand which was fast. Over time, the absence of an article and book news was making Charley more comfortable. However, her general sense of optimism was about to be seriously challenged.

25

While nothing further had happened with respect to the blackmail threat, Charley still watched and waited with trepidation as weeks went by. She hadn't received any more "avengerforamie" emails but didn't know what that indicated in the larger scheme of things. Then suddenly, it was Amie's personal computer which began to receive emails from a "ronshelton.com" that weren't about business. Charley noted that the return address was different from the blackmailer's but didn't know if that meant it were from a different person or if it were simply emailed from a different account. He wasn't interested in accusations or threats. That was a relief. Instead, he was interested in trying to rekindle some long-past intimate relationship with Amie. That was anything but a relief.

He "reminded" Amie that they had been lovers for many years in Boston.

"I have continued to admire and lust for you from afar since. I have never given up on being with you again, my beloved, permanently. When I read about your gallery evening, I knew what you wanted it to say to me. The time for us is now. I'm coming to find you."

He signed his billet-doux with the initial "R."

Charley had never heard of a Ron or a Shelton before, even though over the years Amie had regaled her with many ribald, often hilarious, stories about the many men who had woven themselves through her life. But Shelton indicated they had been lovers for some time. Even though Amie was ten years older than Charley, Charley had known Amie since Charley was a child and didn't recall any long-term relationships, especially in Boston. She didn't know who Ron Shelton was. It all created apprehension for her.

Suddenly, Charley smacked her forehead.

"Oh, damn!" she shouted. "He's coming to find Amie!"

Taking a deep breath, she counted to ten and began to mutter to herself.

"What am I going to do if this person shows up on her door step? I can fake being Amie, given her accident and surgeries, but how could I handle this if he actually had a relationship with her?"

She realized that she didn't really know how she would determine if Shelton had intimately, tangentially, or, perhaps, inconsequentially, passed through Amie's life or not. Or whether it might be a scam.

"If he had had this flaming romance with Amie for so many years, it wouldn't take him long to discover that I'm not Amie," she groaned. "Unfortunately, I can't swoon like a Southern belle, or narcoleptic goat," she chuckled "every time he asks me a question or waxes poetic on something indelicate that they supposedly did together."

Shortly thereafter, a second email arrived for Amie. It was Shelton again. That, she thought, was overdoing it. While she begged the computer not to inundate her with soppy remembrance emails, his message continued his protestations of their unrequited love. He indicated that Amie and he had made plans for their future in Santa Fe. To remind her of many of the things he claimed they had supposedly done together early on he took a brief walk down memory lane.

"Do you remember our large one-room apartment on Commonwealth Avenue? I loved all the time we spent there together. And how you made your special Quiche Lorraine in the tiny, one-person kitchen to have with Chateau Lafite Rothschild. And how we said we'd always be one, no matter what, because it was karma. Your frequent love letters have helped me keep that hope and promise alive. And when you recently accepted my proposal of marriage, it thrilled me beyond words. I can't tell you how long I have waited for you and this."

That sounded more than slightly suspect to Charley. Since the beginning of Amie's lengthy decline, she had been handling all

Amie's correspondence. There had been no emails, post, texts, or calls from a Ron Shelton—and certainly no emails, post, texts, or calls, much less love letters, from Amie to him.

Furthermore, Charley had never seen any sign of this relationship going on when she and Amie were in Boston. Amie had lots of male friends and dated occasionally but spent most of her time painting and teaching. And she had lived in Chestnut Hill in her own house for decades. If she had ever lived in an apartment in Boston, it wouldn't have been in *his* apartment because Amie was smarter than Charley about moving into a lover's apartment. No, she liked her freedom too much and wasn't shy about asserting it.

Charley knew that the only time Amie had "lived" in Boston was when she stayed for a couple of weeks with Saksia Hibbs on Commonwealth Avenue while her house interior was being repainted. Although it was still too soon to tell, more and more Charley wondered if the emails were indeed preliminary to a con game.

"But what," she asked herself aloud, "would be the possible purpose of it? That makes no sense."

This question bedeviled her. He had made what appeared to be strange assertions. Simply making these assertions didn't make them true. He would have to provide proof that supported his preposterous claims. Charley didn't see how any of what he contended could be possible, even if he had known Amie in some circumstance in Boston. That was a predicament. If he really did seek out Amie and make these pronouncements, Charley had no idea what she would do to counter them and successfully dismiss him.

Additionally, when "Amie" would tell him "no" to their being married, was he going to declare breach of promise of marriage? Checking online, she learned that breach of promise was not actionable in most jurisdictions, but it could possibly be considered a tort. If he were to pursue that legally, he'd have to provide proof that she had said "yes" to him. If he tried, that meant that Charley as Amie was going to have to deal with that in public. Charley slumped and sighed at the trickiness of the situation. She needed to take a break.

After making some herbal tea, she grabbed a box of large, salted pretzels and sat at the kitchen table, loudly munching and cogitating on it. Minutes passed as her brain whirled, trying to logically parse what he had said and match it with her memory.

"Whoa! Wait a minute," she exclaimed, shaking her head the sighing, "I need to slow down. I'm getting way ahead of myself. Before going off the deep end, let's see if he really shows up. Let's see what so-called 'proof' he has. Good grief! There's no need for me to act prematurely. It could be a flim-flam. Maybe even a mistake. Actually, a mistake seems much more likely."

Taking a deep breath, she began to feel slightly less discomfited. After she finished her repast, she went to her computer to write an email to Ron Shelton, hopefully before she received another one from him.

"Mr. Shelton, I'm afraid you've confused me with someone else. I do not know you and have never had a history with you in Boston or elsewhere. You've made a mistake. Please stop emailing me. Sincerely, Amie Benison."

Another two weeks went by as Charley worked on some of the paintings she had started as Amie before Amie died. There was no rush to get them all done. Besides, the online instruction videos, coaching, and website business were taking up a lot more time than Charley had imagined. As the weekend approached and Charley was putting posters into mailing tubes to be mailed, the doorbell rang. She thought that was strange because the mail carrier had already been by to deliver her mail, although he hadn't picked up her shipments because she had forgotten to put them out.

Standing on the front step was a five-foot ten-inch-tall, balding with a graying fringe, slightly heavyset man with doughy features, deep-set brown eyes, and heavy dark eyebrows. He was dressed in a navy sport jacket, light blue dress shirt with open collar, and tan slacks. Not getting an immediate response to his ring, he began to knock on her door and ring the doorbell again. Charley who had been in the back of the house hurried to answer it, muttering.

"For crying out loud. Keep your shirt on. I'm coming!"

No sooner had she opened the door than the stranger immediately bear-hugged her, lifting her off her feet.

"Let go of me. Now!" Charley indignantly loudly exclaimed, anxiety tumbling forward to take over as she thought she was being assaulted.

"Amie, what's the matter with you? It's Ron, your loving husband-to-be. I couldn't have changed that much since we were last together. Don't you recognize me?"

Once again standing, she pushed herself away from him. As she looked at him, her peripheral vision caught sight of two large suitcases on the step.

"Who are you?" she demanded, her heart racing. "What is going on?"

"Darling."

She squinted her eyes as she looked him up and down. Raising her voice, she was brusque.

"Don't 'darling' me. I said, 'Who *are* you?'"

"Stop joking with me, sweetheart. You know me. Sure, I've gained a little weight, lost a little hair, and shaved off my moustache, but I'm still your love machine."

"Love machine"? That made her want to put her finger down her throat. As she stood there figuring out her next move, the muscles in her shoulders began tensing. She clenched her fist. It was more to demonstrate her anger which was reddening her face as her blood pressure rose than to cover her fear.

"We've loved each other for many years," he continued, "and made many important plans together. Now don't tell me, you little tease, that you didn't repeatedly beg me to come. And I'm here as promised."

"Look, whoever you are." She could feel her hand wanting to shake. "I already told you that I do *not* know you. I don't know how this happened but you've made a very big mistake. Now please leave."

Her heart tripping, she was hanging on to some semblance of her anger because she was afraid that in her increasing panic she might hyperventilate enough to pass out. And that would be dangerous given his behavior. She could picture him carrying her inside, doing whatever, and never being able to get rid of him. What her assertive side wanted to shout was, "Get lost, creep!" But, instead, she bit her tongue because she was not sure how the stranger might respond, which could be dangerous.

"Why do you keep saying that, darling? I don't understand. That auto accident couldn't have wiped out your memory of me because you've been emailing me. I have saved every last one of your emails, texts, and your beautiful handwritten letters and love notes because I cherish them."

Charley was gradually growing angrier as he pressed on with his repetitive, off-the-wall soliloquy. She kept telling herself to remain calm and retreat into the house as soon as possible without provoking him.

"I received two emails from you on Tuesday, the eighth. I responded by telling you *I do not know you.*" She paused, taking in a deep breath, reminding herself she could handle this. "Seriously, I mean it. You have mistaken me for someone else." She looked him straight in the eye. "Please leave now. If you don't leave, I'll have to call the police."

"Now, wait a minute." There was anger in his voice. "Is this some of kind of game you're playing? If so, it's not very funny. You're Amie Benison, aren't you? Then you are the love of my life. There's no mistake. I've waited, pining for you for years. What do I have to say to prove it?"

"Please just leave."

In a stressful voice he continued, "You must remember I gave you your beloved Saatchi. You acted as my model for my nude series of Nature photographs. We rode motorcycles together to New Hampshire. Now you're not going to try to tell me you didn't say that as soon as you were settled in New Mexico that I should come after you?"

Charley was taken aback, feeling puzzled but even more suspicious.

"When I got your last email, I dropped everything to be here with you. You even set the date of our wedding, June 12. You must remember."

He was so adamant and so sincere sounding. Albeit slightly deranged. It made no sense to Charley. For someone who allegedly had known Amie intimately for years, he couldn't really think she looked like Amie.

"I'm going back inside. I want you to leave and don't come back. I *will* have you arrested. Period."

Ron wrinkled his forehead, looking perplexed and downcast.

"If you're playing hard to get, I'll play along even though I don't understand. You know I'd do anything for you. I'll be back, darling. Our love will never die."

He stepped back, quizzically examining her face, then smiling.

"You're not fooling me. I can see your love for me in your every facial gesture."

"Good-bye," she quickly responded.

Then Charley started backing inside, pulling the door with her, but stopped in the decreasing doorway to watch him. She braced her right foot behind the slightly ajar door just in case.

He didn't move. He was shaking his head sadly, looking forlorn, like an abandoned puppy, hopeful its family had made an error in dropping him off on this lonely rural road in the dark cold.

"It sounds as though my beloved Amie still has remnants of her memory loss from the accident. Maybe you've even developed retrograde amnesia from your car crash. That's okay. I can help. We can find a specialist to assist you in remembering. I'm here for you, darling. Our love will conquer any obstacle, even this."

Charley glared at him. His second mention of Amie having had memory loss pricked her antennae. Suddenly she felt even more wary of his motives. Her fear of his immediate actions had receded. It all sounded like a hustle, one she was not willing to play along with.

He leaned forward and reached out his hand to grab Charley's neck so he could pull her close to kiss her. When she roughly removed his hand with a look of shock, he backed up a little. She likewise withdrew farther into the foyer, still holding the door only partially open. His lower lip drooping, he straightened up, gathered his suitcases, and turned toward the car.

Turning to look back for an instant, he sighed and whispered, "Sweet dreams, darling," to the door that was shutting.

Then he placed his bags inside the rear of the car, settled himself in the driver's seat, and started down the drive. As Charley noted, through the remaining door slit, the car had New Mexico, not Massachusetts, plates. Quickly closing the door all the way, she locked it and slipped on the dead bolt.

Now she wondered if he had flown in from Boston and this vehicle were a rental. But did they rent Mercedes? For some reason the fancy dark blue car looked oddly familiar. She realized she'd seen it, or one very like it, numerous times before in both Santa Fe and in Glorieta over some time. Momentarily relieved that he was gone, she still felt nervous about his probable return. There was no question after the encounter, irrespective of his motive, that he was determined and would be frighteningly persistent.

Charley spent the rest of the day trying to focus enough to paint after she had taken all the new shipping items to the post office. Because it was the weekend, she didn't want to wait to mail them on Monday. She prided herself on getting everything that customers ordered to them as quickly as possible, as a form of respect.

Every time she took a break, she began to dwell on what Shelton might be up to and try to do next. She wanted to immediately rid herself of this stranger's attentions but hadn't a clue how to do it. While she could ignore his phone calls, texts, posts, and emails and not answer the door if he were to come by, that definitely wouldn't solve the problem. Despite his departure, she felt he was going to be steely in his doggedness about moving in and having an intimate relationship with her, even though she clearly wasn't Amie. That meant she *had* to do something ... and fast.

As she contemplated her as yet unfocused options, her brain felt baited by some things he'd said that didn't feel right. They buzzed around like a horsefly, nagging at her. She couldn't shake their sense of infelicity. That evening as she was curled up on the sofa with Saatchi and iced tea she had made earlier, trying to make a plan about what to do next, she had an aha.

"Of course!" she exclaimed, chastising herself, smacking the seat cushion, startling Saatchi who squinted, scrutinizing her. "How could I have not remembered and realized this sooner? It was so obvious." She laughed, feeling confident in her discovery

Mentally, she began ticking off the inconsistencies that were finally revealing themselves to her now in her now relaxed state.

First, he'd made reference to Saatchi, stating that *he* had given that now-famous cat to Amie. That was dead wrong. Charley had accompanied Amie to the Boston animal shelter where she had looked for, found, and adopted the scrawny, scruffy kitten who was to become the "one and only paw-print-signatured cat."

Second, he said they had shared an apartment on Commonwealth Avenue. But Charley was sure Amie had never "lived" in an apartment on Commonwealth, much less in Boston. Amie had moved from her home in Burlington, Vermont, directly to her house in Chestnut Hill and had lived no place else before she moved to Santa Fe.

Third, he said Amie made Quiche Lorraine for them. Amie's mother, not Amie, made that for parties, but never for or by Amie. Poor Amie had had intolerances for milk products, cheese especially, since childhood that could double her over in abdominal pain, and worse from only a bite. There was no way she would indulge in anything containing cream, Parmesan, Swiss, and Gruyere cheeses. That idea must have come from Amie's having shared her mother's recipe for it once with a reporter.

Fourth, Amie would not ride a motorcycle if her life had depended upon it. When Charley was still a teen, Amie and she had taken a ferry over to Nantucket Island, south of Cape Cod, to vet a gallery for them. While there, they also rented motor scooters as a lark to visit this famous seaport. However, as Amie was rounding a curve at twenty miles per hour, her scooter slid in sand. She crashed into a painstakingly-refashioned traditional stone wall lining the road. She broke her ankle and seriously abraded her left leg. Post-healing, the scarred, indented area on her leg was frequently painful. After that blighted Saturday, she eschewed riding in or on anything that didn't have four wheels.

Fifth, Amie would never have posed nude for photographs, Nature or otherwise. It wasn't just her aversion to being photographed. While she found most paintings of nude women as celebrating their intrinsic beauty, she saw photographing nude women as objectifying them and the photos too often being destined to be used as whacking material. Not exactly the aesthetic she had in mind.

Sixth, his reference to Amie's "amnesia" was likewise incorrect. Amie had suffered a temporary period of traumatic amnesia because of the blow to her head in the car accident which had rendered her unconscious until she arrived at the hospital. It was commonplace for an accident victim to have that simple memory loss which was quickly resolved. It certainly had no effect on her past or present memories, aside from her already-existing, Huntington's-impaired memory deficit.

After the "avenger for Amie" scare, Charley didn't need another complication like that in her life. Having to contend with someone who was either scamming her or romantically mistaken was simply too much. Yet, she was determined that she wasn't going to allow herself to be emotionally victimized a second time, irrespective of whatever was going on with that person who called himself "Ron Shelton."

26

The big question now for Charley was: What exactly did he have in mind? And how would she discover and successfully deal with it, whatever it was?

Everything he had said struck her as if he were trying to gaslight her. None of it made any sense … unless he thought he could convince an "amnesiac" Amie of their having had a past so that she would marry him, thus allowing him to take control of her business and finances. She was a well-known, valuable commodity. Charley shook her head. While she couldn't dismiss that scenario, she couldn't quite accept it either. That was more like a 1940's black-and-white movie melodrama she would have seen on late-night television.

After much consternation, she decided that since there had been no actual crime committed—not even trespass since he had finally left after having been asked several times—there was nothing at this point she could tell the authorities that would make any sense or that they could act on. Perhaps, she figured, her best route would be to hire a private detective because Shelton seemed very fixated on her, having every intention to persevere in their coupling. He would be back again and again. The very thought made her palms sweat.

If she hired someone, he or she could delve into who Ron Shelton was, learn his background, and, hopefully, expose what he might be up to. Having someone do a job personally for her could be more profitable than involving the police, assuming Shelton continued, because the detective would be focused on Shelton alone, with nothing else interfering with his or her specific task.

Besides, she was leery of calling the police into what *might* become a stalking situation but, as far as she knew, wasn't one yet.

In spite of the film, *Minority Report,* she couldn't report "precrime." Besides, in view of how strange the situation was, she wasn't confident the police would believe her anyway. In the meantime, she knew she should document everything that had happened. Keeping notes on his behavior and their interactions could be helpful.

Now that Shelton had suddenly thrust himself into Amie and Charley's life, irrespective of whoever he was or whatever he had in mind, he might just upset everything they had created. Charley couldn't allow that. With a glass of cold Pinot Grigio in hand, she ensconced herself in her office in front of Amie's computer to do a search for private detectives. Even in her dotage, Saatchi jumped onto her lap and curled up, purring. While Charley could gain some information on Shelton on her own through one or more of the personal search websites, she wanted someone working for her who could also do interviews and investigate him in person, if necessary and possible, with all that might entail.

The most informative and impressive website she found belonged to Best U.S. Detectives. It was a national firm, established thirty years ago, with investigators in New Mexico and, as she had hoped, in the Santa Fe area. Using their online chat, she briefly communicated with someone ostensibly named "Ben," explained the situation, and asked if there were an investigator she could speak with about her problem.

"I'll have someone call you shortly" was Ben's typed response.

In the interim, Charley looked for articles that would tell her what private investigators generally could and couldn't do. What she found said that a detective *could not*:

1. Enter a house or hotel room without permission.
2. Open or read a person's mail.
3. Wiretap a person's phone without consent.
4. Record private conversations.

5. Trespass on private property.

6. Obtain protected information.

7. Make arrests.

8. Bribe, abuse, or use deceitful means to gain information.

9. Put a tracking device on a subject's vehicle.

What a detective *could* do was:

1. Interview/question people to ask for information.

2. Run license plates, but to do so they had to have a legal justification (which was unexplained).

3. Observe a person in public places and take photos or videos of the person.

4. Take photos and videos of the person in his or her home *if* they were doing so from public property and through a window (at least that was in some states).

5. Use a GPS tracker but only if there were a permissible purpose (but it didn't spell out what a "permissible purpose" was or to what degree that could vary from jurisdiction to jurisdiction).

Charley snickered, "The detective's motto should be: 'If at first you don't succeed, pry, pry again.'" Then she groaned at her bad pun.

Then she took a piece of notebook paper and a pen from her desk to list what she wanted to know about their service for her.

Ten minutes later, Franco Ortega from U.S. Best Detectives called to introduce himself and ask for clarification of her problem.

"Tell me in detail what you want investigated."

Feeling anxious, Charley forced herself to speak slowly and distinctly, giving a full but succinct chronology to date, so there would be no confusion or misunderstanding of her problem.

"A man who said his name is Ron Shelton emailed me two weeks ago claiming we had been lovers and were scheduled to be married. I emailed him back stating I did not know him and he had mistaken me for someone else. He emailed me back to say he was coming to see me. Early today he arrived at my door reiterating his claim that he and I had had a long affair many years ago, that we had lived together in Boston, that we have been frequently communicating ever since, and that I have agreed to marry him. However, not a single word of that is true.

"When I received his emails, I was shocked. I have no idea who he is, if he has confused me with someone else, *or* if he is playing some sort of game."

"What precisely would you want me to do?"

"Find out who he is, what makes him think I'm the one he is pursuing, and if this is some kind of confidence game."

"In order to get a complete picture, I'll want to interview and investigate you as well as him."

That sent a shiver down Charley's spine. It gave her pause, immediately reminding her of what personal documentation she had had to get from Amie to back up her impersonation. But, simultaneously, it occurred to her that he wasn't going to be interested in her Social Security number, birth certificate, and her license which had been updated with Charley's picture. That was dumb but at the same time the thought of being investigated made her uncomfortable. There wasn't any way he could discover her identity switch with the real Amie. Yet, anxiety and guilt were jockeying for supremacy.

Moreover, the idea of his interviewing Shelton made her likewise feel uncomfortable because she was afraid that he would tend to believe Shelton in spite of anything she would say. It wasn't that unusual for a man not to believe what a woman said if it were about what another man had "allegedly" done to her. But in this situation, she assured herself, his investigation would be done at her behest. She would be the one paying him. Perhaps that might make him less biased, in case he was an unrepentant male chauvinist, which she doubted if he were a successful detective.

"How will you interview him? Do you have to tell him why you're doing it, that you're investigating him for me?"

"Oh, no. Not to worry. I'll have a reasonable premise for asking him a few questions. I can pretend I'm almost anyone except a law enforcement officer or a public official. But, it's important to note, that I can't legally compel him or anyone to give me the information I request. In addition, you should know that I can't impersonate anyone in order to obtain his records from a service provider, like from his bank, credit card, utilities, cell phone, or landline. The bulk of what I do is collect facts before talking with the subject and any others that I deem necessary."

"Would investigating him include following him?"

"It might, depending upon what you want to know … as well as what I find out."

"If you surveil him, can you make absolutely sure he doesn't discover what you're doing or for whom? I'm sure you're a professional but if he noticed an unfamiliar car or person following him or a stranger taking pictures of him, his car, or where he went, he might somehow relate it to me and how I responded when he approached me."

"That won't be a problem. If I tail him, believe me, he won't see me doing it."

Charley debated with herself about asking the detective not to interview Shelton. She knew Shelton would talk about Amie's "amnesia." That signaled that she had better prepare the detective for it. She didn't want him assuming Shelton had a logical point thinking Amie simply didn't remember him because of her head injury.

"Something important I think you should know. One of the things he said to me, when he suddenly appeared at my door and I told him I did not know him, was that 'maybe I did not recognize him because I had had amnesia as a result of a car accident' I'd had not long ago. I felt that was a strange thing for him to say. It made me suspect his motives. While I did have very brief moment-of-impact amnesia, it passed quickly and did *not* affect my past or present memory."

"That's good to know."

She hoped Ortega knew that not all amnesias were as dramatic, frequent, or long-lasting as what you tended to see on television dramas and in the movies. In her head she could hear Charles Boyer trying to convince Ingrid Bergman that she was losing her mind, that what she thought had happened, hadn't. But now it would be instead: "Of course, you don't remember, darling. You still have the lingering effects of your amnesia."

Hopefully, she thought, investigating him would give her enough information so she could determine if he were up to no good or just resolutely mistaken. They had to accurately and empirically determine that he wasn't who he said he was, a former-lover and live-in companion of Amie in Boston or anywhere else, and that there was no support—whether emails, pictures, notes, texts, calls, or letters—for any of his outrageous claims about their having now, or ever having had, any kind of serious, intimate relationship and plans for marriage.

Before she could consider hiring Ortega, she had questions to ask about him and his private investigative service. What she needed to know would take up most of the time of their conversation:

1. Was he licensed and insured?
2. What was his background and experience?
3. Did he belong to any relevant professional organizations?
4. Did he have work references and reviews she could see?
5. Did he have a local office?
6. What hours would he be working?
7. Was everything he did for her confidential?
8. Would they have a contract that spelled out everything ahead of time?
9. Could she see a typical report he provided to clients?
10. Could they meet in-person before she made her hiring decision?
11. Did he subcontract any of his investigative work to others?
12. Would he testify in court if her situation became a legal matter?
13. Did he offer a money-back guarantee?

To Charley's relief, Ortega answered all her questions with exactly what she needed to know. But while he came through as she hoped, Charley nevertheless found herself at an impasse. Thinking ahead, she worried about what she could actually do once she had the accumulated information in his final report. Probably not much unless Shelton continued to pursue her against her will. If he did, she would continue to keep records of his activities and turn that plus Ortega's report over to the police ... and anticipate the best.

Emphasizing that he could customize the investigation in any way she wanted, Ortega also answered her unasked question.

"As a trained agent, I can collect all possible data and analyze it to answer your key questions. This will then allow you to make well-informed decisions about what you want to do next. I can also provide you with options if necessary."

They then met in two days' time at Java Joe's coffee shop in Santa Fe where she saw copies of the documents she had requested to review. At that point she gave him printouts of Shelton's two emails to her, her responses, and a typed, detailed summary of the interaction that took place at her front door.

Ortega was six feet tall with a medium build, dark close-cut hair, clean shaven, and attired in a white dress shirt, dark blue tie, highly-polished black oxford leather dress shoes, and gray off-the-rack business suit. She was in her usual loose artistic garb. Looking dubiously at his apparel which wouldn't be likely to make him blend in with the scenery, she hoped he wouldn't be clothed that way all the time he was investigating because he might be very noticeable.

"Despite your assurances that you'll be invisible," Charley's face reddened as she asked, feeling a tinge of embarrassment, "will you be dressed as you are?"

He let out an ebullient laugh.

"Absolutely not when following Mr. Shelton. Other times it will depend on the circumstances. Believe me, I've done this successfully for many years."

After they further discussed her problem, in case there was anything else she wanted to add, a last-minute question crossed her mind. Charley inquired.

"Might you have to fly to Boston as part of your investigation?"

"Yes, that's possible as well as any place else it takes me to comprehensively answer your questions. But no matter how much I believe it's necessary to travel, it will be included in my quoted investigation price of six thousand dollars."

"How long do you think this might take? Will you be in touch with me during your investigation?"

"Working on this fulltime, which I will be, I expect it to take between eleven and fifteen days, depending upon how much travel I have. And, no, I don't expect to be in touch with you unless I need to change the time frame or report something urgent. But you can contact me—here's my email address—with any further information you might acquire."

Satisfied, Charley hired Ortega on the spot.

Fortunately, his interviewing her turned out to be less intrusively painful than she had imagined. He had obviously already checked her out online. Mostly, he asked her questions which focused on her memories about men she had known in Boston.

"Did you ever live with a male in Boston?"

"No."

"Are there any males you have since kept in close touch with over the years?"

"No, not personally. It has been primarily former clients, students, and gallery owners with whom I have had only business relationships. Any correspondence with them has continued to be about business And, some casual friends."

"Have you ever written personal letters to any men?"

"Well, not since I was very young when I wrote to friends and relatives, some of whom were male. No one named Ron Shelton, however. And, no, I have not written anything that could be looked upon as very personal and certainly not as a 'love letter' to anyone I have dated."

"What about social email?"

"I don't keep up with social email in general because I don't have the time or interest. I merely scan it for business and don't encourage it unless it's related to business."

"You do have a website on Facebook and other social media sites?"

"Yes, I also have a business website, 'amiebenison.com' where correspondence is via 'amie@amiebenison.com.' I do keep track of that, responding when it's business."

"How did you feel when you received the email from this 'Ron Shelton'?"

"I was totally confused. I did not know the name. Everything he said about what allegedly had happened between us was wrong."

"So, there is absolutely no doubt in your mind whatsoever that you never had any kind of relationship with him."

"Not the remotest hint. I have an excellent memory for names, even from the past, of my clients, business colleagues, friends, and students. I'm known for it. I'm reasonably sure we never met, even in passing, at a gallery or other event in years past, whether in Vermont, Massachusetts, or New Mexico."

As Ortega left her, she was afraid both that he wouldn't find anything significant about Shelton … and afraid that he would.

27

In the days after her meeting with Ortega, Shelton sent Amie numerous emails, asking to see her, professing his love. Charley didn't respond but collected them in a file to be emailed to Ortega. When Shelton called, she let the answering machine record his messages. And saved the recordings. He came by in person four times that Charley knew of but she didn't answer the doorbell. All this information she recorded and emailed to Ortega every couple of days.

In sixteen days, Ortega called Charley to meet with her to give her his twenty-plus-page, single-space-typed report. When he arrived at the house, he no longer looked like the middle-class businessperson who had met Charley when she hired him. Now he was very casually dressed, in blue t-shirt, jeans, and Rockport walking shoes, with nothing particularly distinctive about him. Instead, he almost blended in with the furniture in the living room, which was precisely what she had wanted in an investigator.

Charley provided them with coffee, paper napkins, and a large plate of chili-flavored mini-scones in the living room. She placed them on her glass and wrought iron coffee table which sat in front of the gray-colored three-seater sofa. As Ortega placed his report on the glass top, he complimented her on the rug under the table. It was a Navajo four-by-six-foot Ganado wool rug with a black border on a gray background, covered with geometric shapes in classic burgundy red. Then, after biting into one of the scones, he began to verbally summarize his report.

"Ronald Shelton is his real name. Your so-called 'boyfriend/fiancé' never lived in Boston. He was born in California where he lived most of his life. After the age of five, he lived in San Diego. He moved to Santa Fe about a year ago, after you did. That New Mexico license plate number you gave me was for his own car.

"He is a lawyer who had attended California Western School of Law and who did a judicial clerkship, a post-graduate position for nearly two years, with a California state judge, both in San Diego." He paused to have another bite.

"A lawyer? I would never have guessed that though it matches his car. Lawyers have always struck me as coming across as professional, objective, and unemotional. That certainly doesn't sound like the one who contacted me by email and in person."

"As I'm sure you're aware, presentations can be deceiving depending upon a person's situational goal and motivation."

"Sure. Of course."

"While he was a law clerk, he did *everything* as the judge's right hand, totally ingratiating himself. He researched and analyzed issues presented by the pleadings; wrote memoranda recommending dispositions; drafted, proofed, and edited opinions; observed court proceedings and assisted; spoke with attorneys and conducted settlement conferences; and wrote jury instructions. Everything was top drawer, making him an acknowledged superstar. He was someone you'd think a judge wouldn't want to lose no matter what. This is important to note. I'll get back to it."

He sipped his coffee as Charley pondered his words.

"After he passed the California Bar, he set up a small practice in San Diego, working primarily on torts, wrongful acts or infringement of rights leading to civil liability. This included participating in class-action suits for victims of mesothelioma against companies which used asbestos in their work or for ovarian cancer victims who had used asbestos-contaminated body talcum. This was what he was best known for. Although, he also did some work with opioid, defective earplug, and weed-killer suits."

"Does he still have his practice in San Diego?"

"No. He closed that office and set up a new office here in Santa Fe. But here's where it gets especially interesting, and important, as

I mentioned. When I located and checked with that judge's office in San Diego, I got a peculiar vibe from her. When I inquired further, she was reluctant to say much … until I explained why I was asking.

"What I finally heard, in confidentiality, was that Shelton had been a big personal complication for her. For some reason he had believed he and she were madly in love and were having a torrid affair. This was not true. There was nothing romantic between them. The judge said that, at first, she did not spot his unfounded beliefs—or unintentionally overlooked them—because she had been so thrilled with his intelligence, unstinting dedication, and superior level of work."

Ortega paused to sip his coffee.

"That certainly sounds familiar. What alerted her to the genuineness of his belief—or what sounds more like a delusion?"

"When he started leaving her Post-It notes with lines of romantic poetry. She spoke to him about it, that it looked to her as if he thought she were interested in a romantic relationship with him, which she wasn't. She told him specifically that she did not allow fraternization in her office. Besides, she already was in a long-term relationship outside the office. In addition, she clarified that his behavior was verging on the unprofessional and must not continue.

"Unfortunately, she said, he seemed to take it all with a knowing wink and a nod, that she *had* to say it so no one in the office would know the 'truth' about them. Paradoxically, he seemed to feel even more sure of her love for him after she had told him his attentions were unwelcome and his related behaviors had to stop."

"That was an awkward situation. What did she do?"

"While, she said, he had become indispensable to her as her clerk, she became very conflicted about having him around. Because she was so stressed as a result, her fiancé urged her to tell him what was wrong. When he heard, he became enraged, wanting to beat Shelton to a pulp. However, she managed to convince him to do nothing because he'd be sure to be arrested for assault and battery. Not only that but she was also afraid of what Shelton would do as a result. Without question, she wanted to take care of it herself, and as quietly as possible."

Charley refilled their cups. "What did Shelton do then?"

"Shelton ceased leaving poetry but after that, his every glance and gesture hinted that each time they interacted it was a preamble to a sexual interlude. Soon, she said, he seemed to read romantic interpretations into everything she did. If she wore a particular outfit under her judicial robe, he took that as a sign of her love. Any office-related email she sent him or note she left for him on legal matters, he took as a secret affirmation of her returning his love. He thanked her for a silk tie she hadn't given him and asked if she liked her own grandmother's cameo ring that he said he had bought for her."

"His behavior sounds so obvious. Didn't *anyone* else in the office see it?"

"She said she thought they must have. But when she later very carefully questioned her staff about him, they all said they thought he was the ideal clerk, a nice and very bright, conscientious person who was headed for a stellar law career. There seemed to be no clue among them as to his beliefs and intentions."

"That's too creepy."

"If you think that's creepy … In her life outside the office, she said she began to notice him wherever she went, making her very uncomfortable. He would show up in the grocery store, at her dry cleaners, *even* at her gynecologist's office, and make a point of getting her attention so he could smile, nod, and wink at her. Other times she spotted his car where she was. As you might surmise, it only took a few of these encounters for her to know for a fact that he was stalking her and she became very afraid."

Charley offered Ortega another scone which he took.

"That is so frightening. I'd be terrified to go anywhere after that. Who knows how long he had been doing that and what he might have done next? So, what did she do?"

"She decided she didn't want to go to the police and have it all become public—as a 'she said/he said'—which would have been very ticklish for her in her position. As a result, the only thing she felt she could do was let him go. This was also difficult for her because it raised lots of questions in the office and the courthouse given his acknowledged superlative legal performance and socially pleasant, trustworthy demeanor with everyone else. Men and women alike had nothing but praise for him. No one could understand her action. She said her peers asked about it but she brushed their queries aside, no doubt leaving them wondering who had done what to whom."

"That sounds incredibly delicate and stressful."

"Then he asked her to write a reference for him. Again, not wanting to air their personal difficulty publicly, especially for fear of his reprisal, she gave his legal work high marks but said nothing else. Apparently, this circumscribed reference was considered unexpected and slightly unusual."

"I don't know which I'd be more panicky about. Having him constantly around me or having him dismissed and feeling rejected by me."

"That was what she said. After she dismissed him, she said she was even more nervous that she would be overwhelmed by emails from him expressing his adoration of her … or his anger at her because she had spurned him. She had nightmares about him coming to her home and threatening her and doing who knows what."

"So, did any of her nightmares come true?"

"Well, someone did smash her car's windshield while it was parked outside her home and keyed the length of her vehicle. Someone also tried to poison her dog with strychnine-tainted meat when the animal was outside her home in its fenced in yard."

"Did the dog make it?"

"Luckily, she found dog in time and it had barely touched the meat because it had just eaten. The vet saved him. She said unmarked packages arrived at her home but she either refused them or threw them away unopened for fear of what they might contain. Unfortunately, even if she had wanted to have him arrested, she couldn't prove Shelton had stalked her or was behind the vandalism. She said that was the only time she wished she had had outdoor surveillance cameras at her home."

"He sounds very vindictive. I hope I haven't enraged him. Did that situation continue?"

"As far as she could tell, after a month of all that, he seemed to have stopped stalking her. At least, she never saw him doing so again or his car nearby. Still, she stayed on the alert, always surveying her surroundings. And she received no more packages."

"Did she have any idea why he might have initially focused on her?"

"She said she thought it might have been because she was a well-regarded judge, who had status and power."

"I guess I'm well-regarded in my field and have some status. But no power to benefit him, except via my income. How long did it take for her to start to relax again?"

"Many months with counseling. She said she hoped he had found something else to occupy his mind. But," Ortega laughed sadly, "she emphasized that she did *not* wish his distorted affection to attach to any other woman. She said she felt very sorry for the next object of his desire, which she was sure there would be, but didn't know of a way to warn potential targets that wouldn't prompt his retaliating against her further."

Charley shook her head then asked him.

"What about me? What did you learn about his obsession with me? Does it look as if had he actually targeted me?"

Ortega said that when he spoke with Shelton a second time, which was in front of an art gallery, he made a point of admiring Amie Benison paintings.

"In response he proudly told me he had a collection of your work and wanted me to see it. I then asked if he had ever had the chance to meet you. He claimed that he had not only met you but that he had also been your lover for a decade, and that you two were to be married in June. I pooh-poohed it and said he must be kidding. He couldn't wait to show me 'your letters and emails,' anything that would support his case of a hot relationship with you in Boston and beyond."

"I can't imagine what in the world he could possibly have shown you."

Ortega sighed and finished his coffee. Charley offered and poured him some more.

"This guy is something else." He munched on another scone. "Grinning from ear to ear, he showed me a *Boston Magazine* article, from several years ago, about you and your art. While I read it carefully, I couldn't find anything about your past or present relationships with any male, or to suggest you even knew one another, much less anything even obscurely romantic between him and you. He seemed to think it was obvious what it indicated. Being enthusiastic, I asked what else I could see about you and him—any 'love letters' from you?"

Aghast, Charley said, "Don't tell me he actually had something to show you."

"This will really curl your hair. What Shelton confidently provided me was a big surprise. His 'emails' from you were actually the results of online searches he had done on 'Amie Benison,' your painting style, critical reviews of it, your events, and where your work was being displayed that he had saved. Your 'emails' to him consisted of responses from your website, galleries, articles, and catalogues where he could order your paintings or commissions, all of which he said expressed your love for him. Apparently, he has believed and acted on this for a long while."

Charley felt a little nauseous. So, Shelton truly believed all he had said to her.

"And these 'handwritten love letters' I'm supposed to have sent him?"

"You're not going to like this. Somehow he has been able to rummage through your trash to find handwritten lists and notes."

"That's so gross and unnerving. How could he have done that undiscovered?"

Ortega shrugged his shoulders.

"There's something else. It seems he went to a local publisher because he wanted to use what he says he has written to you and what you allegedly had written to him as the basis of a book about you and your passionate relationship with him."

"Oh my God! Seriously?"

"Yeah. Even stranger, somewhere along the line he decided for whatever reason someone was forging your paintings and he was going to out the forger."

"What? So, he was the 'avengerforamie'? He tried to blackmail a former student of mine because he thought she was copying my works."

"He told me all about it. He was very pleased with what he'd done."

"When I heard about it, I sent him a 'cease-and-desist' letter because there have been no forgeries. I thought he must have been a crack pot."

"Initially when you explained your situation to me, it sounded like he really had made a mistake. But you were right. While he never knew you in Boston, I couldn't find any evidence you two ever met, socially or otherwise, anywhere. His collection of your paintings in his home was purchased from galleries, et cetera, but not from you directly. The good news is that he doesn't appear to be trying to scam you."

"Given the alternative," Charley laughed, her stress level rising, "I wish he were."

"The bad news, however, is that he is truly delusional about his having had a romantic relationship with you. I'm no shrink but I think he could be very dangerous, especially since he has been constantly stalking you."

"Oh no! Really?"

"I suspect his coming to your home to talk to you was the consequence of his having finally worked up the courage to do it after stalking you for about a year. I followed him drive slowly by your driveway numerous times and on seven separate occasions he actually pulled up to your house. I don't know if you were home at the time to see him arrive."

"Yes, unfortunately, a few of those times. That's very scary."

"But that's not all. Just for the short time I was watching him, he followed your car repeatedly when you went to your paint supplies store, grocery store, and your gallery, for example, as well as visited them to ask about you. While you were in a store or wherever, he'd sit in the parking lot or on the street until you came out and follow you home, frequently snapping pictures of you."

Charley shivered as Ortega finished, recalling having noticed his dark blue Mercedes many times when she was out but having no clue what it meant. While she was glad to know what Shelton had been up to, she was worried about what he'd do next.

"I'm suddenly feeling out of control and very at risk."

"You need to get the police involved immediately. Explain to them what has happened and show them my comprehensive, detailed report. From my little psychological reading on this behavior, which I did recently because I hadn't encountered this situation before, it appears that his delusion can be very hard to treat."

"Meaning that he's psychotic? That's great!" Charley sighed deeply.

"That reminds me. There's something interesting that I stumbled upon when checking out his early background that may or may not be relevant to his delusion."

"I'm not sure I want to hear it. Okay, what?"

"When Shelton was five years old, he and his single mother had just moved to San Diego from Brawley. It was the weekend before Christmas when his mother left him in their second-floor duplex apartment alone trimming their Christmas tree while she went out to pick up a pizza she'd ordered for dinner. However, no sooner had she approached the fast-food restaurant's location than she was killed by a drunk driver who swerved into her car as she entered their parking lot.

"Apparently, while waiting for her, Shelton heard something in the outside hallway and, thinking it was his mother with the pizza, went out to greet her on the stairs. The apartment door swung shut and locked him out. It left him abandoned for three days all alone, with no food, water, or bathroom while their downstairs neighbors were away for an extended holiday visiting with relatives."

"How awful!"

"He knew no one else in the area and had no access to a phone though he knew how to call 911. He was afraid to leave the building. When the neighbors returned, they found him cold, limp, and sunken-eyed on the lower stair steps and contacted EMTs. He was rushed to the hospital with serious dehydration. When the police told him about his mother's death, he refused to believe it. He was confused and kept looking for her. After his hospital stay, they handed him over to social services.

"Because they couldn't locate any of his relatives, he went into the foster care system. But by this time, he was almost mute with shyness, afraid of being alone, and clingingly dependent. Sadly, it turned out that this situation reduced his chances of being fostered because he seemed either distant and unsocial or unable to let go of any female adult. I'm no shrink but I wouldn't be surprised if this further underpinned his current psychological issues."

"Poor little kid. That sounds so terrifying," Charley said, choking up.

"Sounds as though he had a very sad childhood."

Charley nodded, feeling her vision begin to swim with tears.

"Absolutely."

"Please understand that I'm not trying to make excuses for him or make you feel sorry for him," Ortega stressed. "And I'm not suggesting that there's a cause and effect here. Who knows why he has acted as he has toward you and/or the judge? Obviously, all kids with sad childhoods or who have abandonment issues don't have crazy delusions about people or stalk them. But it does make you wonder."

Charley sat back against the sofa cushion. She wasn't sure how she felt. While she empathized with the grief-stricken, helpless little boy who had been dealt a truly horrific hand and needed constant reassurance, she knew that Shelton as an adult wasn't helpless. Since she couldn't make better what had happened to him so many years ago, that was really irrelevant to her own situation.

"But irrespective of his childhood trauma," Ortega noted, "my reading about his delusion has also indicated that no matter what you, doctors, and the authorities would tell him that his relationship with you doesn't exist, he would be unable to see that his beliefs were unfounded. As a result, I think you have only one real option because there have been cases where people with this kind of delusion have become lethal when thwarted in their pursuit of their love object. It's probably best to think of him as a ticking time bomb."

"Resulting in a smashed windshield and poisoned dog? And who knows what else he might have done to get even with the judge that she didn't mention."

Charley knew she was not exempt. He likewise would keep stalking her for as long as he believed she loved him. But when he finally accepted that she had rejected him, he would wreak vengeance upon her as well. Momentarily, she felt faint. Leaning forward, Charley let her head drop toward her knees. Her possible future played before her like a movie preview of things to come and it wasn't pretty.

"You okay?" Ortega asked her.

"I was thinking about my future: being constantly afraid and feeling helpless to do anything about it."

As her lightheadedness quickly subsided, her thoughts ricocheted around her brain, pinging off synapses like a pinball machine. Her life had gotten very precarious. And all because she had become Amie Benison. She couldn't miss the irony.

After he finished his report, answered her questions, and enjoyed the last scone, Charley thanked him for a great job despite what it had revealed. As she took his report and gave him a check for six thousand dollars, she noticed her hand was shaking.

"One more thing," he said. "I strongly urge you to let the authorities know about this and take over, and I mean right now, as soon as I leave. Now that he's come face-to-face with you to reveal himself, he's undoubtedly working on what he's going to do next to cement your relationship. Given how very serious this situation is, you need to be extraordinarily careful and alert while the police act on it."

As soon as Ortega left, Charley made a copy of the report in her office and, keeping her eyes on the rearview mirror for Shelton's car, drove to the police station on Camino Entrada. Even though everything had been spelled out in it in great detail, she didn't want to have to try to convince the police she was in peril.

After passing through several underlings who didn't seem to understand the potential danger she was in, she asked to speak with Police Chief Antonio Rodriguez. Surprisingly, he invited her into his office, offered her a chair, and listened to her fully without a hint of dismissiveness. He even took notes. Then he carefully read the copy of Ortega's report she had given him—every single page of it. Not quite believing her good fortune, she found it wasn't as difficult as she thought it would be to convince a higher-level male authority figure of the direness of her situation.

That afternoon late the police arrived at Shelton's office with a search warrant for his home. His secretary had already left for the day. After closing up, he escorted them to his home where they commenced inspecting all his rooms. It was his bedroom that said it all. There they found he had created a shrine to Amie, with emails and at least a hundred photos he had taken of Charley as Amie as he followed her around Santa Fe and Glorieta. Everything was tacked up on the wall in the shape of a huge heart, dramatically decorated in a sheer red silk drape. Beneath it on a small oak table were lavender-scented candles and dried roses. Below that on a shelf was a four-inch-thick album of newspaper and magazine articles about her, her paintings, and gallery brochures, and print outs of related online information.

As soon as he was taken into custody, Charley had him slapped with an injunction in case he got bail. She wanted to legally prohibit him from getting anywhere near her or communicating with her in any way. To her relief he was not given bail because of his being a continuing threat to her. That lowered her stress level a few notches.

It was months later that he went to trial. Testifying on his frightening criminal behavior were Charley, Franco Ortega, and Police Chief Rodriguez. But what really made the difference and capped it all off was the riveting testimony of a clinical psychologist who was an expert on erotomania—the delusion that another person loves you.

She explained how the delusion often played out with persistent surveillance, stalking, and frequent lethal results.

"When there is perceived rejection by this desired other, the consequence is resentment and rage, which often results in extremely dangerous behaviors against the rejecting person. One example is the July 18, 1989, murder of actress and model Rebecca Shaeffer who was shot and killed at her front door by a fan, Robert Bardo, who had stalked her for three years. He had been convinced that she loved him and couldn't tolerate her rejection of him."

She mentioned how John Hinkley in 1981 had shot President Reagan to seek the fame he thought would impress actress Jody Foster with whom he was obsessed. And she concluded with convicted rapist Dana Martin in 2012 who, from prison, hired hitmen to kidnap, strangle, and castrate his fantasy lover Justin Bieber with a pair of garden shears. He likewise felt he had been unjustly rejected by Bieber who had not answered his fan letters to him. Fortunately for Bieber, the assassins-to-be were apprehended before they could kidnap him, or worse. Having an obsessed fan was not without its dangers.

Charley could tell by the look on the jurors' faces that somewhere in the back of their minds they worried that that peculiar situation could unknowingly, and just as easily, happen to any of them and their loved ones, men and women alike.

Throughout the trial, Shelton smiled lovingly at Charley. After the jury was out for only three hours, they found him guilty. However, his sentence of five years hardly seemed sufficient to Charley after all he had done. Unfortunately for her as well as for others in similar situations, it was a common sentence for stalking convictions.

Behind the prosecutor's table she sat there stunned. Then a chill ghosted up her spine. While she was grateful that he was going to jail, she worried about what she would do when he got out. Five years would go by quickly. What if he escaped? What if he got out early due to good behavior? Was that even possible?

The good behavior scenario seemed like a reasonable possibility. She thought that he could be exceedingly credible as a model prisoner because he deeply believed that he was innocent, had been railroaded, and that he had no place in prison. Moreover, being a lawyer, he was smart, savvy, and skilled at influencing others to his way of thinking.

She wondered if his delusion would change over time. And if so, how? When he apparently didn't continue to further retaliate against the judge, did that mean he had gotten over his delusion about her? Could he get over his obsession with Amie, in spite of her rejection of him, without trying to destroy her car or kill Saatchi?

Would it have been helpful to have known if there had been other females in between the judge and her and what had happened to them? Would it be worthwhile to have Ortega investigate that? No, she recognized, it didn't really matter now.

As she dwelled on it, awaiting Shelton to be led by guards from the courtroom, she felt that over time within the toxic atmosphere of prison he'd undoubtedly replace his adoration for Amie with unmitigated rage. Only minutes after the verdict had been rendered, she could visualize him forever being a sinister albatross around her neck, leaving her in constant fear. How could she live and work under those circumstances?

As Shelton was being removed, he tried to reach Charley to embrace her. When he couldn't because of his restraints, he threw her a kiss. He called to her over the din of shuffling feet leaving the courtroom.

"I know they made you lie about us and all we've meant to each other."

As they moved him toward the exit, to enjoy his next five years without her, he continued his farewell.

"I won't be gone long, darling. Then we'll be back together. Till death do us part."

Charley swallowed hard, hoping that the death to which he referred wouldn't be hers ... prematurely.

28

A week after the trial, the Chief of Police Rodriguez contacted Charley. He explained that he had become interested in her paintings after the Shelton investigation. He wondered if he could commission a smaller painting by her of turbulent clouds, similar to one in Shelton's home. Fortunately, Charley had several such finished paintings on hand. Since she had promised not to *start* any new paintings as Amie after Amie's death, she didn't feel she could do a new commission. That reminded her that she had been remiss about removing the offer for commissions from Amie's website.

"I have some cloud paintings I have just finished I could show you."

"Great. When can I see them?"

"I can bring them to your office. By the way, that reminds me. I wonder if the police department would sponsor an outdoor art show for my painting students. The public would be invited at no charge. Your officers could be there to meet with the public and hand out public safety tips or anything else you feel would benefit everyone. We could go halves on the food and drink. It would be good for my students to get exposure and good community relations for your department as well."

"That could work. I'll give it some thought," he said. "So, you give painting lessons? You know, I've always wanted to try my hand at painting, other than paint-by-numbers." He laughed. "Do you have any openings?"

"Looks like it but let me check. Why don't we talk about all of that over coffee?"

"If you can stand cop coffee, let's do it in my office as well. I have a backlog of work I need to address and can't get away right now."

"Fine. Tell me when."

They met the next afternoon in his small, cramped, file-filled office. It was nearly as bad as Charley's Boston office had been even with her extra floor space. She had the plans for the art show with her so they could discuss more fully how the department could participate. He had to clear a space on his desk to look at them. She also explained how lessons were being provided via video with personal coaching by phone, Skype, and webinars although at some later point she might take students on at her home studio. Rodriguez seemed eager to start his painting lessons right away. They agreed on the following Thursday for him.

In case he had really been interested in having one of her finished cloud paintings, she had brought with her five of them in various sizes, starting with five-by-seven inches. As he considered the artwork, she expressed how very pleased she had been with his testimony in her behalf.

"I so appreciate your rapid action on Shelton and what you said in court. You seemed to truly understand what was going on, the risk, and the impact on me. When women are being stalked, we're not always sure how the police will relate to it and respond to us."

"Amie, may I call you that? You can call me Tony. I do understand it. My sister went through that kind of hell too."

"I'm so sorry to hear that."

"Only her stalker was very clever how he tried to make it look as if it were my sister who was the one doing the stalking. He put a GPS tracker on her car—you know, duct-taped it to the undercarriage—so he could make sure to be wherever she was but have it look as if she were the one following him. He always had witnesses with him to verify it."

"She was very lucky to have you on her team."

"She was very lucky we could gather enough evidence finally to put him away. It wasn't easy. Not every woman who is stalked is so lucky."

"Or comes out of it alive," Charley added.

Charley was impressed, not only by his understanding but also with his looks. Probably in his middle fifties, she found him very attractive. He reminded her of actor Esai Morales. Dark wavy hair, graying at the temples, about 5'10" and slim with slightly-hooded brown eyes, straight nose with a strong jaw and chin, and a dazzling, easy smile, all set in an olive complexion. Before she left his office that afternoon, he had bought her eight-by-ten painting and she had agreed to have dinner with him on the weekend.

29

Saatchi was now over sixteen years old and showing it in her gait and her unwillingness to move around. Charley noticed she was beginning to hesitate in walking, tottering slightly, with resulting lapses in her litterbox habits. Even climbing over the plastic litter pan lip appeared to be uncomfortable for her. To make it easier Charley created a low-sided, cardboard litter box which she covered with a large trash bag before adding the litter. She had extended the plastic beyond the box in all directions to catch the litter that flowed over the edges from Saatchi scratching to cover the spots she'd made before she had left it. Lowering it seemed to help her a little.

While she still enjoyed being petted, she didn't want Charley to handle her. That was new and totally contrary to what she had always enjoyed. As soon as Charley recognized it, she made a veterinary appointment for her in Santa Fe. However, having to manipulate her body to take her to it was problematic. Saatchi wouldn't enter the carrier through the front gate. Trying very carefully to wedge her in only hurt her, making her even more resistant. That left Charley with the only other option of picking her up to put her in the carrier through the top grate opening. Saatchi cried piteously as she did it. Choked with guilt, Charley had to reverse the process at the clinic to remove her for her examination when she wouldn't exit the carrier through its front gate.

There Dr. Carlie Klepach did radiographs of Saatchi's body which showed that her hips and elbow joints had been severely affected by arthritis, creating stiffness in her movement and decreased flexibility. Dr. Klepach prescribed gabapentin for her pain, glucosamine and chondroitin to be mixed into her food for cartilage repair, as well as medical acupuncture. Charley wasn't sure how she felt about acupuncture being useful for the cat. She wasn't sure she believed it was anything other than a placebo effect for humans. However, she was willing to try almost anything to reduce Saatchi's pain and improve her mobility.

But after her first treatment, Charley decided to hold off on further sessions because of Saatchi's resistance to the placement of the acupuncture needles. Despite their not penetrating her flesh deeply, they created enough irritation in her already uncomfortable body that she tried to attack them with her mouth. One needle landed in her mouth which required a quick response from the therapist. That was too close for comfort for Charley.

There was a myriad of treatments for cats with arthritis from which to choose, such as therapeutic joint exercises and hydrotherapy with an underwater treadmill. Charley decided to employ both. However, when a therapist carefully manipulated Saatchi's joints, the cat screamed in pain, biting and scratching anyone and anything as she tried to get away. When they tried having her walk on the underwater treadmill, she panicked. Limbs flying, plunging her momentarily under the surface, she soaked Charley as she desperately splashed, trying to latch on to the side of the tub to escape.

In this one circumstance, it was too bad Saatchi wasn't a dog. Being buoyed by water was helpful to those suffering from arthritis. She remembered a man who in 2012 created an Internet sensation when he was photographed taking his nineteen-year-old, severely-arthritic dog, who couldn't sleep because of his pain, to Lake Superior each evening to float in the water to lull the dog into slumber.

It took Charley a half-hour after each therapy session to calm the poor cat. Reluctantly acknowledging that Saatchi was not pleased with either therapy and harming herself further by exercising a panicky retreat, Charley considered adding another proposed approach to her pain med: therapeutic laser treatment.

Since it didn't involve her being jabbed, screaming in pain, her being nearly drowned, and further stressing her heart and joints in the process, it was acceptable to the cat. As long as no one moved her, she became cooperative. Charley was surprised that it even seemed to help a little. But given that Saatchi was on two treatments—pain med and laser—it was hard for Charley to determine which specific treatment was really working well or if they both were.

Upon investigation, Charley discovered that while no medical researchers apparently knew for sure why the laser therapy seemed to work, what it appeared to do was improve circulation and support cell health, release pain-fighting endorphins and reduce inflammation, and, perhaps, even encourage the growth of new healthy tissue. How much of that was wishful thinking Charley didn't know because there seemed no way to measure its positive effects on Saatchi or to distinguish its effect from everything else that was being done for her. Charley was not going to experiment to find out. Saatchi was feeling and doing better and that was all that mattered.

Ironically, what obviously seemed to help mostly was providing her with a soft-padded bed, a slowly-inclining ramp to reach higher surfaces, and raising her food and water dishes so she didn't have to bend over to reach them. When she still seemed somewhat distressed, Dr. Klepach increased her pain med dosage. But it wasn't long before she reached the point where nothing seemed to make her comfortable enough. Despite her having maxed out the gabapentin dosage and then having tried a Fentanyl patch, Saatchi had begun to moan and whimper. The moment Charley heard her agony, she acted.

With a knot in her gut as she held back torrents of tears, Charley grudgingly agreed with Dr. Klepach that her sweet fur child needed to be released to go over the Rainbow Bridge. Sleep had become nearly impossible and there was nothing that Saatchi was still enjoying, not even her favorite, pieces of deli roasted turkey Charley had purchased just for her.

Standing by her side, Charley stroked and spoke softly to Saatchi, reminding her she wasn't alone—her mom was with her; she was loved, and she would always be remembered for herself and her painting paw-print. As the vet administered her final injection, the light in Saatchi's eyes dimmed and her body went limp. Charley held and hugged her painting buddy and covered her with wet apologies for not having been able to save her from all her pain.

Charley had brought with her some plaster of Paris to make another impression of Saatchi's right front paw. As insensitive and inappropriate as Charley felt about what she was about to do was, she needed to make a new mold to replace the current rubber paw model which was becoming stiff and unwieldly from all the dry air and heat of New Mexico. At present there were numerous Amie's paintings that Charley had been working on that required the paw-print be added to her signature. She hadn't wanted to make the new cast while Saatchi was in so much discomfort and couldn't bear being moved even slightly.

While Charley had carefully saved the original mold for making a replacement whenever it was necessary, it no longer existed. That, however, was not the result of the dryness and heat. Instead, it was the result of one of Amie's rages where she had pulled open the drawer in the studio which contained the plaster cast and slammed it to the floor, shattering it the plaster to powder.

After having the animal clinic take care of Saatchi's cremation, Charley immediately sent the cast away to have a new rubber model made. Then when she received Saatchi's remains, Charley scattered her ashes where Amie's had already nourished the scarlet pine leaf penstemon, pink feathery apache plume, claret cup cactus, and carmine Indian paintbrush that embellished the property-line foothills.

Two months went by before Charley could finally get herself emotionally ready to look for another black, long-haired rescue kitten. One reason for adoption was for business. The public expected a Saatchi clone because she had always been Amie's companion at gallery shows, a participant in her instructional videos, and an integral part of any painting and new-product promotion. Her photo graced the website. That meant Charley would have to have her own picture taken with the new cat in the same pose as the early photo of Amie with the young Saatchi.

Also, Charley had been considering other cat-related projects. One thing she wanted to do was add an event in which younger children interested in art could participate. She thought a contest might fill the bill. The winner would receive painting lessons with "Amie." Each contestant would have to provide (1) a new name for the cat replacing Saatchi which was in keeping with her role as Amie's painting pal and (2) a very brief essay for why the youngster wanted the painting lessons.

However, in reality the primary reason for Charley wanting to adopt another kitten was her personal need for a feline companion. The pain of Little Bit and Saatchi's deaths still endured in Charley's heart. She wanted another fur child to love and grow old with. And not inconsequentially—something that was foremost in her thinking—was that her doing so was also saving another adoption-ignored black cat. For her and the cat that was a big win-win.

When she finally forced herself to visit the no-kill animal rescue shelter in Santa Fe, she found so many wonderful cats and kittens, who needed and wanted loving homes, from which to choose. Charley felt torn. So many of them appealed to her. But the sticking point was that she knew that at present she didn't have the time to devote to multiple cats, even though their being in her home and cared about individually by one person would be better than their being at the shelter and one of many.

In addition, she told herself if she had more, she couldn't keep track of all of them, that multiple cats would always want to explore what was on the other side of the front door. When people came to her home for painting lessons, that would give the cats the opportunity to try to break free and explore, which would put them at risk. Outside, she lectured herself, there were all manner of dangers represented by humans, vehicles, insects, plants, poisonous reptiles, dogs, and wild animals. At least, that was her current justification for not giving in to their hopeful anticipation. At the moment, she had to remind herself, she was at the shelter for one reason only: to find a replacement for Saatchi.

Charley found it so sad to contemplate that there would always be a replacement for Saatchi available because so many people were either superstitious of or biased about black cats and kittens. At kill shelters they were among the first to be euthanized and the last to be adopted, if at all. That hurt her soul. At this moment she wanted to be their Mother Teresa, to rescue and love them all—outside risks be damned—but remembered what the missionary-turned-saint had said.

"It's not about how much you do, but how much love you put into what you do that counts."

When she spotted a long-haired black kitten, it had thin legs and an enlarged abdomen. Charley knew what that meant. Her distended belly was full of worms which were sapping the kitten's food energy, leaving her body malnourished. As disgusting as the feline's visiting internal parasites were, that was hardly a reason to bypass this under-weight and lethargic kitten. They could readily be eliminated. Being an acknowledged patsy, especially for disadvantaged black cats, she readily adopted her.

However, rather than buy a de-worming product off the shelf, she would have Dr. Klepach take care of the procedure. It was better to have the vet gauge what to use and how much of it she needed to de-worm the baby. Furthermore, the vet needed to check out and address any other problems the kitten might have.

Temporarily-named "Saatchi Two," the kitten's test for feline leukemia was negative which pleased Charley. She had seen some FeLV-positive cats suffer terribly with respiratory difficulties, anemia, or lymphoma when the virus became active. Some didn't live long as a result while others overcame it or shed the disease and prospered. It was a potentially-lethal crap shoot for cats, one for which Saatchi Two had happily rolled a seven on her first throw.

Shortly after going home with Charley and on a regimen of special nutrition, the kitten's abdomen shrank and her body began to fill out properly. When she was healthy at last, she was bright-eyed and much happier and more frolicsome without her former meal-sucking companions. Pleased, Charley ran a number of names past her. "Saatchi Two" wouldn't do; it didn't suit her. But when her new kitty mom said "Sushi," the kitten meowed and patted her pantleg.

Getting stronger by the day, she began leaping around. If Charley hadn't known for sure Sushi was a cat, she would have thought her more likely a kangaroo or gazelle hybrid. For her everything begged to be explored. Everything was bright, new, and shiny. Everything delighted her.

Now Charley wasn't the only one with a switched name. Sushi essentially would become a "Saatchi" clone in-name-only to most of Amie's fans. And then she would also become whatever the contest winner named her. Sushi didn't seem to care. She had no doubts about who she really was. She'd respond to "Saatchi" as well if she had to. That is, when her kitty mom took her to gallery or other art gatherings.

Soon Charley would announce the kitten naming and essay contest for children aged six to seven. Broadcast on flyers and Amie's website, it was a big success, drawing nearly a hundred entries with all manner of names provided, from the commonplace of "Ebony," "Charcoal," "Licorice," and "Midnight," to the more unusual of "Saatcharino" to "Crunchy Black," stage name of an American rapper and Hype man, and lots of duplications. Surprisingly, there was even one vote each for the southeastern European country "Montenegro" and the Greek personification of primeval darkness, "Erebos." Those surprised Charley and made her wonder if adults, who hadn't quite gotten with the program, had submitted those for their children. Some suggestions for the name made Charley cringe. Those she didn't share with Sushi. And others which tickled her made her guffaw. Those Sushi got to enjoy as well, sitting on Charley's lap, pawing at the entries.

After all the contest slips had been turned in, Charley looked at the stated ages for their creativity in both the cat names and reasons for wanting lessons. The one that not only captured her heart but also made her cry was from a six-year-old named Wynton. Cleverly he had also incorporated Saatchi's name. He wanted to call the kitten "Saatchmo" for his deceased father who professionally played the trumpet. The reason he wanted the painting lessons was so he could finish the beautiful paintings his mother hadn't been able to complete because she too had died.

When Charley fact-checked his woeful story to make sure it was true, she discovered that his parents had passed away recently in a small commuter plane crash in Anchorage, Alaska, where they were going to pick up an adopted baby sister for Wynton. He was currently living with his godparents, just off Old Las Vegas Highway, and would stay with them. So "Saatchmo" it was for Sushi's cat-paw-print promotional name.

It was time to proclaim the winner.

"Congratulations, Wynton!"

Saatchmo's photo was displayed everywhere along with Wynton's. Charley made sure it was even in the papers, on PBS station's local news, and on local broadcast news. For the big photographic celebration Wynton wore his Sunday best, even with a necktie, and held his five-year painting lessons' certificate above his head with pride. Saatchmo, sitting on the stool beside him as he smiled, lifted her whiskers for the camera.

After that, at galleries and art-related events the cat was on display in person. But unlike the original Saatchi, Sushi loved the crowds and attention. Such that there were times when she would hop off her stool to do her own feline version of a quasi-Michael Jackson moon walk to get their attention and, maybe, some well-deserved petting. She was becoming a real ham. Just observing her, one could tell she knew that Charley and her public reveled in it.

Things went along smoothly for about a year as Charley's own paintings were attracting attention. She presented them *as if* they were a new line of paintings by Amie without actually stating it as such. They bore the new signature of "Mana." At first, she had considered presenting them as having been done by one of Amie's protégés, but the accounting on it would have been complicated to work out, especially at tax time regarding who was being paid from their sales as documented by their Social Security number.

Charley had decided that these Mana paintings didn't fit within the parameters of her promise to Amie. They didn't have Amie's signature and they weren't in Amie's style or on her topics. Moreover, Saatchmo didn't sign them, though Sushi showed she was more than eager to do so if only given the opportunity.

In the meantime, Sushi was growing into a gorgeous, affectionate green-eyed cat who still bounced around, showing her perpetual joie de vivre. She even relished having her photo taken, something which Saatchi had always shunned, turning her backside to the camera. Whenever that had happened, Charley had to laugh.

"At least," she snickered, "Saatchi has had the good grace to never raise her tail when the camera snapped her picture."

Charley was also spending a good deal of her time now instructing in-studio classes in abstract painting with brush or palette knife, with and without the use of computer modeling. By now, she also had a large following of children as a result of the contest. She was having success in getting the works of some of the more promising students into shows at regional events, having their works hung on the walls of local businesses, especially restaurants and banks, and on display in a special section created just for them at some of the local galleries.

However, she made a point of making sure that *all* of her students' artwork, irrespective of their current level of skill, was being displayed somewhere in public, like at the Benison-police co-operative second annual art event in the park. She wanted everyone to be able to see them and have the students feel they were being recognized for what they'd done. The children took great pleasure in being seen and appreciated, often dragging friends and relatives to view them where they were proudly being hung.

Gradually Charley, who was really a Bostonian at heart, was becoming a Santa Fean in spite of her not having been born there. Many things were evolving and changing … but, as it turned out, not necessarily for the best.

30

Out of the blue a disturbing email arrived on Amie's computer from Amie's cousin Davy. They hadn't been in touch since they were youngsters. As a result, he had had to trace her via the Internet. Ostensibly, he said he was writing to her to let her know that his father, Amie's Uncle Tad, had died of Huntington's.

"It was horrible," he said. "He had suffered for such a long time, unable to move on his own, speak, or eat. I guess that was like your dad before he died. 'The Unspeakable Disease' was always the big secret in our family, something we never talked about openly, even as we watched it ravish the family. When Dad died, I decided I had better get tested. I didn't want to spend the rest of my life worrying about it, thinking each odd movement or thought might be the start of the disease.

"I'm a corporate chief operating officer with Morgan-Saks Investment Bank so I wanted to have an idea how long my career might be. Also, I wanted to have an idea what further I needed to do, besides what I have already done, to protect my family's future. Maybe you can imagine how I felt when I received the results earlier this week which showed that I am carrying the gene for it too.

"When Dad died, I immediately thought of you and how it must have been when your dad died. I'm writing to let you know that if you haven't been tested, you can be. It's very easy to do. It can help you plan the rest of your life and, if you're lucky, get rid of the fear of having 'the family plague.'

"But, mostly, I'm writing because I'm thinking about starting up an information page on 'ourancestors.com' to explore our family's Huntington's heritage. It shouldn't be a secret anymore. I haven't run it past Mom yet. I have some information on granddad, my dad, your dad, Uncle Steve, and Aunt Edith. Would you be interested in being involved in this?"

Charley felt an explosion of palpitations. She realized that this could be big trouble for Amie. She hadn't wanted anyone to know of her familial linkage with the disease, not in *any* remotely conceivable way. Once Davy made their respective fathers' health details available, it would become public knowledge because of the construction of "ourancestors.com" family tree, whether she as Amie participated or not. Even if Amie weren't acknowledged as having Huntington's, there was the mere association with the disease which had always frightened her.

Charley would have to contact Davy right away and try to persuade him to rethink his genealogical plan. She would have to try to convince him to forget it by showing the dangers of having that information made public and the benefits of not doing so.

As the protector of Amie's legacy, Charley made a list of what she considered reasons not to reveal such facts. It was mostly reminding him that those kinds of particulars could be deleterious to his banking position *and* his family. After considering it for an hour, she knew she had to reach him right away. Since he had included his phone number, she decided to call him instead of emailing him.

"Hi, Davy. It's Amie."

"Oh, hi. This is a surprise."

"I'm glad to hear from you after all this time. But I'm so sorry about your dad." Then hoping she was saying the right things, she continued, "He was a good guy. I really liked him."

"Thanks."

"I'm wondering if making our family's Huntington's history public is such a good idea."

"Why is that?"

"From what I've read, most people know little or nothing about Huntington's but have hear that it's bad, a terrible, crippling death sentence. After seeing the Ken Burns' PBS program, *The Gene,* viewers know how the disease destroys the brain, creating great difficulty controlling their body movement for doing the most basic life tasks. The segment on the small village of Barranquitas in Venezuela, with the highest concentration of Huntington's cases in the world, no doubt shocked people by showing how incredibly bad it could be."

"Yeah, I saw it. But they showed only the worst examples of it."

"No, just more of them. Just think how bad your dad's case was. My dad's case was equally bad. The point is that others knowing someone is positive for such a horrible gene could cause them to assume the very worst about that person's future."

"Why would they?"

"Because to the uninformed that suggests a guaranteed, drawn-out death sentence."

"You don't know that."

"I've read psychological research that strongly suggests it. Even if you never developed an observable clinical manifestation of the disease, or a minor one, anyone who knows about your having the gene might be concerned about what you will be able to do over time."

"Like who?"

"Like the banking and investments firm for which you work, for example."

"Come on!"

"Their knowing that your brain could turn to mush might make them worry about your continuing to work for them."

"That's ridiculous."

"You know how even smart people can make invalid assumptions and jump to conclusions."

"That's nuts. I've been with them for fifteen years and devoted myself to them. I've always provided high level of operational professionalism. They need me."

"I'm sure they do ... now. But a bank's bottom line will always come first."

"For chrissakes, Amie. They are smarter than that. Besides they'd want to be careful about being sued for discrimination."

"When it comes to a potentially performance-challenging health problem, they could find other ways to protect themselves."

"Like what?"

"Like giving you early retirement."

"That would be bad for their public relations."

"But only if you pursued it publicly."

"Come on, Amie. That's such shit!"

"Davy, I'm just telling you that there's been a lot of documented discrimination regarding Huntington's. Not only social but also medical. Consider that your firm's health insurance company might not want to continue to cover you if they knew you *could* require lots of long-term expensive medical assistance as you developed the disease."

"They can't just drop me."

"I wouldn't count on that. As you've undoubtedly heard, 'pre-existing conditions' have become a political football, about whether to cover them or not. Once a person tests and learns he or she has the Huntington's gene, that person has, by definition, a 'pre-existing condition.' Once that's made public, like on the Internet, it wouldn't matter if you never showed any really bad symptoms of the disease."

"Well, I have read that some politicians don't want to continue to include health insurance coverage for 'pre-existing diseases.' But that's stupid since at least half or more of the U.S. population has some sort of 'pre-existing' condition, like hypertension, diabetes, asthma, arthritis, etc."

"I agree. It's also important to note that making your gene status public could affect your family's health care coverage. Since each of your children has, by definition, a fifty-fifty chance of developing the disease, that could stigmatize them and potentially harm them psychologically and, ultimately, financially."

"But it's only 'ourancestors.com,' Amie."

"Yeah, but millions upon millions of people access it. Information gets around. As for me, Davy, I do not want people to know about my familial association with the disease. It could negatively impact me."

"I think you're overly dramatizing this … but, I hear you. I'll give it some thought and get back to you on it."

The question now was how would Davy respond. Charley thought it unlikely that his mother would want what he said had long been a "big secret" in his family to be aired in public. She undoubtedly had a sense about how people would react to it. Even though Davy had been enthusiastic, she hoped that some of the possible consequences she had provided would cause his enthusiasm to wane. He hadn't really considered how something so seemingly trivial could affect his work, his family's life, as well as Amie's.

For some reason he seemed to believe that people would be more knowledgeable, understanding, and willing to accept his pre-dispositional genetic status and its implications with equanimity. From all Charley had read about it over the years, she thought he was gravely mistaken.

Six days went by before Davy responded by phone. He said that he had reconsidered announcing his and his relatives' Huntington's status on "ourancestors.com" or anyplace else.

"While I still don't think you're right in general, I did read an article about health insurance and pre-existing conditions. As you suggested, just having the gene is considered the same as having the disease itself. I don't want to do anything to risk our losing our health insurance over this. Besides, I sort of mentioned it to Mom and got a very definite 'no' response."

Charley thought that was a wise move and was so relieved.

"Thanks, Davy. One last thought. If you are still considering having our family's genealogy on 'ourancestors.com' anyway, please remember that other relatives may respond to what you put in our tree—and what's their family tree as well—with their own information page about our family's Huntington's heritage. I don't know how likely that would be. Others may not be as circumspect about it as you would want them to be. It's possible that could be just as bad as your announcing it there yourself."

Davy sounded deflated. "You know, not everyone puts additional information on their family tree even though they're given the space to do so."

"Do what you think is right. However, I don't want to be associated with it at all or mentioned as a relative in any way."

"I'll give it some more thought. I didn't think it was going to be such a big deal."

"Either way, let's keep in touch so I can know how you're doing."

Sighing deeply, Charley came away from Davy's call feeling that nearly rubbing elbows with Amie's being outed on "ourancestors.com" had been too close for comfort. However, in the meanwhile, she would keep her fingers crossed that if any of Amie's relatives should ever go the genealogy route that they would skip any health annotations on their family tree. Some actions have serious consequences and implications. She felt there was a lot to be said for carefully maintaining some personal privacy on the Internet.

31

Everything seemed to be going somewhat smoothly as the months sped by. She had agreed to having fine art reproductions of Amie's paintings which would be another profitable income stream. The original coffee table book of Amie's paintings had been finished was still selling well. While it had taken nine months' gestation to be born, the final publication was gorgeous, with full-color, beautifully rendered photographs of each of her pieces. And because of the popularity of Saatchmo, she had decided to do a separate book on him and Wynton for children. A small section of the first coffee table book had been dedicated to the original Saatchi which included photos and a biography.

Charley's own paintings were gathering more and more fans. The website had become so busy that she had hired an off-site computer technician to act as webmaster. Her website designer, Geoff, was frequently designing new pages of photos of new products and paintings for her webmaster to upload. She also hired her young painting students who wanted after-school jobs to handle the processing and shipping of all the items sold, except for the paintings.

Now most of Amie's inventory, aside from the paintings which needed environmental control, were ensconced in a nearby rented storage unit. Moreover, when enough people demanded t-shirts with Amie's most popular paintings on them, she began having those made up as well. Originally only available on her website, they were now also available on the "ecoart.com" catalogue website which was associated with public broadcasting.

Much to Charley's delight, everything with Tony was moving along nicely as well. Despite his being in the police, he wasn't as authoritarian as Charley had at first feared, even with his sympathetic story about his sister. Like Amie, she valued freedom and flexibility over dogmatism and inflexibility. To her pleasant surprise, he was actually sensitive, kind, and democratic in his attitudes and beliefs which especially revealed itself in his painting.

He had continued his lessons with her and was progressing, as was young Wynton. Charley could see Tony had talent as well as his many other attributes. His vision and unique painting style intrigued and impressed her. It was a contradictory combination of the flurried brush strokes and play of light of Impressionism with the vivid colors, simplified shapes, and gestural marks of emotion of German Expressionism. She had no idea how he accomplished that antithetical melding. Some of his works were hung in the State House, informally known as "the Roundhouse," where they were getting a lot of attention. In addition, she anticipated promoting and selling his paintings along with her own and Amie's on Amie's website.

Recently, while they were cuddled on her sofa, watching the end of the DVD of James Garner's 1985 classic, *Murphy's Romance*, the lyrics of the theme song echoed in her ears as the credits rolled: "He kissed me like a lover and loved me like a friend." Charley resonated to that. It spoke to her as a relationship ideal. Just then Tony moved Sushi, who was snuggled on his lap, to put his arm around Charley. Looking into her eyes, he grinned and asked an unexpected question.

"You know I'm retiring in about a year? I've been thinking about starting afresh with a new game plan. What would you think if I asked you to consider my becoming a painting partner and active in some part of your current or expanded business?"

Smiling broadly, Charley said, "Hmmm, I think I'd take it under advisement. You're already a well-respected painter and painting partner. Ask me again when you retire. But, in the meantime," she winked at him, "we can roll the idea around a little."

With that they grabbed their wine glasses and retired for the evening, to explore that and other things. They were followed by Sushi who was not about to be left out of their nighttime activities.

32

Despite her young age, Sushi's health had begun to strangely decline. The situation was depressingly occupying Charley's mind as she tried to keep all other aspects of her life in balance. Nearly finished with her shopping in Santa Fe on this glaringly bright, roasting summer's day, she had paused in front of the plate glass window of the Alameda Pharmacy on Galisteo Street to consider what else she might need to get. She wanted to hurry so she could return to her painting and her sick cat as quickly as possible. But then suddenly everything was turned upside down.

She felt something small, hard, and circular thrust into the middle of her back. Momentarily stunned, she couldn't wrap her mind around what was occurring.

"Don't move!" came a squeaky voice from what sounded like a youngster close to her.

She shuddered. Reflected in the glass now were two short, skinny late-adolescents wearing black acrylic ski masks, black t-shirts, and low-slung pants, standing mere inches behind her. Squelching the impulse to turn around, she held her breath and waited.

In semi-pubescent voices the two whispered to one another about what they were supposed to do next and exactly how they were supposed to do it. The knitted masks which clung tightly to their faces, covering all but their eyes and mouths, restricted their facial muscle movement, and muffled their words. But one thing was clear to Charley from what they mumbled. They were about to rob her. And not for chump change. Instead, they were expecting to extract a sizable chunk of money from her.

Money? she thought, examining the situation and its possible consequences. She mentally shook her head. Why in the world would they think *I* had any money? Have they taken a good look at what I'm wearing? Even though it isn't frayed or replete with holes, it could have come from a 1960's secondhand store. I don't have any wealth-oriented status symbols on display to tantalize them. No diamonds, furs, gold, signature-styled designer shoes or handbag, or a flashy car. And, surely, they don't know who I am. They will be sorely disappointed with the few singles I'm carrying. Uh oh! Will their failure to achieve their goal put me in more physical danger?

Seconds ticked by as she continued to observe their reflection in the drugstore window. It was then she noted that one of the potential robbers was holding an iPhone and attempting to film every nuance of the dramatic encounter. Great, she ruminated, I hope this won't turn into a neo-noir crime drama like *Dog Day Afternoon*, with first-time robbers mucking up everything and taking hostages.

"Don't move, lady, if you want to live," squeaked the voice directly behind her with the gun.

His partner sniffed and snickered as he moved around her to get a shot of the frightened victim's face. But she looked more puzzled than scared.

"This is your big day. Fork over two hundred dollars in cash and you'll see the sunrise tomorrow." His partner sniffed and chuckled as he moved around again to re-line up the shot.

All Charley could think of was that he was attempting to impersonate the ruthless, psychotic robber and killer James Cagney in the 1949 *White Heat*, though she suspected he had never seen, or even heard of, the crime film classic much less of the starring actor. The changing voice of the one with the gun was getting in the way of his successfully masquerading as a tough and experienced gangster.

"Sorry, fellows, but I don't have anything like that kind of cash on me. Let me show you. I'm afraid you've picked the wrong victim."

Once again, she mentally shook her head at these two John Dillinger wannabes. Opening her wallet to show them, she waited until they decided what to do next.

The filming partner looked around and noticed that people across the street who had been looking in shop windows under the pale green awnings were now beginning to turn, stop, and stare at them. It seemed to have skipped their minds that they were attempting this theft on a public street in broad daylight. Scratching his sweaty, itchy chin, he whispered into James Cagney's ear.

"Shit! What do we do now?"

"Wait a minute. Let me think."

Minutes passed. Charley was getting annoyed with this elementary-school theatrical performance. In the pharmacy's glass she could see the gunslinger looking up and down the sidewalk.

"Okay," he said, nodding, "it looks like there's an ATM in the front of the handbag store two doors down." He pointed with his free hand because his partner was continuing to scan the general neighborhood. "We'll have her get the cash from it."

They nodded in concert. It was going to work after all. They snorted in relief, high-fived, and accompanied Charley to the ATM.

Outside the glass-fronted shop, past its glass door, they stared blindly at the ATM screen and the keyboard. The primary robber made his demand.

"Get the two hundred dollars for us here. And don't do anything funny. We're watching your every move."

As if showing concern for them, Charley said, "You know that the ATM takes videos of everyone using it. So, if I could get the money here, you'd have your mug shots taken by it for the police."

Being anywhere between twelve and fifteen respectively, the would-be robbers shifted their bodies and looked at the screen and its instructions. They showed some concern about possibly being identified and captured because of the ATM's recording them. The videographer was tugging at his mask to scratch his cheek as his gun-toting partner looked around the street and into the leather goods store. While they wanted a video of themselves pulling this off, they didn't want it via an ATM.

As they chewed over what to do, sniffing, they seemed to forget that their wearing their balaclavas would probably make them unrecognizable. Furthermore, in their consternation they were also unaware that more people on the street and in the shop were taking notice of their behavior, but apparently unable to decide if this were some street performance or, maybe, something else. The ambiguity of the situation seemed to glue these observers right where they stood, leaving them conflicted. As a result, they did nothing but watch.

"Well," the thief with the gun hypothesized, "maybe if only one of us is behind you and the other is at the side, the video wouldn't catch us."

"Okay," she concurred and began to search her handbag. "Uh-oh. We have a problem. I don't have an ATM card for this bank."

"Are you shitting us? Well, fuck it!" exclaimed the one with the gun.

His videographer shook his head.

"Fuckin' A. Our plan is in the crapper. Why didn't you think of this?"

"Why didn't you, you moron. You're the one who wanted to do this in the first place. Get ourselves millions of likes on YouTube. Christ! Do I have to think of everything?"

It was obvious to Charley from their squabbling that neither one of these "Most Wanted" post-office-poster-masterminds knew that if you had a debit card from one bank, you might be able to withdraw cash at another bank's ATM because banks were often part of a network that provided that convenient service. Maybe she was lucking out, so far. Even though this was a risky situation, Charley felt like laughing. She had been wallowing in the waters of despondency for some time since Sushi had begun to develop seizures.

Her first witnessed convulsion had been a shock. As it tapered off, Charley had rushed her to the vet as an emergency. There Sushi received a prescription for a phenobarbital regimen and a follow-up appointment. While the medication seemed to help a little, Charley noticed that Sushi's gait was becoming unsteady. Following that were loud noises, suggesting she was in constant pain whenever she tried to lie down.

It was back to the animal hospital where Dr. Klepach manually detected a tumor on her back. When x-rayed, it revealed what appeared to be osteosarcoma of her vertebrae. The vet said that the seizures were likely related to the tumor's location, that it had invaded the spinal canal and was severely compressing the spinal cord. To be sure of the diagnosis, a sonographer would explore it further and do fine needle aspirations of the tumor cells which a pathologist would then examine under a microscope.

Days later the analysis was that it was, indeed, an osteosarcoma. In a week's time a surgical oncologist performed the very delicate procedure to remove as much of the tumor as was possible, given the tumor's location, and that it had developed adhesions to the spinal cord. That meant some of the tumor remained.

"If only the osteosarcoma had been in one of Sushi's legs, as is frequently the case," Dr. Klepach told Charley, "we could have amputated that leg and saved her life because these tumors rarely metastasize in cats. If a cat, or a dog, were unfortunate enough to develop any malignancy, this is the better one to have. While it sounds awful, leg amputation is considered the Gold Standard for eliminating this cancer, allowing the animal to go on to have a long and happy life."

Despite the rarity of metastasis, Sushi's cancer had spread to her lungs, perhaps because of the location of the original tumor. As a result, chemotherapy followed. The cat acted like a trooper, patiently accommodating to the toxic chemicals and their side effects. However, within a few weeks she had begun coughing, losing weight, and becoming lethargic. Her bouncy behavior had become a thing of the past.

As Sushi was dematerializing before her human's eyes no matter what she and the vet tried, Charley felt she had been like a jinx for all these sweet cats that she had taken under her protection. She adopted them and they developed painful conditions, being forced to go over the Rainbow Bridge before their allotted time.

Notwithstanding her being on various strong pain medications, Sushi's pain was becoming excruciating. Charley begged the vet for the dosages to be maxed out.

"Depending upon the pain med used," said Dr. Klepach, "if it were strong enough to actually alleviate her extreme pain, she would likely be sedated all the time or have her breathing depressed."

That meant that Sushi would have been left "alive" quantitatively but not able to experience *any* part of her life qualitatively. That would be cruel because it didn't benefit anyone—not Charley or Tony, and certainly not Sushi.

Charley had an appointment with the vet for later that day, after this pathetic robbery attempt was stifled, to say a final good-bye to her beloved cat. Consequently, she discovered she couldn't quite feel afraid of these two delinquents. And, if it weren't for the gun, she thought, she would simply have walked away to spend Sushi's last hours with her.

Unlike moments in years past, despite her despair now, she wasn't flirting with serious depression, and certainly not contemplating suicide. Indeed, she had no inclination to fling herself off a several-story building or lie down in a water-gushing arroyo. Now she knew she had too much to live for in spite of her grief about her current feline love ... and her repeated sense of cat loss.

There in the center of Santa Fe, where she could be killed as the result of some addlepated teenager's whim, she was not about to take that chance. With her luck that underage bozo would shoot her in her painting arm making it nonfunctional or in her leg's femoral artery, causing her either to exsanguinate on the sidewalk or have to have her limb amputated because of significant but non-lethal blood loss. While she didn't savor death, she didn't welcome any of these two lesser options either.

Exasperated, the two stopped bickering long enough to inquire.

"So where is *your* bank?"

"It's about ten miles away."

With slumping shoulders demonstrating their thwarted desires, they muttered in unison.

"Shit! Shit! Shit!"

Apparently, the probability of one not having local access to a bank less far away hadn't entered into their thinking.

Touching his face to feel the now dripping sweat, the armed desperado appeared to recall that he's wearing a mask. He shifted the fabric with his free hand. His partner was pushing his mask up to wipe the wetness from around his mouth. They both seemed to be considering what they should do at this point. They could take off their masks and be recognizable or continue to wear them to keep their identities hidden but publicly continue to draw attention to themselves, as they oozed un-gangster-like sweat. It didn't appear to occur to them that they might also be continuing to risk heat prostration in this day's sweltering temperature.

"What do you think about the masks?" he asked his filming partner.

"The video needs us to act like real criminals. Real criminals wouldn't take their masks off. But we're boiling in these things."

His partner nodded in agreement.

The gun-toting thief turned around to look at his camera operator.

"So, I guess we keep them on for a while longer."

Then he turned to Charley and sniffed.

"Okay, lady, we aren't going to have you drive us to your bank. It would take too long. But you must have cash as your house. You can take us there."

"Actually, I don't keep cash there. Besides, you don't want to go to my house."

"Oh, yeah? Why's that?"

"My dog, 'Sweety Pie,' is a Rottweiler who doesn't like strangers. He gets very angry when they appear on his property. He broke through the screen door last week to try to savagely maul two Jehovah's Witnesses who came around. Blood and pamphlets were everywhere. It wouldn't be safe for you to show up even if I had any money there. Besides, I don't want you to hurt my dog."

The two became highly distressed. The videographer turned off his iPhone.

"Fuck it, Walter! This isn't working out how we planned. This isn't going to be our great crime documentary after all."

"Dammit, Donny! Don't use my name."

Donny quickly responded aloud for everyone around them to hear.

"Uh, Walter isn't his real name. It's his *code* name."

"Jesus, Donny! Shut the fuck up and let me think."

Charley could see they were getting even more anxious and angry. She didn't want them to do something even more stupid and dangerous because of their increasing stress.

"I have an idea that could work," she shared. "My business partner is on her way to the bank right now to deposit some money. It's close to five hundred dollars."

"No shit?"

"No shit. I could have her bring it to you instead. Would that kind of a haul work for you?"

She glanced at them for agreement. They smiled broadly behind their balaclavas and each stood a little taller as if they were given the opportunity to breathe new life into their plan for their desired YouTube stardom.

"I take that as a 'yes'?"

They both nodded with eagerness.

"Okay then. That means I'll have to call her to get her back here before she reaches the bank."

"Five hundred dollars? Jesus Christ! That's more than we could have hoped for. Hell, yeah, call her."

"But," Walter paused as if trying to remember what those who pull off hold-ups always say on TV crime dramas, "Oh, yeah. Don't do anything cute. We're going to be listening."

They nodded to one another again as Charley pulled her cell phone out of her tunic pocket and pressed the number.

"Hi, Linda, this is Amie. No, things are not okay. I'm in town with two robbers who have a gun on me. Yeah, I know, really. They want the five hundred dollars that you're taking to the bank for us. Uh-huh. Where are you now? Good. Well, can you turn around and meet us? What? Hold on a second." She paused her call to ask them something, "She wants to know if after she gives you the money that you're demanding that you'll promise not to hurt her or me?"

They looked at each other and Walter replied, "Why the fuck should we?"

"Should we what?" asked Donny. "Promise or hurt them?"

"Stupid. Of course, I meant 'why should we hurt them.' God, what an asshole."

"Who me? Or them?" Donny asked.

Walter rolled his eyes.

"Look," addressing Charley, "tell her we just want the money for our   video."

Charley, looked up as if beseeching God to give her strength, and spoke into the phone again.

"Promise. No harm. It's just the money. They're ransoming me as part of a crime video they're creating. Okay, can you meet us in the parking lot at 777 Bishops Lodge Road at the far-right end as soon as possible. We can be there in about seven or eight minutes. How about you? That's good. Okay. Please don't make us wait too long. These are two determined, dangerous criminals."

Charley could see the two of them smile behind their balaclavas at her labelling them "dangerous criminals," what they so wanted to think themselves to be.

It took Charley ten minutes to arrive at the lot. When she pulled in, there was another car, a silver Toyota sedan, at the far end with someone in it who looked to be female. Charley honked, parked next to the sedan, and alighted. Slowly Linda exited her car to meet her "business partner."

The instant both were free from the cars, Tony and three police officers, including Officer Linda McAllister, surrounded Amie's vehicle with weapons drawn.

They shouted, "Drop the gun. Hands up. Get out of the car slowly. Keep your hands in front of you."

Unbeknownst to the robbers, they were parked at the nearest sheriff's satellite station. Walter and Donny were furious about the outcome, swearing, and assigning blame to each other for this snafu as they sat in the back seat, unmoving except for raising their hands. Something dropped.

"Fucking Christ! You goddamn ass-hole bastard! Motherfucking stupid shit!"

"Put a sock in it!" interrupted Linda brusquely as she began pulling the still unmoving Donny out of the car in order to handcuff him while Walter glared and grumbled behind him.

"The bitch lied to us and ruined everything."

"Now," said Donny, with a whimper, "we can't finish our crime video. How will anyone know how we pulled off our brilliant robbery?"

Walter just shook his head as Donny tried to evade the handcuffs to reach back to grab for his iPhone which lay on the back seat. It contained what they thought of as their "riveting Scorsese dramatic footage." With Donny cuffed Officer Mc Allister confiscated the phone. As Tony pulled out Walter and patted him down, he found no weapon on his person. But then he spotted a yellow marker that Walter he had used as a gun muzzle which lay on the backseat floor. Handing off a cuffed Walter and the "gun" to other officers, Tony put his arm around Charley. After giving the robber-kidnappers their Miranda rights, the officers convoyed the handcuffed pair away.

"Thanks for your help, Linda," Charley called to the disappearing officer.

"Anytime," Linda answered as she raised a hand of acknowledgment, "I like a little cabaret now and then," as she continued into the station.

Then Charley nudged Tony to remind him.

"Glad Linda called you to come by too. Today is the day …," she paused to stifle a sob, "that Sushi has to go to the vet."

He nodded dispiritedly. It was something he hadn't wanted to remember. He and Sushi had grown very attached to each other. Before Sushi had become so extremely ill, whenever Tony visited Charley, she had always welcomed him at the door with a leap into his arms. As soon as he gave her a big pet and put her down, she followed him around. And the moment he sat down, no matter where it was, which included in the bathroom, she was in his lap, on her back, awaiting his special brand of tummy rubbing. It made Charley happy that Sushi received so much attention from Tony.

Squeezing Charley's shoulders, Tony said softly, "Let's go get her."

Together in her car, they drove to Charley's house, picked Sushi up in a large fluffy towel which Tony lay on his lap in the car, gently stroking her, and accompanied her to her last appointment.

Later that week, still trying not to let tears run down her grief-inflamed cheeks, Charley forced herself to visit the no-kill cat shelter to find another overlooked black kitten. When they spotted each other, she didn't need to think twice about it. They would be alter-egos. Unless someone asked specifically if this were a new cat, she decided not to broadcast that the first "Saatchmo" had died.

Immediately, she called him "Saatchmo," "Saatch" for short, for Wynton's winning name. As she pampered her new housemate, Charley hoped she could somehow spare this fur kid the bad luck her other cats seemed to have had. Cuddling the long-haired baby who gazed up at her with vibrant blue eyes, filled with the passion of curiosity, she remembered a quotation she kept close to her heart and always resonated to when contemplating adopting a needy cat:

"Saving one cat will not change the world, but for that one cat … the world will change forever."

If only, she sighed, she could provide that change for all the needy black cats.

33

Over time, Charley recognized that she had been Amie for so long that she had nearly forgotten how it felt to be Charley. It was only when she re-dyed her red hair brunette and re-cut it that it vaguely occurred to her. It was almost as if Charley had been reincarnated into Amie. Occasionally, a healthy Amie appeared in her dreams to check on Charley and how her life and the business were going, critiquing them where necessary. Charley was always so glad to see her, having so much to share with her. Sitting in her lap was the original hearty Saatchi looking on, taking it all in. Typically, she listened and licked her right front paw to show her approval of whatever was said or groomed her nether region to show her disapproval of it.

Then, one night after a week's hiatus of Amie dreams, Amie re-appeared to Charley, looking distraught.

"I want you to be aware. To be careful. There's danger on the prowl."

Even Saatchi who seemed to mimic Amie's wrinkled brow, looked ill at ease. Their presence lasted less than a minute but left Charley awake, feeling sweaty and uneasy, with a pulse rate of ninety-seven. Saatch, who had been curled under her chin, looked up at her with distress.

Sitting up in bed alone, she tried to construe what the dream could mean. Tony hadn't stayed over that night, though he normally did. He had become a caring fixture. However, his elderly mother in Farmington, about two hundred miles northwest of Santa Fe, was moving into an assisted-living home for active seniors and he wanted to make the emotional and physical transition for her as smooth and comfortable as possible. That was one of the things Charley liked about Tony: his compassion and empathy.

In a way, Charley thought his not being there to witness her distress was fortunate because she had no idea how she could explain the dream to him. It wasn't that he'd doubt or ridicule her but she knew it sounded flakey unless she could tie it to something. Saatch pawed her and softly meowed for them to go back to sleep. Charley snuggled the growing kitten into her arms and lay back down, though sleep came only sporadically as the waves of agitation rose and dipped.

The dream stayed in the back of her mind all morning after she got up and as she went about her chores. It was probably nothing yet it badgered her, exacerbating her anxiety. She told herself firmly that she should forget it. Then the post arrived.

Among the mail orders, gallery brochures, EcoArt's product ad masters, and supermarket flyers was a professional-looking letter with the return address of Penitentiary of New Mexico, which was just fifteen miles south of central Santa Fe. It was from a Dr. Daye, the prison psychiatrist.

"Ms. Benison:

"I have been Ronald Shelton's psychiatrist while he has been incarcerated in the Penitentiary of New Mexico. Mr. Shelton is being released early on parole, for good behavior, on July 25, in spite of my recommendations to the parole board to the contrary.

"In our sessions he spoke repeatedly about you. Initially it was about his love for you, but it quickly changed to angry rantings about 'your flagrant rejection' of him. Over the last three years, his rage has been accompanied by increasingly violent fantasies about extreme harm he wants to inflict upon you. Consequently, I feel he is even more a danger to you now than he was before.

"In keeping with the 1989 Supreme Court of New Mexico's 1989 'Wilschinsky v. Medina' Decision, like California's 1976 'Tarasoff Decision,' it is my mandated-by-statute duty to warn you, as an actual as well as a potential victim, that there is a very real risk to you of lethal violence from Mr. Shelton.

"His delusion now is that you never really cared, were always leading him on until you could reject him publicly. He sees himself as the innocent victim, that he was too loving, and that you cruelly mistook his love for weakness and threw it back in his face in the worst way possible. He is unable to believe you had never known one another.

"I have also registered my complaint with the warden of Penitentiary of New Mexico and the Santa Fe Police Department about his release, in case the parole board chooses not to reconsider their decision based upon my second warning to them about him. I urge you to be very careful and not try to deal with him yourself should he appear in your area. Please feel free to contact me about this.

"Sincerely,

"Dr. Jack Daye, MD"

In a second of anguish, Charley began to crumple the letter then stopped. She felt trapped. What she had worried about in the courtroom was actually playing out. It was now July 10. That indicated she had fifteen days to figure out what to do. As much as she wanted to call Tony, she knew he was tied up with his mother and didn't want to interrupt that. There was time. He'd surely be back within a day or two. Instead, she called the Santa Police Department to check to see if they had received the notification.

"This is Officer Jepson." He sounded old, probably nearing retirement. "Yes, honey, we received that letter but Shelton has had plenty of time to realize you don't love him. He wouldn't be released if he were dangerous."

"Officer Jepson, I don't think you understand that this man is psychotic, delusional. He told his psychiatrist he wants to kill me. He is very dangerous."

"Look, sweetheart, I think the psychiatrist is just being overly dramatic and cautious. Maybe he's just trying to cover his ass in case anything should happen which, I suspect, is unlikely."

"Even though you seem to think this isn't serious, can you send a patrol car by my home every few hours after his release on the 25th just to check?"

"I'll have to see what manpower we'll have available. Maybe we could do a drive-by every six hours."

"Is that the best you can do? This is very serious."

"There's no need to get hysterical about this. We don't know for sure he's coming back to see you. If we learn something more, perhaps we can do it more often, but don't count on it."

Charley didn't feel consoled by that. And his sexist attitude didn't help.

A half-hour later the phone rang. She had been trying to relax after the discouraging response by the police. Wiping off her brushes with a clean cloth, she walked to the landline in the kitchen without checking caller ID and picked up the receiver.

"Hello," came the voice she so vividly remembered and hoped to never hear again.

Charley turned on the answering machine to record the call.

"Hello, Mr. Shelton."

"Mr. Shelton? Now you're pretending you don't know me? You treacherous bitch. You said you loved me but you led me on for years with all those letters and emails. And after all our time together in Boston. I believed everything you said and did."

"Mr. Shelton—"

"I believed you when you said we'd be married and be together forever. I did everything you wanted to make you happy. And for it, you denied and rejected me, pretending we hadn't had our relationship, or even knew each other. Dastardly lies! You did precisely what they wanted. You blatantly rejected me in court."

"Mr. Shelton—"

"You are so unworthy of my love. You've ruined my life. I want you to know I'm going to show you what happens to traitorous, deceitful whores like you as soon as I get out of here." He laughed harshly.

"Mr. Shelton, the police have been informed. Furthermore, I won't be here when you get out. I'm going out of town. Just leave me alone."

"Stupid fucking slut bitch. You can't avoid me. You are going to get what's coming to you. So, you'd better prepare yourself. And I guarantee it won't be pretty. You'll be seeing me very soon and you'll regret every single false-hearted thing you've ever said and done to me."

After he hung up, the first thing a shaking Charley did was try to call Dr. Daye. Shelton's threat to her surely would make a difference in his parole. When there was no answer in the psychiatrist's office, she left a brief message on the machine:

"Dr. Daye, this is Amie Benison. I received your letter about Ronald Shelton and his early release. You need to know that he just called and threatened my life. He has to be stopped. I'm going to make an .mp3 copy of his call and email it to you."

Charley hung up, changed her sweat-soaked, short-sleeved top, made a copy of the recording, emailed it to Daye and took it to the police department.

As she entered, approached the front desk window in the yellowish receiving wall of the reception area, and sat in a molded black plastic chair, she asked for Officer Jepson. When he came forward to the window, she handed him the recording.

"Ronald Shelton called me from prison. He sounded full of rage and exceedingly paranoid. He threatened my life. He said he's coming to see me as soon as he gets out. I need protection once he's released on the twenty-fifth."

"Okay, sweetheart, we'll see what we can do. But we're not the people you should be talking to. You need to talk to the parole board, maybe even the prison warden."

"But once he's released, they can't protect me. You can. And don't call me 'sweetheart.' It's Ms. Benison."

She was annoyed. Unfortunately, Jepson didn't tell her there was an Office of Victims of Crime webpage with a number that she could call to report a threat by a prisoner or if she were worried about a prisoner who was about to be released. It was possible that it might have helped Charley deal with her situation, but she would never be able to find out.

Charley left the beige stucco building, with the American and New Mexico flags on the nearby flag pole, flapping in the hot wind. As sweat ran down her back, she was not feeling assured. None of it looked promising. All that she had feared, and apparently more, was coming to pass. Her albatross was already weighing her down.

Back home she retrieved a pen and paper and, standing at the kitchen counter, began considering what she could do to rid herself of Shelton. Saatch was playing with her platform shoes to get her attention. Charley needed to distract her. She had been teaching the cat from kittenhood different commands, such as to stop, to go, to come, to move backward, to sit up, and stand up. Tony had joined in the training, making it a game, because Saatch delighted in doing almost anything Tony requested. For a minute, she issued commands to him.

"Saatch, go backward."

He went backward.

"Saatch, come here."

He walked forward.

"Saatch, sit up."

He sat up.

Then, without her asking him, he did a jumping stretch for "standing up": his version of initiating a high-five. That acrobatic movement was something he was doing more often whenever there was something above him, like Charley's hand, to reach toward. That was with or without her command. With his right front leg elongated past his head, his toes splayed, he jumped, elevating his body which was curved slightly backward. His left front paw was bent at the elbow, shoulder height, closer to his body, with his toes in a semi-gripping position. His tail, also elongated, curved widely back toward his body. Best of all, his eyes were wide open and as was his mouth in anticipation. She gently "slapped" his right front paw with her right hand. He meowed. As soon as he landed, he sat quietly, awaiting his reward. It sometimes seemed to Charley that Saatch was watching too many YouTube videos because he was picking up all sorts of "cool," non-feline moves.

After getting his treat, he looked for a sunny location to which to retire, and left Charley to return to her problem at hand. Her solution had to be clever and not be associated with her in any way. If only she had a blow gun and curare-tipped darts, she could sneak up on him and send him on his way. She could slip pieces of puffer fish into his tuna salad, toss a cone snail into his bath water, or give him a green bouquet hiding a poisonous dart frog. If she knew what he'd be driving and could locate the car ahead of time, she could puncture his brake line and, using quick-drying glue, adhere his accelerator pedal to the floor. She could anonymously send him a Starbuck's caramel macchiato laced with thallium, garlic dip oozing with selenium, or botulinum toxin in a tube of toothpaste. After she had finished her long list of murderous intent, she sighed. She wasn't going to try to kill him, no matter how the thoughts of revenge lifted her spirits and made her smile. That wasn't who she was. Well, maybe, just in this one instance …

"Dammit!" she uttered.

As Saatch rejoined her, he jumped up onto the counter beside her as if to reinforce her ethical decision. She gave him a pet as she stood there a while longer contemplating her actions. However, if Shelton attacked her and the only way to save her life were to somehow kill him, that would be different. That was true self-defense.

She chuckled to herself, "Besides, who'd know if it weren't?"

After she had grabbed a chair to sit down at the kitchen table to jot down some ideas, Saatch jumped onto the back of her chair and encircled Charley's neck with his tail in agreement.

As nothing came to mind, she groused, "Crap!" She had scribbled a few useless notions then scratched them out. She'd have to think about it some more, maybe something would come to her when she wasn't so anxious. Looking at Saatch who had migrated to the table to try to sit on her list, she complained to him.

"Why don't you come up with something brilliant? You're supposed to be a top-notch predator."

Looking back at her, Saatch lifted his whiskers in a grin.

"That's a great look, but it doesn't help. Put on your thinking cap. Maybe together we can come up with something that might work."

Time hung heavy as Charley tried to rev up her imagination. She had been known for her spur-of-the-moment creativity, always immediately targeting the right element to snag voters' attention and make them take note. So, why was it failing her now? she silently asked herself. As she mulled it over, she made herself a glass of iced tea and a tuna fish salad sandwich with gherkins with kale leaves, which Saatch shared, minus the kale, pickles, and bread. When she had finished her last bite, she went to Amie's computer to google a few things but it bore nothing. Then clicking on Amie's Facebook page, she checked among posted trivia for something to spark an idea.

While most of the posts were political statements, selfies, photos of children putting diapers on their heads, or some questionable delicacy made from insects, there was an ad for a dating site. About to leave it, Charley paused, then chuckled as she remembered something. Back in Boston early on, she had tried an online dating site.

"Pathetic," she said aloud, "hardly described its process and results."

Despite specifying what she wanted and didn't want, she ended up being matched with men of all ages, educational levels, political and religious stripes, from a Brahman snob to a Neo-Nazi Party disciple. However, the promotional item plucked the harp strings of inspiration.

What, she wondered, if she could send an email to Shelton and act like an admirer. She could talk about how she had known of him from San Diego, that she had been a lawyer on one of the other judges' staffs and thought he was so intelligent, legally beyond compare, and attractive. She could say she had come to Santa Fe because she knew he had moved here, and then happened to hear about his case. She couldn't believe that someone as brilliant and clever as he was had been arrested and convicted. It obviously had been a big mistake. And maybe she could visit him in the prison.

At this point, Charley stopped. Stuck, she couldn't decide where to go from there. Maybe she could finish by saying that she was hoping that he would be released sometime soon. Then she could suggest that he return to San Diego because she wanted so badly to get to know him. She could also include an attractive photo.

That really appealed to Charley's perverse desire to get even so she searched for "sending emails to prisoners." However, what she discovered deflated her balloon of enthusiasm. To send one she would have to set up an email account on a site that promoted email communication with prisoners. Furthermore, she would have to pay for it with her credit or debit card. That meant he could know or find out her real identity. That wasn't workable. But what, she wondered, about sending him regular posted mail?

More research showed her that she would have to get Shelton's prisoner ID, which might be his booking number, from the penitentiary's online inmate database. The only thing she'd have to remember was that any incoming mail would be opened, read, and investigated before being delivered to the prisoner. Moreover, there were restrictions about what she could send, but that was okay. She wasn't going to send him anything sexually-suggestive, gang-related, candy or food (so much for sending the macchiato or garlic dip), checks or cash, glue or white-out, a cell phone, or hard-cover book.

The envelop would have to have a return name and current address. She would have to figure that out quickly so he could receive the letter and she could get one back, assuming that what she had written intrigued him. If not, it was back to the drawing board and, perhaps, in desperation, tapping into her assassination strategies. After all, ethylene glycol in lemonade could work too.

She would need the sender's name and local address for seven days as well as a post office box in San Diego for after that. She'd also need a photo of a good-looking woman in her thirties. That she could get from one of the photo-selling websites. Or, better still, have her website designer photoshop a casual picture of one of Charley's former-associates so it would not be of a recognizable real person. She felt the woman's first name should be common, like Marie, Kathy, or Elizabeth as should the last name, like Barton, Gardiner, or Martin.

Since she didn't want to impose on any of her gallery colleagues or clients for an in-care-of address, she decided her local address could be a post office box. But, as she found out from calling, accessing those boxes tended to take too long. Besides, the annual fee was prohibitive. A box at a UPS Store could be immediately available and she could have it for seven days or longer. She could privately pick up any mail that he sent at any time. The same could work in San Diego, except they could send it to her.

The more Charley thought about it as she found a photo of Anne to send to Geoff with instructions for minor feature changes, the crazier it sounded to her. She drove into the city, located the UPS Store, and set up a box under the name of "Beth Martin" and paid for ten days—three extra days, just in case. Having a box with a combination made it so much easier to check for a return letter without having to be "Beth Martin" for the proprietor. That was also safer.

When she arrived home, she found Geoff had left an email for her to which he'd attached a .jpg file of the altered photo. Anne, who already was very attractive, would never have recognized herself in his Hollywood-glamour head shot. He made her cheekbones more prominent and her heavily-fringed eyes larger, gave her a pointed chin, and pouty lips. He'd also made her a golden blonde. Charley printed it on photographic paper. It looked good. It even had Anne with dilated pupils showing her interest. She smiled and sent him an email.

"Geoff, you never disappoint. It looks great! Thanks."

Charley used some heavy, expensive vellum paper and handwrote her letter to Shelton with an ink pen, using a slant to the left so he wouldn't recognize her handwriting from her notes he had pilfered and collected.

"Dear Ron,

"You may not remember me from the Judge Howell's office in San Diego but I remember you. I read some of your work product and was so impressed by you because of your quick, agile mind and legal brilliance. I admired your skills and vast knowledge. I don't think we were ever formally introduced. My office was down the hall. While I was in and out of your judge's office, unfortunately you were always tied up with your judge when I stopped by. She was so lucky to have you as her judicial clerk. Everyone raved about everything you did there and we were devastated when you left. I came to Santa Fe ostensibly on vacation but really to search for you since I'd heard you had moved here after you left. I'm here only seven more days.

"When I read about what had befallen you, I was shocked. Someone as clever and professional as you arrested and imprisoned? Inconceivable. I couldn't believe it. It must have been a huge mistake, a tragic miscarriage of justice. However, I hope that whenever you're released, you'll come back to San Diego. I really want to get to know you better and explore your incredible mind.

"Until I leave, I have taken a mail box at UPS, Box 34789, 1015 S. St. Francis Drive, Santa Fe, NM 87505. I hope to hear from you before then. To help jog your memory of having seen me around the courthouse I'm enclosing a photo of myself with an inscription. Please don't disappoint me.

"Yours,

"Beth."

After she finished the handwritten letter, Charley placed it in a matching vellum envelope with the photo, sealed it, addressed it to Shelton's penitentiary, and stamped it. She grabbed her keys and wallet and was about to leave for the post office when something instantly clutched her gut. It stopped her cold like the jolt of severe colic. It reminded her of her younger Boston days when she, Karlene, and Anne had pigged out on a large pepperoni-sausage-bacon-and-three-cheese, stuffed-crust pizza, which had obstructed her, doubling her over. Of course, the real Amie could never have touched that. Charley's gut was telegraphing her that she needed to stop and think. Fortunately, she always paid attention to her gut.

As she stood in the kitchen, she re-ran the plan's details through her mind's wash and rinse cycle. Immediately, she was astounded by what she had almost done. All her eagerness drained away. She hadn't fully considered what the possible repercussions of her letter might be.

"Wait a minute! What," she now asked herself aloud, "if Shelton actually responded positively to Beth's letter and went back to San Diego to search for her? No matter how fervently he searched, he wouldn't find her. If he sent letters to her proposed UPS mailbox there, he wouldn't get any answers. Frustrated, he'd probably become enraged. Since he had retaliated against the judge and was ready to retaliate against Amie for rejecting him, how could he not want to act the same way, and even worse, with Beth for leading him on and then abandoning him?

"Dammit! What this letter would have done is set up a scenario that would make him like an incendiary device for any woman he encountered and obsessed over."

She could also envision him, when he was unable to locate Beth, coming back to Santa Fe with even more ferocity directed toward Amie.

"Damn! Damn! Damn!" said Charley as she dropped the letter on the counter. "I thought I'd really aced that. But that was stupid raised to the nth power. So now what? He'll be here on the twenty-fifth. I'd better get my butt in gear and come up with a real, rational, and workable plan to deal with his arrival."

After having finished setting his mother up in her new accommodations, Tony called Charley that evening.

"I'll be back tonight between ten and eleven. If you're going to be up, would you like some company?"

Charley grinned, comforted that he'd be around to help her decide what to do about Shelton.

"I'll be here, waiting with bated breath. Saatch is eager to see you."

When Tony arrived at ten-fifteen, he gave Charley a big hug and a protracted, toe-curling kiss. At that moment, Saatch clawed at his pantleg for similar attention, though not necessarily of the lip-lock variety. He picked him up. As they walked into the kitchen together, Charley spotted the envelope on the counter that she had so casually discarded there earlier. She'd forgotten about it. Now she felt a palpitation. She didn't want Tony to see it and have to explain why she was writing to the penitentiary, again. Since she was about to tell him what had already transpired in his absence, writing twice would make no sense. Besides, she didn't like lying and she didn't want to do it. Especially with Tony. She preferred not to have to address the topic of the letter at all. It had been a dumb move in the first place.

Nonchalantly she walked over to that portion of the counter and stood with her back to it as she talked with him. Since he wasn't looking her way as he spoke to her, being preoccupied with stroking Saatch's wriggling tummy, she eased her right arm behind herself. There she wrapped her fingers around the envelope, drew it forward, and surreptitiously slipped it into her tunic's side pocket.

Over some local wine, she listened to his story of moving his mother before she stunned him with the voice-from-the-past tale of happenings in Glorieta. Bit by bit, she revealed her having received the psychiatrist's letter, which she gave to Tony to read, and her first trip to the police department. Expressing her disappointment that they weren't sure that they could help her, she then replayed Shelton's threatening call and related her second trip to the police. Tony's facial expressions changed radically from jaw-dropping upset to a temporal-artery-pulsing angry scowl. This was the first time Charley had witnessed this degree of temper in him. She was glad she wasn't on the receiving end of it.

"He said he'd see you on the twenty-fifth." Controlling himself, Tony spoke slowly and calmly but the tendons in his neck were standing out. "No, he will see *us* then. I will be here with you so *we* can welcome him back, together."

Charley smiled grimly, imagining the "gunfight at the OK Corral." But Shelton wasn't likely to have a gun just getting out of prison, was he? As far as she could tell from Ortega's report, he didn't carry or have a gun, or have a permit for one. But that could change. After the judge of whom he was so enamored had rejected him, he didn't threaten her with a gun, as far as Charley knew. He didn't shoot her dog. However, he could have used a gun butt to smash her windshield if he didn't have a baseball bat or paving brick.

For a male with low self-esteem, like Shelton, who had already been rejected by the judge—and who knew how many other times before or after that—he could feel he had to be physically retaliatory, to brandish his masculinity, by acquiring and using a weapon. He could get it from former inmates or the black market. She suddenly remembered a quotation from an academic article she'd read on the likelihood of his coming after her.

"Stalking has been described as murder in slow-motion."

She knew in the back of her mind that he'd be released someday. But "someday" was, in the courtroom, in a total of five years. Now, unexpectedly, it was in under fifteen days. From the receipt of the psychiatrist's letter, she had been marking off the days on her kitchen calendar which she had hung near the refrigerator. Feeling the need to be hypervigilant, she had begun checking the house, garage, and property every morning and night and every time she had returned to the house after she been away, always carrying Mace, as was allowed in New Mexico. As the date approached, sleeplessness and a knot in her stomach became her daily companions.

"Until the twenty-fifth!" Tony stated. "But first thing tomorrow morning I'm calling the penitentiary to speak with the warden. I mean, what the hell is this? Shelton is not even out on his parole yet and he's already violating it by issuing physical threats to his former stalking victim. His parole should be revoked immediately."

It was early the morning of the twenty-fourth. While Tony was back at his office on Camino Entrada, Charley worked hurriedly as if she were on amphetamines. She filled and shipped orders and painted. But as the morning wore on, she didn't think Amie's paintings looked quite right. The upheaval being depicted appeared to be too calm for the way she felt. In a slap-dash fashion she added to, subtracted from, and totally erased some portions of the canvases she was working on. Suddenly she gasped. Stopping her frenzied activity, she stood back from what she'd done. Staring now at the disasters she had been producing, she shook her head as she castigated herself.

"What the hell am I doing? What have I done?"

Objectively, she couldn't believe how she had screwed up perfectly okay canvases. She knew she had to take a break before she lifted another brush and did any more incomprehensible damage. Walking around the studio didn't help. So, she tried a stroll around the back garden. It didn't work either. Maybe, she thought, switching activities was the solution.

Since she hadn't finished the separate book on Saatchmo, she thought she could spend her time more profitably adding to it. But as she trudged to her office, she knew her heart wasn't in it. At the computer keyboard, she uploaded what she had already written and read it, unimpressed.

"Not great. It could definitely use some work."

But before she added or deleted a single comma, something put up a mental stop sign to stay her hand. She chastised herself for being ready to act senselessly here too.

"For heaven's sake, Charley, don't mess with it! You're not in the right frame of mind to improve it. You can do that when it's finished. Right now, just see if you can add anything else to it."

However, nothing revealed itself. Forcing herself to sit there, she typed a jumble of thoughts that looked like gobbledygook. The longer she sat, the more she fidgeted.

"Okay," she said aloud, "that's it. This is probably crap. But I'm in no position to judge it accurately now."

With that she took in ten deep breaths which she let out slowly and saved the file. She knew she had to do something. Something to help expend all her excess energy because it was blocking her mind and creativity. Maybe exercise, she thought. That made sense to her. She could go for a jog. Regretfully, however, she hadn't done that for a while, not since she had received the warning from Shelton's psychiatrist. It had left her feeling both anxious and torpid, unwilling to even do stretching much less set foot on the public road. As a result, she had lost her athletic edge. That meant there was no way she could perform like a well-oiled machine in her run, as she had in the past when she ran, when she stretched and exercised every day.

Even after her twenty minutes of warm-up, she felt tight and sluggish. Trying to feel more optimistic, she pushed herself to fast-walk down her dirt driveway until she reached the street. On the right side of Log House Road, she jogged slowly, uncomfortably, west past the multi-branched cholla cactus which was reaching out its spiny arms to snag anything near the road edge. There with the cholla were long-limbed, light green, feathery chamisa shrubs, aka "rubber rabbitbrush," with their tiny yellow flowers beginning to release their pollen to have the bees help them rapidly duplicate themselves. The sharp bitter resinous scent of the silvery and woody salt bushes, which appeared here and there along the road, was filling the air. While the summer heat wrapped her in sweat, she was grateful that her being at a higher elevation made it a little less oppressive, though still not tolerable enough.

In spite of her struggling to keep up her retarded pace, she was heading toward the dark coolness of the conifers which lined the unpaved portion of Fire Station Road ahead. Reaching them would have been a welcomed reward for all she was suffering. But her physiology was against her. After she had gone only three-quarters of a mile, her legs were cramping, screaming at her, and her lungs had been set on fire. Doubling over with her hands braced on her knees, gasping for breath, she winced, really wanting to cry, as her legs' large-muscle spindles contracted involuntarily with exquisite pain.

Her body was behaving as if she had just completed a full marathon, including Heartbreak Hill in Boston which rose eighty-eight feet in half a mile at a three-point-three percent grade. Standing back up, she tried to jog in place, hoping to make the cramps subside. Her stabbing calf muscles began to release but the tightly twisted knots in her thighs seemed to have no such intention. Despite the pain, making her want to cry out, she hobbled all the way back to Log House Road.

A short distance from her driveway she found herself stuck in place for a few minutes again, massaging and begging her thighs to relax enough to allow her make it to her house. Then she heard something.

A car slowly approached her from the rear. It was a battered and paint-crazed silver-green 1980s Chrysler LeBaron mid-size sedan, a far cry from what had at one time been considered a classic luxury car. The vehicle crept by as the driver and passenger stared at her. Pretending she wasn't interested in them, she viewed the two males out of the corner of her right eye, wondering why they seemed to be watching her. If they stopped, she was ready, hamstrung or not, to crawl, if necessary, to her left. She was motivated to do whatever it would take to try to get away from them. She was not going to allow them to assault or kidnap her. After a minute of pacing her shambling vertical movement, they sped up. The twinges in her legs were superseded by the heavy galloping of her heart.

As she falteringly reached her driveway, she emitted a sigh of relief ... until the car reappeared. It was coming back. It crept by her as the gaunt-looking passenger with dark fuzzy eyebrows and wearing a long-billed ball cap low on his forehead stared at her, smirking.

Using her best militaristic stance despite her current disability, with her shoulders back and with fists on hips, she glared at them until they finally sped up again, wheels spinning grit, and disappeared. This time she remembered to catch their license plate number. After they'd gone, she shouted to their dust cloud.

"It's not bad enough that Shelton is being released tomorrow, still threatening to harm me, but now you two clowns are trying to do what? Terrify me?" Then she mumbled to herself, almost sobbing, "And you're doing a fine job." She glanced up at her house in the small distance, "Now, if I can only make it up my driveway."

After work, Tony appeared. He hadn't heard back from the penitentiary yet in response to his call and the .mp3 copy of Shelton's call he had also sent to the warden. When she related the Chrysler incident, he suggested that until the Shelton problem were resolved, she might want to reflect upon not leaving her house. In the mean time he'd check the plate number she gave him.

"They might have been some local jerks attempting to give you a bad time ... or," he paused and stared up as if seeing something else less pleasant, "maybe, even prisoners Shelton knew, laying the groundwork for him."

Charley gasped silently.

"I don't mean to frighten you, but that has to be considered. The former, however, is much more probable than the latter. But, either way, you don't need that kind of harassment or risk."

Eager to change the subject, she asked him.

"How about some dinner? I've made the enchiladas you like, some fresh guacamole, and a salad of greens and herbs, especially cilantro."

Following dinner, they did the dishes then played several games of five-card stud for matchsticks, as they sipped a local sweet wine, which had a huge honeysuckle nose. It had been produced from a blend of Vidal Blanc, Seyval Blanc, and Muscat Canelli. They'd have to get it again. They then watched the news. While Tony relaxed, Charley squirmed. She kept getting off the sofa to check her email, make sure all the curtains and large-slat wood Venetian blinds were closed. Tony said nothing. He knew from his experience with the aftermath of his sister's stalker incident that suggestions and comments "to relax" were unhelpful, and best left unsaid.

By bedtime, Charley felt exhausted. Initially falling asleep in Tony's arms, she quickly began to toss and twist in her covers for the remainder of the night. Saatch, who was trying to cuddle under her arm, had to keep moving to keep from being rolled upon. Each time she awakened she was feeling breathless and damp. She could feel her calves trying to cramp again. Tomorrow was the day Shelton was to be released. She simply didn't feel prepared to face whatever was coming, and she knew it was undoubtedly coming out of left field, fast, and low.

34

While Charley and Tony awoke early on the twenty-fifth, Tony was still waiting to hear from the warden at the penitentiary about what he was going to do to act on Shelton's pardon breach. Tony's plan was to work from Charley's house for as long as he could so he would be present if Shelton were able to get transportation to arrive there. But, as was so typical of his days, he received a call that he was needed immediately at his office.

After Charley and Tony had finished saying an anxious good-bye, she closed all the blinds and curtains and made sure all the doors and windows were locked. She'd remain in her office, with the air conditioner on, not answering the phone unless the caller ID indicated it was Tony, and work there until he returned.

Around noon as she was getting antsy, she heard something roll up her driveway. Since Tony would have called first so as not to startle her by arriving unannounced, she sneaked into the living room to peek through a tiny slit in the curtains and blinds.

Before her was the old silver-green Chrysler. The driver, whom she couldn't see, wasn't moving but someone was getting out of the passenger's side. It was the man with the dark fuzzy eyebrows and ball cap slouched low. He had a gaunt face. His navy sport jacket, light blue dress shirt with open collar, and tan slacks hung on him. His pants were held up by a tightly-cinched belt, like a drawstring on a sack of corn, which wrinkled his pants at the waist. No gun was visible. His angular face almost looked distorted as he grinned. When he raised his head slightly, there was a savage gleam in his eyes, similar to a CGI trick to designate an evil being in a horror movie.

He looked familiar. "That couldn't be Shelton, could it?" she asked herself, confused. "But he was the passenger I saw yesterday. How is that possible? How could I have seen him yesterday when he wasn't released until today?"

There was a heavy knock on the front door, rapidly followed by a ringing doorbell. Barely breathing, Charley moved back from the window to the security of the center of the living room. More fist-pounding and bell ringing. The next thing she heard was the solid wood door being stabbed and reamed, making screeching and crunching sounds as the agonized wood splintered. It was complemented by mumbling and cursing. While he may not have had a gun, he certainly had a large knife or wood chisel as a weapon. Both of which could quickly dispatch her if he were given half a chance to use them on her. She began to feel cold sweat run down her thighs.

His attacking the door seemed to Charley to take forever. At times it sounded as if he would penetrate the old, one and three-eighths-inch wood. Charley's imagination began to run wild. If he could make a large enough hole, he could stick his hand through to try to open the locks. But if he did, she could counter him with … what? It was only seconds but seemed to take an eternity for her to answer her question. Maybe, she thought, a hot clothes iron would work! That notion made her run on tip-toe to the utility room off the kitchen to grab the iron. Once back in the living room, she plugged it into the electrical outlet nearest the door and set it on the brick floor on high. As the minutes of gouging the wood dragged on, it sounded as if he were moving his digging implement from place to place. That didn't suggest he was creating a single hole. By the time he stopped his excavation it had been only fifteen minutes by Charley's watch. That didn't seem possible. Hunkered down, she crept back to the slit in the curtain, hoping Saatch would stay curled up on the large work table in the studio.

As the perpetrator was sliding back into the passenger seat, his driver revved the engine and raced forward onto Charley's grit-covered property. Then he hit the emergency brake, locked the back wheels, turned the steering wheel sharply one hundred and eighty degrees, released the emergency brake, and sped down the drive, raising a dense cloud of dust behind him for celebratory effect. As soon as the sound of the car could no longer be heard and the dust cloud settled, Charley opened the door.

It hit her like a thunderbolt. On the door was a crudely incised threat. It said, "Say good-bye bitch." She snapped a picture of it with her cell phone and called the police to have his vandalism on record.

Shaking, Charley went back in, unplugged the iron, and walked back to the kitchen to put it on the counter to cool before replacing it in the closet. Then she got a glass of water to wet her dry mouth. Leaning against the counter, she called Tony.

"That car with the plate number I gave you just left. The passenger, who was clearly Shelton, attacked my front door and carved a threat in it. But this was the same guy I saw in the car that harassed me yesterday. This makes no sense if he was to be released today. Somebody mucked up somehow."

"Sorry to have to tell you that it probably was Shelton both times. When the warden called me back, he told me there must have been a clerical error or typo for the release date which his psychiatrist received. Shelton was actually released yesterday morning, the twenty-fourth. So, by the time they'd received my message and listened to the tape of his threat, they'd already processed his release."

"Dear God! I was out in the open, on the road when he came by yesterday. He could have killed me then."

Tony ignored the validity of her statement. There was nothing he could say that would make her feel better. She had been very fortunate at that moment, for whatever reason, but there was no reason to think it would last.

"By his calling, harassing you, entering and damaging your property, he has committed a number of crimes as well as having violated the restraining order in his parole about contacting or coming near you. The warden said they have issued an arrest warrant."

"That's good. Does that mean he'll be back in jail immediately?"

"Not necessarily. Since the warrant was issued today, he probably won't know about it until he checks in with his parole officer. That's the first working day after his release date, so I suspect he will hear about the warrant today. That's assuming it's been communicated promptly to his parole officer."

"Then he could be out wandering around for days, carrying out his revenge on me."

"There's no way to know how long it will take to get him back in prison. It's not as easy as just putting him behind bars again."

"What do you mean? Why can't they just pick him and put him in jail again?"

"They can arrest him but there needs to be a probable cause determination within two days of that arrest. Then to make revoking his parole legal they have to have a due process proceeding in court and show probable cause to revoke it. You'd likely have to be a witness in court and provide documentary evidence of his parole violations, like the tape of his call and a picture of his damage to your door."

"And will that finally do it?"

"Well, … as I understand it, depending upon the nature and severity of the violation and if probable cause is established, there will be a final hearing to decide if the preponderance of evidence supports that the allegations are more likely to be true."

"That's appalling. It sounds as though he's getting more legal protection than I am. I'm the victim here. And I'm the one being threatened all over again but this time he's not just stalking me. He's threatening my life. He even told the psychiatrist he wants to kill me!" Charley took a deep breath then resumed more calmly. "Okay, so if the court thinks there's enough evidence, then what?"

"If so, his parole is revoked. If that happens, he'll forfeit all credits for good behavior he had previously earned to reduce his sentence and go directly back into the slammer."

"In other words, he might get away with it if they don't think what he did was serious enough? What does he have to do to make it *serious* enough?"

"He's shown himself to be a real physical threat to you ... all over again. I think it's probable he'll have to stick it out in prison for the remainder of his sentence."

"Is that all? And what about after that? Doesn't he get any additional time?"

"That's anybody's guess. Meanwhile, we're checking the license plate number. Knowing who has been ferrying him around should help us find Shelton."

"But until his parole officer informs the police and the police find him ..." she sighed despondently, "he could kill me."

"We'll keep you safe as we handle the Shelton situation. At least you've been lucky so far." The second Tony uttered that phrase, he regretted it.

"Sure," Charley responded dully as she rolled her eyes. "Yeah, lucky," she exclaimed with a harsh laugh. "If I were lucky, Shelton wouldn't have randomly glommed onto 'the illustrious painter Amie Benison' and turned my life upside down."

When she hung up, she didn't feel any better. Moreover, she now needed a new front door which could cost her between five hundred and eight hundred dollars, if she could find a great bargain, otherwise ...

"Too bad," she muttered to herself, "they couldn't take that expense out of Shelton's hide, well, whatever hide he has left on the mere shell of his former self. ... But wait a minute!"

Something suddenly occurred to her, causing her to slap the ceramic tiled counter.

"He's not some poor indigent living on his Social Security or welfare checks. He had been and still is a tort lawyer. Those guys rake in lots of dough with their contingency fees that often take at least a third of each personal injury or class-action suit. At the very least, he owes me a new door. I should sue him. But can I sue a prisoner, whether on parole or not, in civil court? I'd better check and if so, get on it right away."

After she did some searching on the subject, she returned to her front door to assess the damage. While she wanted some wood putty to temporarily repair the front door surface, she knew she shouldn't repair it before the police saw it. Instead, she decided to search the garage for something to cover the epithet. A sixteen-inch-wide lavender, statice, and boxwood wreath lay in a marked box on a shelf in the righthand corner. Hammering a small nail in place, she hung it over the gouging. While it left "Sa" on the left and "itch" on the right, it covered most of the message. It was a good choice. Besides being colorful, it smelled clean and fresh and temporarily perked up her sagging spirits.

While she was outside, she had the overwhelming desire to work in her garden. Maybe, she thought, it was because she wanted to assert herself, to tell Shelton that he wasn't going to control her life. But maybe it was also because she really needed to feel in contact with Nature and the universe, among the flowers, trees, bees, hummingbirds, and occasional velvety tarantulas. However, since she wasn't going to test fate, she decided to work in the back garden. There she could still hear a car approach out front and slip inside quickly through the back door under the portale.

Grumbling about the restrictions on her possible behaviors, she lamented.

"Too bad I can't plant a blast mine or a fragment mine, like a 'Bouncing Betty,' half-way up the driveway such that Tony would know to miss but Shelton couldn't."

She allowed herself a small, sadistic laugh, harkening back to her assassination list, and shook her head, muttering, "If only." With that she gathered her garden gloves, pruners, trowel, cultivator, and a trash bag and entered the back garden to distract herself and try to relax.

35

Shelton's driver, Howie, a former cell mate of his, had picked up Shelton at the prison on Sunday to first drive him through Glorieta to spy on Amie before he did anything else. Then he took him to attorney Martin Borstall's office on Sandoval Street in Santa Fe. Before he was released, Shelton had called the attorney to meet with him as soon as possible in order to gain access to his house, office, and car. Before he was sentenced, Shelton had hired Borstall to handle the trust into which he had put all his assets and possessions, including his Amie Benison paintings. With Shelton's power of attorney the law office had taken over his finances: paying insurance bills, the mortgage on his home, the rent on his office, and his taxes while he was incarcerated.

When Shelton then arrived at his home, he found to his irritation that even after his call to his lawyer all the utilities had not as yet been turned on. He hadn't requested it but merely assumed it would be done. With no electricity, he'd stay with Howie until the next day. He was finding his being out of prison a little disorienting.

With no utilities, the only things that would be immediately available to him at the house would be his clothing. As he looked around, he was at least pleased that Borstall's office had hired someone to keep the place safe and reasonably clean. So, minimally, there weren't any broken windows or door locks, fright-night cobwebs, a refrigerator interior covered in gray mold, or a carpet mired in inches-deep mouse droppings and dead centipedes.

Staring at himself in the full-length mirror on the front of the bedroom closet door, he couldn't believe how he now appeared. He was no longer even a little heavy. In fact, clothes on him looked as if they were still hanging from a wire hanger. He had found it difficult to eat in prison. While the food was unpalatable, it was more than it's being flavorless starch fillers, overly-steamed vegetables, and tough, cheap cuts of meat disguised by greasy gravies. It was more than his missing indulging his palate with the rich French foods and fine wines he had normally enjoyed on his clients' dime. Mostly, it was a terrifying worry that kept him furtive, sleepless, and unable to eat much throughout his tenure at the prison.

From the moment he arrived at the penitentiary, he agonized about being physically taken advantage of. He'd read about the atrocities of having his front teeth knocked out in order to be made someone's BJ bitch. He'd also heard about the demands to "bend over and grab your ankles" and the resulting internal injuries inflicted by sexual predators who would rape him whenever they chose.

In hopes of keeping them at bay he immediately offered his legal services to anyone and everyone who was interested in his reviewing their sentences for technical errors or for making appeals or anything else they wanted regarding their cases. Maybe, he had thought, if he could be valued for helping them work toward their freedom, he wouldn't be as valued as a potential sex slave. While the positive response to his legal offering lessened his panic and dread, it never totally eliminated it or his heart palpitations.

Over time, his being a brilliant lawyer, so open and generous, seemed to have raised him onto a pedestal, untouchable for anything other than his professional skills, as far as he knew. His fellow prisoners who knew about him happily took advantage of what he had to offer because he wasn't just a jailhouse lawyer, he was the real, bona fide deal. And rather than his taking work away from the jailhouse lawyers around him, he smartly gathered them together and made sure they had all the profitable legal work and glory they could handle. Still, he could never be sure if it were enough.

Now that he was out on parole, he could resume his legal practice. The stalking accusations, of which he truly considered himself innocent, constituted a felony but it hadn't been bad enough for the New Mexico Bar Association to take away his law license. He would have his small office on Montezuma Avenue up and running well within a couple of weeks. But first, his focus was on Amie. He had to finish taking care of her as ingeniously and quietly as possible. However, he wasn't sure how he wanted to do it.

Despite his overwhelming desire to do so, he had decided he wasn't going to kill her. Well …, not right away. He wasn't going to shoot her, stab her, put poison in her Ovaltine, or hang her up and use her for archery practice. *If* he let her live, he wanted the psychological and physical consequences to linger so recovery from them would be impossible. She had gone out of her way to destroy him. And all he'd done was love her. She had to be repaid for all he'd suffered since then. There had to be balance in the universe. His extreme anguish and his Old Testament sense of justice demanded it.

Shelton knew he had to check in with his parole officer but felt disinclined to do so. Yet, he wanted to get on with his life so he figured he'd better not botch it. He was finally free and would do whatever was necessary to remain so. After he changed his clothes, he unlocked his garage to get his beloved 1995 Mercedes-Benz E-Class, Midnight Blue four-door sedan. His tires were nearly flat. His car's engine whirred for a few minutes then surprisingly barely caught, coughing. The battery should have been dead after all that time. He couldn't believe it. Gasoline evaporation had undoubtedly taken place. Everything had dried out. That suggested the fuel pump and drive belts needed to be replaced and the tank drained and refilled. He found that discouraging. But, he wondered, given that, could he get his car to a service station under its own steam?

After pumping up his tires, a miracle happened. Bucking all the way, the car slid on vanishing fuel fumes and intermittent electrical current into the station a half-mile away. By all rights, the car shouldn't even have started. Shelton took that as a good omen that his plans were on the right track.

As he waited for his car to be worked on, he put together a list of things he had previously contemplated in his prison cell that he could do to torment Amie.

1. Break out the driver's side window to leave maggots, feces, and/or vomit.
2. Smash her windshield.
3. Puncture all four tires when she was away from home.
4. Cut the wiring in her car's electrical system.
5. Throw acid on her car's paint job or key fully both sides of the car.
6. Put her name and phone number along with a picture of her head on a woman's spread-eagle, ravished naked body on a porn website.
7. Put up salacious and defamatory posters everywhere.
8. Rig remote explosive devices on her car and at her home.

While he liked the list, which was good for a laugh, those items were lame gestures. They were okay to start with but he needed stronger, more fearsome actions as well. Furthermore, he really wanted to do something truly spectacular as a climax. But when nothing dawned on him at that moment, he began muttering too loudly to himself. Over the sound of impact drivers removing lug nuts from wheels, his vocalizations attracted the attention of the mechanics who were working nearby in the garage.

"I have to figure out exactly what I want for my pièce de résistance. In the meantime, I have to stay calm and not worry. The more often I see her and review the depths of her treachery, the more it will revitalize my retaliatory juices."

Looking maniacal, he suddenly burst out laughing, slapping his thigh repeatedly.

36

Two hours in her backyard garden weeding and dead-heading long-past flowers made Charley feel more like herself. Going back inside, she grabbed a chair at the kitchen table in order to make a list of what tasks she needed to do. As she glanced back at the calendar on the wall, she reminded herself it was approaching the first of the month. That meant she had a number of bills to pay. As the bills came in, she had them stuffed by the Maxwell-like pink pig-with-pinwheel cookie jar, which held cat treats, sitting on the counter near the stove.

Her personal and business credit card bills were kept separately from the others. She always checked them online immediately for errors, for purchases she hadn't made. Once upon a time she hadn't been so vigilant and had suffered for her lax behavior.

When the paper copy of her business credit card bills arrived one month, there was a listing for the purchase of an airline ticket from Accra, the Republic of Ghana, to Vancouver, Canada, to the tune of eighteen hundred dollars. Shocked, Charley couldn't reach the credit card company fast enough. This had happened to Anne Lane once too. As she had hung on the phone, she wondered if someone had gotten her number when the computer of a business she patronized had been hacked and customer data stolen. There was a lot of that going on and the public didn't always hear about the thievery or, more precisely, the extent of its damage.

The result of this brouhaha had been a super-inconvenience. After eliminating the charge, she had to have a new card issued. That meant that anything that she had already set up to be automatically paid monthly, like her merchant account bill, would be interfered with, requiring her to contact each company or service and provide them with the new card number as soon as she received it. In addition, whenever she would use her new card online where she already had an account, she had to go through the process of deleting the old card number and adding the new one.

Making the whole situation worse, the card company had said it would over-night the card but Charley hadn't received it. After two weeks and phone calls to get another new card, she had found the original package. It was under the large lavender bush next to the front step which had been soaked by weeks of scheduled drip-irrigation.

After she lined all the non-automatic-paid bills up on the table, she paid them one by one by check. While she could have paid them all automatically online each month, she still preferred to have a paper record for some of them, like her taxes, mortgage, utilities, and medical-, health-, house-, and car insurance. It was better for her peace of mind to know that she had her own documentation of having paid it.

Saatch who had been keeping Charley company in the garden, leaping at butterflies and lizards to assist them in getting their exercise, jumped onto the kitchen table. Sitting on the array of paper, he wiggled his bottom to read whatever interested him until his human received his unmistakable message: "How about that pet?"

It was obvious that Saatch knew that Charley was a member of a species cognitively slower than felines. As a result, he had trained her well to be aware not only of her own deficiencies but also of his behavioral prompts. She always responded on cue. After all, how could she refuse that long silky coat, kneading paws, and seductive purr?

Keeping close to the house while Shelton was still on the loose, Charley put off going to the art supplies store. Instead, she would give the house a quick cleaning, process orders, then give them and the paid bills to the postal carrier who came around 2 p.m. The afternoon would be devoted to painting.

Paintings by Mana were catching on, better than Charley had hoped. Several galleries were displaying, and even selling, them. Tomorrow she would need to create another online painting video for her students. Her in-person students had been asked to use the online videos until she could have them in her studio again. Rather than tell them she was at risk from a former-stalker, she told them that there had been a septic tank problem which needed to be repaired. The construction project would take several days. While her students indicated disappointment, they acceded to her request.

Nevertheless, Wynton was especially saddened because he was working on what he considered his best canvas to date and wanted her to see it right away. Up-close and personal, not by his phone. When he begged her to let him just come over to show her, Charley, fearing for his safety as well as her own, turned him down with a perfunctory excuse.

"Wynton, the driveway and the front of the house are being torn up. It's dangerous to navigate. I'm sorry. But I really do want to see your painting. So please send me a pic right away."

With regret, he did as she asked. When she saw what he had sent her, she was extremely pleased. His talent was shining more brightly every day and she felt proud that she had helped facilitate its growth. Praising his achievement with a "big thumbs up," she promised to take his canvas to the Vida Hermosa Gallery to be hung there as soon as it was convenient. Tom, the owner, had told Amie he could always fit in a painting by one of her prized pupils. There was no question in her mind that Wynton had a bright and profitable artistic future if he kept pursuing it. She only hoped her own future would be as bright. With Shelton free to lurk about she was not that confident it would be ... or if she'd have one.

37

When Shelton arrived at his office, he picked up his phone to call his parole officer to check in. Forgetting again that all the utilities had not as yet been turned on, he found the line dead. Opening his desk drawer, he found his cell phone, which hadn't been charged in three years, as well as his pre-prison heart-related prescriptions: his anti-platelet clopidogrel and his anti-lipid lovastatin. He looked at them disdainfully. He felt that he had done fine without them for those three years. Consequently, there was no reason to believe that he really needed them, irrespective of what the alarmist doctor back in San Diego had claimed.

Irrespective, what he needed now was to find a phone. The closest public phone was at the gas station where he'd just had his car serviced. Protesting, he drove back there and dialed his parole officer. The traffic noise made it difficult to hear that it was an answering machine responding. After a fitful start, he left a message.

"This is Ronald Shelton checking in. I'm going to be living in my old house but don't have phone service yet. I'm also going to be opening my law office as soon as I can. You have those addresses. I'll let you know my numbers when I stop by next week."

After that, he scoured the booth's phone book, which hadn't been vandalized yet, for his utility companies. One by one he reinstated service for water, electricity, gas, trash collection, and telephone so he could move back into his house and office fulltime. When he finished, he felt he was back in control and luxuriating in it. Until early the next day when he would be back at his house and then his office awaiting whatever service people who were to arrive early, he would buy a few groceries and stay in a motel. His own bed sheets hadn't been laundered in three years. That was unacceptable.

When he was finally lodged in his motel room for the night, he re-charged his cell phone and had a snack. Then as he worked on his Amie revenge schedule, he spent his time untwisting a wire clothes hanger as he watched a forensic program on the television for hints. He wanted to start retaliating against her as soon as possible.

"Stronger than a lover's love," he laughed, quoting from Euripides' *Medea*, "is a lover's hate."

Around midnight, he drove toward Amie's house. Parking his car at the bottom of the driveway, he quietly walked up, keeping to the sparse vegetation at the right side of it. But not having surveyed the driveway area when he and Howie arrived to attack Amie's door, he tried unsuccessfully to avoid the painful spines of prickly pear cactus awaiting him in the dark. Removing them from his shoes, socks, and pantlegs required him to pause frequently. While this irked him, it didn't overwhelm his excitement for performing his first planned task.

The dark sky was filled with stars and a quarter moon. Lights from Santa Fe glowed dimly to the west. A cool breeze encircled and further invigorated him. He was psyched because he was on a mission. As he reached the top of the driveway and quietly approached her house, he saw there was only one car present. It was parked in the open garage. Hooding his flashlight so as not to be easily detected, he could see the license plate said, "Amie B." He smiled, gratified that she was there and alone.

Inside the garage he pulled on leather gloves and carefully removed the untwisted wire clothes hanger from under his belt. Using it like a Slim Jim, he tried to slip it down past the driver's side window to reach and release the locking mechanism. But he couldn't get the door lock to snap open. After a few minutes of swearing under his breath and grappling with it, he realized that the car had power locks. And maybe a lock rod. He berated himself for his failure. It was clear he wasn't going to be able to open the door this way. That meant he couldn't release the hood either to cut the wires of the electrical system.

"Shit!" he stifled a shout.

For a moment he was undecided what to do. Then it struck him. He'd go for the tires. He'd already decided to do it too. He could slice her car's wiring another time. There was no set schedule for these operations. With the utility knife he'd brought with him, he vigorously and brutally slashed all four tires, over and over again, pulling a muscle in his left shoulder and chest as he did it. Each stabbing razor slice was like raping Amie, again and again. Feeling almost orgasmic about this evening's accomplishment, he silently left the garage and made his way down the driveway, that time racewalking through its dusty center. As he opened his car door, he let out a small whoop of joy, feeling satisfied, and rushed off to retire to his motel room.

Early the next morning Charley decided to again water the foundation plantings she had put in three days before. Slowly opening the front door, she checked her surroundings. Finding nothing about which to be worried, she slipped out and passed the garage in order to turn on the water faucet for the hose on its outside wall. She had yet to put in the drippers for the new lavender bushes and attach them to the already existing irrigation system. She didn't want to spend the time doing it out front just yet.

As she walked by the open garage door, she faulted herself for having forgotten to close it. Then she noticed something strange out of the corner of her right eye but didn't stop. On the way back, to replace the hose and turn off the faucet, she took a closer look. Her back tires were cut in ribbons and flat. Stunned, she stood there, feet glued to the concrete. Then she looked around to see if she were alone, if anyone were watching to see her reaction. Hesitant, she walked around the car. The car was sitting on its wheel rims. Frightened, she took cell phone shots of the damage for her Shelton records and called the police as she raced inside.

When they arrived, they took photos and a report from her. She told them she was sure it was Ronald Shelton and jogged their memories about the arrest warrant issued for his vandalism and death threats against her. They advised she keep her garage closed and locked—which she considered "brilliant advice"—but could add nothing assuring.

That afternoon a vehicle transportation truck she had ordered arrived to take the Honda to a service station to fit it with new tires, as long as the wheels were still in round. She also left a message for Tony about the incident and her car's removal.

As soon as he received her message, Tony drove a cruiser out to her house.

Saatch was so glad to see him again. Tony had insinuated himself into Saatch's life. The cat couldn't get enough of his play with a laser light on the walls or floor or a string with a piece of folded paper tied at the end that he dragged around for the cat to chase, and ultimately catch. He clamored for more of Tony's delicious tummy rubs. Charley was convinced that if Tony could have marketed his famous kitty massages directly to cats, he would have become a millionaire many times over. He had a real talent for connection. What she delightfully discovered was that the more attention Saatch received from Tony, the more attention and love the cat had to share with her.

However, at this moment, Tony had something else more pressing on his mind so he gave Saatch only a small pat on the head. The cat just looked at him, puzzled, as Tony spoke directly to Charley.

"I'd like you to stay at my house for a few days."

"I appreciate your concern and offer," she shook her head, "but if I hadn't left the garage door open, he couldn't have slashed the tires." She looked at him for understanding as he raised his eyebrows. "Seriously, I have lots of work to do and can only do it here. Besides, I don't want him to be able to make me hide from him."

"Okay, I'll be by tonight," he nodded, unconvinced that what she wanted to do was for the best. "If he comes by again, I can arrest him."

"You know you can come by tonight whether he does or not." She smiled at him and comically fluttered her lashes at him.

Not relieved, he kissed her and said, "Later." Then hurried back to his patrol car and his office.

In the meantime, Shelton had gotten his phone service for both his house and office. Because he didn't as yet have electricity, he couldn't use his desktop computer to search for service stations where a car with slashed tires might have been conveyed. Instead, he had to rely on the Yellow Pages which he had just received. At each station he called he asked about Amie's car.

"My Honda Fit was transported to your station for new tires for all four wheels. When do you expect the car will be ready?"

"Sorry. That wasn't here."

His third call hit paydirt.

"Sir, you can pick it up tomorrow morning."

That evening he planned on making a visit to the station. But first he had to go to a hardware store to get what he needed. In his motel room he laughed as he borrowed a towel and prepared his gear for his midnight operation.

"She will never ever forget this," he quipped as he gathered all his paraphernalia.

At the service station, he found the car just inside a five-foot tall cyclone fence which had a lock on its gate. It was located at the right side of the building. Rather than try to use a lock pick he had acquired from Howie to release the Master lock, he decided it was quicker to climb over the fence with his bundle, tied in the large bath towel with the nylon rope he'd bought, slung over his shoulder. The fence swayed as he tried to find footholds in the small wire openings for the toes of his shoes. A muscle pulled in his chest. When he irritatingly acknowledged that he couldn't bring everything that way as he climbed over because of the awkwardness and fifteen-pound weight, he climbed back down. Then, unhindered, he climbed over again and struggled to pull on the rope until the bundle reached the top of the fence. After disentangling it from the knuckle selvage at the fence top, he grabbed it and lowered it slowly to the ground, his muscles protesting.

Once by the Honda's driver's side which was blocked from street view by a metallic-beige Nissan SUV, he untied the bundle. Inside it was a heavy bucket and a five-pound brass-headed hammer which he removed. Wrapping the hammer in the towel to damp the sound, he began to pound the tool on the tempered glass of the driver's side window. Under the concussion, the glass broke into tiny shards which clung together. With more pounding he was able to remove enough shards to make a large hole. Now wearing elbow-length rubber gloves, he lifted the unwieldy bucket to the window and poured its contents onto the driver's seat, the clutch, brake, and accelerator pedals. Then with a gloved hand he reached through the hole to smear the dashboard and control panel with handfuls of the mixed cement.

When he was content with his job, he hid the bucket and hammer behind the station, wrapped the rubber gloves in the towel, and began to climb the fence with them again. But mid-fence he paused as if having a second thought. Jumping back down and sidling up to the car, he pulled out his utility knife. For five minutes he engraved his new name for her, "fucking bitch," on the driver's door in eight-inch-high letters.

Afterward, he stopped at a local bar to toast his achievement with their best single malt Scotch, giggling to himself, drawing patrons' attention, as he polished off two glasses neat.

When Charley didn't hear the next day from the service station about the car being ready, she called.

The owner answered and said, "I talked with your husband last night when he called to ask if the car was ready for pick up."

"Husband? I don't have a husband. What did he say?"

"Nothing. He just asked. And I told him."

Charley felt her heart sink into her lower abdomen. It had to have been Shelton. Immediately she called a cab to take her to the station. When she announced herself to the office that she was there to retrieve the Honda, the attendant unlocked and opened the gate and directed her to her car. When she saw the destruction, she nearly vomited.

She shouted at the top of her lungs, "Son of a bitch!"

The attendant raced to her side, his lower jaw slamming his chest when he spied it.

"I don't understand what happened."

"I do." Her face and neck reddened as her blood pressure spiked. "That bastard! Get your manager for me and call the police." She took pictures of the Honda with her cell phone.

Once again, the police photographed and made a report on the damage to her car. She reminded them of Shelton for what now seemed like the millionth time. As the officers surveyed the damage, some said they couldn't believe someone would actually do this.

"This guy must be a psycho!"

Charley wanted to exclaim.

"Gee, you think so? Really?" Calming herself so as not to sound snarky with "I told you so," she offered, "Perhaps you can see why I wanted protection from him."

A sympathetic officer took Charley in the police vehicle to a car rental agency where she rented a dark green Subaru Forrester. When she arrived home, she immediately called her insurance company and Tony to inform him.

"Tony, can you find out who his parole officer is? I don't understand why Shelton hasn't been arrested yet. This needs to stop ... and now!"

"No problem."

Tony checked with Corrections and received the parole officer's name, Steve Hollander, and his number. He called him. He was in.

"Mr. Hollander, this is Santa Fe Police Chief Antonio Rodriguez. Have you heard from your new parolee, Ronald Shelton?"

"Yes, he left me a message on my machine that he was going to be living at his old address and setting up his law practice again. I'm waiting for him to give me his new phone numbers."

"Have you received a warrant issued for his arrest for parole violations?"

"No. This is the first I've heard of it. Unfortunately, they don't trickle down to me as fast as they should."

"Since his release, he has committed additional violations."

"I'll get on it right away."

Tony knew that Hollander could arrest Shelton because he was also a Commissioned Peace Officer with arrest authority unlike some state parole officers. He sighed and thought of poor Amie. It never seemed to stop. Shelton ruined her front door, destroyed her tires, and now he had demolished her car. When she took him to civil court, which she had already started the process to do, she had to sue him for all he was worth, not only for all the physical destruction but also for all the extreme emotional cruelty and pain.

First thing the next morning, Hollander traveled to Shelton's house. When he rapped on the front door and rang the bell, which was now electrified again, he received no response. He left Shelton a message taped to the door to see him immediately. At Shelton's office, where he likewise wasn't present, Hollander did the same. When Shelton returned to his home from the motel, he saw the note and called Hollander back. His parole officer explained about the arrest warrant that had been issued and asked Shelton to come to his office. Shelton amiably agreed to come in to discuss it in the afternoon. He took the phone opportunity to frame his situation with Amie Benison.

"Dammit! Not again! I can't believe it. It was her baseless delusional claims that sent me to prison. And now that I'm out, she's attempting to harass me again? This woman is certifiable. She has a vendetta against me and I have no idea why. She's the one who should be in jail instead of me. My God, when will it end?"

This arrest news put a new complexion on Shelton's long-term plans for slowly ratcheting up his abuse of Amie. He was suddenly at risk of going back to prison and she was getting away with her persecution of him all over again. He knew he could not let her. Already having made his life miserable, she was now actively attempting to make it even worse by having him re-arrested on another trumped-up charge. Why, he agonized, was she continuing to torture him?

The little pranks he had played on her since he had been released were so mild by comparison, he absolved himself. They were certainly not tit for tat. Her evil had twisted her into slavering, rabid beast, attacking him every chance she got. Her ruthless goal was to continue to crucify him. Feeling a sob stuck in his throat, he moaned.

"Haven't I endured enough agony already?"

But now the time he needed to complete his mission was getting much shorter than he had expected. Unforeseen events were closing in on him. He'd have to do something to quell her tyranny … and do it ASAP! Otherwise, she would relentlessly follow him to the ends of the earth to terrorize and destroy him.

As soon as he regained his advantage by exterminating her, he'd have to leave. Wishing he could do that under the cover of night instead of in the revealing illumination of morning, he looked for and picked up several items in his kitchen, got back into his car, and stopped at a hardware store. Driving to the nearest gas station, he filled his newly-purchased steel-pressed jerrycan with fuel. Then he put his pedal to the metal in the direction of Glorieta.

Wearing wireless headphones, Charley was in her office, processing orders to the sound of reggae by Bob Marley. Saatch sat on her shipping table. He was "helping" by jumping onto the cut wrapping paper to "smooth" it out for her as well as swatting the poster mailing cylinders around to make sure no rodents or insects were inhabiting them. Swaying to the Jamaican beat, Charley didn't hear a vehicle that slowly rolled up her drive.

Shelton scanned for her rental car but it was nowhere to be seen. The garage door was closed. He alighted from his beloved car, leaving the driver's side door open, and walked to the garage to check the lock, and then to the side of the garage. The window there showed the car was inside. That indicated to him that Amie was very likely home as well. Tiptoeing back to his car, he opened the trunk and retrieved the jerrycan.

Since newer pueblo-style houses in the area were not made from adobe bricks but were stick-built, covered with chicken wire and cement-mix stucco, he searched for the best places that would allow gasoline to seep in and reach the underlying wood structure as rapidly as possible. That meant the front door, around the window casings, the canales, vigas, and the portale out back.

Wearing his long rubber dishwashing gloves and a forty-gallon garbage bag over his clothing, he began to splash gasoline on Amie's house, particularly soaking the front door. However, reaching the vigas and canales overhead was harder than he thought as the gasoline splashed back on him. A ladder would have been helpful but slow to use … and would probably have made enough noise against the stucco to alert her. The portale in back, however, was accessible because of the carved wooden columns holding up the roof. After drenching them, he struck a wooden match to start the columns ablaze. Then he rushed back to the front door to throw a match at it as well. When it hit the thin layer of flammable liquid, flames sparked, the vapors ignited, and it began to burn. His objective was to block both exits.

"Deal with that, you depraved fucking bitch!"

Even with her earphones, Charley heard the smoke alarms in the living room and back hallway go off. She grabbed her cell phone, called 911 to report the fire, dropped her cell into her pocket, and scooped up a panicked Saatch. She raced him to the back bedroom. Slid open the window. Knocked out the screen. Placed Saatch on the ground outside. Slipped herself over the embedded window track. And closed the window behind her to prevent outside air from fanning any flames that reached the inside space.

Then she ran to the water faucet on the garage side, turned it on, and dragged the hose to the back. There she sprayed the columns full-blast. She could not let the fire reach her studio with all her and Amie's paintings, the workshop with inventory for shipping as well as all her business electronics and records. Despite water tending to spread gasoline, the hose's stream was sufficient to blanket the flames, cutting off the fire's oxygen supply. In a few minutes, it put them out. As she heard sirens approaching from the distance, she dragged the hose to the front to attack whatever was on fire there.

Reaching the garage, she saw a dark blue car start down the drive. Quickly she snapped a picture on her cell phone then attended to the fire-ravaged front door. As the Glorieta Pass firetruck rolled up her driveway minutes later, she was already on to further spraying any place that smelled of gasoline. The firefighters unrolled the two-inch, double jacket fire hose, to attach it to fire hydrant located near the bottom of her drive. They began to douse the entire house until she begged them, shouting above the commotion, to avoid the two rooms in the rear because of the perishable artwork they contained.

Then she called Tony who couldn't leave at that moment and explained that the fire had been contained. Fortunately, as the firefighters inspected the building, they determined that the fire had not penetrated as deeply or widely as they had at first imagined. As a result of her swift action, water hadn't seeped through the ceilings or into the walls, thus missing the wallboard and floors. Aside from the scorched, gasoline-reeking front door and the portale columns, the damage was minimal, mostly smoke residue settling on the exterior and interior walls, floors, ceilings, rugs, and furniture.

Suddenly it occurred to Charley that Saatch wasn't around. Anxiety seized her heart. Terrorized by the fire, smoke, siren, truck, water, and strangely-dressed people, the cat had probably run away. Charley immediately began to walk around to the back of the house to search the back garden. She then explored every square inch of the property. With no success. Attempting to keep tears from obscuring her vision, she thought about how a seriously frightened cat might never return.

Like so many others, he could wander around and lose his way home. He could be attacked by wild animals and dogs. Or struck by a car. Through her now torrential tears, everything was a blur. Calling Saatch's name, she looked over, under, and around any place a freaked-out cat could hide.

When she reached the property perimeter, she scanned the area for as far as she could see for any movement which could be Saatch. But even with the binoculars she retrieved from their case in the house she saw nothing. That meant traversing and inspecting all the areas around her. Off she went immediately to look, asking the few nearby homeowners, including the ones who owned her old house, for their permission to check their gardens and outbuildings, calling Saatch's name until her voice was hoarse.

After nearly two hours of scouring the land well beyond hers and walking along the road in both directions, she sorrowfully slogged back to her property. There, sweaty, gritty, and exhausted, she plopped herself down at the base of the black locust tree on the property line at the back of the house. Putting her wet, red face in her hands, she sobbed, even more inconsolably, until she had no more tears to shed.

As minutes passed, her eyes burned and her head ached. Something deep inside her wanted her to lie down, circle herself into a fetal position, and let the world pass her by. While Shelton hadn't burned down her house, he had won. Saatch was gone ... perhaps forever. That meant she had failed another cat. She was bereft.

Then suddenly there was a rustling sound. It seemed to be coming from everywhere. Charley looked around, trying to locate its direction. She couldn't see any movement. There was no wind to upend leaves. She waited, straining to hear and reconnoiter. Then another sound occurred. Charley quickly stood, checking everywhere. When she finally looked up, she saw him. Saatch was about twenty-five feet up in the tree slowly making his way around the tree thorns of a branch toward the trunk.

"Saatch!" Charley gravelly called to him, gasping for air, hoping it was not a hallucination.

The cat looked down for a moment then attempted to speed up his movement, occasionally slipping as his paws barely avoided the flesh-penetrating spines. The branch jounced, again making the rustling sound. When he reached the trunk, he was meowing loudly as he looked down. Undecided. Frightened. She guessed he was trying to figure out how best to descend. Since his curved claws were designed to climb up, they were useless for climbing down head-first. Descending was a daunting task.

If only he were closer, she agonized, she could retrieve and open her old PBS umbrella and encourage him to jump into it. Minutes hung heavily. Then something else occurred to her. Her now raw throat begging for relief, Charley called to him.

"Climb down *backwards*, Saatch!"

Saatch looked at her, confused.

"Go *backwards*. Come on, baby." Her voice nearly gone, she croaked, "*Backwards*. Do it for me."

Saatch sat against the trunk, his head cocked to one side, and continued to stare down at her. Frustrated, Charley thought it would have been so much simpler if only she could speak "feline." After a few more excruciating minutes of Charley whispering to the cat, Saatch ceased meowing and appeared more relaxed. Very slowly he shifted position to reach out to grab the rough trunk, first with his right front paw and then his left front paw.

"Good boy, Saatch!" She strained to make herself heard. "Now go *backwards*."

When Charley saw him put his right back paw below his right front, she almost leapt for joy. With choreographed movements the cat began to haltingly climb down, looking cautiously over his left shoulder as he did it. Charley breathily cheered him on.

"Good boy! Good *backwards*. Come to me."

Occasionally slipping, Saatch made it down twenty feet of the trunk's creviced bark. Then twisting and dropping the last five feet, he landed into Charley's awaiting arms. Overwhelmed with happiness, despite a few of his unintended claw punctures in her flesh, Charley nearly suffocated Saatch as she hugged him. Then she wrapped him around her neck as she surveyed and assessed the exterior damage of the house.

"Not too bad," she squeaked to him, barely above a murmur, as she stroked his head. "The front door has been trashed. The stucco will need repainting with its acrylic latex here and there. But, in general, we were really very lucky."

Then Charley walked inside to check the walls and furniture of each room and get some acetaminophen for her head. When she came to the studio, she found that some paintings smelled a little smoky but at least the residue was minimal. And nothing had been harmed in any way. The door to the back room having been shut helped keep them from reeking. She whipped out her cell phone to call Tony.

"Do me a big favor. No, it's Amie. A-m-i-e. Lost my voice calling for Saatch. No, S-a-a-t-c-h. Sorry. I'll send you an email. E-m-a-i-l."

At Amie's computer her email told him that Saatch and the house were fine but asked him to call a well-regarded fire restoration service that he knew of in the area. They needed to come as soon as possible to remove the soot and smoke residue from the house's interior as well as clean all the furniture. In the meantime, she would launder all washables then gather everything else that could go to the dry cleaners.

While steaming and washing the walls and other surfaces could permanently remove the smoke smell, Charley wasn't sure if she should clean her and Amie's paintings herself. If she did, she'd have to use a neutralizer and emulsion cleaner with cotton balls, moving in one direction only, being very careful to follow the brush strokes. But she was exhausted. It would be easier and smarter to have a professional do that. So that was her plan ... until whenever Shelton struck again.

38

Back at his house Shelton had no way of knowing how much damage the fire had created … and if Amie had died in it of smoke inhalation or been fried to a crisp. He really wasn't choosy now and could settle for either, though the image of her scorched body pleased him that much more. Just as long as she had ceased to be and it had been frantic and deservedly painful for her. Maybe, he thought, it would be in the Santa Fe paper tomorrow. But it didn't really matter because he couldn't see it. He'd have to read it elsewhere, whenever. The death of Amie Benison would definitely be news outside the city. What mattered was that he had to leave … right now.

Since he had departed her place, he had been gathering his most essential possessions together. There wasn't much in the house that mattered, except for his clothes, primarily his well-tailored, expensive suits and monogrammed shirts, and Amie's paintings. He thought it was ironic that while he hated the artist, he still loved her art work. However, to put it in its proper perspective, what he now loved was his investment in them. They were worth a bundle, always increasing in value.

"And with her death," he chuckled to himself, "they will be priceless."

Most of what he'd save was in his office. It was his office equipment, law books, and two boxes of files. Carrying it all out of the office and packing "Mr. Benz" was both awkward and more strenuous than he had imagined. The haul was heavy and unwieldy. Leaving his expensive ball claw, cherry-veneer desk was heartbreaking but he could neither carry it nor fit it into his car. There was no way he was about to take the time to rent a U-Haul for it or even his file cabinets which he couldn't jockey out of the building himself anyway.

When he finished, the rear end of the loaded vehicle dragged from the extra weight. His chest and left shoulder felt as if he'd strained himself again by overdoing. But there wasn't time try to work out the kinks at that moment. From his office he drove to the bank to withdraw all his money, empty his safe deposit box, and close his accounts. The process took longer than he expected because of the lines of customers. His desire was to be on the road as soon as possible, but he still had other things to do first.

Somehow, he managed to sweet-talk himself into seeing Martin Borstall without an appointment. There he needed to sign papers for his attorney to cancel his office rental agreement, turn off the utilities, and sell his house as soon as possible for a pre-set price. But since he had just returned from prison and moved back into his house, he realized the situation would look odd and be tricky to explain. He felt it was necessary to supply a plausible excuse for his quick change in plans so Borstall wouldn't question them or be suspicious. There was no need to alert him that something was amiss. He had no idea if the attorney had heard about his arrest warrant but doubted it when Borstall seemed his normal self and said nothing about it.

Laughing, Shelton told the attorney that the most amazing thing had happened.

"A large tort firm in Denver wants me to join then as soon as possible. They had heard about my work on asbestos class-action cases and want someone with that experience and expertise right away with them in Colorado, rather than my working with them from here. The move's a pain but what a great opportunity!"

Borstall seemed to accept Shelton's excuse and offered his congratulations.

"It's fortunate that the offer came before you started up your practice here again. Will you be moving everything out of your office and house before you leave?"

"Yes, I'll be taking care of it in a day or two. So, put it up for sale as soon as possible. Right now, however, I have to catch a flight to Denver."

Shelton cut the conversation short. He wanted Borstall to hurry up preparing the contract for the house sale. Things were taking more time than he wanted. Still, he had to be careful not to look as frantic as he felt about the delay. All the while, he could feel his anxiety spiking. As they were finishing, Shelton reminded Borstall that the house price was non-negotiable.

"For no less than five hundred thousand dollars. Given its size and location, at that price it's a bargain and should go fast. You have my cell phone number. I'll tell you where to send the check as soon as I get settled."

Once everything was completed, he thanked Borstall and left to grab a quick bite to eat. He was beginning to panic. The bank and legal work had taken too much time. Regretfully, he wouldn't be able to locate a restaurant with fine French cuisine to dine leisurely to celebrate his future. It was too early anyway. His schedule now made that kind of "dining" out of the question. He almost had to eat on the run.

As he searched his iPhone, most of what he could find in a hurry were fast food places. Those were not acceptable. As far as he was concerned, those were not even providing real food. And he wasn't interested in Slovakian, Mexican, Persian, or Indian food that the city offered. What he needed was a small family restaurant. Then he caught sight of the Chandler Family Dining on Galisteo.

It was cozy with fifteen cloth-covered tables. The menu actually looked tempting, considering what it was. They offered a juicy, third-of-a-pound, marbled-Angus-ground beef hamburger garnished with sautéed onions, melted real cheddar cheese, three pieces of bacon, red and green chili salsa, and guacamole on a Ciabatta roll. That wouldn't take long to make, serve, and eat. Given the time available, he thought it could do. If necessary, he could take what he hadn't finished in a doggy bag for later.

The burger masterpiece was over five inches high and solidly packed. While not haute cuisine, it was better than prison food and surprisingly even better than he expected. Eating every tasty bite, he washed it down with a chocolate milk shake with chocolate ice cream. The large dollop of real whipped cream which decorated the top he spooned onto his plate. It was too much after everything else.

With all that had happened that morning he had needed something triumphant at that moment and his meal came close to being it. Coincidentally, it reminded him of what he had had to eat to celebrate his becoming an emancipated teenager at eighteen. He had finally become free of what he considered the torturous foster care system. That was the start of his real life. And this was the start of his next real life.

Back in his car, feeling satiated, he loosened his belt and comfortably anticipated that the meal would last for the seven-hour ride ahead of him. He wanted to drive straight through to Fort Collins and definitely didn't want to have to stop for food again before he reached his destination.

Then he stopped at a service station. Even though he had had everything checked before when he took his car from storage, he wanted to make sure everything was ready for his trip, that no car problems could interfere. He had his car's fuel tank filled and his radiator and transmission fluids, oil, and tire pressures re-checked. As the attendant was doing that, he purchased three large-mouthed bottles of sports drinks. Two would keep him hydrated and the other he would use as a urinal after he'd drunk its electrolytic contents. He had to be ready for any contingency.

At long last, he was good to go, but his anxiety was resurfacing. His departure was taking way too much time. Any moment a patrol car might wander by, spot him, and start its siren wailing. Keeping his eyes peeled, he slipped out of town. With an obligatory tip of his imaginary hat, he bid "adios" to Santa Fe and the biggest mistake of his life, Amie Benison.

"Amie," he laughed hard enough to cause his unhappy muscles to twinge, "I can't tell you what a major and bitter disappointment you turned out to be after all. You got what you royally deserved, sweetheart."

With a map of Colorado at the ready, he took Route 84 north. Fort Collins, which was north of Denver, was about four hundred sixty-four miles from Santa Fe. That was where he'd set up shop, to take up torts once again. Colorado had handled some very profitable class-action suits. But unlike what he'd told Borstall, he would be working by himself and involving other tort lawyers only as need be. That was how he liked it. He was pleased with what he'd done and the promise of his future. He'd put all this previous pain behind him … at long last. Grinning, he sighed with relief.

As he looked at the map, he knew that because of his late start he might not be able to make it all the way through. And, given his heavy meal, he might have to stop sooner if he grew too sleepy to drive safely. But as long as he was in Colorado and away from his parole officer and New Mexico police, that would be okay. He just wished he could snap his fingers and already be there. Speeding away from Santa Fe, he was feeling upbeat, contemplating getting into the money-making product-injury suits that he loved.

But as he put miles between Santa Fe and himself, for some reason his meal wasn't sitting well. He noticed that heartburn was slowly revealing itself. He grimaced, rubbing his sternum.

"Damn! Well, that's what you get when you eat at a greasy spoon. Thankfully I asked that the chili salsa not be added but, then again, I didn't check. If only I'd had the time to do so," he regretfully replayed, "I would have tried to locate a suitable restaurant offering what was more fitting: Veal Cordon Bleu with Asparagus Hollandaise, a French Pinot Noir, and Crème Brûlée. Ahhh. But that fucking Amie ruined everything again. Just another reason to be glad she's dead. At least," he smiled, his taste buds recapturing his ideal meal's delicate taste, "it won't be long before I can indulge in haute cuisine and expensive wines again. Living la dolce vita, which I deserve now more than ever."

Quickly he approached the small town of Tesuque which boasted the ancient Tesuque Pueblo, a member of the Eight Northern Pueblos. It was listed in the National Register of Historic Places and dated from Twelve Hundred Common Era. He had no intention to take time to look around as he charged through. Besides, he thought, who cares about ancient buildings? He pushed on and miles flew by.

Next came the town of Pojoaque, which as the major employer in the area owned several business enterprises, including gaming operation in three casinos. From the highway he couldn't see any of it but guessed it tried to outdo the glitz of Las Vegas. The town and most of its buildings were off the highway but reachable by the Pojoaque Overpass.

As he passed the overpass sign, he felt the heartburn increasing, searing his esophagus. "Damn!" he uttered. Maybe, he contemplated, after avoiding so much of the inedible prison food, he'd just eaten too much and too fast. His poor stomach wasn't prepared for the rapid onslaught. Undoubtedly it releasing too much acid to deal with it. Sighing at the inconvenience, he decided that perhaps the best thing he could do was look for a pharmacy to get something to settle his delicate stomach. However, that would further mess up his schedule. Still, his condition was getting progressively worse.

"Oh, shit! I missed the overpass exit."

As he glanced at his map, he saw another exit was coming up but was several miles away. That meant he'd have to essentially retrace his steps, wasting more time. He pounded the steering wheel with his fist.

Finally, the next exit arrived and he found himself heading through neighborhoods of small houses back toward the small town without a clue of where to look. Slowing down more than he wanted, he carefully eyeballed both sides of the street just in case. As he crawled along, his attention paid off. On the left side of the road he saw a sign for a drug store. Pulling off and parking askew in its lot, he yanked on his emergency brake, and hurried inside. His esophagus felt on fire. He could taste peppers. Damn! Damn! Damn! He no longer had to wonder if he had unknowingly eaten some of that flaming hot chili salsa that he had eschewed. The fire in his throat reminded him. For an instant Amie flashed into his mind.

Quickly, he walked up and down the aisles of the small establishment looking for antacids. In his haste it hadn't occurred to him to look for any overhead signage demarcating product categories. When he discovered the antacids, they didn't have the name brand he wanted. He thought, that figures. All that was available was a bismuth subsalicylate generic, the label of which claimed it would do the same job as the high-priced brand. He didn't have the time to search for something else. He had no choice. He snatched up a bottle and ran for the register.

However, when he reached the register area, there were four Native American customers ahead of him. He couldn't believe he'd have to wait in line as well. He muttered obscenities under his breath. That was totally unacceptable. His heart racing, his anxiety, like his heartburn, was making itself known. He needed to get away as soon as possible. The police would have already been alerted to be on the lookout for him.

He thought about tucking the bottle into his pocket and leaving or just throwing a ten-dollar bill at the register and racing out. But, giving it a second thought, he realized that the last thing he needed was to draw attention to himself. Waiting impatiently, tapping his foot, he watched each person in front of him slowly finish his or her friendly conversation and purchase.

Jesus! Just get on with it!" he muttered again.

Nearly twenty minutes later he was back in his car, unscrewing the black cap of the thick, pink liquid to take a big swig. He hoped it would coat his esophagus and stomach sufficiently so he could continue his journey without further gastric annoyance. It was well past two o'clock now and he still had a very long trek ahead of him.

That suggested it would be quite late when he arrived in Fort Collins where he didn't have a hotel or motel reservation. He had no reservations anywhere, not even in Denver where he'd most likely have to spend the night.

Hoping he'd encounter no more distractions, he pulled out of the parking lot and floored it, crossing his fingers that no pueblo- or state police were lurking about, unseen, as made his way back to the highway. His anxiety was peaking as he sped along.

By the time he approached Española, his heartburn was easing off a little. That was a big relief. However, it seemed to have been replaced by a touch of nausea. This made no sense to him.

"Shit!" he talked aloud to himself. "The heartburn I can understand because of the hot peppers, the greasy onions and bacon, but feeling sick to my stomach? What's that all about? Maybe it's only momentary because it was such a heavy meal, something I'm not used to."

In spite of how he felt, he kept his foot adhered to the accelerator and plowed ahead. Slowly as he passed acre upon acre of vacant sandy land on either side of the highway, dotted with scrub, stunted junipers, and dry native grasses, the more he noticed he was also becoming sweaty. That was odd because the temperature in the car hadn't changed.

About to turn on the air-conditioner, he felt a single chill that enveloped his body and erupted into massive shivering. Frowning, he questioned what his body was telling him. Was the nausea a significant sign of something other than just the size of the meal he'd ingested. Was it more than the grease and peppers? What about food poisoning? Could he be suffering from that? While he wasn't sure of its symptoms, he thought that abdominal pain, diarrhea, and vomiting were a part of it. Maybe the nausea was the start of it. Yes, he decided it probably was. But what would have caused it?

"Kee-rist!" he shouted. "Maybe I shouldn't have eaten the guacamole too. It could have started to turn," he complained. "Or even the hamburger. It could have been not properly refrigerated, tainted with E. coli, and hadn't been cooked enough to kill it. But it tasted all right. Wouldn't it have tasted off?"

He tried to belch but couldn't. Unscrewing the bismuth bottle again, he took another large swig. It was obnoxious stuff. His tongue felt coated and his mouth tasted gross—a fake bubble-gum flavor. As he glanced in the rear-view mirror at his tongue, he could see it was painted black by the bismuth.

"Jesus, what if it really is food poisoning? That could be bad."

He had heard of an older relative who saved scraps from meals in the refrigerator and tended to forget when he had put them in there. The old turkey corn bread stuffing from Thanksgiving that he ate in February had turned, making him desperately ill. When he couldn't call 911, he died.

"Does that mean I have to stop to look for a doctor? Crap! I'm out here in the boonies. Where would I even find a doctor? Shit! I don't have the time to do that. I have to get out of New Mexico." He tried to calm himself. "Okay, maybe, I'm being overly concerned. It still could be just an upset stomach. If it gets worse, it might be a good idea to pull over to the side of the road and make myself vomit. That might eliminate some of the problem."

By the time he arrived the intersection of Route 84 and Route 285, heading for Ojo Caliente's mineral springs, which was another twenty-four miles, his nausea was increasing. It now felt as if it were patting him under the chin. Saliva was collecting in his mouth. It was definitely time to find a safe place to pull off the highway. He repeatedly swallowed, hoping to keep his stomach content in place for a few more minutes.

Adding to his discomfort, he had started to feel dizzy. Strangely, he noticed, his shoes were feeling tight. As his symptoms seemed to multiply, he kept his gaze sharp for a place to pull off. He had to act fast. He most assuredly didn't want to vomit in Mr. Benz, his prized toy.

When he located what appeared to be a convenient and safe strip of grass and dirt, he begrudgingly swung the vehicle off the highway onto it, hoping he wouldn't accidentally drop a wheel off the far side where the land appeared to decline.

Now sweating profusely, he glided to a stop. But by the time he had turned off the ignition, he was also having trouble breathing.

"Son of a bitch! If I could ingest that ungodly prison swill, I should be able to handle toxic civilian food! What I really need is a snifter of a 1968 Armagnac brandy. That cures whatever ails you and would delightfully settle my stomach."

However, sitting there stopped, he noticed a pain in his gut. He thought that perhaps he really did require a doctor's attention. But where could he find medical help? He was in the middle of nowhere and had no idea how large any of these little towns or villages were. Would they have a medical clinic? But would this Podunk clinic do? Maybe it would have to. It seemed improbable that they'd have a hospital. As his discomfort increased, checking his phone didn't occur to him. He still needed to vomit.

Before he could undo his seat belt to do it outside the car, his breathing difficulty worsened. It felt as if all the air had been sucked out of the vehicle. He had to strain to get enough oxygen into his lungs. Panic gripped him. His thinking felt fuzzy.

When his left hand felt for the door handle to open it, a sharp pain stabbed his jaw like a red-hot rotisserie spit rod. Simultaneously, an excruciating pain encompassed his left shoulder through to his back. Rapidly it radiated into his left arm and spread across his chest. His eyes widened in horror. His heart was beating hard and irregularly. It felt like a caught fish flopping on a dock, trying to save itself.

He truly needed help. He finally remembered his cell phone. It was in the console just inches away. All he had to do was seize it and call 911. But his right hand couldn't reach it because the equivalent of a cinder block wall had suddenly landed on his chest. Heavy pain and pressure enveloped his upper torso. The thought of his phone slipped away. His hands desperately clutched his chest as his heart felt as if it were doing Olympic gymnastics on a pogo stick. His body motion forcefully pressed his head back against the headrest. He was like a ripe melon being crushed to a pulp.

Despite the afternoon sun shining through the windshield, illuminating his twisted agony and pinpointing all the squashed bugs on the glass, darkness was encroaching upon him. Starting with his peripheral vision, it was gradually engulfing his visual field.

The last thing he saw in his mind's eye was his mother smiling at him. She was beside a fragrant, colorful, tinsel-draped, balsam Christmas tree in their San Diego apartment. She was handing him a piece of his favorite sausage pizza.

"Mommy!" The word barely escaped his lips.

Hours later when the State Police found his car, his body, and checked his license plate and driver's license, they discovered that he was wanted. Checking vital signs, they duly contacted the nearest ambulance, the penitentiary, his parole officer, and Santa Fe police. When Tony received the notice, he almost felt like shouting.

"At last, no more delusion-oriented, psychopathic behavior. Thank you, God. It couldn't have happened to a more worthy fellow."

Feeling a little guilty about his lack of charity, he knew that if his mother had heard her son be so sacrilegious and without compassion, she would have looked to God for understanding, crossed herself, and said a little prayer for him.

Since Shelton hadn't left a will, most of the money from the sale of his house and what he had with him would go to the state once Charley's civil suit was settled. Besides compensation, she would also gain possession of his Amie Benison paintings. Because Borstall seemed to be the only one to mourn Shelton, he used part of the house sale money for his open-casket funeral and headstone.

"You know," said Charley as she and Tony were driving to Shelton's funeral service, "some say that getting rid of a delusion makes us wiser."

Tony laughed, "But getting rid of the one with the delusion makes the rest of us a whole lot happier ... and safer."

Charley unexpectedly felt a touch of sadness. Philosophically, she added, "I wonder if one imprisoned by such an idiosyncratic belief can really ever be rid of it."

Tony dovetailed on her sentiment, "It *is* sad he had such serious problems, but it's even sadder that he felt compelled to sadistically impose those problems on others."

Charley and Tony were present at his sparsely attended ceremony—mostly a few former clients and Borstall—at the Santa Fe Congregational Church. It was a short service.

"I guess Isaac Asimov was right," Tony said solemnly to Charley outside the church. "He said, 'In life, unlike chess, the game continues after checkmate.' I'm grateful for that."

They skipped the interment at Fairview Cemetery. Shelton was out of the picture, once and for all, and that was all that really mattered.

39

Charley's house had been cleaned top to bottom so the smoke residue was mostly a thing of the past. When it seemed to re-appear because some piece of fabric-covered furniture, even after its having been professional cleaned, retained some hint, Charley put out a dish of white vinegar and water laced with a stalk of lavender to temporarily eliminate the odor. She had had a local professional art restorer clean her and Amie's paintings. And later, after she had won her civil suit against the now-deceased Ronald Shelton, she had purchased another solid-wood front door and another Honda Fit in orangey-gold on which she re-used the license plate "Amie B."

By now Tony and Wynton's paintings were surpassing all her expectations. Wynton especially was living up to his desire to finish his mother's paintings when he was ready. Both Tony and Wynton were being shown, via "Amie" as their agent, in local galleries and beyond. Charley and Wynton's godparents saw to it that most of the money from the sales of his works was put into trust for his education. The rest was parceled out to him, through his guardians, for his weekly allowance and artistic supplies. He shared with Charley, out of the hearing of his godparents, that his most heartfelt wish was that his parents could see what he was doing for them. Charley could only nod, hug him, and try to smile.

They would have marveled at his also becoming a local celebrity. Not just because of his art work but because he was contributing to his community by showing elementary school children during his recess how to paint like him. At one point he shared with Charley that he was thinking about becoming an art teacher, maybe even for kids like himself. He was demonstrating that he was much older than is age.

She was very pleased with everything he had done but, like him, wistfully wished his parents could have seen what they had set in motion and how much he had accomplished as a result. He was so motivated. It was as if he knew what his potential was and he was striving to reach it. Charley was continuing to mentor him and would do so even after his five-year painting lesson certificate ran out. By helping him in every way she could, she was duplicating what Amie had done for her

Tony retired from the police department, sold his home in Santa Fe, and moved in with Charley. Together they worked on the Amie Benison business, though not as legal business partners. He was very serious about his art. She knew he had promise and wanted him to singularly focus on pursuing his late art career. As a consequence, she was working hard to get Tony's paintings even more exposure via regional and national art shows and important hangings. This included one in the governor's mansion. It was quickly becoming apparent that painting was his true calling. Constantly trying new techniques, he was receiving praise for everything he did. Charley couldn't believe the scope of his talent. He, in turn, couldn't believe that he was starting to receive occasional requests for commissions. Charley handled the transactions for him.

"Not bad for a paint-splattered ex-fuzz," he'd laugh. "Now this is what I call a successful retirement."

It wasn't long before people were clamoring for posters of his most popular works which would be seen on the Amie Benison website, on the "ecoart.com" site, and in their mailed catalogue.

Charley started the poster process rolling. It was likely that Wynton's would be as well as she spread the visibility of his works.

A new coffee table book was in the works, expected to be available soon. This was of the popular works of Tony, Wynton, and Mana, with a much-deserved section on Saatchmo. Even though his paw-print was no longer on all the site's paintings, he took very seriously his role as the symbol of "amiebenison.com" and all it produced.

Charley's in-person painting classes had become popular enough to require a waiting list. When she didn't have room for new students, she sold even more packaged DVD programs of her lessons, especially to the youngest and oldest painters-to-be. As awareness of her studio spread over time, she was also looking for some of her accomplished past pupils to teach. Given the interest in their abstract art, Tony and she deliberated the cost-benefit analysis of establishing a painting center in Glorieta dedicated to it.

Together Tony and Charley decided not to marry any time soon. As they joked whenever they were asked, "Maybe some time, but it would be a shame to spoil a beautiful friendship with benefits by wrapping it up in the state's bureaucratic red tape." Tony's mother, however, still hoped she would be attending a wedding. Remaining healthy, Saatch spoiled Charley's former cat medical track record. When over time nothing had changed in Charley's annual mammograms, that pushed her breast cancer worry a little farther away. The Post-Shelton Period had a sense of normalcy about it that they fully relished as they tried to eighty-six his memory.

While Charley continued to consider adopting more cats, she finally opted instead to become a patron of her favorite area no-kill homeless cat shelter and help it construct a cat café. There the public could interact with and photograph the felines available for adoption over coffee, tea, hot chocolate, or lemonade. She had heard that those in Japan and increasingly across the U.S. were helping create more adoptions.

Furthermore, she and Saatch sponsored an annual "Black Cat Appreciation Day" to be held at the café. To help celebrate the first one they invited the popular YouTube star "OwlKitty," a black cat rescue adoption, to demonstrate how her antics were delightfully added to segments of popular movies and TV shows. On that one special day, only adoptable black cats were present at the cat café to play with, enjoy, and adopt with Saatch regally overseeing the festivities from his special stool. The many fun "OwlKitty" videos played in the background on a wide screen on a loop.

After all this time, Charley had decided to let her hair gradually grow out to her original red color but keep it short and tousled. Additionally, she would incrementally add more style and color to her wardrobe as she represented more paintings by Mana than by Amie. As she was superficially re-inventing herself, which Tony encouraged because of her enjoyment of it, Nova Libre Publishers contacted her. Shelton's former rep, James Shannon, said he thought that all that had happened to her would make a best-selling book and wanted her to write it.

"It would include Shelton's previous attempt to do your relationship biography which we bypassed for his outlined exposé about revealing some non-existent phantom forger of your artwork. We'd want this new book to cover how he obsessed about you, physically pursued you, went to prison, and then tried to kill you."

Charley winced, asking herself if he were serious. Why, she wondered, would she want to relive all that? Even though they promised a hefty advance, she wasn't moved. At this point, it wasn't so much protecting Amie's privacy any longer since it wouldn't come into play with the book. It was no longer at risk of being invaded. It was that what he was proposing was really Shelton's biography. She was only incidental as that which spurred him on. But, irrespective of whose bio it was, she wanted no part of it.

However, she knew that because of the story's seductive horror, it would definitely be written by someone and be a best-seller. Because it was so strangely mesmerizing it was sure to appeal to the unquenchable thirst of a voyeuristic public.

Sadly, she mused, it would probably be written by someone who hadn't a clue about what had actually happened, who Shelton was, or what his motivation might have been. That author would end up fictionalizing everything, especially since input from her would be totally unavailable. Still, given the book's inevitability, she hoped that it would be penned with a slant toward the *Diagnostic and Statical Manual of Mental Disorders,* and not like some pulp fiction magazine crime story. It would be best tackled by the clinical psychologist who had testified for her at his trial. Her deepest desire was for Nova Libre to forget about it. She surely neither needed nor wanted that kind of notoriety and remembrance.

Now as Charley looked back upon her own bizarre journey, dealing with an amalgam of incongruous, painful, and frightening business and personal situations, she had to laugh out loud. Early on she was like Don Quixote tilting at windmills to keep her political image consulting alive. Then, as the years passed, she had become the stalwart "keeper of the flame" for Amie, meeting every challenge to protect the promises she had made to one whom she had held most dear. And now, she was building on all that, creating what she hoped was her destiny.

As she imagined Amie and the original Saatchi smiling down on her, she shook her head at the irony. Even she couldn't believe what she had done and all that had happened. Ultimately, it seemed to her to have come down to one nearly impossible and barely incomprehensible thing, to which Amie would raise a righteous fist and Saatchi, a paw. It was only because she had attempted the absurd that she was capable of achieving the impossible.

ABOUT THE AUTHOR

Signe A. Dayhoff, PhD, MA, MEd, is a social psychologist who was graduated from Boston University with post-graduate training in counseling, emotional intelligence, and positive psychology. For thirty-eight years she has been a cognitive-behavioral coach specializing in alleviating social anxiety and enhancing social effectiveness by overcoming obstacles, removing limiting beliefs, and maximizing confidence. An applied feline behaviorist, she is "mom" to twenty-six senior, chronically ill, and disabled cats. She also writes about human-cat relationships and the human-animal bond.

She has taught social and organizational psychology at Boston University, University of Massachusetts, and Framingham State College and has done research at Massachusetts Institute of Technology (U.S. Bureau of Standards' project on textile information retrieval), Scripps Clinic and Research Foundation (Upjohn diabetes clinical research trial), and Fairview State Hospital (behavioral therapy to help those with developmental disabilities get necessary exercise).

She is author of nineteen books: twelve of which are self-help and five of which are cat memoirs. This current book is her second novel.

Check out her books at http://effectivenessplus.com/books